SINNING for SANTA

SARAH JD

Content Warning

Please note this is a Dark Mafia Christmas standalone MF romance
from the Marx Mafia world.
You do not have to read any other books from that world to read this.

Sinning for Santa contains subjects that maybe triggering to some
readers and is intended for mature audiences.
Reader discretion is advised.
They contain, but are not limited to:
Graphic Violence, Explicit scenes, Reference to childhood trauma,
Trauma from Religious Extremism, Gaslighting (not between H & h),
Past sexual assault (not between H & h), Reference and use of date rape
drugs (not between H & h), Dub-con, Kidnapping.

PLEASE NOTE:
*This book is written in Australian English, therefore
some words will appear slightly different for my beloved
US readers*

Chapter One

Jaxcen

The sky lights up overhead as I leap from the curb, the reflection of the lightning bouncing off the hundreds of windows lining the tall buildings surrounding me. I count in my head, trying to prepare myself for the pending clap of thunder, quickening my pace as much as my pencil skirt will allow.

I ignore the chill of the water splashing up from the road as I run, knowing my Tony Biancos are going to need some TLC when I get home later. As much as I love these pumps, my need to get this over and done with is my top priority right now.

It wouldn't matter if you had gone straight home, Jaxcen.

Shoosh, I silently snap at my internal thoughts while I run, being careful as I hurry over the tram tracks so I don't get my heel caught and fall.

Thankful that the Melbourne city streets aren't busy this late on a Tuesday night, I don't have to continuously check for oncoming cars, instead keeping my focus on the church up ahead, and the large metal doors that hint to mediaeval times Australia never saw.

St Catherine's Church is never open this late, but I clearly saw a couple of men slip inside from where I was across the street, and since Father Peters is obviously working right now, I'm sure he can spare me some time.

Darting around the two blacked out Land Rovers parked on the street in front of the church, I hurry through the gate and up the path, holding my breath just as the sky lights up everything around me again.

Reaching the door, it creaks a little as I heave it open and quickly dash inside to get out of the rain just in time for a loud clap of thunder to rattle the very foundation I stand on.

Damn. The sky is angry tonight.

Taking a moment, I shake my feet and arms to dislodge as much water as I can in the small foyer, annoyed that I didn't think to grab my raincoat when I left work earlier.

Of course I didn't think about a coat when all I could think of was....

No.

This has to stop, Jaxcen.

Shame burrows deep in my gut, reminding me why I made a detour here instead of heading straight home.

Father Peters will help.

Glancing down at my ivory blouse clinging to my white lacy bra, I tug my thin black blazer tighter, trying to cover myself up as much as possible, before heading inside the main building.

As I step in, another flash of lightning illuminates the whole interior of the church in a rainbow of colours from the stained glass windows.

"Wow," I whisper to myself, taking a moment to appreciate the beauty of it, something that's not typically seen on my regular visits during the day.

The towering height of the cathedral-like ceiling looks haunting as it's plunged into darkness before the dull glow coming from the dimmed wall lights shows hints of its beauty. I take a moment to appreciate just how impressive St Catherine's is, and the history held within the walls.

So many secrets.

Especially the confessionals.

That thought draws my eyes in that direction, and my gaze catches on Father Peters standing at the other end of the aisle talking to a man who's sitting in the front pew.

From here, it looks like Father Peters is offering the man comfort, the sight tugging my lips into a smile.

He's such a kind and generous man, his greying hair always styled into the same respectable short back and sides with a subtle side part, reminding me of what a grandad would look like if I had one.

Ignoring the puddle I've just left behind on the slate tiled floor from my rain drenched clothes, I move forward towards the man I came here to see, my heels clicking loudly echoing through the celestial structure, making my presence known.

My steps slow as Father Peters and the man he's talking to in hushed tones both dart their heads in my direction, and for a moment I feel like I shouldn't be here.

But that can't be right, can it?

This is my church.

It's not until Father Peters' frown turns into a smile, that the niggling feeling that I've walked into something I'm not supposed to see diminishes and I hurry forward again.

I don't get a chance to really see the other man, his head turning to face the altar at the front, giving me his back, but for some reason as I near, I get the awkward feeling again that I've just interrupted something.

"Miss Summers. What a lovely surprise." Father Peters beams, giving me his full attention as he steps forward to meet me. "Is everything alright?"

"Yes, Father. I apologise for coming in so late. I saw that you were open and I needed to..." I trail off, my gaze shifting to the man sitting in the front pew who can most definitely hear me.

My cheeks flush, my inner humiliation taunting me.

What would he think if he knew why you're here, Jaxcen? He'd be disgusted.

"You needed to?" Father Peters urges, gaining my attention again to finish my sentence.

"I-ah." Again my eyes snap to the other man before I lean in closer to Father Peters. "I would like to use the confessional," I whisper, and Father Peters nods, his smile warm, his gaze understanding.

"Of course." He gestures to the confessional booths built into the left wall. "Head over. I'll be right there."

"Thank you." I sigh, shooting him a grateful smile as relief washes over me.

This is good. I'll confess and do my penance and everything will be okay.

Father Peters steps aside for me to pass, and as I do, I get the first look at the man in the front pew, his gaze shifting in my direction as if he's tracking my movements in his peripheral.

His dark hair is damp, probably from the same rain storm I ran in from moments ago, and his white shirt is soaked, especially along his broad shoulders and back. The fabric clings to his skin, clearly showing dark inky patterns underneath, that run up to appear on the side of his neck, finishing just below his ear.

His jawline is dusted in dark facial hair. Not enough that you can't see how chiselled it is, but enough to make me wonder what it would be like to touch it.

Really, Jaxcen? You're in a church!

I'm walking too quickly to take in much more than that, and I'm a little disappointed to be frank because there's something about his presence that has me intrigued.

Does he always come to church this late?

The one thing I definitely notice is the air of danger that swirls around him, and a shiver runs up my spine.

Maybe coming here was a bad idea.

Turning my focus on the confessional before me, I hurry forward, my heels clacking once again as I hear the deep rumble of Father Peters and the man talking quietly behind me.

Opening the heavy door of the booth, I step inside and turn back, my eyes landing on the man in the front pew as Father Peters heads my way.

My breath hitches as the man's dark gaze catches mine, a small smirk tugging at the corner of his lips as he leans his forearms on top of his knees, the long sleeves of his white shirt rolled up to reveal intricate tattoos snaking down both forearms and onto his hands.

Damn. Is it hot in here?

He doesn't really look like the type of guy that would deliberately come to church. The creep of my blush heats my cheeks, giving my ogling away, so I quickly close the door blocking the man's view from me, and mine from his, and then, with a sigh, I kneel.

I hear the moment Father Peters steps into the other side, the door clicking closed before the small slot in the wall dividing us opens, revealing a decorative vent.

"Join me," Father Peters says, and together we recite, "In the name of the Father, the Son, and the Holy Spirit," and I sign the cross.

"May the Lord be in your heart and help you acknowledge your sins, and trust in his mercy." He precedes and I respond.

"Amen."

Then, I let my mind shift back to why I'm here.

"Bless me Father, for I have sinned. It has been one week since my last confession."

"What ails you this evening?" he asks, and I clear my throat before I begin.

"I went back, Father."

"When did this happen?" he asks, his calm tone not scolding, yet I know if I could see his face, he'd surely look disappointed.

"Tonight," I admit. "And Sunday night."

"Two nights since last week?" he asks, and this time I can hear the surprise in his tone.

"And Friday night," I rush out, feeling the shame heat my entire body.

"I see. What is it that you think keeps drawing you back?"

"My thoughts," I admit quietly. "They are so impure, Father. They are getting worse and I'm afraid."

"Afraid of what?"

"Indulging," I admit.

Father Peters clears his throat, and not for the first time do I wonder if he's at a loss with me and my disturbing desires.

"Temptation is acknowledged by God, because resisting it can bring about strong personal growth, however, just as we discussed last week, the Lord does not wish us to face temptations that are beyond our ability to resist. I'm concerned that place may be beyond your ability, and that if you keep giving in to your temptation to go there, especially given your upcoming nuptials, that you will eventually give in to the temptation to indulge."

"Yes, Father. I cannot explain why I returned," I say, but the truth is, I know why I returned.

I'm curious.

Intrigued.

Wanting.

"What feelings were evoked when you went there?" he asks, and my thoughts return to the club, the dark atmosphere, the masks, and the acts committed.

Although humiliating, I'm about to explain about my need and arousal when shouting out in the church forces my confession to end abruptly.

"What on earth?" Father Peters mutters right as I hear him open his door, so I quickly stand and do the same.

"Get down!"

The deep command comes a second before I realise there are two men standing across the other side of the church, pointing large guns in my direction as the man that was sitting in the front pew runs towards me.

A gasp lodges in my throat and my eyes widen, Father Peters in my peripheral holding his hands out in front of him right before the man from the pew slams into me, sending us back into the booth.

A scream escapes me as loud gunfire echoes out in the church, bullets slamming into the booth door as the man shuts us into the tiny space.

Oh my Lord. We are going to die.

"Fuck," he hisses, pressing me against the back wall with his tall, firm body, his hands still gripping my shoulders in the tight space. "Do me a favour, love. Reach around to my back pocket and pull out my phone."

What? Why would he be asking me that right now?

"We're going to die," I whimper against his chest, my fingers gripping the front of his shirt like he's my lifeline.

"The doors are bulletproof. We're safe in here." His breath fans over the top of my head, and I risk a glance up to see a smirk pulling at his lips.

Why the hell is he smiling?

We are about to die.

And why would the doors in a church confessional be bulletproof? Surely he's just saying that to make me feel better.

"My pocket," he snaps as another round of bullets pelt the door, jolting me out of my chaotic thoughts.

With a trembling hand, I peel my grip from his shirt and graze my hand over his side, feeling the strong ripple of muscle underneath that speaks of hours in the gym.

"So Miss Summers, what's your first name?"

Is he really making small talk right now? Although to be honest, I'm kind of glad for it since the deep gravel of his voice seems to seep into my veins like the heat of a strong drink does, somehow calming me.

"Jaxcen." The quiver in my tone gives away my fear as my fingers brush over his backside, finding a hard object under the fabric.

"Jaxcen Summers. What a stunning name."

I scoff at his compliment, before focusing on finding the opening of his pocket.

"You don't think it's stunning?" he asks and I give my head a small shake.

"It's nothing special, but thanks for the compliment," I rush out, still trying to find the pocket opening.

"You're copping a good feel there, Miss Summers." He chuckles, this time his breath brushing over the side of my head as he gives his arse a little shake.

"Stop moving," I snap, my fear controlling me as I try to get into his back pocket until finally I find the opening and slide my fingers in.

A deep chuckle rumbles in his chest, and as I grip what I assume is his phone, he tilts his hips forward right against my pelvis, making me very aware of *all* of him.

The gunfire out in the church has died down, but the explosions of my thundering heart rush past my ears with the heat of my cheeks just the beginning of the burn that ignites my entire body.

This isn't right Jaxcen. You're going to die at any moment and you're getting turned on?

This has to be adrenalin, right? I can't honestly be more focused on how it feels to have a man, *this man*, pressed against me, rather than the fact there are men with guns out in the church.

Think about Eddie. Not this man.

"Got it," I mutter as I start tugging the phone from his back pocket, my voice raspy from fear and something else I refuse to analyse while I'm in the middle of a shoot out.

"Atta girl." His words do something entirely inappropriate to me, and I nearly drop his damn phone as I try to bring it between us in the tight space.

Taking it from me quickly, he dials a number before pressing his phone to his ear.

"Be a love and get the gun I have tucked in my back waistband," he orders quietly while he waits for whoever he called to answer.

My eyes widen, my gaze darting up to his as he winks and then turns his attention to whoever just answered his call.

A gun?

No. Surely he said something else.

"Where the fuck are you?" he snaps into his phone, his tone no longer playful but then he gives his hips a little wiggle against me in the playful manner he had only moments ago, reminding me that he asked me to do something.

Glancing up again, I hadn't realised I'd looked away when I find his dark gaze pinning me.

"Gun, Jaxcen. Now."

The demand in his tone is unmistakable.

Dark.

Menacing.

Terrifying.

Not an ounce of playfulness there.

Something shifts in the air between us, and I'm no longer sure if I'm safer in here, or out in the church where the gunmen have fallen quiet.

"Figure it out. I'm under fire. Two shooters." The man barks into his phone, and I don't delay any further, quickly reaching around his back again, this time up higher until my fingers brush cold metal.

A quiet gasp escapes me. I don't know why. Maybe I didn't believe him when he said he had a gun. Or maybe because it is a gun, and I've never actually touched one before. People don't just have guns here in Australia.

A little scared that by touching it, it'll somehow shoot me, I grip the hilt of the metal, my palm sweaty as I tug it free. It's heavier than I thought it would be. Bigger too as I try to quickly slide it between the back of his body and the door.

"Get it fucking done." The man snaps into the phone before ending the call, and with a trembling hand, I produce his weapon, hoping that'll make him less angry.

"Thanks, love." He winks again.

What the hell... he's playful again. Is he flirting with me?

"Open the booth!" a voice yells from out in the church and a whimper escapes me as I duck my head into his chest.

"Shhh." The man whispers against my ear, "You're safe with me."

"Maybe we got him," another voice says.

"Man, look at the door. The bullets didn't go through. He's in there."

Was he telling the truth before? Are the confessional doors really bulletproof?

"Looks like it's time for me to go out there," the man says quietly shifting in the small space, before pressing his phone to my chest. "Look after this for me, love."

"What?" I whisper-yell. "You can't go out there. You'll die."

"Probably," he agrees, still bloody smirking. "Give us a kiss then."

"What!" I squeak and he chuckles.

"If I'm going to die, I'd like a last kiss." He leans in closer, his lips hovering near mine.

"You can't be serious," I say breathlessly as his nose brushes mine, his warm breath fanning over my lips.

"I'm deadly serious, Miss Summers. You're not going to deny a dying man his last wish, are you?"

Even though the men out in the church are still yelling for him to come out, all I can focus on is the way he presses into me, the way his spicy scent envelops me, the way his lips hover so closely near mine that I can feel their heat.

Is it cheating if I do this? It's his dying wish and he's absolutely about to die. Surely Eddie would find this acceptable.

"No." I breathe, giving in so easily, and the next second, his lips claim mine.

Everything I have been fighting against, my urges, my sinful desires, my past, fall away as I finally give in to temptation and indulge.

This man might be having his last kiss, but I'm having my first.

Well, it feels like that anyway, because I've never in my life been kissed like this before.

He parts my lips with his tongue, diving in and brushing against mine, and oh, a familiar ache shoots between my legs as I moan into his mouth.

His fingers delve into my blonde hair, tugging the strands at my nape, causing my head to tip back in a way that has him deepening the kiss.

I'm hot. From head to toe a fire licks underneath my flesh, my tense muscles melting away like butter as I take everything he's giving.

The moment he shifts to nudge his knee between my legs, the ache in my core rejoices, and I find myself grinding against his thigh, sending a wave of pleasure through me, all thoughts of my fiancé vanishing.

A loud rattling makes us both stiffen, and I realise someone is trying to open the door.

"Fuck." He breathes against my lips, slowly pulling back. "Lucky the lock is working, hey love." His grin is mischievous, his straight white teeth flashing at me as he wags his brows. "It's time for me to die now. With a hardon I might add." He chuckles to himself, holding his gun up next to his head and bringing his other hand up to check it, for whatever one does to check a gun in a small space.

"I don't think you should go out there," I whisper, dread settling in my gut as reality sets back in.

"Don't worry love, this will all be over in a flash."

I open my mouth to protest, but he has already reached behind him and flicked open the latch, and before I can beg him one more time to stay, he spins with his gun raised and shoves the door open.

CHAPTER TWO

Devon

With well trained precision, the moment the door swings open, I've fired my Glock and shot dickhead number one between the eyes.

It's just too easy sometimes.

Dickhead number two is a different story.

He shoots, his aim off because of my 'tada' act, and the bullet merely scrapes my shoulder before I fire two rounds, one into his arm, causing him to drop his gun, and the second in his leg, so the fucker can't run.

Then he cries out like a whiney fucking cat is being strangled.

"Shut the fuck up!" I boom, storming towards him and kicking his weapon across the room where it slams to a stop against a pew end.

"P-please don't k-kill me," he fucking begs, and I sneer at the nerve of him.

"Who the fuck sent you?!"

"I-I can't s-say."

I shoot his other leg, and this time I don't just hear his cries, but a whimper behind me from the sweet little blonde mouse still in the confessional.

Fuck.

I've never seen a woman so sweet yet so made to be a man's plaything before. It could be her plump pink lips that has me imagining them wrapped around my cock. Or maybe her satin smooth skin that flushes so brightly there's no mistaking her arousal. Or perhaps those big doe like eyes, so blue yet so dark from her nearly blown irises, giving away her lust.

As the man before me tries and fails to drag himself in the other direction, I refocus on him and put the little mouse to the back of my mind until later.

"You fond of your tiny cock?" I hiss, taking a few steps closer to loom over the ratty looking fucker. "Because it'll be my next target."

"P-please Mr Marx. I had no choice. He said he'd kill my family if I don't do this."

"Boo-fucking-who," I snap. "Give me his name." I aim my gun.

"I don't know it!" the man rushes out, holding up his only uninjured hand. "I've never met him. Only spoken to him on the phone. But he calls himself Mr V."

"And what were his orders? Word for fucking word!"

"K-kill Devon Marx at the St Catherine's Church on Tuesday evening or else my sister and her three kids will die."

Taking a moment, I study the guy who's probably a low income earner given his basic clothes and lack of dental hygiene. Could even be as close to homelessness as one can be before it actually happens.

I may not know him, but I don't think he's lying.

"Your name?" I demand, and he starts sobbing.

"Phillip Randall."

Nodding, I lower to my haunches and lean in close. "I'll make sure your sister and her kids remain safe."

Relief washes over his features only to rush away a moment later when I press the muzzle of my gun to his head, and pull the trigger.

The shot is so fucking loud, echoing in the space, and it takes a moment for my hearing to return.

That's when my men finally fucking burst through the doors with their guns raised.

"The fuck happened?" Finn snaps, charging towards me as the others fan out.

"What the fuck does it look like?" I ask my best mate, who is my second in command as I straighten and shove my gun back into the waistband of my pants.

"Ahh, Dev?"

The question comes from Miles, one of my soldiers, and I turn to find him hovering by the open door of the confessional. And then to her.

Those big blue eyes are round with what's most likely disbelief, and a shit ton of fear, my little mouse clearly in shock over what she just witnessed.

The blare of a phone ringing stiffens us all since none of us ever have our sound on our ringtones, and we look around to find the source.

"It's coming from the dead guy." Finn points down to Phillip Randall's lifeless body.

Bending down, I search his jacket to find the source and see the name "Mr V" flashing across the screen.

Fuck. It's the man that ordered my hit.

"Check Father Peters," I bark to whoever, pointing over to the pew closest to the confessional where I noticed him hiding.

Well, I hope the ball he was curled in under the seat was him hiding, otherwise he's either injured or dead, and I can't fucking comprehend the possibility that he got killed instead of me.

Two of my men move towards the pew Father Peters is under, while I hit answer on the phone speaker and wait.

"You're a hard man to kill."

My eyes meet Finn's, and he steps closer to listen.

"Wanna tell me who the fuck has broken one of our most sacred fucking rules?" I snap, and the man chuckles.

"And what rule is that? Daring to go against a Marx family member?"

"No. The fucking rule where churches are sacred ground and we don't bring our wars to them!"

"Well since I don't live by the rules put in place by made men, I can do whatever the fuck I want."

A low deep growl reverberates in my chest, and a flash of heat rushes over me as I fight to keep calm.

I want to point out that I'm not a made man since I'm not Sicilian, or residing in America, but that lesson will have to wait for a later fucking date.

"Who the fuck are you?"

Again, he chuckles. "Someone you shouldn't have fucked with."

"That doesn't narrow it down very fucking much," I point out, and Mr V clucks his tongue.

"No, I don't suppose it does. Maybe you should stop fucking with other people's lives."

Fuck. That still doesn't narrow it down.

"And you most definitely shouldn't kill people's loved ones," the man says darkly, and again, it still doesn't narrow it down.

This shit comes with the territory of being a part of Victoria's most ruthless crime family. People die. It's as simple as that.

If they fuck with us, or run with those who are the truest forms of the scum that walks this earth, then yeah, they are gonna find themselves fucking dead by a Marx hand.

"You sound like nothing more than a coward if you are blackmailing other people into doing your dirty work for you." I point out and he scoffs.

"Looks like you're a coward too then, since blackmailing people is one of your specialties."

"You know what else is my specialty? Chasing fuckheads like you to the ends of the earth until you're begging for mercy, only to die by my hand."

"Maybe," he hisses, "but until then, you'd better keep looking over your shoulder, *Devon*." He draws out my name like it's a foul taste on his tongue. "Oh, and to make it interesting, just so you can have a taste of your own medicine, I think I'll start killing people you care about before I get to you." He chuckles through the line. "You know, just for the hell of it."

"Nice try, arsehole. You'll never get close enough."

"Oh really? What about your little blonde side piece still trembling in the confession booth? I bet I can get to her."

My wide eyes dart to the little mouse trembling with fear, her arms wrapped over her chest as she stares at the slate floor, before I shoot them back to Finn.

Fuck.

He can see us.

"And the things I'd do before I kill her," he continues. "I'll even record it and send you the video once I'm done. I might even insist she keep those sexy fucking heels on."

My eyes mimic Finn's, wide shock before I mouth, 'cameras'.

Realisation crosses Finn's expression, and he steps away, probably to find Dominick, who's not only really fucking talented with a gun and knife, but is a hacking wizard.

"She's not my girl," I snap, trying to keep this fucker talking in the hopes he gives something about himself away.

"Isn't she? Then why save her and not Father Peters? You dived into that booth on her like your very existence depends on hers."

"She is nothing but an innocent woman that was in the wrong place at the wrong time." I point out.

"Oh how unfortunate for her," Mr V says empathetically before his tone fills with nothing but hate as he yells. "It looks like she's just another bystander that becomes collateral damage in everything you fucking touch!"

The line goes dead then, and for a long tense moment, there's not a sound to be heard in the church.

What the fuck just happened here?

My gaze drops to Phillip Randall as I remember the promise I gave him. Not that he deserves to get a promise, but his sister and her three children don't deserve to suffer.

"Lenny!" I bark, dragging my gaze from Phillip to find our shortest soldier, but just as fierce as everyone else, charging my way. "Do an ID check on both of them," I order, and as he nears I lower my voice to a whisper in case Mr V has audio feed into the church. "Find out who their families are and send a crew to do a welfare check. We may need to provide them protection as well."

"Yes, boss."

I roll my eyes. "Cut the shit, Lenny. How many times do we have to go over this? You're not in the police force anymore. Just use my fucking name."

He smirks, nodding. "Yes, boss."

He doesn't even flinch at my glare, the fucker not scared of anything. Not even me.

I'm not sure I like that.

"Cameras and audio are down," Dom calls from the doorway as he hurries in with Finn, and even though it's a relief to know the arsehole that ordered my hit tonight can no longer see or hear us, it doesn't fucking ease my tension, because what the fuck! Someone tried to kill me on sacred fucking ground!

"I want everything you can find on these two," I bark at both Dom and Finn as they stop before me. "Go through their phones, computers, contacts, fucking everything and find me Mr V!"

"On it." Dom nods, before dropping to search Phillip's body.

"Now tell me why the fuck you took so long to get in here from the street?" I snap at Finn.

"I already told you on the fucking phone. We couldn't get out of the car."

"Why? Because your hair would frizz in the rain?" I snap, and Finn smirks.

"Besides that." The fucker chuckles before turning serious. "We couldn't unlock the doors. We were locked in, and since the windows are bulletproof, Lenny had to slash through the back seat and smash his way into the trunk to break us out."

"The fuck. Why wouldn't the doors unlock?"

"Fucked if I know. Both cars were locked down."

Fuck. This doesn't make sense. How could that happen?

"Get the others and do a sweep of the vehicles. Mr fucking V knew we would be here. He's been tracking us somehow. The vehicles have obviously been compromised."

Finn nods. "I agree. Want me to ask Conrad to send some cars?"

I don't particularly want to involve my cousins but since they are at the top of the food chain here in Melbourne, if I don't, it'll probably end up biting me in the arse if I don't fill them in.

"Fuck it, yeah. Call Connie."

Finn chuckles. "He's gonna kick your arse if you keep calling him that."

I shrug. "I'd like to see him fucking try."

Conrad is one of eighteen spawned by the head of our family, Ewan Marx. My old man Leon, Ewan's brother, doesn't exactly see eye to eye with his older brother's ruling, mainly because my dad prefers to cause chaos wherever he goes, and Ewan demands compliance and adherence to strict rules. Rules which some of his own children fail to comply with.

"You're still in the Lord's house, Devon."

Father Peters' voice draws my gaze from Finn, and I take in the old guy looking more frail than I've ever seen him, yet the scowl in his expression remains firm.

"Apologies Father." I offer for my bad language. "Are you alright?"

He waves me off. "Just a bump on my head. Nothing serious."

That's a fucking relief.

Even as I think that, Father Peters wavers on his feet, and Miles hurries forward to catch him.

"Shit. Call the doc. Get him over here," I demand and Finn hurries to do that.

The hurried click of heels on the stone floor of the church draws my attention to see blonde hair fanning out behind the slender body of the little mouse I'd been enjoying the company of in the confessional as she tries to flee.

"Miles," I bark, gaining his attention. "Stop her."

CHAPTER THREE

Jaxcen

My heart thrashes wildly as I hurry forward, the glass door leading to the foyer in sight. I have to get out of here. I have to get home, lock my door, and hide.

"Hold up." A deep voice rumbles right before a wall of man steps into my path.

"Excuse me." I dart to the side, trying to round him, but he steps in my path again.

Huffing, my gaze travels up to lock onto the dark menacing eyes of a man so tall and wide that I feel dwarfed.

"Sorry, Miss. I can't let you leave."

"Please," I rush out. "I need to get home."

He answers with a simple and annoying shake of his head.

Dammit.

If I don't get away, they are going to kill me.

Weighing up my options, I know that staying here isn't one I'm willing to give in to, so I do what any smart minded woman would do.

I stomp on the man's foot with the heel of my Tony's.

The deep timber of the man's voice has disappeared as a broken squeak flies from his lips, and I don't waste another second, darting to the side and shoving through the doors.

Heavy feet pound the stone floor behind me, moving faster than these damn heels and pencil skirt will allow, but the mediaeval looking doors are in sight, so I charge forward, my arms outstretched ready to shove them open.

A moment before my hand touches the door, a strong arm snakes around me from behind and a scream lurches from my lungs as I'm lifted and I start kicking my legs wildly, trying anything to get free.

"No! Let me go!"

"Calm down, love."

It's him.

I only heard his deep rasp for the first time just minutes ago in the confessional, yet it has a profound effect on me.

An unhealthy effect.

You're engaged, Jaxcen! Get your head out of the gutter.

"Please let me go," I whimper as I continue to struggle, quickly realising my attempts to break his hold are futile.

I can't overpower him. His strength far outmatches mine.

"Come and sit down, little mouse."

What did he call me?

Still trapped in his arms, my back to his chest, he spins us and carries me back through the foyer doors, humiliation flaming my cheeks as all eyes turn to us. Well, more like they turn to me as I get carried like a useless doll.

"I won't tell anyone what I saw," I plead, my fingers trying to grip his arm to pry him loose. "Please. I just want to go home."

He ignores me, carrying me easily to a nearby pew before lowering me to my feet and releasing his hold. I immediately spin to face him, our gazes locking. Mine pleading. His deadly.

Dark eyes. Damp hair. Wet shirt.

"Sit."

"But—"

"SIT!"

His cold demand sends my arse to plonk on the pew and a pleased smirk tugs at his lips. Bending, he leans down, putting his face level with mine and stares into my eyes.

Can he see what I hide?

Can he see who I really am?

I gulp.

"Thanks for taking care of this for me." He winks, slipping his phone from my grip.

Dammit. I forgot I was holding it. I could have used it to call for help.

"Bag," he demands.

"What?"

"Give me your bag, love."

Naturally, I squeeze my bag to my chest, unwilling to hand it over. "What do you want with my bag? I don't have much money."

He chuckles, although the grin that pulls at his lips doesn't reach his eyes.

"I don't like repeating myself, little mouse. Bag. Now."

I don't know why, but everything in me is screaming not to hand it over to him, so I squeeze it tighter to my chest.

"For fuck's sake," he mutters, right before he grabs the strap off my shoulder and tugs. I hold firm, which makes him grunt, and before I know what's happening, the arsehole tickles my ribs, and a second later, my bag is no longer in my possession.

"Give it back," I demand, but all he does is shake his head, smirking as he takes a step back out into the aisle before rummaging through it.

Once again my cheeks are on fire from humiliation.

Why did I think this man was attractive? He's insufferable.

Pulling out my wallet, his eyes light with amusement as he glances at me while shoving my bag under his arm to hold it before he opens my wallet and pulls out my driver's licence.

Shit.

"Jaxcen Isabelle Summers. Date of birth…" he trails off, his brows shooting up before those dark eyes are on me again. "Twenty four years old. You look younger."

"And yet you still kissed me." I point out because I know I look young. Some might say too young, especially with so little makeup on. Like tonight.

My mum used to tell me it's a blessing and that I'll appreciate it when I'm older, but so far it's been a pain in my arse.

"Given you are roaming the streets so late on a Tuesday night in heels and corporate attire, I assumed you were at least of age." He shrugs, like the possibility of me only being eighteen is alright despite his age, clearly so much older than me, and how he pressed his thigh between my legs and...

Dammit. My cheeks heat and he notices, his lips twitching, and I just know he knows I'm remembering the few heated minutes we shared inside the confessional.

Turning his sights back onto my ID, he studies it some more. "Your apartment is only a couple of blocks from here."

"Yes." I straighten hopefully. "I'll go straight home. I promise. I won't go to the police."

All he does is smirk. No reply. No come back. No disagreement.

I want to smack that smirk right off his face.

Tugging my bag from under his arm, he slips my wallet back inside before bringing out my phone and sliding it into his back pocket, ignoring my gasp of protest.

"Please don't take my phone. I need that."

"I'm sure you do, to call someone for help. To be honest, I'm surprised you haven't already." He grins and I shrug.

"Maybe I have."

He chuckles. "Nice try, Miss Summers." Then, with that infuriating shit-eating grin he wears so well, he hands me my bag, his gaze refocusing on my ID still in his hand.

"What about that?"

Again, he doesn't say anything, but spins on his heel and walks off with my phone in his pocket and my ID in his grip before speaking to one of his men.

What is he doing?

Dread unfurls in my gut as my mind races to come to a conclusion.

There's no way I'm getting out of this unscathed. I witnessed him kill two men with ease. Not an ounce of remorse was on his expression as he took their lives as if he's done it a thousand times.

I bet he has.

I should have left the moment I recognised the aura of danger around him. Hell, I should never have gone back to that club. If I had just gone straight home after work and ignored the gnawing fire inside me then I wouldn't have needed to come here and ask the Lord for forgiveness for my perverted sins.

The man that begged for his life before it was brutally taken called him Devon Marx. That detail and the part about some guy ordering those two men to come and kill him is all I heard before my heart beat so wildly that I fell deaf to anything but the rush of blood in my ears.

I'd come to church seeking absolution, but instead I found the devil.

Speaking quietly with one of the men that came rushing in after he killed the shooter, they both eye me as they converse, not trying to hide the fact their discussion is about me.

Devon hands the man my licence, before turning his gaze back to me, and I suddenly can't swallow the lump that's lodged in my throat.

He's going to kill me.

A chill travels up my spine as he continues to stare, and hot tears prick the back of my eyes as I fight the need to cry.

Don't let him see, Jaxcen. Never let them see.

If I'm going to die, then I'll do it with dignity.

I jump with fright as the doors behind me fly open, and more men fill the space, moving to Devon like he's their captain. It only takes a second to recognise that he is definitely the ring leader here as the men listen and take orders from him.

That's when they start removing the dead bodies.

I squeeze my eyes shut as the lifeless eyes of one man come into view while two men lift him onto a tarp. There's a bloody hole in the centre of his forehead that I just know I'll never be able to unsee, along with the sound his body made earlier when it thudded to the stone floor, the life ripped from him.

My stomach churns.

Think happy thoughts. Think happy thoughts.

My sister comes to mind. Her hair and looks similar to mine, looking closer in age to me than we actually are. She's older, and much wiser, and has always had all her ducks in a row.

My ducks are an unsymmetrical zigzag of chaos that makes it hard to decipher, which is a never ending war inside my head.

Never quiet. Never at peace. Always disruptive.

"Are you alright Miss Summers?" My lids flash open at Father Peters' voice, and I watch as he comes to sit by my side.

"No, Father," I whisper, not trusting my voice to give away how close to tears I am. "That man is going to kill me."

His smile is warm, as he shakes his head, his hand coming to rest over mine, which is trembling so obviously that I'm surprised I didn't notice until now. "No, he won't."

"How do you know?" I lean in conspiratorially and he meets me halfway.

"Mr Marx may be the devil, but despite his reputation, he has morals."

My brows hitch. "Could have fooled me."

"There is no need to fear him, Miss Summers. All will be well." He offers, and now I know he's lying.

I want to point out that lying is a sin, but I suspect Father already knows.

"Do you want to continue the discussion we were having in the confessional while we wait?"

Do I want to discuss how I went back to the sex club tonight? How I was so close to giving in and participating?

"No," I rush out, remembering how I confessed what I'd done, and the shame that washed through me knowing how disappointed Father

Peters would be given I promised him just last week that I wouldn't return to Cloud 9.

It's too late for him to save me now, though. Especially after what happened in the booth with that man.

The devil.

My eyes, the traitors that they are, automatically seek out the man that holds my life in his hands. A man fit to be the devil just as Father Peters suggested.

It's like he knows when I'm looking at him, those dark pools darting to mine and flaring with something sinister.

I'm going to die.

It's in this moment that more people arrive, bursting through the doors like they own the place, and perhaps they do with the way they wear their expensive suits. Even the female accompanying them oozes power.

Why do I feel like I'm on the movie set for the Godfather?

A couple of them eye me, one of the younger men peruses me playfully as they all walk past, clearly checking me out before the deep gravel of Devon's voice scolds him.

"Keep your fucking eyes to yourself."

His glare is fierce as he stares down the newcomers, who don't seem the least bit worried.

"You call us out so close to Christmas to help your prickly arse, and yet you treat us so disrespectfully?" the peruser says with humour lacing his tone, and the others in his party laugh.

"Don't pretend like you were busy doing important shit." Devon rolls his eyes.

"You got that right." The only other female here giggles, standing next to the peruser. "He was trying to work his charms on a couple of wine stupored women that stumbled into Marick's from a Christmas party. His charm wasn't working."

"Hell, Liam. Fallon knows you too well." Devon smiles, and wow... that smile.

The way his lips pull wide, his white teeth flash, and dimples sink into the dark facial hair lining his jaw and lower cheeks is a sight to behold. Even his eyes seem to smile, which is such a contradiction to the cruel mask that he's had on most of the limited time since meeting him.

"Pfft. My sister is just jealous she wasn't getting any action." The peruser, whose name is apparently Liam, tries to brush it off, but the fact he leans in to whisper something in his sister's ear a moment later, gives him away.

He's pissed.

"Conrad." Devon nods to the oldest guy as they shake hands. "Thanks for dropping by."

"You need some cars?" Conrad asks and Devon nods before he starts filling them in on what happened.

Well, at least that's what I think he's doing since they stroll out of ear shot.

A minute later, another man walks in dressed all in black like he's some sort of Special Ops guy. Not that I'd know. I'm only jumping to that conclusion from TV shows and movies, but as I eye the gun on his hip and another in a holster on his upper thigh, it really is the only thing I can think of as to why he's dressed like that.

"Miss Summers." Father Peters regains my attention, and I peel my eyes from the military looking man. "The Marx family is... Let's just say, above the law."

As Father Peters gestures his head to the newcomers, my brows disappear into my hairline at his words.

"No one is above the law," I whisper and he shrugs.

"Some people are."

I scan the space again, taking in the many bodies and noting that they all seem to work seamlessly as they clean up the evidence of what happened here.

They *are* above the law.

Maybe the Godfather scene wasn't that far off from what is happening here.

I clear my throat, the lump forming seeming to get bigger with every breath I take.

Turning, I study Father Peters, taking in how tired his ageing eyes seem in comparison to when I first arrived earlier.

"Are you hurt, Father?"

He waves me off, "No. No. Nothing but a small bump on the head. I'll be fine. It's you I'm worried about."

I swallow thickly. "I thought you said I don't need to fear him."

"And you don't. That is not what I'm worried about." He leans in closer. "It's your struggles with temptation that have me concerned."

My cheeks heat. "I don't think we need to worry about that right now." I dismiss his concerns in the hope he'll drop it.

I know it's him I confess to in the booth, but it's easier to do it that way so I don't have to see his face. This, right here, being face to face is too confrontational for my liking.

"On the contrary, Miss Summers, I've been watching the way you and Mr Marx look at each other."

Oh my fuckety fuck.

It's that obvious?

Kill me now.

"Father, you remember Riggs?" Devon's voice breaks our little bubble, and I'm actually grateful this time for his interruption.

"Of course." Father Peters stands politely.

"I'll get my team to install new cameras and security measures in the morning, Father," Riggs, the black clad military man explains. "In the meantime, I'll leave a team of four men to stay on the property tonight." He hands Father Peters a card. "Call me if you have any concerns."

"Bless you, Mr Riggs." Father Peters bows his head in thanks.

"We'll help your men get the Range Rovers back to one of our workshops to go over with a fine tooth comb." Riggs explains as he turns his attention to Devin who nods.

"Excellent. I need to go. How likely is it that Connie will loan me one of his Corvettes across the street?"

Riggs smirks. "Well, he's right into Christmas, so maybe use that shit as an excuse when you drop to your knees and beg."

Devon scoffs. "I don't fall to my knees for anyone."

And hell, I believe him. I can't imagine anyone would have the power to make him do that.

The men walk off, having a discussion about cars, and Father Peters gets led away with discussions of security, leaving me alone on the pew.

Glancing around, I notice everyone is busy. No one is paying me a lick of attention. Maybe if I slip my heels off, I can discreetly disappear before anyone notices.

Devon has my licence which has my address on it, but I still have my handbag. I have enough cash to pay for a hotel for the night, and then tomorrow, maybe I can go to my sister's until I can figure out what to do.

With a somewhat sketchy plan in my head, I subtly lean to the side, reaching down to slip off one of my heels, before doing the same with the other. Just the thought of trying to run again has my heart thundering in my chest, my pulse so loud in my ears that all noise from inside the church gets muffled.

You can do this.

I glance around again, still noticing everyone busy and preoccupied.

Just go, Jaxcen!

Slowly, I stand, my legs shaky as I glance around to see if anyone notices.

Nothing.

I take a step to the side, slipping out of the pew.

Still nothing.

This is it.

My gaze locks on the doors, and I run.

Vida Loca
Trust

Chapter Four
Devon

"Are you planning on keeping that delectable blonde?" Liam asks with a smirk, and I glare at the fucker.

He's always trying to pick up chicks no matter who they belong to.

"She is mine. Stop eyeing her like she's your fucking dessert."

He shrugs like he doesn't care either way. "I just thought you might care to know she's running."

My eyes dart to the pew I sat her on earlier, noticing it empty, and then to her blonde hair as it disappears through the fucking doors.

"Fuck," I snap. "Time to go. Can I borrow one of your babies or not?" I ask Conrad as I hurry forward, and his "whatever," reaches my ears as I start to run.

Storming through the doors into the foyer, I find the exterior doors just closing. Another curse flies past my lips as I shove them open to see my little mouse running as fast as she can in bare feet up the path, her skirt which tapers in at the knees making it hard for her to lengthen her strides.

I grin, storming forward with my prey in sight, ignoring the heavy drops of rain that still fall.

My strides are twice as long as hers, so it doesn't take much for me to catch up to her as Liam calls out behind me.

"Run, run as fast as you can! You can't outrun Devon, the devil man!"

I'm going to kick his arse.

His laugh meets my ears as Jaxcen squeals in alarm, and a second later, I have my arms wrapped around her middle again.

"You'll never escape me, little mouse," I growl, right before she screams at my contact, flailing just as she did earlier, but this time I spin her in my arms and hoist her over my shoulder.

"Put me down!" She protests, one of her dainty fists pounding my back, warranting the slap I give her arse as I turn to face my cousins with a shit-eating grin.

"Right, Connie. Lead the way to my new ride."

"Call me Connie again, and the only ride you'll be in is a fucking hearse."

I roar with laughter at my cousin, who fights to hide his own smirk with his brother Liam and Liam's twin sister Fallon at his side.

"Put me down you... you... monster!" Jaxcen continues to pound my back, so again, I slap my palm onto her perky globe which is so fucking close to my head that I'm tempted to sink my teeth in.

That'll really make her squeal.

Fuck. I'd love to hear that.

"You really do have a way with women." Fallon smirks, and I spin to walk ahead of them, noticing my little mouse has now fallen quiet.

"You doing okay there?" Liam asks Jaxcen as we walk, and she grumbles.

"Just peachy."

They all laugh.

Passing my compromised Land Rovers, I grit my teeth in frustration at how someone was fucking able to get close enough to fuck with them. Whoever this Mr V fucker is, he's done his homework, and I don't fucking like it.

Hurrying across the road and tram tracks, we walk in silence up the path to the side entrance of Conrad's performance car dealership.

Once inside, he lights up the space revealing the cars in the showroom.

"Where's the good one?" I ask as I lower my little mouse to her feet, only to score myself a harsh glare.

Shit. It looks like she wants to hit me.

How fun.

"You don't need the good one. Just take one of these," Conrad grunts but I shake my head.

"No way. Give me the red Corvette."

Conrad rolls his eyes. "Fine. It's in the back, but if you so much as scratch her, I'll fuck you up."

I chuckle, taking Jaxcen's hand in mine and pulling her along with me. "I'd like to see you try."

Ignoring Conrad's grumble, I lead my little mouse into the back section of the dealership to find the sexiest fucking car I've ever seen.

It's Conrad's favourite, which is exactly why I'm insisting on taking it. Annoying him is worth his bitching.

As he hands me the keys, I notice Fallon eyeing Jaxcen, and I just know she's about to start shit.

"You're not his usual type."

And there it is. Fallon being fucking Fallon. Always causing trouble.

Jaxcen scoffs, "I'm not with him."

"One hundred bucks says you don't last a day." Fallon giggles and I roll my eyes, wanting to take the bet on a matter of hours instead of a day given what we shared in the confessional.

"Leave her alone, Fal." Liam chuckles, before turning his sights to my little mouse. "Ignore her, she likes to stir shit."

Fallon rolls her eyes. "As if he's not going to be balls deep inside her as soon as he can. Look how protective he was of her when you were checking her out."

"True." Liam fucking nods, and I want to punch the fucker.

One glance at my little mouse shows how uncomfortable she is with this entire conversation. I could join my cousins in stirring things up, because that's how we roll sometimes, but my need to get inside the car and out of here is eating at me.

Maybe it's because I want to get her alone. But then there's also the fact that this Mr V fucker is out there somewhere and I have no idea if he's gearing up to hit again tonight.

He made his intentions clear, though. He noticed her. He noticed my reaction to her. And now it's put a target on her back.

"Come on, love." I ignore my cousins and open the car door. "In you get."

Frantic eyes dart to my cousins and then to me, before her timid plea reaches my ears.

"Please, I just want to go home."

Gritting my fucking teeth, I don't miss the curiosity on my cousins' expressions. They're waiting to see how I react. They're waiting to see if I'll give in and take my little mouse home. But I can't do that. Not now that she's attracted the attention of someone who is clearly out for revenge.

"For now, your home is where I say it is. Get in the fucking car," I snap, and a whimper escapes her as she takes an uneasy step back.

"Wanna clue us in?" Conrad asks, this time concern creasing his brow.

"Later," I bark, returning my furious gaze to my little mouse. "Get in, Jaxcen."

She takes another fucking step back and a savage growl rumbles in my chest as I point to the seat inside the five hundred thousand dollar car.

"Either get in willingly, or I'll put you in there myself and tie you to the fucking seat."

"This just keeps getting better and better." Fallon snickers, and I'm about to rip my cousin a new one when Jaxcen beats me to it.

"I'm glad the fact this arsehole is kidnapping me amuses you so much!" she snaps, her glare harsh and fuck, just the sight has my dick stirring.

She looks so innocent and sweet, yet there's fire in her, and fuck if that doesn't make me want to devour her even more.

While I stare at my feisty little mouse, my cousins chuckle as Liam nods.

"She got the arsehole part right, hey Dev."

I roll my fucking eyes.

"She's a bit too feisty for you, Dev. You sure you can handle her?" Conrad asks and I scoff.

"I can handle anything."

"Cocky much?"

The retort comes from my little mouse, right before she glares at me like she wants to stab my eyeballs out with the sharpest knife she can find. Nevertheless, she gets in the car with a huff.

My arsehole cousins' *ooooh's* meet my ears, but I can't take my eyes off my little mouse as I notice her hands glide over the soft leather of the seat and I just know she's enjoying the luxury of the expensive car.

Closing her in, I dodge a few more questions my cousins throw my way as to who Jaxcen is and what exactly is going on, before I'm sliding into the car with her and closing us in together.

Our eyes meet in the confined space, and I get the feeling she wants to say something, but it's almost like now that we're alone together, she's lost her nerve.

The thought tugs at my lips and I try to hide my smirk.

"Seatbelt," I say and I start the car, the engine roaring to life.

As if she's just remembered that we're about to drive in a car, she quickly feels for her seatbelt before tugging it across her body, her eyes wide like she's about to go on a rollercoaster ride.

Hell. Perhaps she is.

Conrad presses a button to the side of the garage, and the door starts to roll up as I rev the engine a few times making sure to fit my own seatbelt. The lights from the dash illuminate the cabin, the warm glow dancing over the flawless skin on Jaxcen's delicate cheeks, making her appear more angelic than human.

"What do I have to do for you to let me go home?"

Her question takes me by surprise. For some reason, I figured any argument about what was happening here had finished, but she's not giving up.

I have to say. I like that about her.

She's a fighter.

"There's nothing you can do. You're coming with me."

"Where?"

A slow, sinister smirk tugs at my lips as our eyes remain locked, and I rev the engine a few more times, just for effect before I answer.

"To hell."

It's then that I shift gears and plant my foot, shooting us out into the dark night, the rain soaked street adding to the effect of the tires sliding as I turn the wheel.

A squeal escapes her and I laugh maniacally as I plant the gas and speed through the streets of Melbourne, heading towards the eastern suburbs.

Her dainty hands grip the sides of the seat, her knuckles turning white as she holds on for dear life. Where I can, I accelerate fast. Much faster than what is legal, which spikes my adrenalin to life.

There's just something about speeding up the freeway in a five hundred thousand dollar car that has me wanting to see just how fast this baby can go.

"Please slow down."

The quiet plea from my little mouse brings my gaze to hers and the fear etched across her face is what has me lifting my foot off the accelerator to slow to a normal speed.

"You don't like going fast?"

"I don't mind fast things," she mutters, "I just prefer not to be another statistic wrapped around a tree."

I chuckle. "There aren't any trees out here on this part of the free-way."

"A concrete bollard, then." She scoffs, and my gaze manages to catch her eye roll.

She has a point. I don't exactly want to become another road fatality statistic either, so I maintain the legal speed limit, keeping an eye on my mirrors to make sure we aren't being followed.

"So, Jaxcen Summers. Tell me why you just had to utilise Father Peters for a confession, so late on a Tuesday evening?"

If the lights were better inside the cabin, I just know she'd be blushing right now. She shifts nervously in her seat, and when I risk a glance, I notice those pretty pink plump lips sealed together in a tight line, like she's trying to hold back her answer.

"Oh, come on, love. Would it really be so bad to tell me why you were there?"

"Maybe." She responds quickly, and I chuckle, checking my mirrors as I change lanes to go around a truck.

"At least tell me what sort of confession it was." I continue, not ready to give up. "Was it like, bless me, Father, for I have sinned. I didn't eat all my vegetables today."

She shoots me a 'really' glare before turning her sights back out to the window.

"Or was it, bless me, Father, for I have sinned. I let someone eat *me* today."

Her gaze shoots back to me wide eyed in disbelief, and I'm grinning from ear to fucking ear.

"That was it, wasn't it? You totally went there tonight to confess a sex sin, didn't you?"

"No, I did not." She rushes out, panic lacing her tone, and I can't help but laugh.

"Yeah, you did. That's exactly why you went there tonight." I snicker teasingly. "What's wrong little mouse? You feeling guilty about getting all down and dirty with someone?"

"No! That's not what happened!"

"Yeah, I think that's exactly what happened." I deadpan. "Was it someone from work? Perhaps your boss?"

"No, it wasn't my boss. I mean... no, that's not what happened."

My laugh is loud in the confined space of the Corvette as I throw my head back, which just seems to annoy her, a scoff flying past her lips as she shifts uncomfortably in the seat and wraps her arms angrily over her chest.

That's when I see it. The glint of a diamond ring on her finger.

An engagement ring.

"You know, there's nothing wrong with a bit of workplace romance, little mouse." I tease, dragging my gaze away from the small rock and gaining her glare.

"Would you stop calling me that?"

"Why? What's wrong with little mouse?" I ask innocently before shooting her a wink. "I think it suits you."

"It does not. It makes me seem like I'm weak."

My brows shoot high. "Hell, love. There's nothing weak about you. You're a feisty, fiery little thing, I'll give you that."

At my words, her own brows shoot up for a beat before her scowl returns.

"Where are you taking me?" she asks, trying to change the conversation, and I bite back my laugh this time.

"I'll tell you what." I grin as we pass another lone truck on the freeway. "I'll tell you exactly where I'm taking you, if you tell me exactly why you went to see Father Peters tonight."

She scoffs in disbelief. "How about I tell the first person I see that you just killed two men in a church."

And again, I'm fucking laughing.

This girl. She's hilarious.

I'm not sure I've ever met someone that can be so timid, yet so sensual and so feisty in one sexy little package.

"And what do you think will happen to you if you go around telling people what you saw tonight?" I ask.

"What does it matter? You're going to kill me anyway. You're probably driving me out of town to do just that," she snaps. "Will you make me dig my own grave in the middle of the bush somewhere before you shoot me in the head?"

"Well, someone's been watching too many true crime dramas." I point out.

"That's why it's called true crime, because it actually happens in real life." She counters, and I can't help but laugh again.

"Since you think you've got me all figured out, little mouse, what have you got to lose by telling me why you went to confession tonight?"

"How about my dignity?"

"You didn't seem to have much dignity when I had my thigh pressed between your legs."

Her dark lashes flutter as she shoots her gaze out the passenger window again, trying to hide the fact that her cheeks are most likely on fire.

Fuck, I wish I could see them. I wish I could see how the red tints her skin. I wonder if it travels up her neck and reaches the tips of her ears, giving her feelings away to anyone that is watching.

"Come on, love. You didn't seem that shy in the confessional. Why have things changed now?"

Anger flares to life as her head darts back in my direction, those big blue eyes wide with fury.

"You tricked me," she snaps. "You told me to kiss you. You said that you were about to die, and yet you knew damn well you weren't going to." She shakes her head like she's angry at herself. "I know now you knew you weren't going to."

"I might have died. Those men might have had one up on me that could have killed me before I even fired my gun so that may just have been my last kiss."

"But it wasn't."

I frown. "So you wish me dead, is that it? You give me a kiss and wish me dead." Her expression contorts into shame, but I stop that in its tracks. "Ah, woman. You are so cruel." I slap my hand over my chest, feigning a wounded heart.

And that's when I see the slight tug of her lips.

I nearly made her smile.

"I have to say, love, as far as last kisses go, it was fucking hot. Sent the blood straight to my cock which made it really fucking hard to leap out like a hero and shoot those motherfuckers."

She rolls her eyes. "You didn't seem to have much trouble from where I was sitting."

I wag my brows. "Were you checking out my arse?"

"Are you always so crude?"

I shrug and nod at the same time. "Well, yeah. Pretty much."

She huffs in frustration, her eyes staring out the windscreen again, but I'm not ready to give up on her just yet.

"What would you say to a deal?" I ask, as the freeway lights slowly lessen the closer we get to the regional fringe. "A trade of sorts?"

"What do you mean?"

Damn. Is that curiosity I hear in her tone?

"How about you tell me exactly what you said to Father Peters in that confession booth, and in exchange, I agree not to kill you."

Knowing I'll likely get a less than stellar reception from my idea, I keep my eyes focused on the road ahead and a moment later, I can feel her eyes boring into the side of my head. They're like a sharp knife stabbing right through my temple.

If looks could kill, Jaxcen Summers would have just murdered me, but thankfully she doesn't have that power.

"I think it's a pretty good deal," I continue. "You want to live, right?"

"How do I know you won't just kill me anyway?"

Smart girl.

"You don't." I shrug. "But what's the alternative? You stay quiet and I take you out to the bush, make you dig your own grave and shoot you in the head."

"Why are you doing this?" she whimpers. "I swear I won't tell anyone. Please just let me go home. My family is going to be worried."

She's right. Her family will be worried. Especially whoever put that ring on her finger. They'll be wondering why she's disappeared, which is why I've already arranged for Finn and Dom to dive into her background and see if we need to come up with a story until I can get this shit show fucking sorted out. I didn't contemplate her having a fucking fiancé though, given how young she is.

It's a problem, but one my men can handle, so for now, her family will simply think she's decided to spend Christmas with a friend. Or perhaps she's run off with her new lover.

Yeah, I like the sound of that better.

I mean, it's not that far from the truth, right?

"I can't let you go, little mouse, but I can keep you alive. All you have to do is tell me what you confessed."

The cabin falls quiet. The only sound is the rev of the Corvette as we travel towards country Victoria.

At first I think she's not going to answer, and hell, I'm not going to force her. I was just hoping I could use a little blackmail to find out what makes her tick. But when she clears her throat and shifts nervously in her seat, I know she's about to reveal her secret. The one that has her so ashamed that she had to go to confession on a wet and stormy Tuesday night in December, only five days from Christmas.

Chapter Five

Jaxcen

The way my skin flushes can't be normal. Yes, I'm humiliated about what I'm about to do. But is that really why I feel like I'm burning up from the inside out? Maybe it's because I've never had to admit these things face to face before. Or maybe it's because I'm admitting them to *this* man. *The devil.*

But what's the alternative? If I don't tell him, he's going to kill me. So to hell with my dignity. I have to do this. I have to survive.

"I went to see Father Peters tonight because—"

"No." He cuts me off. "Don't explain to me why you went. Confess to me exactly like you did to Father Peters."

"What?" I squeak.

"You heard me, little mouse. Confess to me. Pretend I'm Father Peters. Pretend I'm the person on the other side of the confessional for you to divulge your most wicked sins to."

"I don't want to do this. I've changed my mind," I rush out, shaking my head.

"So you'd rather die?" he asks, dark brows raised. "Okay then."

Flipping on the indicator, Devon veers across four lanes of what would normally be packed with traffic, and speeds up an exit.

"What are you doing?" I stiffen, glancing out the windscreen.

"I'm taking you bush." He shrugs, like it's no big deal. "What do you think I'm doing?"

"But…"

He chuckles darkly. "But nothing, little mouse. The deal was, you confess and you get to live. But since you seem to have so much trouble doing that, then let's cut the shit and get the killing part over with."

Oh my God, he can't be serious. Is he really going to force me to treat him like he's a father? Like he's a man of the cloth?

My stomach churns. Unease rushes through my whole body, my palms so sweaty that I need to wipe them over my skirt to dry them off.

At the top of the exit, he pulls the sleek red car to a stop before turning his dark eyes to me.

"So what's it gonna be, little mouse? Are you going to confess? Or shall we turn left and head to the mountains to find you a nice place to rest for eternity?"

Tears well in my eyes. My chest aching from the fear racing my heart at knowing I have to do this. I have to tell him.

"Fine," I snap, waving my hand in the direction of the freeway we just exited. "I'll tell you. I'll confess."

"Atta girl." He grins, and then plants his foot down on the accelerator and speeds straight through the intersection, and back onto the freeway.

"Don't even think about making your confession up, little mouse. I'll know if you're lying." He shoots me a warning glare that sends a chill up my spine. "Which is one of the twelve cardinal sins. Don't forget that."

I roll my eyes. "Yes, it is. You must have forgotten that murder is also one of the twelve cardinal sins."

I can't believe I just said that to a man that has the ability to kill me before I take my next breath. But then the wicked grin he shoots me tells me he's not at all angry. In fact, he looks damn proud about the fact he murdered someone.

What kind of sick and twisted man is he?

A sick and twisted man that will kill me if I don't do what he says.

"Bless me, Father, for I have sinned." I start, my voice shaky with embarrassment as he nods in satisfaction. I want to punch him. I want to dig my nails into his unfortunately attractive face, and tear his flesh from his bones. "It's been one week since my last confession."

"One week?" he asks, dragging his gaze from the road momentarily. "Is that all? You seem to be a little *sinner*." He draws the word sinner out like it's a delectable treat. Like it's something to be proud of. Like it's not the bane of my existence.

"Yes." I nod, trying to ignore his curious gaze. "One week. Can I continue?" I snap, and even though he's smirking, he nods.

"I went back." I repeat the words I said to Father Peters, and Devon's brows shoot up, his dark gaze darting to mine before returning to the road.

"Back where, little mouse?"

"I don't have to tell you that part. Father Peters already knew."

Devon chuckles, his teeth flashing briefly as he bites his lower lip.

"Well, Father Devon doesn't know. So how about you tell me?"

My God, he's really gonna make me do this, isn't he?

"I went back to the club," I rush out, wanting this to be over already.

"What club?"

"Cloud 9," I admit, and at the mention of one of the city's most exclusive sex clubs, I risk a glance to see his brows have shot high as his foot lifts off the accelerator, the car slowing before he realises what's happened.

Holy shit. Did I just shock Devon Marx?

"*You* went to Cloud 9?" he asks in disbelief, and I glare at him.

"Yes, *I* went to Cloud 9, and not for the first time I might add."

Dammit. Why did I say that like I'm proud of that fact? I'm not. It's... wrong.

"Wow, little mouse, you don't really look like the type of girl that would go to a sex club."

"Haven't you heard the saying you shouldn't judge a book by its cover?" I retort.

"Oh, I've heard it all right. And now I'm fucking intrigued to know what happened in Cloud 9 when little Miss Jaxcen Summers made an appearance."

"That's not part of my confession," I snap, hoping to God he doesn't dig for more information. This is already humiliating enough.

"Of course." He lifts his hand from the steering wheel and waves it in the air. "Miss Summers, continue with your confession."

I roll my eyes so hard it brings on an instant headache which is the last thing I need.

I clear my throat. "Father Peters asked when it happened, and I admitted that I went there tonight. And Sunday night. And Friday night."

Throwing his head back, Devon's laugh is loud in the confined space. "Oh wow. You're a frequent flyer. I would never have fucking guessed." He shakes his head, his grin wide. "Damn, little mouse."

"I'm not a frequent flyer. I just go to watch."

The words are out of my mouth before I can stop them, and I slap my hand over my lips, completely mortified. This is utterly humiliating and my gaze darts to the door handle.

Open it and jump, Jaxcen.

Before I can follow through with my inner demon's demand, my gaze travels back to Devon to see the most sinister gaze staring back at me.

"So my little mouse is a voyeur."

My lips thin, and I force them to remain sealed shut, not wanting to admit to that, but Devon simply shakes his head, pointing out the window to a road sign we pass on the side of the freeway.

"The next exit has an even better place I can bury you."

Ugh. This man.

Never in my life have I wanted to punch someone more than I want to punch him.

"Fine." I huff. "I guess I am kind of a voyeur."

And there's that shit-eating grin again.

Goddamnit.

"So, little mouse, what did Father Peters have to say about you going to Cloud 9 so frequently?"

"He asked me what keeps drawing me back," I divulge, not sure that I care about my pride anymore.

"Hell, I know what keeps drawing you back." He nods, "But please continue. What is it that keeps drawing my little mouse back to Cloud 9?"

For another moment I contemplate opening the door of the Corvette and just slipping out to my death. Surely that would be less painful than having to admit my most darkest secrets to this animal. But then again, I get the feeling he probably wouldn't be all that shocked by the thoughts I have. By the needs that drive me so many times back to a sex club despite the fact I'm engaged. Despite the fact my fiancé shames me for getting aroused and wanting to do more with him.

Maybe Devon Marx is exactly the right person to confess these types of sins to.

"My impure thoughts are what send me back," I finally admit.

"So you have impure thoughts, and you go to a sex club to indulge a little, yet when you leave, you have the urge to confess this for God's forgiveness?"

"Yes."

"Why?" he asks so seriously, and this time I'm not that ashamed to admit the reason why.

"I'm scared."

There. I've said it out loud to this wicked man. Nothing can be worse than that.

Well, I guess death by his hands could be.

"Scared of what, little mouse?"

"Indulging," I admit so freely. It's like he has a hold of me. Like I'm a puppet he's controlling.

I guess I really would do just about anything to save my own life.

"What did Father Peters say about indulging?" Devon nudges, his tone laced with curiosity.

"He said something about temptation being acknowledged by God. That resisting it can bring strong personal growth, but that the Lord does not wish us to face temptations that are beyond our ability to resist. And then he pointed out that Cloud 9 seems to be beyond my ability."

"And what do you think about that? Do you think going to Cloud 9 is beyond your ability to resist?" The deep gravel of his tone, no longer harsh or playful, but rather utterly mindful, penetrates beneath my flesh, settling over me like a second skin as I part my lips to answer in a whisper.

"Sometimes I think the temptation will suffocate me if I don't give in to it."

Something that sounds a helluva lot like a growl rumbles in his chest, and I notice his hands gripping the steering wheel, his knuckles white like he's trying to strangle it. I'm not sure what it is about my words that has him reacting this way, but I don't think it's good.

"So you go to Cloud 9. You watch but you haven't given in to temptation. The temptation of what little mouse?" he asks. "Of joining in? Of stepping into the throes of an orgy laid out before you? Of letting other men and women touch you in places you ache to be touched?"

"Stop." I rush out as heat pools between my legs, reminding me of my devious desires.

"What's so wrong with that?" he asks in all seriousness.

"What do you mean?" I snap, staring at him in disbelief. "It's so inappropriate."

"For who exactly?" he asks, his eyes watching something in the rearview mirror before he returns his attention to the road. "Is it inappropriate for the people that are there because they want to be? They're there because they want to indulge, little mouse. They are there because they want to be explored and to explore. To push their boundaries and give in to the temptations. Why is that wrong?"

"It just is," I rush out, my lower lip quivering as shame washes over me.

What would Eddie say if he knew? Would he cancel our engagement? Would he insist on counselling with Father Peters? Hell, I know Father Peters has already offered so many times, knowing the struggles I have. Knowing I'm about to be married.

I know Eddie would cancel our engagement. Without a doubt.

Hell, he hasn't even let me kiss him properly. Nothing more than a peck. How many times have I practically begged him to even touch me? Sometimes I wonder why we're even getting married. And yes, I know it was always something that's meant to happen. Growing up together, our parents always threw us together, smiling and talking about the day we would get married. So is that really why I said yes to him? To appease my family?

It's not the first time I've had that thought, but it's the first time I want to scream. Because yes, I think that's exactly why I said yes. Everything I've been doing, my schooling, my work, my friends, my relationships, are all to appease my family and Eddie. No one's ever asked me what I want to do. No one has ever asked me if I even want to be married. If that's the type of future I want for myself.

Everything is just expected.

"So I'm guessing by your reaction that you don't go to Cloud 9 with your fiancé."

My eyes dart to his and his gaze shoots to my hand telling me he's noticed my engagement ring.

Even though it's too late and I know he's seen it, I still shove my hand under my thigh, covering up the evidence like it will somehow make a difference.

"Why don't you go to Cloud 9 with your fiancé, little mouse? Surely you would both get some enjoyment out of it and you wouldn't have to only watch. I'm guessing that's why you stand on the sidelines because you're a taken woman and adultery is a sin you're not willing to commit."

My cheeks flare remembering how I kissed this man not that long ago.

Yes, it was because I thought I was giving him his dying wish, but it doesn't change the fact that I did that. I still gave in and pressed my lips to his despite the fact he's not my fiancé.

I internally scoff. Eddie thinks kissing before we are married is a sin.

"Eddie isn't like that," I rush out, for some reason trying to defend the man that isn't even here, that would so quickly throw me under the bus and shame me for my thoughts and desires. For my attendance at such a club.

"Your fiancé doesn't like sex clubs?" Devon asks, surprise lacing his tone, like it's absurd.

"He's a very religious man." I point out.

"Is that why you go to church, little mouse? For your fiancé?"

I want to say no, but the fact of the matter is that is exactly why I go to church. It's exactly why I've been going to church since I was fourteen years old. For Eddie. For his parents.

"Like I said, he's a very religious man."

The car is now surrounded by darkness, not a light in sight as we travel further into the country. I still have no idea if I can take his word that he won't kill me, but I have to hope that wherever he is taking me, isn't to my grave.

"Am I to take it that your fiancé, given he is such a religious man, also doesn't believe in premarital sex?"

Oh my God, is he really going there?

I want to slap myself just for wondering that because of course he is going there. He's been on a mission to get inside my head, to see my darkest thoughts since the moment we got inside this car.

"You don't need to know that. It's not part of my confession." I rebuke, but he just snickers.

"Since your life is in my hands, little mouse, then you'll tell me what I want to know," he snaps, an air of danger lacing his tone.

Goddammit.

"Fine," I huff. "Eddie doesn't believe in premarital sex, okay? Are you happy? Does that make you feel better?"

"Fuck, no. That only makes me feel sad for you. That your arsehole fiancé has been holding out on you. No wonder you're going to a club."

"That's not why I go to the club."

"Isn't it?"

I worry my lip as I consider it. It's absolutely why I go to the club. My curiosity got the better of me. Watching things online just wasn't cutting it anymore. I wanted real. I wanted to see how people actually behave when they aren't in front of a camera filming a scene. I wanted to see it in the flesh since it seems so far from anything I've experienced.

"I guess perhaps it's part of why I go," I admit, but I don't dare look at him.

I can see in my peripheral that he watches me every now and then, dragging his eyes from the road. But I can't bear to see those dark eyes. Smouldering, sinfully dark eyes.

"Are you a virgin, little mouse?" he asks, and I nearly choke on my own saliva as my gaze darts back in his direction.

"That is none of your business," I snap, and he chuckles.

"Actually, right now it *is* my business. Answer me," he demands and another shiver runs up my spine.

I hate him.

"Fine, if you must know, no, I'm not a virgin."

"Huh. Why do I feel like you're lying?"

Shame engulfs my cheeks as memories swarm me. I have never told anyone this. As far as everyone knows, I am a virgin and I'm not exactly sure how I'm going to explain it to Eddie on our wedding night.

Will he notice the lack of blood?

I'm sure it will still hurt to an extent given it only happened one time, but I haven't been able to tell my fiancé. I haven't been able to tell my sister. I haven't been able to tell anyone.

"I don't understand why you need to know this," I snap, crossing my arms over my chest again. "I've confessed. I told you what I went to see Father Peters about."

"Yes, but that just opens up so many more questions, little mouse." He points out. "You said so yourself. You've been going to that club on the regular. You're engaged. You don't engage in premarital sex, yet claim not to be a virgin. So why not push your fiancé for a little bit of intimacy?"

"He doesn't know," I admit, almost hating myself for saying it out loud

"He doesn't know you're not a virgin?" Devon asks and I don't need to look at him to know he's surprised by that. It's in his tone, so I nod. "How interesting, little mouse."

"I wouldn't call it interesting." I deadpan, feeling the weight of that lie settle in my gut.

When Eddie finds out, will he ask for an annulment? Will he demand our marriage be dissolved?

And will I care?

Sometimes I wonder if perhaps that's all I'm waiting for. For Eddie to find out the truth. For Eddie to find out that I'm not pure. That I'm not innocent. That I haven't abstained.

It's easier for me to accept him walking away from me than having the courage for me to do it myself. Which just makes me a coward, really.

It makes me that weak, little mouse.

"From where I'm sitting, it's very interesting. You're getting married to a man who's very religious. Abstains from premarital sex and who assumes his wife will be a virgin on their wedding night. How exactly do you think you're going to get out of that, little mouse? Because I can guarantee, he will notice."

"Will he?" I ask, genuinely curious. "He's a virgin. How will he notice? How will he know if he has nothing to compare it to?"

I glance over to see Devon nodding. "You have a point, if he is indeed a virgin then he won't notice. But how do you know that he is one?"

I frown. "We've been together since we were kids. Officially since we were fourteen. He hasn't been with anyone."

"But he could have." Devon continues, and I really get the feeling he just likes fucking with people's emotions. "How would you know? How do you know that while you're at Cloud 9 he's not with another woman? Because you have secrets too, you know, little mouse. So why wouldn't he?"

The thought makes me feel sick. And then I want to slap myself for even feeling that way because I have been lying to Eddie for so long.

Why do I even care if Eddie has been with someone else when I know deep down I don't even want to marry him? Hell, I don't even know if I want to kiss him. Not anymore. Not the way I used to want to. But he's turned me down so many times over the years, and now I just look at him like he's my brother or something. Which is a whole other issue that I'm going to have to get over before our wedding in a couple of months.

"I guess I don't know," I admit, kind of hating to say the words out loud.

"How old is he?" Devon asks.

"He's the same age as me. Older by a few months. He'll be twenty-five in the new year."

"Did you both go to university?"

I nod. "Yes. We attended universities in the city, but we didn't go to the same one."

"So in a way, you have your own lives outside of your relationship."

"Well, yes, doesn't everyone?"

"To an extent, but what I'm about to say to you, little mouse, isn't to make you feel like shit. I'm not saying it to be a mean motherfucker, even though I am most of the time." His serious gaze locks with mine for a minute before he returns it to the road. "I'm saying it to be honest."

I gulp, not sure if I'm ready to hear what he has to say.

"There's a ninety-five percent chance that your fiancé hasn't been a virgin for a long time."

"You can't know that. You don't know him. He's... different."

"Unless he's an ugly fucker, I'm gonna tell you right now that he's already given in to temptation and sunk his dick that he refuses to use on you, into some bitch in the city. Hell even if he's a little on the dorky side, he probably paid for it."

I gasp. "Eddie would never go to a prostitute."

Devon throws his head back, laughing. "Oh little mouse, you have so much to learn. He probably went to a prostitute before he was even 18 years old."

"If that's the case, then why wouldn't he want to have sex with me?" I snap, feeling proud that I've put a kink in his theory. That is, until he speaks.

"Well, there's a few reasons that could be." He glances at me, and I'm expecting that infuriating shit-eating grin again, but all I see is something that looks a helluva lot like sympathy. "One, because he's likely a lying arsehole. Two because he could be gay, and you are his beard. And three, some men see their wife as the mother of their children, and they can't imagine doing the things to their wives that they like to do to the whores. He could be seeking his dirty desires elsewhere, outside the marital bed."

I feel sick.

Not because his words are a lie, but because I feel like they are so close to the truth.

Have I really been abstaining for someone who doesn't really want me?

Would it really be such a sin to give in to my desires and just indulge?

I consider that for a moment. The fact that tonight I nearly did it. I walked up to a man and woman at Cloud 9 and was about to let them touch me, and then not an hour later, I kissed a man inside a confessional that wasn't my fiancé.

I've already sinned, and in return, I was nearly shot and somehow wound up in the lap of the devil himself.

At the sound of the indicator, I glance out the windscreen to see that we are turning off the freeway, taking the exit that has a sign reading, *Welcome to the Timber Valley region.*

I've never been out this way before, but I know it's surrounded by pine trees. Lots and lots of pine trees and bushland. A lot of good places to bury someone.

"Where are we going?" I ask again, hoping this time he'll tell me the truth.

He chuckles wickedly. "I've already told you, little mouse. We're going to hell."

Suddenly, the idea of going somewhere that is most likely my final resting place with this savage is an unbearable thought. If he's going to kill me, then I'll make him work for it. I won't die without a fight.

As the dark pine forest flashes past the window, I reach for the door handle while simultaneously unclipping my seatbelt. The moment it unlatches, a ding of warning sounds in the car, and as Devon yells a surprised '*hey*,' I open the door and prepare to jump.

Vida Loca
Trust

Chapter Six

Devon

The fuck is she doing?

"Jaxcen!" I yell, my hand snapping out to fist her blazer in my grip as the door swings wide. On instinct, my foot lifts off the accelerator, slowing the car's pace as the god damn pine forest passes by in a rush.

"Just let me go!" she cries, fighting against my hold.

"If you jump, you'll fucking die, woman! What is wrong with you?"

"I would rather die this way, than have you lead me to my grave and shoot me in the head!"

Jesus fucking Christ, has she lost her fucking mind?

With her blazer still in my grip, I'm surprised she doesn't try to shrug out of it to get away. Perhaps she hasn't even considered she could do that, or perhaps she really doesn't want to jump. Either way, I hold her with one hand while I steer the wheel with the other, easing the car to a stop on the side of the road.

The moment I release her, she runs.

For fuck's sake, can this night get anymore painful?

"Goddammit, Jaxcen," I hiss, throwing my door open, nearly choking myself on the fucking seatbelt because I forgot to take the fucking thing off.

When I wrestle my way out of the car, I storm around the front to see her trying to navigate the ditch on the side of the road in bare feet, her fucking heels clutched in one hand as she sets her sights on the dark forest.

"Are you fucking crazy, woman? You won't last five minutes out in the pine forest. Now get your arse back in the car!" I demand, my tone deadly.

"No. I'm not going with you. You're just going to kill me." She cries before slipping in the mud as she tries to scramble up the embankment.

"Fucking hell," I snap, before storming towards her.

Once again my strides are double the length of hers as I close the distance.

This woman is hilarious as she holds those goddamn heels up high like she can't bear to get a speck of fucking mud on them, and I'd be laughing if it wasn't so fucking annoying.

"Stop, Jaxcen!" I yell, tired of chasing her, but my demand has her scrambling harder in the mud.

It only takes me two more strides to catch up with her once again. For the third time tonight, my arms wrap around her from behind as I stop her from fucking running.

A scream lurches from her lungs, so loud it echoes around us, disturbing something that has wings deep in the pine forest.

At hearing the wings flap, my little mouse stills, a quiet whimper flying past her lips, and I know now she's beginning to realise that I'm probably the better devil in this scenario.

"We made a deal, did we not, little mouse?"

"Yes, but..." She squirms in my arms, still trying to get away, but I hold firm, pressing my lips to her ear and inhaling her intoxicating scent.

It's fruity, but has a spice to it that I can't quite place. Whatever it is, it makes my fucking cock stir, and I have to fight the urge to nip at her lobe which is so close to my lips.

A deep rumble sounds in my chest as I fight against all of my carnal urges to give in and just take her right here, right now, in the mud against the embankment.

Lucky for her, I shake it off.

"But nothing, little mouse. We made a deal." I remind her, and even though she whimpers, I swear she presses her ear closer to my lips.

"I don't know if I can trust you," she murmurs breathlessly, fear lacing her tone as I carry her back to the car once again.

This whole thing feels like deja vu, and for a moment I wonder if she likes running. If she likes being chased. Because I sure as shit know that I fucking love chasing.

Lowering her to her feet, I spin her and press my palms to her shoulders to urge her back down into the car. It's then that she starts crying. Fat tears popping from those big blue eyes that look up to me pleadingly.

"Why are you doing this? Please, I don't want to die. You killed them in self defence and I promise I'll never tell anyone what I saw."

I chuckle. "The first guy was in self defence. The second guy was because I could."

She pales.

"A deal is a deal. You told me your confession, little mouse. I'm not going to kill you."

Not that I was anyway. I could tell her that and alleviate her fears, but that will bring about other drama that I don't have the patience to deal with right now. She's better off not knowing she's become a target. She's better off not knowing I've brought her here to protect her.

"If you're not going to kill me, then why am I here? Why can't I just go home?"

Lowering to my haunches in front of her, those blue pools follow my every move, her pink lips so plump and kissable that I have to fight every fucking urge inside me not to just lean in and claim her lips again.

"I may have said I'm not going to kill you, little mouse. But that doesn't mean I don't want to keep you for a little while. It's boring out here at Christmas time." I shrug with indifference. "There's nothing to do out here in the pine forests, and I want something new to play with."

Her lower lip trembles at my words, my insinuation clear.

"So you're going to rape me, is that it?" she snaps, that little fire inside her returning.

"Love, when you spread those pretty thighs for me, it'll be because you beg me for my cock."

Even though her lips part in a shocked gasp, the fire brushing over her cheeks gives away how much I think she would love that scenario.

"I'm engaged!" She protests like her upcoming nuptials are going to stop me from taking my fill of her sweet, sexy little body.

"Engaged isn't married, little mouse. So until then. You're all mine."

I've never said that to a woman before. *You're mine.* I've never claimed a woman to be mine. Never wanted to. But for some reason, the idea of making her mine has my cock hardening, my balls tightening, and my heart racing.

Can this day get any fucking weirder?

"Seatbelt, little mouse. We are nearly at our destination," I bark, and even though she looks like she wants to argue, she shifts back in the seat and starts tugging her seatbelt on.

"Don't you mean hell?" she snaps, sending my lips wide as I laugh at her retort.

Such a feisty little Catholic girl.

Standing, I close the door and watch her as I round the front of the car.

Once back inside the sleek Corvette, I strap myself back in and the first thing I notice is all the mud my little mouse has brought in with her.

Connie's not going to be happy about that.

The next thing I notice is that Jaxcen still has those damn heels in her hand. I'm surprised she hasn't tried to stab me with them. Maybe she hasn't considered that the stiletto could be used as a weapon. Since I'm not keen to get stabbed right now, I keep that to myself and plant my foot on the accelerator once again, speeding into the darkness ahead.

Woodall Ridge is a small mill town that sits on the cliffs overlooking Timber Valley. A couple of years ago, the little town became mine.

It was crumbling and old. The remaining occupants in the town were too elderly to work anymore to maintain it. There were no job prospects, no tourism. It was fast becoming a dying ghost town, which just so happens to be the perfect place for someone like me to call home.

So I acquired it. Made some upgrades to most of the main buildings and some of the homes, and turned it into a kind of gated community.

At the time, the ten or so elderly residents that remained were happy to stay. They were already willing to die in this place, and I knew they weren't going to be any trouble, so I let them stay and upgraded their homes, and ever since, I've made sure there's enough food and medicine for them to live out the rest of their days comfortably.

Why would the devil do that?

Well, like they say. Better the devil you know.

As we approach Woodall Ridge, my gaze shoots in the direction of each armed post I know is hiding in the forest. Normally they would shoot the tires out of an unknown car arriving in the dead of night. However, I already know Finn would have called ahead to let them know what car I would be arriving in and that I would have a guest with me.

Nearing the town's edge, the gates of Woodall Ridge loom ahead, the men guarding it all armed to the nines, on alert as we approach.

"Are you sure we're in the right place?" Jaxcen murmurs, and I flick my gaze to her to see those big blue eyes wide as she takes in the armed men up ahead.

"Of course, little mouse. This is hell."

Her blue gaze darts to mine. "Woodall Ridge is hell?"

Smirking, I shrug. "Depends who you ask. But I prefer to call it home."

Surprise flickers over her face, her gaze staring back out the window as I ease the car to a stop while the big gates slowly creak open.

I nod to my men standing guard as we wait, and as soon as the gates open wide enough, I drive through and up the dark steep road that leads to the main township.

Given the early hour of the morning, which some might say is late at night, no one is around but those on duty to protect the township. All the houses are dark. All the businesses are dark. All except for the large building up ahead.

The Palace.

The Palace Hotel has become my home. It's also the main hub of activity in the township where people gather, drink, eat, and celebrate. But the top floors are all mine.

Jaxcen remains quiet as I pull the car to stop outside the pub. She seems to have shrunken in on herself. Whether it's from fear or the unknown, I'm not sure, but since I'm dead tired and fucking starving, I don't have it in me to pacify her.

Getting out of the car, I round it and notice she watches my every move right up to the moment I crack her door open and wait for her to climb out, but she remains seated, her seatbelt securely fastened.

"Time to get out, little mouse."

She shakes her head.

"For fuck's sake, Jaxcen. Get out of the car."

Her big blue eyes shoot up to me. "Promise you're not going to rape me."

"Fucking hell, woman. I already told you that when you part those thighs, it'll be because you want to. Now get the fuck out of the car."

She scoffs, shooting one of her vicious daggers at me as she unfastens her seatbelt and slowly eases out of the car with those god damn heels still in her hand.

Pressing my hand to the small of her back, I lead her up the steps of the old hotel. My men standing guard on either side of the grand doors give me a nod as they open them to let us through, and Jaxcen takes it all in, looking back over her shoulder at my men who close the doors behind us.

Then her gaze roams over everything in our path.

"Who owns this place?" she whispers like she's worried we will wake someone.

"I'm the king of this palace, little mouse." I grin and wag my brows at her as her gaze snaps to mine.

"This is yours?" she whispers again and I nod.

"Yes. The Palace is mine. This is hell."

Her brows shoot high like she's surprised my home isn't a fucking dungeon, and a part of me wants to take her down into the cellar to show her where I do have an actual dungeon, but given everything she's been through tonight, I don't think she'd appreciate my killing cave that much, so I lead her into the hotel kitchen, where a very tired looking Mabel stands.

"Mr Marx." She smiles, giving me a welcoming nod before shooting a warm smile to Jaxcen.

"Mabel, please tell me you didn't get out of bed just for me?"

She waves me off. "I couldn't sleep anyway and heard you arrive, so I thought that perhaps you'd like some supper before you turn in for the evening."

Smiling, I glance down at Jaxcen who seems to be stunned given the way her lips are parted and her brows have disappeared into her hairline.

"Are you hungry, little mouse?"

"Oh, umm." Her dark lashes flutter like she's just woke from a trance. "I don't want to impose."

I chuckle. "Perhaps just some sandwiches, Mabel. Could you bring them up to my suite please?"

"Of course, Mr Marx. Would you like a hot chocolate as well?"

"Would my guest like a hot chocolate?" I ask teasingly as I turn my sights back to Jaxcen who slowly nods.

"If it's not too much trouble, that would be lovely, thank you."

Fuck, she's so damn polite.

So polite. So sweet.

And all I want to do is corrupt her.

As Mabel starts on her task, I lead Jaxcen out of the kitchen and towards the staircase that leads up to my suite. It's a grand old staircase, the railings a deep mahogany, and the carpet runner a royal red befitting a palace.

Large painted portraits line the walls as we ascend, and Jaxcen's gaze studies each one as we pass like she is trying to learn something about me.

Unfortunately, those portraits are not my lineage. They were here when I took over the place, and they say something about the history of the town, and the previous owners of the pub, so I thought they deserved to stay.

At the top of the staircase, a set of double doors are ahead, and off to each side is a single door. One of the single doors is access for the staff lift. And hidden away behind the other door is another staircase leading up into the attic.

But the double doors straight ahead lead into my suite, which is where I take Jaxcen.

Going inside, she remains quiet, taking in the open plan space of the main living area. Her eyes are unable to hide her surprise, and I take a moment to study the space I've been living in.

The walls are papered in a texture that almost looks like a linen fibre with greys, creams, and taupes through it. All the doors are a rich brown, almost black, and the light switches match with the centre, a stainless steel look. The floors are a light sandy brown timber look, with large rugs at the foot of the lush grey couch and underneath the rich brown circular dining table.

The drapes are heavy, a greyish black, and I know behind them are white sheers that Jaxcen will get a glimpse of when the sun rises.

Her eyes roam over the kitchen, which is one of my favourite parts of my suite, aside from what lies waiting behind my bedroom doors. The stone benchtops wrap from the floor, their dark granite speckles with silver that makes it sparkle. The cabinetry is a lighter timber to the doors in the suite, creating a contrast with the black handles and sleek black appliances, including the fridge.

"Shocked little mouse? Or is that disappointment I see in your eyes that my apartment doesn't resemble more of a dungeon?"

A laugh bubbles up her throat, and as if the action shocks her, she slaps her hand over her mouth, her eyes widening like she is disappointed in herself that she found humour in this situation.

"You're safe here with me, Jaxcen. It's okay to laugh." I grin, and she drops her hand from her mouth.

"You kidnapped me. There is nothing funny about this." Dragging her gaze from mine, she turns in a full circle, her eyes travelling over my suite. "I think perhaps I'm a little delirious."

She's right. I did kidnap her, but with good reason.

"Well, what do you think? Is your new prison up to your standards?"

Her eyes narrow, the fire returning to them as my words remind her that she is indeed my prisoner.

"It looks easy enough to break out of." She counters and I laugh.

"You can try, little mouse." I gesture to the double entry doors. "But just remember I have armed men inside this building. I have armed men outside this building. And I have armed men at every exit point of the town. So while this building might be easy enough for you to get out of, do you really think you'll be able to get out of hell?"

"You know, sometimes you seem like you could be a decent guy and then you go ahead and say stuff like that, reminding me that you're an arsehole."

I throw my head back laughing, surprised by the venom in her tone.

"I never said I wasn't an arsehole, Miss Summers. But I'm not so sure I've ever been a decent guy. I think you must be confusing me with someone else. Maybe that loyal fiancé of yours?"

Her cheeks flare in anger but I ignore her, moving into my bedroom as I start to undo the buttons of my white shirt.

The fucking thing is ruined. Not only soaked through, but there's blood on it from my kills and mud from chasing this little wildcat into the fucking pine forest.

Glancing down at my shoes, I sigh. My Aquillas are looking worse for fucking wear. I'll have to see if Mabel can polish them up and see if they're salvageable.

"You don't know my fiancé. Stop talking about him like you do." Jaxcen's words gain my attention again.

"My apologies." I turn and give a mocking bow to my guest, which just seems to infuriate her more, but as I reach the final button on my shirt and peel the fabric open, her fury seems to disappear.

Her lips part, her gaze searing as it rakes over my chest.

It's like she's in some sort of trance as she watches me ease the shirt off my shoulders and drop it to the floor. Next, I start with my belt buckle, undoing it slowly, waiting for her to protest, yet still she remains on the spot, watching like she's hypnotised by what I'm doing.

I can see it now. The voyeur in her. The woman that goes to Cloud 9, one of Melbourne's most exclusive sex clubs. I can imagine the mask she wears, probably covering the majority of her face, not willing to risk being recognised.

I imagine how tightly peaked her nipples would be under the white lacy bra I glimpsed beneath her soaked blouse earlier this evening. I bet her panties were soaked through, and not because of the rain.

What would she do if I walked up to her right now, hitched that pencil skirt up to her waist, and slid my hand into her panties?

Would I feel her absolutely saturated?

The thought has my cock stirring, and I lick my lips, so fucking tempted to find out just how slick Jaxcen Summers can get.

What would she do if I took my hardening cock out right now? Would she spin and gasp in horror? Or would she drop to her knees, desperate to wrap those pretty plump lips around my girth?

Slowly sliding my belt off, I drop it to the floor watching how she tracks the movement like it's in slow motion. And then her gaze, dark and hungry, returns to where my hands are working down my zipper.

"Are you hungry, love? Would you like a taste?"

Chapter Seven

Jaxcen

"Yes." My murmur is quiet, and it takes me a hot second to comprehend what I just did.

A gasp rushes past my lips as my eyes go round in horror, and I slap my hand over my mouth.

What is happening right now?

I'm standing here, in this utterly divine suite, which is annoying to say the least, that this man has such good taste, and I've been staring at him undressing.

My cheeks are on fire, yet my gaze drops back to his bare chest, and oh my God, he does one of those peck flexes like he's wagging his nipples at me.

I cover my eyes.

"Stop. No." I rush out, trying to cover up my huge fuck up.

His deep raspy chuckle meets my ears, clearly finding my embarrassment hilarious.

"Are you sure? You do look kind of hungry." His tone teasing, I spin on my heel, giving him my back.

What the hell is happening right now? I should punch him. Or knee him in the balls, yet all I do is stay rooted on the spot, for some reason not wanting to put any distance between us.

A knock on the main door of the suite makes me jump, and I hear Devon's zipper behind me as he obviously does up his fly. A second later Devon strides past me, the tanned inked skin of his back rippling as he moves. I can't seem to take my eyes off him, finally able to see the intricate design that adorns his skin covering most of his back and down his arms.

The urge to follow him and trace my fingers over his tattoos is almost overwhelming, yet I somehow manage to keep my feet planted on the spot as he moves to open the door, revealing the little old lady he calls Mabel, that I met in the kitchen before.

"Here you go, Mr Marx." She smiles warmly at him, and I have to wonder why she doesn't seem scared of him. "My apologies for taking so long."

I'm not sure why she's apologising. She didn't take long at all, but I get the feeling she may do that a lot as Devon waves her apology off, which makes me think she has past trauma.

"No apology needed, Mabel. Thank you very much." Devon offers her a warm smile back, and I frown.

Strange. I didn't peg him to be civil.

Mabel places the tray of food down on the round dining table, and her eyes meet mine, shooting me another warm smile before disappearing back out the door.

The smell hits me then. Something like bacon? Perhaps chicken?

I'm not sure, but it floats across the room, engulfing me. Teasing me. Urging me.

I want to follow the smell. Go over to it, lift the lid off the tray and devour what's underneath. But I don't. I remain standing rooted in the same spot I've been for a few minutes now, watching as Devon moves to the table.

"Come and have some food." He gestures for me to join him, before lifting the lid of the tray to reveal heaven.

A large serving plate is filled with small toasted sandwich triangles.

Oh my god, are they BLTs?

My mouth waters.

"No, no, thanks. I'm not hungry." I lie, scared I'm about to drool and give myself away.

His dark brows hitch as he shoots me a 'really' look.

"Come and have some food, Jaxcen. It will make you feel better."

I shake my head. "Thank you, anyway, but I ate earlier today."

He frowns. "Don't you mean yesterday? It's already Wednesday."

"I wouldn't know. You took my phone, and I don't wear a watch." I deadpan, and his lip quirks up.

"Don't tell me you're one of those women that only eat meals at a certain time of day and the meals you do eat are basically rabbit food."

My cheeks flush.

Dammit.

How does he know?

"Jesus Christ," he mutters. "It astounds me that women do this to themselves. You are basically starving yourself. All for what? To look slimmer for a fucking guy that won't touch you?"

I gasp at the insinuation, but he's not finished yet.

"You know he's not a real man if he doesn't appreciate a woman's curves. It makes him nothing but an arsehole." He holds his finger up as I part my lips to retort, halting my words. "And before you say it, yes, I know I'm also an arsehole, but I'm not *that* sort of arsehole."

"No, you're just the sort of arsehole that kidnaps women."

He nods, and shrugs at the same time. "Yes. Exactly."

I roll my eyes. "That wasn't a compliment."

He chuckles, flashing those white teeth before picking something off the plate and tossing it in his mouth.

"Miss Summers." He starts as he chews the food. "My cook has prepared the most delicious BLT sandwiches for us. I think it would be extremely rude for you not to eat at least one."

Dammit.

He's right.

I nibble on my lip as I consider the best way to accept defeat, but as he picks some more food off the plate, and the aroma of it teases me, my shoulders slump.

"You're right, that would be rude." I agree, and move in his direction.

As I pass him, his hand snatches my heels from my grip, a gasp flying from me as I reach for them.

"Give them back."

"You don't need them in here." He shakes his head, moving towards the entry door. "Calm down. I'm just going to put them by the door."

Calm down? He just took my Tony's.

Does he have no mercy?

One look at my expression has him snickering, and he points to me.

"You still have your bag, love. Now come and sit down. Have a sandwich and the hot chocolate. It will make you feel better." He gestures to the seat he pulls out, before taking the one next to it.

Reluctantly, I join him, my gaze fixed on the BLT.

Bacon.

I love bacon.

I shouldn't eat it, because when I do, I only want more, but oh how I love it. I could eat it for breakfast, lunch and dinner, and even find a way to work it into a snack and it still wouldn't be enough.

Fight the temptation, Jaxcen. Gluttony is a sin.

"Are you trying to count how many calories are in one triangle, little mouse?" Devon teases, drawing my attention.

"No."

He grunts. "Then stop staring at it and eat it."

But I can't. If I start, I may not stop.

Maybe I can pick the lettuce and tomato out of it and just eat that.

"Jaxcen, if you don't eat that fucking sandwich right now, I'm going to shove it down your throat myself."

He's being a little dramatic, but it does the trick, because the next second I reach for one of the triangles before bringing it to my lips.

I nibble at it first, terrified of overindulging.

Gluttony can be seen, Jaxcen, worn on the outside of your body, showing the world you have no self control for what you put in your mouth.

Eddie's voice fills my head, his disapproving tone like a spy on my shoulder, always there keeping me in line.

I can feel Devon's eyes on me, and I just know he's about to yell at me again, so I take a bigger bite this time. The flavours burst on my tongue, and my eyes widen as I realise I'm not going to be able to hold back.

This is it.

I'm stepping over the line of temptation and indulging.

With the next bite, I can't help it. I moan. The explosion of flavour too much for me to deny, and my lids fall shut as I chew, wanting nothing more than to engorge.

As I eat, all my fears and worries seem to fall away. My only concern is with my next bite and how good it feels to be ingesting something that I know isn't good for me.

Devon remains silent as we eat. I try not to look at him too much, but each time I do, his dark gaze is on my lips, watching me as he eats his own food. I have no idea what he's thinking. I can't tell by his expression if he is angry or turned on. Maybe both.

When we are done, Devon packs up the tray and sets it outside the door like you would in a hotel. I guess Mabel or someone else will remove it.

It takes me a moment to realise that he's flicking off the lights in the suite, and the only light remaining is the glow that flows out of his bedroom.

"Time for bed, little mouse," he says, and I stiffen in my chair.

"Where is my bed?" I ask, glancing around to find another door. There isn't one. Not off the living room.

There's only one bed. And a couch, which I'm happy to sleep on if I must.

"Your bed is right here." He gestures over his shoulder to his bed, and I frown.

"And where will you be sleeping?" I shift to peer back into his bedroom at the large four poster bed, the timber thick posts a similar sandy brown as the floors.

"In my bed." He deadpans as my eyes widen, panic rushing through me.

"But I thought you said you weren't going to—"

"I'm not going to fucking rape you!" he booms, clearly sick of having to reassure me, but what else am I supposed to think?

"But…"

"But nothing! There is one bed big enough for the two of us," he mutters, clearly trying to calm himself down as he pinches the bridge of his nose. "Now, I'm tired and I want to go to sleep so let's stop fucking around."

I can't sleep in the same bed as him. That would be yet another sin against my name. Eddie would never forgive me, not that I know if I care about that, but for some reason I feel like I'm doing something wrong if I accept this and sleep in the same bed as another man.

"That's okay," I rush out. "I'll sleep on the couch."

Suddenly, his dark eyes glare as he storms towards me, and a squeak leaves me as I try to sink back further in the chair, squeezing my eyes shut as I brace for impact.

The impact I was waiting for never comes, but another embarrassing squeak leaves me as I find myself getting hoisted up off the chair and over his shoulder like he did earlier at the church.

This time, when my fists pummel his back, they meet the searing heat of his skin.

"Stop! Put me down!"

"You know your punches are like a form of foreplay for me, don't you? They're making my cock hard."

As his words register, I quickly cease my assault which only makes him chuckle, before I find my world the right way up as he flips me, my back bouncing off his mattress as he looms over me.

"We are sleeping in the same bed, little mouse. I'm too fucking tired to argue with you about this. I will get you a shirt to sleep in, and you can use the bathroom to shower and wash off the mud you decided to play in earlier." He gestures his thumb over his shoulder where I notice an open bathroom door. "And then, little mouse, you will get into this fucking bed and go to sleep. Am I making myself clear?"

I open my mouth to protest, but the savage glare he shoots me has me snapping my lips shut.

Your life is in his hands, Jaxcen. Stop infuriating the devil.

Before I know what's happening, he flips me face down and settles his weight over me, my heart thundering in my chest as I brace for what's about to come.

This is it, he's going to rape me.

"The only word I want to hear from you right now, is yes." He rasps against my ear, his breath hot, sending an unsolicited shudder down my spine.

I nod into the mattress, "Y-yes."

"Atta girl," he rasps before his weight shifts off me and the palm of his hand slaps my arse.

I squeal, quickly rolling over to watch his retreating back as he enters another door, which looks like a walk-in wardrobe. For a brief moment I glance through the open bedroom door, to the living room, and wonder how easy it would be for me to run.

I've already tried numerous times tonight to get away from this man, all unsuccessful, and I get the feeling now that I'm surrounded by his loyal followers that the possibility of me escaping is unattainable.

As I shift to sit up on the bed, Devon re-enters with a white t-shirt in his hand. Tossing it at me, it slaps into my face and he chuckles as I glare with a huff, watching him move into the bathroom.

At the sink, he starts splashing water over his face, and I wait patiently on his bed, taking in my filthy feet and hands.

Ew. My hands. I didn't even wash them before I ate.

Shame fills me at how revolting that is. I never forget to wash my hands before I eat. I've probably just ingested so many germs I'll wake up sick tomorrow.

Shaking off thoughts of my impending illness, my gaze flicks back to the hard plains of muscle that ripple over Devon's back as he bends and starts brushing his teeth.

Outside of Cloud 9, I've never seen a man like this so nearly naked. Aside from my dad, of course, which doesn't count.

I've never actually seen Eddie's body under his clothes. He's never taken his shirt off in front of me. Even when we've been swimming, he wears a rashi, covering up his torso. And now, I realise that perhaps, I really don't know the man I'm meant to marry at all.

Maybe that's why I'm not feeling a connection to him like I should be. Maybe it's more than just the fact that he won't let me touch him, or that he won't let me see him without clothes on. But perhaps the fact that he won't let me get to know him, always telling me we will have the rest of our lives for that.

He hasn't always been like that, of course. As kids, we were best friends. And even when I was shipped off to the 'facility' for those three horrible years, he was still the one person I could count on, aside from my sister.

We wrote to each other back and forth, although my return letters took some time, since I wasn't always in a state to write, but for the most part, things between Eddie and me were good. At least I thought they were, but something happened when we turned fourteen.

He told me I was going to be his wife one day, and like every silly little girl's dream, I was excited for the day I'd have my white wedding, and white picket fence. I wanted nothing more than to marry him. To be his wife and have that dream together.

But now that I think about it, I'm really not sure our dreams align.

Sure, he wants a wife, and I've always thought of myself as his girlfriend since that day when we were fourteen, but aside from hanging out together and going places, we haven't done anything remotely like a boyfriend and girlfriend would.

I remember when I tried to hold his hand once. How he quickly pulled his away and told me it was inappropriate.

Devon's words from earlier come back to me making me wonder if perhaps he knows my husband-to-be better than I do.

Is Eddie just an arsehole? Does he do this just to control me?

There's a possibility that perhaps that's probably it, because he likes to control everything I do. If I do something that isn't considered acceptable by the Church, he makes it his mission to make sure I know. Sometimes, he takes me to confession himself if he has to.

But what if it's more than that? What if he isn't just an arsehole? What if he is really gay and I'm his beard as Devon suggested? What if he's repulsed when he looks at me because he would rather kiss a man than a woman?

Tears well in my eyes at that thought. Not because I'm sad that he might not like me that way, but because he would rather lie to me and condemn me to a loveless life with no passion, rather than admit his truth.

And then, of course, there's the other reason Devon suggested.

Maybe Eddie just sees me as a suitable person to be his wife and the mother of his children, and that apart from the intimacy that's required to conceive children, he may not ever want to be sexual with me.

Is he still a virgin?

Has he paid for sex?

What does he like to do with other women that he could never fathom doing with me?

"What has you so deep in thought?"

I startle at the deep gravel of Devon's voice, my eyes going wide with worry that he has a super power of reading one's mind.

As he stands in the doorway of his bathroom, one arm propped up on the door frame, watching me, I can't stop myself from perusing his taut body. The way the pants have shifted low on his hips. The defined ridges of his abs and the way the vee disappears below the fabric.

I've seen it on men before, of course, at Cloud 9, but I haven't seen it on this man, and I wonder for a minute if perhaps we've crossed paths at that club given he seems to know so much about it.

"Just stuff," I respond vaguely to his question which makes him frown.

"You still think I'm going to harm you, little mouse?"

"No." I shake my head, but then I shrug, "Yes... I'm not sure." I babble, confused by my own indecision.

"Tell me what you were really thinking about just now. Because I get the feeling it wasn't about me."

"This isn't confession." I point out and he smirks.

"True. But I can take you to the old church here. There's an old confession booth inside. Not as nice as the one Father Peters has at St Catherine's, and also not bulletproof, but I can take you there." His smirk turns sinister. "You can go inside. Close the door. Drop to your knees. And pray. And then, little mouse, you can confess your sins."

"Do you have a priest here?" I ask, not sure if knowing there's a man of the cloth here will make me feel better or not.

"I'm the closest thing to God there is here. So when you confess on your knees it will be to me."

My cheeks flush, and heat pools between my legs as an ache I've been trying to ward off all damn night when this man's around, makes itself known once again.

Why does the thought of me going into a confession booth with him listening on the other side sound so... tempting?

"Ah, I see you like that idea, don't you?"

"No," I blurt and he chuckles.

"Yeah, you do." He tilts his head to study me. "What have I told you about lying to me? Do I have to remind you again that lying is a sin?"

"Do I have to remind you again that murder is a sin? Thou shalt not murder."

He chuckles at my retort before responding.

"Lying lips are an abomination to the Lord, but those who act faithfully are his delight."

My eyebrows shoot up at his recitement of Proverbs 12:22.

"So you're a religious man too?"

"Yes, little mouse, why else would I have been in a church?"

"Oh, I don't know. Given the fact there were bulletproof doors, perhaps you were hiding from someone."

He snickers. "Would you believe I was there seeking absolution? Just as you were."

"For what?" I ask, lifting a single brow, and he sighs.

"It's too late to talk about this right now. I want to go to bed." He juts his thumb over his shoulder. "Get in there and have a shower."

I glare at his demand even though I slide off the bed to do as he ordered.

Moving to the doorway of the bathroom, he only steps aside so I can pass, still looming in the doorway.

Frowning, I wait for him to leave, but he doesn't, a wicked smirk tugging at his lips once again as he crosses his arms over his chest and leans against the door frame.

"Well, aren't you going to leave?" I snap.

"I was kind of hoping you'd give me a little bit of a show."

My mouth drops open in shock. "Why on earth would I do that? You need to leave. Hurry up and close the door."

He chuckles. "So you go to Cloud 9. Probably walk around in your underwear, yet you blush at the thought of me watching you undress."

"It's inappropriate. You're not my fiancé."

"That argument is getting old, little mouse. And we've already established that you're all mine. For now, anyway."

"And I thought we established that you weren't going to rape me."

A chill fills the air as he growls. "Stop saying that fucking word. I will never do that!"

"Could have fooled me by the way you're lurking in the doorway waiting for me to take my clothes off."

I thought the growl a second ago was scary, but the sound that comes from him now is purely animalistic before he storms forward, backing me up against the counter.

"Don't pretend like you don't want to get naked for me, little mouse. I can see it in your eyes, how they travel over my skin with nothing but lust in them." He wraps his hand around my neck, giving a gentle squeeze. "I can see it in your cheeks, how they flare to life from your arousal. And I can hear it in your tone, how it turns a little husky just like it did before, when you admitted to wanting to taste my cock."

Releasing my neck, his strong hand grips my jaw, tilting my head back as his eyes bore into mine, his lips hovering so close that I can feel the heat of his breath on my chin.

"I'm going to have fun with you, little mouse. A little Christmas treat to keep me occupied over the break."

I whimper as he shifts, worried he's about to hurt me in some way, but then his thumb glides over my lips, and I watch as his gaze tracks the movement like he finds my lips to be the most delectable looking dessert he's ever come across.

Heat ignites under my skin from the top of my head to the tip of my toes, a fiery ache coursing through me with longing that I know is going to get me into trouble.

"We're going to have to start working on your sins, little mouse. Especially the one where you keep lying."

His thumb pushes past my lips then, sinking into the heat of my mouth and I'm helpless not to react. Helpless not to do the one thing I know I shouldn't.

I suck on it.

And he growls.

"Atta girl, little mouse. Now take off your clothes."

Vida Loca
Trust

Chapter Eight

Devon

I shouldn't be doing this. Jaxcen seems so innocent at times, yet the way her eyes stare up at me right now through the fan of her dark lashes, so submissive and filled with so much need, has me giving in.

She says she's not a virgin, but I'm not so sure. Her experience seems to be minimal given the fact she's been with that fucking douche since she was fourteen years old. But she said she wasn't a virgin which means she is either lying about that, or she cheated on her fiancé. Either way, I get the feeling I'm going to find out.

"Did I stutter, little mouse, or did you not hear me?" I snap. "I said take off your clothes."

She pulls back, letting my thumb pop free of her plump lips, almost looking nervous like she didn't believe my demand was serious.

"I shouldn't." She all but whispers, but the fact is, she really fucking should, and she knows it.

"No one's here but you and me, Jaxcen. No one needs to know what happens inside my home."

"But the Lord will know," she whispers again, and I scoff, rolling my eyes.

"You don't really believe that?" I ask with a single brow raised. "Come on, Jaxcen. Think about it. God's not real. It's just a belief. So if you're not going to do something, it better be because you don't want to do it. Not because you think there's some almighty being watching over you who will judge everything you do."

Her cheeks flush and I'm not sure if it's in anger or embarrassment, but I don't ask. I'm not known to be careful of people's feelings.

"Come on, love. You felt it earlier in the confessional. Doesn't it just feel right? Isn't there just something so fucking hot about doing something you're not meant to do?" I drag my thumb over her lower lip again, tugging on it, pulling it down so her mouth opens, showing me her pink tongue.

Nodding, probably because she can't speak with how I'm manhandling her lips, Jaxcen's gaze softens as she gives in to her feelings, and I grin.

"See. Sinning isn't so bad." I wag my brows. "Sinning is fun, little mouse. Don't you agree?"

Releasing her lip, I hear a breath escape her like she was holding it before she speaks.

"I don't understand." She gives her head a little shake. "If these things are so wrong, then why do they feel so good?"

My grin spreads into a full out smile. "Ain't that the million dollar question?" I murmur as I graze my knuckles down the column of her neck and over her clavicle, watching as her chest rises and falls faster as I get nearer to the swell of her breasts.

"I know you don't understand why I brought you here. But you need to know you won't be leaving for a while. And since it looks like we'll be spending Christmas together, why don't we play?"

"Play?" she asks, her brows tugging inward, her confused expression making her look even younger than her twenty-four years. Hell, she looks barely eighteen at times.

"Yes, love. Play. You know. A bit of role play."

"Role play?" she asks, her brows shooting up this time, and I know she gets my meaning.

"Yes, love. Role play."

"And what roles will we be playing exactly?" She tries not to smirk, but I can fucking see the way her lips are trying to pull outward.

"Given it's nearly Christmas, how about I be Santa, and you be my little helper?" I don't know why I like the sound of that so much when I'm not really a fan of Christmas, but I could definitely get around the idea if it involves her on her knees.

Slowly, her lips spread wide, no longer able to fight her grin, before her teeth show and she throws her head back, laughing.

"Are you fucking laughing at me?" I snap, but still, she continues to laugh, slapping her hand over her mouth like that will somehow control it, but it fucking doesn't.

Without a second thought, my hand wraps around her throat, giving it a squeeze as I tug her closer so we are nose to nose.

"Do you think I'm fucking joking around? I'm dead fucking serious, Miss Summers. And if you want to get through this alive, you'll stop fucking mocking me!"

Any humour she had falls away, replaced with a mixture of fear and that heat she had only moments ago, returning.

Fuck, is her fear turning her on? Does she have a fear kink? Perhaps that's why she hasn't screamed bloody murder yet.

"Is your heart racing, Jaxcen? Is it pounding so wildly in your chest that you fear it might leap through your ribcage and fall to the floor? Or perhaps it's racing so fast you fear it will stop and never beat again?"

When she nods quickly, a lazy and sinister grin contorts my face as I watch her gaze scan my features, taking in every little detail.

"Are you scared, Jaxcen?"

She shakes her head, but then nods, before shrugging, and I chuckle.

"You are scared, aren't you? Are you scared I will hurt you?"

Slowly, she shakes her head, her gaze dropping to my lips. So naturally, I lick them and watch how her lips part as desire floods her eyes, making the blue turn almost black.

"Are you scared that I'll make you feel good, and you'll like it so much, you won't ever want to stop?"

A moaning whimper passes her lips, her chest straining against mine, almost like her breasts have increased in size, expanding like they're reaching out, desperate to be touched.

Releasing her neck, I quickly draw her blazer off her shoulders so it drops halfway down her arms. Then I spin her to face the mirror so she can see both of our reflections before I tug the blazer taut, pulling her arms back with it, effectively making her my little prisoner.

A gasp flies from her lips like she's waking from a daze, the sudden movement snapping her out of her lust momentarily as she comes face to face with her expression that screams, *fuck me please*.

"Look at that woman in the mirror," I rasp. "Look how much she wants to be touched by me. Look how much she aches for something more. Something wrong."

Gripping her chin roughly, I run my nose up the column of her neck, inhaling her sweet, yet spicy scent, and hum.

"Fuck, woman. Why do you smell so damn good?"

A shiver ripples up her spine as she leans closer, desperate for me to do something to her. Desperate for me to step over the line she's tried to put up, but is failing to maintain.

"I wanna watch you come undone." I groan against her ear, and her moan is unmistakable as it fills the space of my bathroom.

Pressing myself against her arse, I move my hips to make sure she can feel my hard length. To make sure she is well aware of what she's doing to me.

"Do you feel that, Miss Summers?" I ask, and she whimpers, her gaze darting between her own reflection, and mine in the mirror. "Wouldn't it feel so fucking good to feel my cock sink deep into your tight cunt?"

Another whimper escapes her, and this time her arse presses harder against my length, causing her back to arch and her chest to push forward, the hard pebble of her nipples straining against the fabric of her blouse, their peaked outlines so noticeable.

Taking a step back, I tug off her blazer and then find the zipper at the back of her skirt, quickly releasing it. Even though she gasps from the sudden action, she doesn't protest, she doesn't try to stop me. She lets me work the fabric down over her hips, to pool around her muddy feet on the tiled floor.

Where the skirt was, I find white lacy panties. They're not a G string but they don't have a wide backside to them, and the globes of her cheeks peek out the sides, teasing the fuck out of me. My palm comes to her arse, rubbing over the perky globe, inducing yet another moan past her pink, plump lips.

"Do you like feeling my hands on you, Jaxcen?"

"Yes," she whispers, almost as if she's too scared to say the words too loud because that would make them true.

"Where do you want my hands?" I ask, catching her eye in the mirror, but her lips thin as she tugs them inwards, like she's trying to stop herself from speaking.

SLAP!

The clap of my palm against her arse echoes through the room, and a squeal escapes her, those blue eyes wide, almost panicked.

"Answer me Jaxcen! Where do you want my hands?"

Trembling, I wonder for a moment if she's going to stop this right here, right now. If she's going to pull away and say 'no, stop, we can't do this.' Because I know it's going through her mind. I just know it. But then she speaks, surprising me.

"I want your hands everywhere."

"Atta girl, little mouse." I grin, pleased, not just from the words she spoke, but the conviction in her tone. "Take off your blouse."

She moves quickly at my order, unbuttoning the ivory fabric before tugging it off and letting it drop to the floor by our feet.

Now standing before me in her white lacy bra and matching panties, I get an image of her dressed like this with a mask covering her face.

"Is this what you wore into Cloud 9 tonight?"

She nods.

Fuuuck.

"It should almost be illegal with how innocent you look in this underwear, Jaxcen." I graze my nose along the column of her neck as I speak. "Yet the filthy thoughts it conjures are the complete opposite."

I can't bring myself to stop sniffing her, like I'm addicted to her scent. Like it's a line of coke I want to snuff.

Snaking my hand around to her front, my large palm almost covers her abdomen, reminding me just how small and dainty she is compared to my hulking size.

Her stomach dips, like the feel of my fingers tickles her, making me think back to the church earlier when that's all I had to do to get her to release her bag. That knowledge is worth keeping in the memory bank for later I suppose, knowing she's so ticklish.

"Where do you want me to touch first, Jaxcen? Do you want me to go up here?" I slowly start to glide my hand up towards her breasts, which are rising and falling in rapid succession with her breathing, "or would you like me to go down here?" I change direction, grazing my digits down past her belly button towards the flesh I know is probably saturated right now.

"Either." She breathes. "Both... I don't know."

I chuckle at her indecision. "My little mouse is greedy, I see. But I can certainly do both if you think you can handle it."

Once again she whimpers, probably questioning herself on whether or not she can handle that, but I don't give her much time to consider it as my other hand joins in and slides up to the swell of her breasts before I cup the heaviness in my palm, while my other hand grazes over her mound between her legs.

"Y-yes." She moans and stutters, her stance moving wider to allow me better access, and I watch her eyes as they watch mine while I simultaneously graze her nipple through the fabric of her bra and do the same to her needy little clit through the fabric of her panties.

She jerks at my touch, almost like she wasn't expecting it, or perhaps not used to it. Which would indeed be the fact if what she said about her fiancé is true.

He hasn't touched her. Why the fuck wouldn't he touch her?

"Do you like that, little mouse?" I rasp against her ear before sucking the lobe between my lips and gliding my tongue over the soft skin.

"Yes," she pants loudly, any shame disappearing since she no longer tries to whisper her words.

Continuing to graze my fingers over the two areas, I'm desperate to go beneath the fabric, but I don't think she's ready for that. Not if she actually hasn't been touched by a man, ever, or perhaps in a long time.

My cock is straining in my pants, aching to be let free and slide between the folds I already know are drenched given the wetness of the fabric I feel beneath the tips of my fingers.

I bet she'd be so fucking tight.

Taking my cues from the signals her body is giving, I speed up my pace, my fingers working faster as her pleasure quickly rises.

I'm not trying to blow my own horn or anything, but I'm a fucking talented man in most aspects of my life. And when it involves sex, I'm yet to hear a complaint from a woman that has been in my bed. Yet I'm not sure any have responded so quickly to my touch. None have ever been so near the edge of climax in such a short space of time, like Jaxcen Summers is right now.

"That's it, Jaxcen. Let yourself go. Let yourself see and embrace how fucking good it feels to have my hands on you." I nip at her lobe again, my teeth grazing this time, and the action seems to send her skyrocketing, her cries fast, loud and high pitched as she nears the edge.

Her hips are moving on their own accord. Thrusting. Grinding. Chasing her pleasure with such desperation, that her eyelids fall shut and her angelic face contorts, almost like she's in pain.

"Eyes open!" I demand, and those blue eyes, nearly black, go wide as her lids part quickly on my order. "Watch yourself, Jaxcen. Watch how fucking beautiful you are. How exotic you are. Watch every moment of when you come."

My words do the trick, her cry loud in the room as my hand between her legs moves so fucking fast that she jerks and shudders before crying out again, and wetness seeps through the fabric of her panties and down her thighs.

Fuck me.

I really am talented.

As her climax subsides, her legs give out and I hold her up, my cock pressing into the valley of her arse as her loud panting fills the room.

"Such a good little sinner, aren't you?" I murmur against her ear once again, which have to be the sexiest fucking ears I've ever come across.

Do I have a fucking ear fetish? Is that even a thing? Fuck, who knows, but I fucking want to devour hers.

Jaxcen makes a noise in response to my question. It's kind of a non committal *yes*, in a moaning type of way, and I can't help but grin.

Her lids flutter open, her gaze lazy as it lands on me, and her own grin pulls at her lips.

"The just fucked look, looks good on you, Miss Summers."

"You didn't fuck me," she points out, her words nearly slurred like she's drunk.

"Not yet, but imagine what you'll look like when I do." I chuckle, and even though she grins, her eyes go wide as if once again, she's waking up from a trance and realising that she's just being a very naughty Catholic girl.

Easing my hands from around her, I let her take her own weight and step back, moving to the shower to turn it on. I test the water, making sure the temperature is hot and then turning the heat up a little more, knowing chicks like it so fucking scolding that it almost peels a man's skin off.

"Have a shower, little mouse. Then put my shirt on, and get your sweet arse into my bed." I tell her, giving that sweet arse a slap as I walk past and close the door behind me, shutting her in.

I want nothing more than to go back in there, tear those white innocent panties from her flesh and part her thighs so my cock can find its own release. And normally that's exactly what I would do. But something has me stalling. Probably the fact that I've declared that she's going to be with me through Christmas. And normally, if I bed a woman, it's only ever for one night. Not to mention the fact that the woman tonight is in my actual home. Usually the fucking happens in the city. I use my apartment there as a base for work sometimes, and it's a convenient place to take women when I want a release.

So why have I brought this woman into my home, and insisted she get into my bed? Why am I not questioning this even more, instead opting to get changed into my comfy boxers, knowing I probably shouldn't go commando in bed tonight, and wait for Jaxcen Summers to finish showering in my bathroom?

These are questions I don't have answers to, so for now, I'll table them as I slip into my bed and wait for Jaxcen to join me.

It doesn't take long, thank fuck, because I'm tired and I'm starting to get moody, but when she ventures out five minutes later, steam wafting around her in the doorway as she flicks off the light, only leaving my bedside reading lamp to illuminate the space, I swear she looks like an angel.

Shifting nervously beside my bed, Jaxcen hovers and I chuckle, realising she needs my demand in order to take the step and get into the bed with me.

"Under the covers, Jaxcen. Now."

She does as I demand, moving to pull back the covers before quickly sliding in, wearing my t-shirt.

Fuuuck, there's just something about her wearing my clothes that has my cock hardening again.

Jesus fucking Christ. Am I going to get any sleep tonight?

Shifting, I flick off my lamp and roll on my side to face her. Slowly, my eyes adjust to the darkness, a faint glow coming in through the crack in the drapes, giving me just enough light to see that Jaxcen is as stiff as a board next to me, her eyes wide, staring up at the ceiling.

That won't fucking do, because if she doesn't go to sleep then I won't either, so I reach out ignoring her gasp and tug her towards me, her small body easy to manoeuvre so I can spoon her, wrapping my large frame protectively around her dainty one.

"Sleep, Jaxcen. This is all this is. Sleep."

My words must give her the reassurance she obviously needs and she quickly relaxes in my hold. Within a few minutes, her breathing evens out and deepens, and her body becomes lax as mine is anything but, primed behind her. Fucking aching to take its fill.

I don't know how long I lay awake going over everything that has happened tonight, but eventually my lids fall closed, and I succumb to sleep, letting it drag me under for hours, and my dreams are filled with a sweet little blonde temptress, and the needy little moans that part her plump pink lips.

I wake several hours later, already knowing that it's probably mid-morning given the way the bright December sun is trying to burst past the thick drapes.

Rolling over, I stretch out, releasing a groan before my mind shifts from its slumber state to awakened reality, reminding me that I had a bed partner last night.

Darting my head to the side to seek out Jaxcen, I blink a couple of times to make sure my eyes are seeing right.

My bed is empty.

My gaze darts to the open bathroom door, noticing the light off, telling me she's not in there.

Sitting upright, I scrub a hand over my face and slip out of the covers, padding through to the living area, almost certain I'll find her asleep on the couch like she so desperately wanted to do when she first arrived.

"Jaxcen?" I call, frowning as I see the empty couch and spin in a circle as I gaze over the living area in my suite.

There's nowhere to hide here. The space is an open plan. There are no large cupboards. There are no other rooms, except for perhaps my walk in wardrobe, so my feet hurry towards that.

Flicking on every light as I go just to make sure she's not curled up in a corner somewhere, I don't find anything, and my wardrobe is undisturbed.

Fuck!

She's gone!

Dashing out of my wardrobe, I leap over my bed, snatching my phone off the bedside table and hit Finn's number.

He answers it on the first ring.

"Sup, man?" he asks lazily like he's only just woken himself.

"She's fucking gone. Lock the whole place down!" I bark.

"What?" Finn mumbles like he's still fucking asleep.

"Jaxcen is gone! Lock the place down. Now!"

My demand is loud through the phone and I hear him curse before I hang up and rush to put my pants on.

I can't fucking believe she's run again after I told her what would happen if she did.

Look out, Jaxcen Summers. You're about to meet the devil for real this time.

Chapter Nine

Jaxcen

A yell from the floor below has me stiffening, Devon's roar clearly recognisable. I guess he's just realised I'm not in his suite anymore. I should probably go back down so he doesn't lose his temper, but I'm curious to see how this will play out.

How will the devil respond to me running?

I haven't run of course. I took his threat seriously, and knew he wasn't making up the level of security around his town. I saw it as we drove in.

There are armed men everywhere.

From up here in the attic, you can see over the whole south side of the township. It's not a huge town, but it seems bustling enough below with people down on the street, some working, others running errands or chatting to others.

When I woke and slipped out of the bed without him noticing, I decided to do a little exploring.

Since I'm only wearing Devon's t-shirt, and my clothes are basically ruined from the rain and mud, I decided to keep my explorations inside the building.

I was a little surprised to find there wasn't an armed guard standing right outside Devon's suite, but one glance over the rail and down the staircase showed some armed men walking around on the ground floor, so I decided to check out what was behind the other two doors on either side of Devon's suite.

One side led to an elevator and a storage closet, and the other door led to a staircase going up. So I went that way to find myself here, in a large open attic space, above Devon's apartment.

A rush of movement in the street below draws my attention, and there he is. The man in question. Or perhaps the devil in question.

My skin prickles with heat at seeing him, so tall, muscular, and sinfully attractive. I imagine he must have been a pretty boy when he was younger, but now, the prettiness has given way to such manly features that it makes me see Eddie as a boy rather than a man.

The things he did to me last night have been at the forefront of my mind, and honestly, it has to be why I haven't tried harder to run, because even though he's kidnapped me, I don't feel unsafe.

Hell, I feel kind of worshipped.

I think there's something wrong with me.

A group of Devon's men gather around him, and I can tell by how animated he is that he's pissed. He looks to be asking questions and barking orders. Some of the men shake their heads, and then the guy Devon gave my driver's licence to last night walks up to the group and passes Devon what looks like a tablet device.

Devon studies the screen as they talk, before he turns to look at the building, and the others do too.

Huh. I guess he does have cameras around the place. I'm guessing he knows I didn't leave the Palace.

I should go back down to his suite, right? I should go and beg for forgiveness and hope he won't shoot me in the head.

The thing is, I don't think he's going to, and I can't for the life of me figure out why I think that.

Maybe it's nothing more than wishful thinking.

I snicker at that thought.

I'm pretty sure they can't see me sitting up in the attic window, so I stay put and wonder how long it will take him to find me, and what he'll do when he does.

You're playing with fire, Jaxcen.

And maybe I am. I think he must have short circuited my brain with that orgasm last night because I'm obviously not thinking clearly. It certainly has done something to me, part of me is wracked with guilt for letting a man that isn't my fiancé touch me, but the other part of me wants to know what it would be like to feel more than his hand.

Like his lips. His dick.

But as for the cowardly, the faithless, the detestable, as murderers. The sexually immoral, sorcerers, idolaters, and all liars, their portion will be in the lake that burns with fire and sulfur, which is second to death.

Revelation 21:8 comes at me, engulfing me with guilt, shame and fear, and tears prick at the backs of my eyes as I struggle with what I allowed Devon to do last night.

But it felt so good.

Devon and some of the men storm towards the stairs that lead up to the Palace, and my heart races with anticipation at Devon finding me.

What is wrong with you, Jaxcen? He will kill you.

No, he won't.

Or maybe he will, and that's really what I want.

Ugh, now even my inner voice is confused and dark and sending me spiralling with thoughts I've fought hard to overcome.

Remaining seated on the window box, I watch the street below and the curious eyes of the locals as they watch Devon's men dash off quickly.

Something I'm only just noticing is that aside from the older residence, most of the other locals seem to be female, or children.

How odd.

Wait... Have I been brought to a cult compound? Or is this like a polygamist colony, and all of these women belong to one man?

My brows shoot up at that thought, and for a moment I wonder if Devon might be their husband.

Heavy feet pound the floors below and my name being called by a few different voices makes me stiffen.

Shit. I'm causing so much drama, aren't I?

My gaze darts to the chapel at the end of the street, or what I can see of it anyway.

That has to be the church Devon was speaking about. My need to run there and seek forgiveness is niggling at me so severely, that tears prick the backs of my eyes.

Perhaps absolution is all I need. Perhaps if I can confess and repent then everything will be okay.

"Jaxcen!"

The deep angered yell of Devon's voice makes me flinch, and when I hear heavy boots pound the staircase up to the attic, I brace myself, bow my head and do the only thing I can right now to remain calm.

I pray.

"Lord, I come before you with an open heart and mind, ready to receive your love and grace."

"Jaxcen!" Devon booms, and I know he must be entering the room.

"Lord, I ask that you cast out all fear from my heart, mind and soul."

"Fuck." Devon pants from behind me, and I stiffen even more, but remain with my head low.

"Help me to trust in your perfect love, knowing that you have a plan for my life."

"Finn, yeah, I found her in the attic," Devon says from somewhere behind me, obviously on his phone.

"I surrender my fears to you and ask that you replace them with faith and hope."

"Jaxcen." Devon speaks again, and this time, I know he's right behind me, and for some strange reason, my eyes fill with tears that instantly pool over and run down my cheeks.

"Lord, I ask that you be my guide and protector. Give me the courage to face the challenges, and help me to remember that I am never alone, and that your love surrounds me at all times."

A sob escapes me as the warm touch of Devon's fingers brush back some of my hair and hook it behind my ear.

"Little mouse, look at me."

"Lord, thank you for your unconditional love and grace which sustains me each day. Help me to share that love with others and be a light in the world, casting out fear and bringing hope and peace."

This time, I feel Devon move onto the window box with me, and a squeak escapes me as he lifts me so effortlessly onto his lap, as I finish my prayer.

"In the name of the Father, the Son, and the Holy Ghost. Amen." I sign the cross before falling silent.

"Let's get one thing straight." Devon's deep voice rumbles right next to my ear. "If by Lord, you really mean Devon, then okay. But if you really think there's a magical being that will be your guide and protector, then let me remind you, there is no such thing." With a firm finger, he coaxes my head around so he can see my face, and the darkness within his eyes should scare me, but for some reason, it feels... safe.

"I will be your guide and protector, Jaxcen. Not some mythical man."

My lids flutter, pushing more fat tears out, and I swallow thickly before I speak.

"Are you mad?"

For a long moment, he simply stares at me, and I almost think he's not going to answer, but then he smirks.

"You were up here watching the whole time, weren't you?"

I nod, and he chuckles, shaking his head in disbelief.

"You watched me lose my cool with my men, accusing them of letting you slip past them, and you didn't consider that perhaps you should come down and diffuse the situation?"

I shake my head. "I was curious," I murmur.

"Curious about what?"

"To see how it would play out," I admit, and he grumbles.

"Jesus, woman, I was ready to shoot some of my best men."

My eyes widen in shock. "No, you weren't... were you?"

"He was." A voice comes from behind us, and Devon's head darts in that direction before chuckling and shifting us, so I can see the man too.

"Jaxcen, this is Finn. My right hand man."

Finn smiles, his whole facing morphing with it and I can't help but smile back.

"He calls me his right hand man, but really he means best mate."

"The best mate title depends on the day and how much you're annoying me." Devon snickers.

"Pleased to meet you, Finn." I smile, swiping at my tears. "When are you going to give me my licence back?"

His brows shoot high and he grins. "I like her." Then he reaches into his back pocket and holds out my ID.

I glance at Devon, as if to ask if it's really okay for me to have it back, and when Devon's hold on me loosens, I hurry to stand and accept it from Finn's grip.

"Thank you."

"A word of advice," he offers, and I gear myself up to be scolded. "If you really want to make Dev panic, try and hide better. I'll introduce you to the Anderson boys, those two eight year olds know all the good hiding spots."

"No, you fucking won't." Devon complains from behind me, and my lips lift high as Finn smiles back.

"Well, I'm heading back to bed for a couple more hours of sleep since this fella woke me spewing orders," Finn says, bowing his head in farewell as I frown.

"Oh. Sorry."

Finn laughs, while Devon mumbles something under his breath, and I turn to face him.

"What was that?" I ask.

He grins. "I said, you will be sorry."

I stare at him and his gaze doesn't waver.

"Is this where you kill me? Because technically I didn't run. I was just exploring and found this place," I gesture to the attic space around us. "And then I was curious about the town, so I was people-watching."

"So why were you praying if you were peoplewatching?" Devon asks, approaching me, and I have to tip my head back a little to keep my eyes on his.

"Well, the prayer was because the devil was coming for me."

If I didn't believe he was the devil, I do now with how utterly wicked his smirk is.

"I will always come for you, little mouse."

I roll my eyes. "You haven't even known me for a whole day. You tricked me into kissing you. You killed two men right in front of my eyes. You held me against my will. Took my ID and phone, carried me like a sack of potatoes, forced me into a car and drove me out into the middle of nowhere and made me eat all of that food before you... you..."

He's grinning from ear to ear. "Say it, love. What did I do?" He leans in closer. "Lit you on fire from the inside out?"

I blush.

Dammit.

He chuckles, and I wave him off.

"My point is you can't tell me you'll protect me when we barely know each other. Why would you care about protecting me? And, hell, you're probably what I need protecting from."

"Damn right I'm the one you need protecting from." He lurches forward and picks me up by my thighs, wrapping my legs around his waist as a surprised squeak flies from my lips.

Stop doing that. No wonder he calls you a mouse, Jaxcen.

"But the thing is," he says, his lips hovering before mine as he walks us back over to the window box. "Do you really want to be saved from me?"

He lowers my arse to the box seat and leans over me, forcing me to nearly lay right back.

"One day soon, I'm gonna fuck you right here in front of this window. I'm gonna let the whole fucking town see how much your cunt craves my cock."

Oh. My. God.

His words are so crass yet do things to me. My skin feels like it's on fire. My core flutters with a level of need I'm scared of, and I have to force myself to remain still and not move, because if I do, and I reach out and touch him, I'm going to cave.

"These lips," he groans, like I cause him physical pain, "I wanna watch my cock disappear past these." His thumb grazes over my bottom lip much like it did last night, yet this time, he doesn't slide his thumb in.

The way he looks at me, makes me feel wanted. Desired. Treasured. All the things Eddie doesn't do for me.

Why can't he be more like Devon? Why doesn't he want me?

"You need to remember you're in hell now, little mouse. God can't help you here."

"What about in church? I spotted the chapel at the end of the street."

A grin tugs at his lips. "Of course you did."

"A church is sacred." I point out. "The devil can't go there."

He chuckles. "Have you already forgotten what happened last night? Devil's gates opened inside St Catherine's last night, and the devil won."

I gulp, guilt washing over me as I remember the two men that died. How Father Peters hit his head. How I was nearly killed.

How could I forget that?

I need to call my sister. My parents.

"Can I please have my phone back?"

He frowns, almost like he's disappointed. "No."

There's a little anger in his tone as he pushes back off me, and I suddenly miss being crowded in by him.

What's wrong with you, Jaxcen? Get a grip.

"Can I at least go to church?" I ask, watching his large form retreat, heading to the staircase.

"Confession isn't until later tonight. You can go then." He grumbles before looking over his shoulder. "Come and have some brunch, and I'll organise some clothes for you so you can venture out later and explore my town."

I perk up at the thought of going out to explore, so I leap up off the window box and follow him back down to his suite, where he calls the kitchen to send up some food before he showers.

I don't know why, but when he's in the shower, I find myself walking past the door numerous times, like I'm subconsciously hoping the door will fall off the hinges, or I'll get sporadic x-ray vision, and see inside the room. At a naked Devon.

I got a glimpse last night. Him shirtless, and then with only his boxers on after I showered and rejoined him in the bedroom to go to bed.

As far as I can tell, there's not a single flaw on him. His height, his broad shoulders, the ropes of muscles that travel his arms and legs, it's all near perfect if you ask me, and when he wrapped his arms around me from behind in bed, tugging me close, enveloping me, I melted and secretly wished to never leave.

As I pass by the door again, a deep, gravelly moan floats out from underneath it, and I freeze.

That can't be what I think I heard... right?

Tip toeing, like he'll somehow hear me walking on the thick push pile of his carpet, I gently press my ear to the door and listen.

Slapping. I hear wet slapping sounds, and from the indecent x-rated online videos I've watched, I know exactly what he's doing.

He's... He's...

Oh my.

My cheeks flush as my heart races and heat pools between my legs.

I picture him, naked, his strong fingers wrapped around his length as he pumps...

Another moan floats under the door, before his deep voice, although quiet, clearly speaks.

"Fuuuck." He grunts and pants, a needy whimper escaping me before I realise what's happening, and I leap back slapping my hand over my mouth.

And that's the moment I want to curl up and die.

"Excuse me, Miss Summers, I knocked."

Mabel. Bloody Mabel is standing in the living room, tray of food in her clutches, her expression reminding me of my second grade teacher that caught me eating a lolly from my school bag.

Shame. Shame. Shame, Jaxcen.

The bathroom door swings open, Devon's expression pinched as he hurries out to find me, probably resembling a deer in headlights as I dart my gaze between him and Mabel.

"What's going on?" he demands, and now I resemble a damn fish, my mouth opening and closing, words lost. "Mabel?" He sighs, clearly giving up on expecting an answer from me.

"I have your food, Mr Marx," she answers, politely.

"I can see that. But what's going on here?" He gestures between me and Mabel, and I shoot a silent beg her way not to dob me in.

Placing the tray on the table, Mabel brushes her hand down over her apron and clears her throat before glancing back at Devon.

"It appears your guest was eavesdropping on your bathing activities."

OH. MY. FUCKING. GOD.

Vida Loca
Trust

CHAPTER TEN

Devon

For a moment there, I wasn't sure Mabel would be honest, even though I've never before questioned her loyalty. But having Jaxcen here is new. Different. And she's extremely likeable, a fact that has been bothering me because I have no doubt she has the ability to befriend my soldiers and get under their skin to coax them into letting her leave.

Not to mention, that women, especially the ones in my town, tend to band together, which I don't hate, but it can lead to some tense moments at times. So really, Jaxcen already getting Mabel on her side was highly likely, but it appears not.

Mabel is still only loyal to me, it seems.

"Is that so?" I ask, keeping my expression neutral as I stand with only a towel wrapped around me, my gaze locked onto the mortified expression contorting Jaxcen's face. "Were you eavesdropping on me in the shower, little mouse?"

She gives me the slightest head shake before my brow shoots high, daring her to continue lying, which is when her shoulders slump and she drops her head in defeat.

"Thank you, Mabel. That will be all."

At my dismissal, Mabel nods and leaves the suite, closing me in with my guest. Or prisoner. It depends who you ask, I suppose.

"Sit. I'll be right out." I order, and notice how quickly she obeys.

There's a part of me, and it's a pretty big part, that enjoys this power play between us. I know I have a dominant personality, but I don't consider myself a Dom, or partake in any such roles. I just demand, and expect obedience.

But there's something about Jaxcen's obedience that doesn't sit well with me.

Don't get me wrong, I'm enjoying her submission, but it's where it comes from that is the troubling factor.

After dressing, I join Jaxcen at the table, noticing that she hasn't touched the food. She's just sitting and waiting as instructed.

"Eat," I bark, and I expect her to jump from the bite in my tone, but instead, she glares at me.

Fucking hell. I can't help but grin.

"Why are you glaring at me? I'm not the one in trouble here." I remind her, and her eyes fall to her lap. "Eat, Jaxcen."

Reluctantly, she takes an apple and starts slicing it thinly on her plate.

Note to fucking self. Tomorrow, ask Mabel for a big greasy serving of bacon and eggs for Jaxcen. She's too fucking thin and needs some meat on her bones.

"So you were eaves—"

"I wasn't. I swear. I heard a sound and thought you might have fallen. That's all."

Not only did she interrupt me while I was speaking, but she still has the audacity to lie.

Taking a sip of my juice, I place the glass back on the table and slowly sit back in my chair, regarding her with a smirk.

"You're certainly wracking up the sins here, Miss Summers. Confession will be a long one tonight," I point out and she frowns. "Lying to me seems to be one of your favourite sins."

Her cheeks flare to life at my observation, and I chuckle, picking up my fork and pointing it at her.

"We both know you were eavesdropping, little mouse. Tell me, did you hear me finish?"

This time, her blush engulfs her whole face and tracks down her neck, giving herself away.

"Going by that blush, I'd say yes." I tease, dropping my eyes to the avocado on my plate.

"I'm sorry I..." Her words trail off, and I glance back up to see her biting her lip.

Fuck, that's sexy.

It seems she's lost for words.

I could press the matter. Really rub it in her face, but I think I'll leave that to her confessions.

"I'll take you to the chapel tonight. You can repent there, love."

At my words, she nods, like that's the most acceptable outcome.

I wonder if she'll find her penance acceptable.

I grin down at my plate, and focus on my meal as ideas come at me from every direction while we eat in silence, until I order her to shower.

While she's in the shower, I don't eavesdrop, but instead, welcome Finn into the suite and take the bag he hands me with Jaxcen's personal items.

"Any sign yet of Mr fucking V?" I snap, and Finn shakes his head.

"Cameras haven't picked up any activity yet."

I sent him and a team to Jaxcen's home last night after I left with her to come here. I asked him to gather a bag of clothes and essentials for her, and install some hidden cameras so we can keep an eye on the place in case Mr V turns up.

I also asked him to gather intel on Jaxcen, so I'm hoping he was successful.

"Okay. What did you learn about my guest?" I ask, making sure my bathroom door remains in my view so I can see the moment it cracks open.

"Well, she has an old school answering machine on a landline phone, and there are already a ton of messages left by a guy called Eddie."

I nod. "Her fiancé."

"Her space is simple. Nothing extravagant until you open her wardrobe." Finn reveals and my brows shoot up.

"How so?"

Finn smirks. "That woman has hundreds of shoes, all kept in clear boxes. There are stacks of them, and Miles seems to think they are the expensive kind." He shrugs. "I don't know about that, but the interesting thing was what was behind all the boxes of shoes."

"What was behind them?" I ask, my mind racing with the possibilities.

"A laptop."

My brows shoot up.

"A laptop?" I ask to confirm, and Finn nods.

Fuck. Why would she hide her laptop?

"Did you look to see what was on it?" I snap, like he might have found something that I don't want him looking at.

"Nah, man. Not my expertise."

Why the fuck am I jumping the gun?

"Sorry man," I mutter, shaking my head at my own fucking behaviour.

"All good." Finn chuckles. "She's already gotten under your skin. Is everything alright?"

"Yeah, everything is fine." I blow out a frustrated breath and glance back up at my best mate. "Did you find anything else?"

Finn studies me a moment, and I know he can see my lie, but he doesn't call me out on it. "Nah, just her laptop. It's with Dom. I told him just to get into it and see if there's anything unusual."

"Okay, thanks," I mutter and gesture my head to her suitcase. "You pack any of her fancy shoes?"

He nods. "A couple of pairs, and some strappy sandals and a pair of the fanciest runners I've ever seen."

"Are they those ones on a bit of a platform, with fucking bling on them?"

He grins. "Yeah, exactly like that."

"Hmmm, she really does like her shoes," I mutter more to myself than anything, and Finn laughs.

"No shit, take a look." He holds up his phone screen and I see what he was talking about inside Jaxcen's wardrobe. There are so many fucking shoes, that it looks more like an obsession than anything, and I fucking smirk.

Another sin, Miss Summers.

Greed.

"Send me those pictures," I order Finn, and he nods, doing so immediately before leaving.

I take Jaxcen's large suitcase, heft it onto my bed and unzip it, revealing some very haphazardly packed clothes, shoes and toiletries. The panties, which are tucked into the sides of the case, are all lacy, and I spot a few bras that match, so I pick a mauve set and lay it out on the bed before moving to my bedside and taking out my notepad to write her a note.

Here are some of your things, little mouse.
Wear whatever you want, but my only stipulation is you must wear the purple panties and bra.
And don't think about disobeying me, because I'll be checking.
Come downstairs when you're ready.
I'll be in the Cliff Top Bar.
x D

Folding the paper in half, I drop it on top of the mauve panties and bra before leaving.

The Palace is bustling with staff and patrons, but the bar itself isn't as busy.

Most are likely out in the beer garden, given the warm December sun shining today, with the few still inside simply getting drinks for outside, or the couple of usual day drinkers, who perch themselves at the end of the bar from opening until closing.

They are husband and wife and have experienced unbelievable loss. They barely talk to anyone, let alone each other, yet every day, they walk in hand in hand, and stumble out hand in hand, and I often wonder if things will ever get easier for them, or if this is where they will die, living the same day over and over.

"Hey Dev." Ronnie nods, wiping over the bar as he gestures his Santa hat wearing head to the far corner as I approach. "Melissa is here to see you."

My gaze shifts to the corner to see the young woman, probably close in age to Jaxcen, her arms wrapped over her chest as she curls in on herself almost like she's cold.

It's not cold.

"How long has she been waiting?" I ask Ronnie, and he shrugs.

"She was here waiting at the door when I came in to open up, and hasn't left since. Just asked for an audience with the devil."

The devil. I can't believe the stupid nickname has stuck.

I can thank my cousins for that, the pricks.

Not that it doesn't work in my favour most of the time.

When people think you're the devil, they tend to tread carefully.

"Thanks, Ronnie. I'll take her into my office. If a skinny blonde that looks like she has no idea if she's in the right place comes in, tell her to take a seat and offer her a drink. Her name is Jaxcen."

Ronnie smirks. "You got it."

I roll my fucking eyes at his grin. I know what he's thinking. I don't bring chicks back here to fuck, so in his eyes, it must mean more.

Whatever. It's nearly fucking Christmas and I wanted a fucking treat.

Approaching Melissa, her eyes widen when she sees me nearing, her spine straightening.

"You've been waiting to see me?" I ask, and she nods.

"Yes, Mr Marx. I..." Her lower lip starts trembling and her eyes turn glassy, so I gesture to my office door off to the side.

"Let's go into my office."

She nods quickly, sliding off the bar stool as she swipes at the tears escaping her eyes.

Leading her to my office door, I grit my teeth at the fucking garland framing the fucking thing, having to brush some of it aside to get to the key pad and type in my code to unlock the door.

As I step inside and hold the door open for Melissa to enter, my gaze travels back out over the bar and I frown.

Garland, tinsel, ornaments, lights. You name it, my bar has got it, thanks to a sassy teenager that has absolutely added more decorations after I told her she'd already over done it.

"Ronnie," I call, and his head snaps in my direction from behind the bar. "Get Allegra in here. I need to have a discussion with her about following instructions."

Ronnie's lips spread wide, his moustache quirking up at the corners as he nods.

"Will do."

Fucking teenage girls and their over the top decorating ideas.

As I turn to close the door of my office, I still at what I see hanging over my fucking desk.

She has to be fucking kidding me.

Mistletoe.

Fucking mistletoe is dangling from a red ribbon tied to the fucking light shade over my desk.

How the fuck did Allegra get inside my fucking office? I told her it was a no decoration zone, yet there hangs a fucking mistletoe.

I want to rant, but Melissa's sobs remind me that she's here needing my help, so I close the door, ignore the fucking mistletoe, and take a seat behind my desk.

"What's happened?" I ask Melissa who fiercely tries to slap away her tears, only to have more fall in their place, the ones on the left side of her face run down the thick scar that runs through her left eye and down to her jawline.

"I've done everything you said. I don't use my old social media account. My new one has a fake name and picture. I don't mention anything about my past, but..." Her face contorts like she's in pain, and by the way she clutches at her chest, I suppose she might be. "You told me he was dead."

My brows hitch. "He is dead. I killed him myself," I snap, feeling a little fucking insulted.

Her ex boyfriend was a piece of shit gangbanger in the city. There was no method to his madness, only that he was completely fucking nuts, and somehow, Melissa got swept up in his chaos. Fit Nick is what they called him. A gym junkie and pumped up on so many fucking steroids, I bet the fucker couldn't find his dick. But his real name was Nicholas Ballen, and his brain painted the street by the time I was finished with him.

"But he messaged me. On messenger on my new secret profile. It leads back to his profile."

Fucking social media.

"Show me," I bark, and she hurries to stand, sliding her phone over my desk towards me.

Taking it, I read the message.

Shit. Someone is harassing her. It's not her ex, but someone that has access to his account, or has made a new dummy account using his identity.

Taking out my phone, I snap a picture of the message, and then go to the profile and snap another picture before handing back her phone.

"Don't respond and send me screenshots of anything else you get," I order and she nods. "I'll have Dom rescan your device to make sure there's no tracker as well."

"Thank you." She nods, standing quickly and offering me a shy smile even though tears are still falling.

"You're safe here, Melissa. I won't let anyone hurt you again." I remind her, and she nods quickly, moving towards the door.

"Thank you, Mr Marx."

I roll my eyes, following her. "How many times do I have to remind you to call me Devon?"

She shrugs. "Miss Barber says it's disrespectful to use your first name, and that even if you insist we call you by that, we should still refer to you as Mr Marx."

"Well isn't Miss Barber a pain in my arse?" I tease, and Melissa's smile grows wider as she giggles.

Reaching around her, I open the door, and we step out only to come face to face with my blonde goddess whose gaze is dancing between the two of us before it narrows.

Huh.

I know that look.

My little mouse is jealous.

She shouldn't be, and not just because I'm not attracted to Melissa or the fact there is absolutely nothing going on between us, but because Jaxcen and I aren't a thing, so whether or not she notices, she's just shown me her cards.

Try to deny it all you want, little mouse, but you like me.

The thought makes me smirk, and I relax against the door frame as Melissa brushes past Jaxcen and scurries out of the bar.

"Who was that?" She has the nerve to ask.

"None of your business." My gaze drops down the length of her body and back up, taking in the strappy dress she chose to wear with the strappy sandals, and my eyes narrow at the fact I cannot see a mauve bra strap which should be noticeable, given the straps of the dress. "I see you've already disobeyed me."

She frowns. "What do you mean? No, I haven't."

Pushing off the door frame I take a step back inside my office and gesture my head for her to follow. She only hesitates a moment before stepping inside, her curious gaze travelling over everything in sight.

I watch as she approaches my desk and runs the pad of her finger over the rich oak wood before spinning to face me.

"So this is where you—" she gasps at my nearness, even as I press myself up against her front and lift her to place her arse on my desk. "What are you doing?"

I don't answer, keeping my eyes locked with hers as I glide my hand up her side before cupping her breast to feel her nipple pebble under my touch.

Fuuuck. Just that simple touch has my cock waking up.

"Where's the bra?" I snap, and she stiffens.

"I... well if I wore it you'd see the straps," she explains, "so I decided to go braless."

I growl, "For all my men to see these?" I pinch her nipple and she cries out, arching her back so her tits press harder against my touch.

"No... that's not why," she breathes, clearly affected by the sensation of having her nipple stimulated, and I want to protest, but all I can think about is the tight peak of her nipple, and having it in my mouth.

Giving in, I lean down and take the hard bud into my mouth, dress fabric and all, and a whimper escapes her.

As I scrape my teeth over her nipple, her nails dig into my shoulders and her legs part wider to allow me closer as I stand between them. Releasing her nipple, I drop to my knees while hitching the fabric of her dress up to reveal the mauve lacy panties I chose for her.

I'm fucking starved, just the sight of the wet patch darkening the satin crotch of her panties has me surging forward and pressing my nose to her core to breathe her in.

"I... what... oh..." She's lost for words, and I wonder if she's ever had a man's face between her legs before.

Just the thought that I could be the first has me shifting away to hook her panties in my fingers and tug them off her legs.

"What are you doing?" she breathes, panic in her tone.

"What does it look like, little mouse?" I ease her legs wider, my gaze dropping to the pink satin flesh, already swollen and wet with arousal, a small neatly groomed arrow of hair pointing towards her clit like it's saying, 'press here.'

Fuuuck. I love a well groomed woman, and I don't mind some hair. It seems unnatural and childlike when women have bare cunts, and it fucking deflates my cock.

But not Jaxcen.

She may be only twenty-four, but she's all fucking woman.

When all she can do is stare wide-eyed at me, I point above us, and watch her head tip back as she spots the mistletoe above us.

"What?" She frowns, her gaze returning to mine. "You're meant to kiss under a mistletoe."

I grin wickedly and nod before closing the distance and flicking my tongue over her needy clit.

"Oh!" she cries out before slapping her hand over her mouth, her wide eyes shooting to the door, clearly worried someone will overhear.

Like I give a fuck.

"Stop, Devon. That's not a kiss."

When she tries to shove my head away, I snag her wrist and growl.

"Isn't it? Your wet cunt seems to like the way I kiss."

Chapter Eleven

Jaxcen

A loud gasp escapes me which turns into a strangled moan when Devon buries his head between my legs and starts pashing my pussy.

Yes, he actually pashes it. Like a full on make out session, and I swear, oh boy do I swear, I see stars.

I can't look away from the sight, not just because he's on his knees before me, something I didn't think I'd ever see Devon Marx do, but because it's all just so... filthy.

His hot lips nibble, nip and suck at me, while his tongue flicks, glides, and dives inside the place aching to be filled.

I have no choice but to give in, heat igniting my entire body from head to toe as I tug on my wrist, needing it free so I can lean back and give him better access.

Getting my silent meaning, Devon releases my wrist, and I brace my hands back against his desk top while his grip shifts to my hips, holding me in place.

Oh wow. The feel of his hot tongue gliding over my most intimate flesh feels unlike anything I've felt before. I've seen this happen in the adult movies I watch, and at Cloud 9, but I've never experienced it personally until now.

I don't have much hands-on experience when it comes to sex, but I already know this has to be my favourite thing ever.

EVER!

My heart thrashes wildly in my chest as I pant and cry out, and I can't even tell how loud I'm being but I don't particularly care right now.

All I know is if he stops, I'll commit murder.

"Yes." I moan, my hips shifting as they work of their own accord to chase this building ache deep inside me before I start grinding against his face.

Yes, I'm actually grinding. That's the only way I can explain it. The need inside digging its claws in and taking over, possessing me like a dark and sinister demon inside me has awoken from thousands of years of sleep.

And now it's hungry.

So, so hungry.

A scream rips from my throat as I explode, a rush of cold tingles sweeping up my legs, and over my hips, and all the way up to my head as my core pulses with the most intense orgasm I've ever had.

I collapse on the desk top, my arms giving way, no longer able to support me, while my hearing floats in and out as I go languid.

My body must be numb, because I don't even feel Devon shift from between my legs before he appears in my line of sight, hovering over me.

"You doing okay, little mouse?"

"I... ah..." I shrug. I think. I still can't feel anything.

Devon chuckles. "So what do you think?"

"About?" I whisper, my lids blinking rapidly as the surrounding sounds start to creep back in.

"My kiss." He smirks, and hell, he could ask me to do anything for him right now, and I think I'd obey without argument.

"I think..." I breathe, a lazy smile tugging at my lips. "I think I like mistletoe."

Throwing his head back, Devon laughs, its deep rich tone seeping into my chest and settling there like a comfortable weighted blanket.

Scooping his hands under my back, Devon helps me to sit up, and it takes a moment for my lightheadedness to fade away. He eyes me with that damn shit-eating grin he wears so well, before taking a tissue from his desk and dabbing at the mess I made on his chin.

And there's my cheeks, on fire once again.

"Sorry," I whisper, and he shakes his head.

"Don't ever apologise for taking what you need and leaving a mess behind. Own that shit." He insists, but all I feel is embarrassed.

I can't imagine Eddie ever wanting to do *that*. He'd tell me it's dirty filth. Depraved. That I should be ashamed to even consider doing it. To ask him to do that.

I kind of hate him right now.

Why is it so bad to want to do these things if they feel so good?

I guess heroin makes people feel good too, doesn't it. But sex isn't illegal.

It's natural.

Isn't it?

It felt natural. My body felt like it would die if Devon stopped. Even now, I feel swollen between my legs but it doesn't feel bad. And hell, I kind of feel like I want more.

Eyeing Devon, my gaze travels down his black tee and how it hugs his impeccably sculpted chest and abs, to settle on the hard bulge hiding in his pants.

He jerks his hips forward and laughs when I flinch back and start blinking, embarrassed that he caught me staring.

"See something you like?"

"I-ah." Getting tongue tied, I take a deep breath, lick my lips, and try again, gesturing my head to his crotch. "Should I?" I can't say the words out loud, because I'm a wimp, but I point to his crotch just in case he isn't picking up my brand of awkwardness, hoping he'll catch on.

"You want to kiss my cock, Jaxcen?"

Do I?

Hell, the idea has a small ache beginning to build between my legs again, so I guess I do, but I shrug, because admitting that is just too much right now.

"Hmmm. Lying to me once again I see," he mutters, taking a step back. "It's okay, little mouse. The fact that you want to suck my cock like a lollipop will remain our little secret for now, because I'm pretty sure you're not ready to handle it."

Turning his back on me, he moves to the door, leaving me sprawled on his desk with my dress bunched around my waist.

"Wait!" I screech, and he turns back, a smirk already present. "I need my underwear."

"Oh, you mean these?" He holds up the mauve fabric, the lace dangling from his finger, and I quickly shuffle off his desk, nodding. "Nope," he says, and tucks them into his pocket.

"Stop. I need them," I protest, but then he's turning and swinging the door open wide, stepping out into the bar with my panties in his pocket.

Chasing after him, as I enter the bar again, I come to a stop as I notice several sets of eyes on me, as Devon starts to chat quietly with the bartender.

What are they staring at?

Glancing down at myself, I make sure my dress is in place and I'm not unknowingly flashing everyone, feeling naked without fabric covering my bits underneath.

Can they tell what we were just doing in Devon's office?

The thought has me glancing up again, to see one man smirking into his beer.

Oh. My...

They all totally heard me, didn't they?

Heat engulfs my cheeks once again, and I wonder if someone can get sunburnt from the inside out.

Is that a thing?

I kind of want it to be a thing right now, because self combusting and turning to ash sounds a helluva lot better than knowing these people heard me... Oh god, they heard me have an orgasm.

It's more than obvious these people know exactly what just happened in Devon's office. Well, maybe all but the couple sitting at the end of the bar, their expressions solemn as they stare into their drinks.

"Jaxcen," Devon calls, turning his dark gaze to me. "This is Ronnie. He's your man if you're thirsty, but he doesn't make those fruity cocktails. If you want one of those, Miss Barber serves them at her house on Friday and Sunday afternoons. The only payment she expects is a plate of treats."

I nod, even though I'm not sure why I need to know that because I'm not staying.

Then it hits me once again.

He brought me here against my will.

Kidnapped me.

And now he's making me into his... his... plaything.

For a moment I feel used, but then I remember that not once has he used my body for his own pleasure. He's only given it to me.

I'm so confused.

"Come on, love. I'll show you around."

Devon starts walking off, and I freak out, feeling the light breeze coming through the door rush up my dress and over the bare flesh between my legs. With both hands pressed to the sides of my thighs, I hurry forward, hoping the damn thing doesn't blow up.

"Devon!" I whisper yell, catching up to him. "I can't walk around without panties on."

He chuckles. "Sure you can."

"Stop. This isn't funny." I complain, as he leads me out to the front porch lining the Palace.

"It is for me."

I slap his arm which just makes him laugh again at my damn expense and keep walking down the steps and out onto the path.

Oh. My. God. He's really going to make me walk around without panties on, isn't he?

Glancing over my shoulder to the large entrance doors, I consider bolting back into the building and up to his suite to get a new pair to put on, but the thought he might catch me and throw me over his shoulder again has me squashing that idea.

My naked coochie will surely be noticeable if he does that.

Dammit.

I concede and follow behind.

As we walk side by side, I keep my dress in my clutches, making sure there's no chance of it flying up with the breeze.

Devon shows me the convenience store, the bakery, the butcher, and all the little shops that make up a small country town, before leading me up the hill to some of the house lined streets, all of which are decorated with Christmas dressings.

I find myself listening contently as he explains who lives where, the deep timbre of his voice having a calming effect on me that I'm not willing to analyse.

I should probably tell him I'll never remember all of this, nor will I ever need this information, but he sounds so proud as he speaks. I can also see it in his confident stride and the tone of his voice. This little community means a lot to him.

Once again, most of the residents I notice are females, and the only men in sight are dressed in back vests and armed with weapons, all bar a few older men that were starting their drinking sessions early in the bar, and a middle aged man that ran the butcher's store.

It's clear Devon is the king here, and this is his Palace.

I don't want to even think it's possible, but I'm pretty sure these women are his.

Like he owns them, or they are his wives or something. They look at him with such respect and admiration, which really doesn't match up to the cocky asshat I met in the church.

Did he kidnap them all like he did me and their admiration is some sort of stockholm thing? Did he groom them into loving him? Did he bring them blinding pleasure too? Is that how he weaves his web?

Am I trapped here forever?

The thought has my heart sinking and my mood souring. I want to ask him, but his reactions are so unpredictable. I'm not sure if he'll pull out a gun and shoot me in the head, or demand I strip where I stand so he can use my body in front of everyone.

Will they stop him?

No. Mabel already proved that to me.

They are loyal to him and it's either because they respect him or are scared of him. I just need to figure out which one rules their behaviour.

"Who got my clothes and things and brought them here?" I ask as we stroll the streets, momentarily stopping in the shade of a tree.

"I had Finn and Miles collect it." He admits easily, and for some reason I didn't think he'd actually answer.

"Why couldn't you have taken me home to pack for myself?"

He shoots me a *'really'* look, but I just stare at him, waiting for a proper response.

He sighs. "What would have happened if I took you back to your apartment? Would you have willingly packed a bag? Would you have screamed? Would you have tried to alert a neighbour?"

I gulp. I would have absolutely screamed and hoped Mr Hickock, my elderly neighbour would have heard.

Seeing the truth on my face, Devon nods and steps closer. "The moment you involve a neighbour or a bystander, you give them a death sentence, Jaxcen. I'd have to cover our tracks, and the only way to do that is by killing them."

Tears prick at my eyes from the severity in his tone, reminding me once again, that I'm with the devil. Not a nice man.

"Why am I here? You don't need me. I swear I won't tell anyone. Please let me go home."

His shoulders drop, almost as if my words disappoint him.

"You're here because that's what I want, and if you want your time here to be easy, little mouse, I'd suggest that you don't fucking ask to leave again."

Spinning on his heel, Devon storms off towards the town centre, not the least bit concerned with leaving me alone here.

I take a moment to let my scared tears fall, waiting for the loneliness to creep in. But it doesn't.

I don't really miss the hustle of the city. The loud car horns and busy streets. I don't miss my apartment other than the few creature comforts I allowed myself. And I definitely don't miss Eddie.

Watching a bee buzz at my side, I smile remembering the hives my grandad had on his farm when I was little, which makes me think of my parents.

I don't really miss my dad, and my mum and I have a strained relationship.

I wonder what my parents would say if they knew what I've been up to lately. What would they say about me attending a sex club? What would they think about Devon Marx?

I think my mum would probably faint.

The thought brings a smile to my face, and my eyes drop back to my surroundings of this weird but cute little town that sits on the ridge overlooking Timber Valley.

Slowly, I meander back towards the heart of the town, which all seems to centre around the Palace. Devon's castle.

Running off Main Street is a big clearing, its grass so green it looks like it must be watered two times a day. There's a children's playground off to one side, and a plaque off to the other, but beyond it, the grass runs right up to the cliff's edge where eight or so park benches face the stunning view over the valley.

I head towards the cliff's edge, taking in the beauty of the townships below.

Fox Pines and Redfield are closest with Redfield Lake off in the distance.

There's another lake close by. I saw a sign for it on our way up the mountain. It's Lake Woodall. And down below are the small dots of people, picnicking by the lake while others swim.

"I hope you're not planning on jumping."

I gasp at the voice, spinning to see a woman, maybe in her forties wearing gym pants and a crop top as she jogs on the spot, sweat beading on her forehead.

"Oh, ah... No." I laugh awkwardly, and she nods.

"Good. It's awful having to retrieve the bodies that go over. Some think it'll kill them instantly, but many have found if the fall doesn't kill them on impact, the injuries they sustain makes them wish they were dead all over again."

"Oh." I lean over a little to get a better look over the ledge which is fenced off with clear perspex, but I guess if someone really wants out, they'll climb it and jump. "Does that happen a lot?"

I glance back in time to see the woman shrug as she checks her fitness watch, still jogging on the spot. "A time or two. Some women just can't handle it, you know?"

Some women?

No, I don't know, but I'm not telling her that.

A cold chill runs up my spine, her words just another convincing factor that these women didn't come here voluntarily.

"I'm sorry, I didn't catch your name." I smile fakely, but all she does is quirk a brow.

"I didn't offer it. But I'm guessing you're Devon's little mouse?"

I nearly choke at her words, my own saliva working against me, getting stuck in the back of my throat.

"What? How?"

She snickers, her eyes roaming me from head to toe before she starts jogging off and calls over her shoulder. "Welcome to the family."

The family?

My heart sinks.

I was right.

This is some sort of a cult, or a polygamist community, and Devon is their husband. And probably not because they wanted to be his, but because he kidnapped them too, and groomed them into accepting a life here.

I peer over the edge of the cliff again, looking at the steep drop that looks pretty lethal to me.

Is that the only way out? Did some women feel like jumping to their death was their only choice?

I back away, suddenly not so sure the view is as beautiful as I thought it was.

I need to keep my wits about me and figure out a way out of this town before I become just another woman Devon claims.

Glancing at the Palace as I make my way back to Main Street, its sheer size compared to everything else in this town is overwhelming. It's named appropriately given how it towers over the rest of the town, with the next biggest structure being the church at the end of the street.

My feet lead me there, my heart hammering in my chest as the reality of my situation settles in my gut. I need to figure out a way to get out of this place. To get away from that man.

Hurrying up the small paved path, I grip the old wrought iron handle and pull, only to have the door not budge.

"It's locked," a woman calls, and I turn to see a younger woman than the last, pushing a stroller with a toddler in it past the church. "Mr Marx is the only one with a key."

Of course he is.

"Do you know why it's locked?" I ask, making my way towards her, my eyes dropping to the dark haired child sleeping with a pacifier in its mouth. A little boy.

My gaze darts back to the woman, who must be in her late twenties or early thirties. Her hair is auburn, not dark brown, so the father must be dark haired too.

Wait... Is Devon the father?

I wonder if the little boy has Devon's eyes?

"We don't practise religion in this town," she states, not seeming to be concerned about that which I find odd since Devon said he's a religious man and we literally met in a church.

"Why not?"

She shrugs, pushing the stroller back and forth as if she doesn't want to stop the movement in case the child wakes. "Mr Marx prefers it that way. He hasn't banned it. Says we can worship and do whatever we want in our homes, but it won't be a communal thing."

Well now I'm confused. A cult would have some sort of worship thing, and as far as I know, polygamy is also religious, so if worship isn't the factor here, then it only leaves one conclusion.

Devon Marx is a monster who steals women and keeps them for his own pleasure.

Oh but what pleasure it is.

Oh shut up inner voice.

"Right." I nod, like her explanation makes perfect sense. "Well thanks."

I go to leave, but the woman keeps talking.

"I'm Marilda, by the way. I live on Oak Tree Lane. Number three." She smiles, offering me her hand, and I take it, because she has to be the least threatening person I've come across so far.

"Hi Marilda, I'm Jaxcen."

"Wow, that's a pretty name. So much cooler than Marilda." She screws her nose up.

"Most people assume I'm a male when they read my name. Sometimes I tell them my name is Jac, and they assume it's short for Jacquie or something."

She nods. "When I was little, I used to tell people my name was Matilda instead. My youthful mind was hoping that by changing it to that, magic would come my way."

I giggle. "And did it work?"

Her smile falls a little. "No. Well, I guess little Damon here is pretty magical and I made him so..." She shrugs.

"Yeah," I smile down at the sleeping child, trying not to get hooked up on the fact his name starts with a D, just like Devon. "That is pretty magical."

"You should come by Miss Barber's house on Friday afternoon. She makes the most amazing cocktails, and all of us ladies have so much fun."

"Ladies?" I ask, remembering how Devon told me about Miss Barber's cocktail sessions.

"Yeah, most of the ladies go and relax. It's a male free zone, so we can speak freely about all our dirty little secrets." She winks.

"Oh, I don't know..."

"Oh come on. You have to. You're part of the family now." She beams, reaching out to give my shoulder a squeeze while my heart just about stops. "I'd better keep moving. When Damon wakes from a nap, he gets pretty moody. Just like his dad."

The smile slips from her face, and she glances over her shoulder like she's looking for someone, but when she faces me again, she smiles like she wasn't just freaking out about something.

"I hope we see you on Friday." She smiles, steering the stroller around me on the path and walking away.

So, I'm part of the family apparently. Two women in the space of ten minutes have said so, and it can only mean one thing.

I was right. Either they are happy and comply because they have been brainwashed by Devon's charm, or they fear for their lives.

I have to get out of here.

Panic grips me as I hurry up the path that wraps around the back street of the Palace, and make my way towards the road we came in on. I've all but forgotten about the fact I'm not wearing any underwear, my need to escape more important than something as simple as a pair of panties.

The road we drove in on is steeper than I realised, and I have no doubt that if it was raining today, I might slip given how quickly my feet are shuffling down the incline.

I know there are armed men at the gates, but maybe I can convince them to let me go. Surely they can't be alright with Devon keeping all these women here for himself.

Does he ever share with these men or do they just stand guard and watch?

That thought makes me feel just as sick as the thought of Devon trapping all the women here does, which is why I have to escape. I have to get to a phone and call the police and save these women.

Rounding a bend, the gates up ahead also seem bigger than they did when we drove through them in the car last night. The men haven't noticed me yet, their stances relaxed as they laugh about something, their deep chuckles meeting my ears as I approach.

"Oh shit." I hear one say as he stiffens, kicks the other guard's foot before standing tall and rolling his shoulders back which makes him appear three times bigger than he did moments ago when he was relaxed.

The other guard looks over his shoulder spotting me, and lurches up, his hand on his gun at his hip, watching me approach.

Plastering on a fake smile, I give them both a friendly wave.

"Hi," I say cheerfully. "You must be hot out here."

They glance at each other before returning their intense gazes back to me, their height becoming more prominent the closer I get.

"Can we help you, Miss Summers?"

Shit, they know my name. I bet they know all the names of the women Devon kidnaps.

"Oh no. I was just going for a walk in this beautiful weather and must have taken a wrong turn."

They nod, and I notice the guy at the back relaxes a little with the way his shoulders drop a fraction.

He doesn't see me as a threat. Which I'm not. I'm no match for them. I've done stupid stuff in my life, but me thinking I can out muscle these men isn't one of them.

"If you turn around and head back up this road, you'll find your way back into town," the first guard offers, shooting me a wink.

Oh. He's a bit flirty.

I can work with that.

"Would you like to join me for a walk?" I ask him, smiling as sweetly as I can muster. "I could use some company."

"Is that so?" He grins, while the guy behind him curses under his breath.

"Yeah. I'm just feeling a little lonely, you know?" I let my smile drop and give him puppy dog eyes. "What with being new here and everything. I'd really like to make some friends."

The guard smirks, taking a step closer. "And you want to be my friend?"

I nod. "Yeah. I'd love to be your friend."

Ugh. Why is he eating this up? I sound fake to my own ears, clearly not used to being flirty, but his eyes drop to my boobs, and I know he notices the outline of my nipples. Maybe I should bend to pick something up and show him what's not covering my butt underneath my dress.

"I can always use new friends." He gestures behind me, but I bite on my lip and glance over his shoulder beyond the gates.

"We could always go that way. You know, just to be safe so no one sees us." His brows hitch at my suggestion, and he glances over his shoulder to the closed gates.

"Outside the boundary?" he asks and I nod, but his eyes narrow a little.

Shit.

I'm losing him.

Panicking, I start fanning myself and gesture my head past the gates again. "There's a big old tree over there. I bet it's nice and cool under it. On the ground." I reach back and scoop up my long hair, holding the blonde locks above my head to fan the back of my neck with my other hand, and his eyes dart to my clavicle where I know a bead of sweat is running down my flesh before disappearing under the fabric of my dress.

The crunching of gravel sounds beside me, right before the barrel of a gun presses against the guard's temple.

"What did I tell you about involving other people, little mouse?"

My eyes widen as a gasp escapes me, my eyes locking onto the dark and sinister gaze of Devon Marx.

Oh shit.

CHAPTER TWELVE

Devon

"**I**... I... I..."

She's fucking lost for words, those big blue pools wide with fear, her gaze dancing between my gun, which is digging into Bruno's temple right now, and back to me.

"What did you want to do under the tree with Bruno, little mouse?"

"Nothing... I..."

"You what?" I snap, and she flinches, her shoulders rolling forward as fear grips her.

The only response she musters is a shake of her head as her eyes turn glassy.

"Did you want to drop to your knees for him?"

"Sir, I—"

At Bruno's attempt to defend himself, I shove the barrel harder against his temple, keeping my gaze on Jaxcen.

"No," she whispers, her lower lip trembling, and fuck, I don't want to make her cry, but I need to remind her that she can't leave. She needs to stay here.

"So why the fuck did I get an alert on my phone from the motion activated camera, even after I've told you time and time again not to run, and what will happen to people you involve, only to find you strolling up to my men, and fucking flirting with them?"

She remains quiet.

"Trying to escape again?" I ask and she nods this time.

"Yes."

"You obviously don't care what happens to others do you?" My words have her scared eyes turning into angry slits. "So again, I'll ask, what did I say happens to people you involve?"

"They die," she snaps in a loud whisper.

"Exactly. You give them a death sentence. Now I have to kill one of my best men." I deadpan and her lips part in protest as Bruno stutters.

"B-but Dev—"

"Stop!" I bellow, causing Jaxcen to squeak and Aaron to curse behind me as I glare at his fellow guard, shaking under the press of my gun.

Leaning in, I whisper in Bruno's ear, so Jaxcen can't hear. "Go along with this and I won't beat the shit outta you for ogling what's mine and considering her fucking offer."

Bruno nods quickly, probably wondering what the fuck I mean by go along with me, but I don't have time to explain it right fucking now. I'm too busy needing to make sure Jaxcen understands the consequences of her fucking actions.

"P-please don't." She starts to sob. "I didn't mean to get anyone in trouble."

"Yet you did. And now, because you were selfish, he's going to die." I shift my stance, like I'm preparing to shoot, and she drops to her bare knees on the hot gravel road.

"Please Mr Marx. I beg you not to harm him. I am at fault. Punish me, not him."

My cock is instantly hard, the mere sight of her down on her knees looking up at me with tears streaming down that angelic face has sent all the blood from my brain to my fucking cock.

"Please. I'll do anything you ask. Just please don't kill him."

With her hands held together in front of her like she is praying, I almost wish there was no one else here but the two of us so I can show her what I'm holding out for tonight.

"Anything?" I ask, and she nods, completely devoted to her response.

Pulling my gun away from Bruno's head, he sighs in relief, so I punch the fucker, watching him stumble back as a squeak falls from Jaxcen's lips.

"That's for all the fucking things that went through your head about my girl!" I snap, letting him see my rage as he scrambles backwards on the ground to put more distance between us, before I then turn my sights to Aaron and point. "You should have fucking stopped it. I'll deal with you later."

He doesn't argue, just nods, accepting his fate, so I turn back to Jaxcen, still kneeling on the ground, her eyes trained on my gun at my side.

Stepping closer, I angle it back and forth, letting her get a good look. "You like my gun, little mouse?" I hold it in front of her eyes, watching her fear filled gaze dart from the heavy metal in my grip to my hard stare. "Do you want to take it from me and shoot me?"

"Yes." Her confession is quick, and I smirk.

"Unfortunately for you, today's not that day." I chuckle, reaching forward to press the barrel to her damp cheek, and she flinches.

There's just something about the way she's looking up at me. The way those big blue eyes shoot hateful daggers at me, like she is imagining my death.

Slowly, I glide the metal over her searing cheek, to her mouth, which parts before I graze the tip over her plump lips.

"Open," I demand, and the trembles rippling through her body increase as she shakes her head just a fraction, her terror gripping her.

I consider pushing the issue, but I'm pretty fucking sure she's received the message loud and fucking clear, so with a smirk, I re-holster my gun.

"Stand up." I gesture with two fingers and she obeys quickly, still keeping her eyes locked with mine.

That's it little mouse, don't let the predator out of your sight.

"Let's put these back on," I say, reaching into my pocket and bringing out the mauve lacy panties I stole from her earlier.

The guards curse behind me, but I ignore them, my sight trained onto the flush engulfing Jaxcen's cheeks at the sight of her panties dangling off my finger.

Slowly, I lower to kneel on one knee, and tap the inside of her ankle. "Step in."

Now it's me who's looking up at her, on my knees, yet I don't feel any less powerful.

She knows who's boss here, so she obeys, lifting her sandaled foot so I can slip the fabric on each leg before sliding it up and under her dress, before I give her arse a little tap.

"Atta girl."

It's hard to know what she's thinking right now. Her gaze remains on me, yet there's no glare, and I'm not even sure there is fear right at this moment.

If only I could see what's going on inside her head.

I brush off the dirt and small pebbles that sunk into her knees from kneeling on the gravel road, before brushing off my pants and standing.

"I'll see you both in my office in the morning." I turn and glare at my guards, who nod quickly in agreement before I turn back to Jaxcen and sweep her up in my arms.

A squeal flies from her lips, sounding more like a squeak befitting my little mouse, and her dainty hand fists the front of my tee as I cradle her to my chest and start walking back up the fucking mountain.

"What are you doing?" she whispers, like she's not sure if she's allowed to speak.

"What does it look like?"

"I can walk," she protests, but I simply shrug.

"And I can carry you. Besides, it'll take you forever to walk back up this mountain, and I don't have time to wait for you."

Even though I'm focused on where I'm walking, I can feel the sear of her glare.

"Perhaps I'm trying to be a gentleman."

She scoffs. "There's nothing gentlemanly about you."

"Hmmm, was I not a gentleman when I made you soak through your panties last night?" I smirk as I glance down at her, and she quickly looks away. "Or how about this morning on my desk? A gentleman eats everything on his plate. I think I succeeded. Don't you?"

"You're so crude."

"Don't pretend you don't like it, Miss Summers. I was simply trying to kiss you under the mistletoe. You were the one that took my sweet kiss and started fucking it with abandon."

"I hate you," she whispers, and I grin at her flat tone, knowing she can't even deny the way she ground against my face this morning.

It was fucking hot.

As I walk, Jaxcen rests her head in the crook of my neck, and a part of me is waiting for her to attack. To bite, and dig her teeth into the column of my neck so she can make her escape. But by the time I make it back to the top, and head towards the Palace, I know she's not going to try anything.

I feel the gazes of the locals on me as I carry Jaxcen, but ignore them, carrying her into the bar where I order a couple of drinks on my way out to the beer garden.

Straightening in my arms, Jaxcen's interest piques, so I ease her feet to the paved ground as I lead her closer to Taylor and Alice, their angelic voices wrapping around us as they sing into the microphones while Natasha plays the guitar behind them.

"What's this?" Jaxcen asks absentmindedly.

"The beer garden. From November until mid-April, the locals turn up to sing, or watch and enjoy the atmosphere." I lead Jaxcen to one of the lounges with a small table and a shade umbrella overhead, urging her to sit, before I slip down next to her.

She doesn't even flinch at the way I put my arm over her shoulders and pull her to my side, her gaze taking in her surroundings, shock playing at her expression.

"What's wrong, little mouse? You didn't think people would have fun in my town?"

She glances at me then, her brows tugging in. "Well... no actually. I thought perhaps you might shoot locals in the head if they enjoy themselves."

I chuckle at her feisty tone.

"Only if they are having *too* much fun." I tease, and she rolls her eyes, returning her gaze to the women singing.

"Why are there so many women here?" She turns her frown back on me.

I've been waiting for this question. Either she's only just noticed how the female gender overpopulates the men in this town, or she's been too scared to ask until now.

"I keep having to kill my men for touching what's mine, so there are now less males." I lie, and her gaze hardens, a single brow hitching high. I grin. "What's wrong, little mouse? You don't like my laws?"

She scoffs. "They are barbaric. What you're doing is illegal."

I shrug. She's not wrong. Most of what I do *is* illegal.

"I don't know how you sleep at night," she snaps, and this time it's me who lifts a single brow.

"If I'm such a monster, how can you stand to sit so close to me?"

"Like I have a choice."

Her words grate on my fucking nerves, and I know she's not wrong, but it doesn't make it any easier to hear.

Better she think I'm a monster than know the truth and think she can deal with things on her own.

Ronnie arrives then with our drinks, placing them on the small table with a bowl of nuts and pretzels. "Finn wanted me to let you know that there's been a new development," Ronnie states, gesturing his head over his shoulder where I notice Finn hovering near the door.

I guess news about my run in with Bruno at the front gate has made its way around now and my best mate doesn't want to be next.

Sometimes he forgets he has the ability to sit me on my arse in the blink of an eye if he really wanted to. We may be a similar height and build, but his skills out throw mine by a long shot given his military special ops training.

I got my skills from a brutal father that liked to use me and my family as a punching bag, and from serving my Uncle Ewan, making sure the crims of Melbourne know which family rules over them.

"Tell him to come over," I advise Ronnie, and turn back to see Jaxcen watching Finn as he approaches.

She likes him. It's not just in the way her face softens, but by the way I feel her tense frame relax as Finn pulls up a seat and nods a hello to her.

"What's happened?" I snap, and Finn gives me his attention.

"The cameras we planted picked up a visitor." He glances at Jaxcen again, so I keep my words vague, realising he's talking about the cameras we planted in her apartment.

"Friend or foe?"

"Definitely foe. He planted his own cameras, but he didn't find any of ours."

I nod, considering my words, so as to not alert Jaxcen.

"Did we get an ID?"

Finn shakes his head. "Nope. He wore a ski mask. Wore all black. Came in armed and ready to kill, but when he found no one there, he installed the cameras."

This Mr V fucker isn't messing around, and he certainly wasn't bluffing. He said he'd come after Jaxcen, and he's now tried, planting cameras when he didn't find her there.

Fuck.

"So we still have nothing?" I snap, and Jaxcen stiffens next to me at my savage tone.

"Not nothing. We were able to follow his path from CCTV. We got a partial number plate, so Dom is working on that. He's also finished with the laptop."

I shoot a sideways glance at Jaxcen, and see her watching the women singing in my peripheral.

She really has no idea we are talking about her apartment and her laptop.

"Also, this is ready." He hands me a black pouch, and I take it, removing my arm from around Jaxcen to peer inside.

It's her phone.

Nodding, I glance back at Finn, handing it back. "Put it in the safe in my office. I'll look at it after."

He nods back, accepting the pouch and standing. "We have another meeting at seven to discuss the other intel." Finn reminds me of the fact they forced Father Peters to give up everything he knows about Jaxcen and her fiancé, Eddie.

All in the name of keeping her safe of course.

"Enjoy your afternoon." Finn nods to Jaxcen who smiles back, and fuck, I want her to smile at me like that.

Leaving us alone, I return to holding Jaxcen close, and eventually she relaxes again, leaning forward every now and then to have a sip of the lemonade I ordered her, or to scoop up a small handful of pretzels.

For a little while, I relax too. Coming out here and listening to the talent in this town is often a way I like to unwind. Usually Finn sits with me and we have a couple of beers, but it's nice spending it with my guest, even if she's probably quietly plotting my death as she watches on.

My peace doesn't last long though, as Allegra sweeps into the beer garden with her best friend Eden, and their sights immediately zero in on me, and my guest.

Fucking hell.

I shift uncomfortably as they come our way, Jaxcen not noticing them until they are upon us, blocking our view of the singers, their smiles huge.

"What do you two want?" I snap, and Allegra rolls her eyes before her expression morphs into puppy dog eyes and a fucking pout.

"We wanted to see who was taking all your attention." Allegra's fucking acting skills are sensational. Really they are. I should give her an award for best bullshitter.

"This is Jaxcen," I mutter, and the two girls beam as they turn their sights to my little mouse, who is now sitting ramrod straight.

"Hi Jaxcen," Allegra says as she pulls up a seat near Jaxcen, while Eden takes the one Finn was in before, closer to me.

"Uh. Hi," Jaxcen mumbles, her gaze dancing between the two teenagers.

Fucking teenagers. These two especially will be the death of me.

"I'm Allegra, and this is Eden."

Eden waves, and Jaxcen offers them a warm but somewhat awkward smile.

"We haven't had anyone new for a while." Allegra continues, and ignores the fucking death glare I shoot her way. "It's always exciting when we get a new lady in town."

Jaxcen's gaze darts angrily to me, and I frown, because what the fuck did I do?

"How often do you get new ladies in town?" Jaxcen snaps, and Eden answers.

"Usually at least one a month, but it's been a while." Eden turns her green eyes to me. "I know it's never good circumstances, but what are the chances you'll bring another teenager home with you soon?"

I roll my eyes, and Jaxcen gasps.

Fucking hell, these goddamn teenagers know how to boil my blood.

"Just remember what they have to go through to come here, Eden," I snap.

"Nevertheless, we're happy Jaxcen is here." Allegra smiles while Jaxcen shoots me the most venomous dagger she can muster.

What the fuck is up with her?

"So when am I gonna get some Devon time?" Allegra asks, pouting again. "It's hard sharing you with everyone."

"What are you talking about?" Eden scoffs. "You had Devon time last week. I haven't had any Devon time for at least three weeks."

I'm about to tell the teenage brats to stop fucking around, when Jaxcen stands abruptly.

"I can't believe the way you two are behaving. This isn't okay." She snarls at the girls before turning to me. "This isn't okay, Devon. You are a disgusting pig!" She all but fucking yells, gaining everyone's fucking attention before storming off, leaving Allegra and Eden snickering with laughter.

"You two fucking proud?"

"What?" Allegra asks like she's done nothing wrong. "It's just a bit of hazing. We do it to all the new girls."

"For the fucking record, Miss Summers is not a new girl. She is simply a fucking guest for Christmas."

Their faces fall. "Oh, we thought—"

"I know what you fucking thought, Allegra. And how the fuck did you get inside my locked office while I was gone?"

A sinister smirk pulls her lips wide. "You found the mistletoe. Have you had to kiss anyone yet?"

I could tell her the truth about who and what I kissed under the mistletoe, that'd really fuck with her, but I'm not that fucking crude, despite what Jaxcen thinks.

Allegra is a child and doesn't need to be fucking exposed to that shit. Especially not after what she's been through.

"Uh, Dev?" Ronnie comes rushing out. "You might want to come in here."

Shooting the girls one last glare, I stand and head inside, to find Jaxcen standing behind the bar, holding a knife out in front of her.

"What the fuck is this?" I snap, watching as she stabs it out in front of her, ready to strike anyone that comes near.

"She just walked behind the bar and grabbed the knife I use to slice the limes." Ronnie explains, "Then she said she'd stab me if I didn't get her a phone."

My brow hitches and I fight to hide my smirk.

She's fucking resourceful, I'll give her that.

"Everyone out!" I call, and the old fellas that rock up before lunch every day slide off their stools, unfazed by our knife wielding guest, and go out into the beer garden, while the old couple, the Burlingtons, remain in place at the end of the bar, not caring if they live or die.

Ronnie moves to their sides and tries to urge them to leave, but they just look at him like he's grown two heads, and return their gazes to their glasses of beer.

"Give me a phone, Devon!" Jaxcen snaps, her eyes wild as they dart around the space.

"Ronnie. You leave too," I sigh.

"But..." he gestures over his shoulder at the old couple, and I just shrug.

"It's their prerogative. Man the beer garden door and make sure no one comes in."

Nodding, Ronnie dashes out quickly, leaving me alone in the bar with a crazy-eyed Miss Summers and an old couple that wished they didn't exist.

"Put the knife down before you hurt yourself," I scold and she scoffs.

"Come over here and let's see who will get hurt."

Sighing, I drop my head back and stare at the fucking ceiling.

I shouldn't have brought her here. I should have palmed her off to my cousins and let them deal with her.

Even as I think it, I know there's no way I would have allowed that. From the moment she walked into the church, she drew my fucking attention. Now, she's stuck with me.

"What's really happening here?" I ask, bringing my gaze back down to see her eyeing the old couple. "Why were we enjoying music one moment, and the next, you're storming off and calling me a pig?"

"You are a pig. I can't believe what you're doing here. It's vile, Devon. They are teenage girls."

My brows shoot up and for some fucking reason, her words have sparked the Burlingtons to life.

"They were teenage girls," Edith hisses. "So innocent and sweet, and those monsters took that away."

Fuck. This isn't good.

Jaxcen's mouth drops open, her gaze darting from the old couple to me.

"See, they agree."

"You don't know what they are talking about, little mouse. Now put down the knife and come here."

"They needed a knife," Gordon Burlington growls. "They could have gutted them all. Cut their gizzards from their bellies."

Jaxcen's expression morphs into confusion, so I approach Gordon, who's slowly rising from his bar stool.

"Hey, Gordon. We got them. Remember?" I gesture for him to sit again, and he does, while his wife Edith nods.

"I remember." Her normally almost gone gaze meets mine, and for the first time in a long time, I see the flame still burning. "But it wasn't enough."

I don't get emotional often, but this is a hard one and I have to stare at the fucking floor for a moment to let the wave of emotions pass.

"No, Edith. It wasn't enough." I glance back up so she can see the sincerity in my eyes. "I'm sorry."

A tear pops from her eye then, and a dainty hand reaches into my peripheral, as Jaxcen hands Edith a napkin.

As Edith dabs at her wet cheeks, and her husband begins to break down, Jaxcen's tear filled gaze locks with mine.

"What are you doing to these people?"

It's a whisper, but I hear it, and I can't blame her for jumping to the wrong conclusion. I did kidnap her after all. Hell, she probably thinks I kidnapped everyone that lives here.

It's then that I know my epiphany is true.

Fuck.

That's exactly what she thinks.

"Give me the knife, please," I ask politely, and she screws her nose up at me.

"Go to hell."

Frustrated, tired, and fucking horny from this temptress always testing me, I pinch the bridge of my nose, willing myself to have more patience.

When I glance up, I know I can spend all fucking day wishing for patience, but it'll never happen.

"You keep forgetting, little mouse. This is hell, and you're in it with me."

My words make her gasp in disbelief, distracting her, so she doesn't see me coming until I'm halfway over the bar top, with my sights set on her.

She tries to turn. To flee.

She's not quick enough, and the moment I fist my hand in her hair, she screams.

Chapter Thirteen

Jaxcen

Swinging my hand out, I try to stab Devon's leg, but all it does is slice over the top of his jeans, his fist in my hair tight and unyielding.

"Stop!" he snaps against my ear, his strong hand finding my wrist before I can take another backwards swipe at him, his grip tightening as he twists my wrist in an unnatural way. "Drop the fucking knife."

I cry out as pain shoots through my wrist, the knife clattering to the sticky tiles beneath my feet before Devon's arms wrap around me from behind, pressing me against the back counter.

"Do you think I kidnapped all of the women that are here, little mouse?" he rasps against my cheek, and I catch his gaze in the mirror lining the back of the bar with dozens of bottles perched on glass shelves.

His eyes are so dark. So menacing that it sends a chill up my spine, and heat to pool between my legs.

Why, oh why does my body respond like this to him? He's a monster. A predator. Am I really that starved for a man's touch that I melt even if it comes from the most vicious beast?

"Why else would they be here with you?" I grit between clenched teeth, curling my lips so he sees my disdain.

"Maybe they chose to be here. Maybe they feel safe here with me. Ever think of that?"

I scoff. "More like they are too scared to tell you how they really feel."

He smirks. "Unlike you, Miss Summers. You're getting good at telling me what you really think. It's a shame your body doesn't hold the hate for me that your mind does."

He cups my breast, and I try to squirm free, but he has me trapped against the bench, his strength too much for me to compete with.

"Fuck, little mouse. Do you feel that?" His hot breath fans over my cheek as his lips graze the blazing skin. "Your nipple is straining under your dress." As if to show me, he gives the pebbled traitor a pinch.

"Stop." I breathe, and he chuckles quietly.

"You say stop, but your body says please don't stop."

Dammit. Why am I like this?

"Do you know how easy it would be for me to slip your dress up, Jaxcen? How easy it would be for me to slide my cock into your tight pussy?"

"Stop being crude," I pant, hating the way my voice gives me away.

"Why would I stop when you enjoy it so much?" His lips press to my cheek then, the kiss gentle yet his gaze still hard in the mirror. "You're such a dirty girl, Jaxcen. So dirty and filthy and it's fucking beautiful."

Tears pool in my eyes.

Not from fear, or because I'm hurt. But because of how much I've yearned for someone to see me. The real me. And not be disgusted.

Why did it have to be this monster?

Because monsters know each other, Jaxcen. Monsters belong together.

"I'm not a monster," I whisper, shaking my head.

"I never said you were."

His voice startles me, and I realise I'd sunken into my torment so far that I must have spoken the words aloud.

We stare at each other for a long beat in the mirror, and I know the moment he feels me relax, because he does too.

"I want to make you feel so fucking good that you forget your own name, little mouse. But I can't do that here." He gestures his head to the old couple at the end of the bar, and the crazy haze that had swept over me lifts as my embarrassment sinks in.

Oh my... I threatened people with a knife. I tried to stab Devon.

"Shit. I'm sorry," I whisper, and he smirks.

"Sorry for trying to stab me or for wanting me to fuck you right here in the bar with an audience?"

My cheeks heat at the idea of people watching. Of the roles being reversed and instead of watching, I'd be the one being watched.

I need my head checked.

"Let's take this upstairs."

Devon suggests, stepping away from me, and hell, why do I miss his nearness?

"No," I protest quietly, eyeing the couple at the end of the bar that are staring into their drinks still. What is with them?

"No?"

I glance up to see Devon frowning at me, then to the knife in his hand. The one that I tried to stab him with.

My gaze darts to his thigh to see the denim sliced a little, but there's not much damage, and since there's no blood, I assume I didn't knick his skin.

Dammit.

"I'm not going upstairs to have sex with you," I mutter, trying to remember what I was even talking about.

"We'll see." He smirks, gripping my arm and leading me out from behind the bar, placing the knife on the counter before he calls out. "Ronnie! All clear!"

The door to outside opens, and I notice there's no music playing anymore as Ronnie steps back in, his eyes scanning the space.

Shit. They must think I'm batshit crazy. And perhaps I am. Perhaps I'm unhinged again.

Again.

What will my parents say?

Words are spoken, but I hardly hear them before Devon is leading me from the room and back up the stairs. I think I can still hear him talking, probably to me, but everything is muffled, as my brain goes back to ten year old me at Sunday School. Back when I tried to help, but it only made things worse. Back when even the scariest of grown ups looked at me like I was the monster, and not them.

Them.

"Jaxcen?"

The deep rumble of Devon's voice shakes me out of my memory, and I blink a few times to find myself already up in his suite, sitting on his sofa as he cups my cheeks, his expression pinched with concern.

"Where'd you go?"

"I..." I snap my mouth closed because I can't tell him. I can never tell anyone if I want them to look at me the same.

My parents know of course. As does my sister.

And Eddie.

He knows everything.

No one else can know.

"What's going on inside that head of yours?" Devon asks, and I wonder if he's not the perfect person to tell all my darkest secrets too.

Monsters would understand monsters, wouldn't they?

"So many fucked up things," I whisper, and his lips kick up.

"I'd love to hear them."

Sighing, I try to shake my head, but his hands are still framing my face, so it doesn't budge until he finally releases me, sitting back with his own sigh.

"I have so many questions," I say instead.

"I'm sure you do." He smirks.

"What are the chances you'll answer them?"

"Slim, but you knew that already."

Huffing, I roll my eyes. "I just need something. I don't understand what's happening here. Why you brought me here? What's going to happen to me, and I just wish you'd stop talking in riddles and give me the truth."

For once, the playful guy that usually lurks on the surface slips away, and in its place is a serious version. Not the deadly version I've met a few times already, but just serious. No bullshitting.

"You can ask me five."

My brows shoot high at his declaration, and my spine straightens with hope.

Finally, I can get some answers.

"I'll answer one."

My shoulders slump.

Damn him.

I swear he likes messing with my emotions. He just takes them and dangles them over a pit of vipers, every damn time.

"Why are you like this?" I mutter and he shrugs.

"Because I am. Take it or leave it, little mouse."

"Fine," I huff, taking a moment to narrow down the hundreds of questions I have to just five.

"Take your time." He rises off the coffee table he was perched on, to sit next to me on the sofa, hooking one foot up to rest on his knee as he relaxes back into the cushion.

He reminds me of a king, sitting lazily on his throne.

I guess he is king of this Palace.

"So I ask five questions and you'll choose one of them to answer truthfully?"

"Yes, little mouse. Correct."

"Okay then. Why is the main population women?" I ask as my first question, watching his expression which doesn't change, so I ask my next. "Why don't you let people practise religion publicly?"

His brows shoot up at that question, and I feel victorious for some strange reason. He didn't know I knew that.

"Are all the women your wives?"

This time, his lips spread wide with that stupid shit-eating grin again.

Ugh. I want to slap him.

"Is Marilda's little boy your son?"

Again his brows shoot high. "You've been busy today haven't you, little mouse. Snooping around and asking questions."

I shrug, like it's no big deal and ask my next question.

"Do women throw themselves over the cliff because they can't stand to be your sex slave?"

This question makes him angry, his brows tugging in as he glares and stands from the sofa and starts pacing.

"All your questions are about my town. Don't you want to know why you're here?"

"Well, der." I scoff, immaturely, rolling my eyes until his hard gaze snaps to mine and I stiffen. "I've asked that before and you refuse to answer so I figured it would be a waste of a question."

"You're right. It would have been."

Ugh. He's unbearable. He starts pacing again, obviously trying to figure out which question to answer, before he responds.

"Religion has a history of creating unnecessary tension. This is a small community, and we don't need different religious beliefs dividing the town, or turning this place into a cultish religious faction."

Of course he chose the religious question to answer. As if he'd give me the truth about the women.

Dammit. I should have thought of something else to ask. Like why does he have teenagers as his slaves as well.

"I'd like to retract that question and ask another."

His feet halt as he stops pacing, his gaze shooting to me as he chuckles. "Not a fucking chance in hell."

I roll my eyes.

As if he'd be reasonable.

"Fine," I huff. "Why do you oppose the religious thing so much if you yourself are religious?"

"I prefer to keep my beliefs and worship to myself. There's no need to rub it in others' faces. And I sure as shit don't want them rubbing their beliefs in my face either." He starts pacing again. "There are a few other reasons why public practise of religion isn't a good idea, but I've answered the main one."

"Funny how you chose that question and not the ones surrounding how sick you are."

I expect his infuriating chuckle, but instead, a frown contorts his face.

Guilt pangs in my gut, and I wish it away, needing to remind the good samaritan in me that this man is a monster, but it doesn't work.

My words have upset him.

"Whatever it is that you think is going on here," he turns his harsh glare in my direction, and I sink back in the cushions, wishing I could hide, "you are fucking wrong. I know I haven't given you any reason to trust me, other than keeping my word and not killing you, but I'm not the monster you think I am."

Standing taller, as if that is even possible, he rolls his shoulders back and glares. "But I can be that monster if that'll help you paint the picture you have in your head. I can be your worst fucking nightmare if you want to be right so fucking badly."

I flinch, feeling like ten year old me being scolded for calling the monster out and having it turned on me.

"I don't want you to be that monster," I whisper, and he lurches forward, gripping my jaw and angling my head up roughly so he can stare into my eyes.

"Why not?" he asks, and all I do is whimper. "I'll tell you why you don't want me to be that monster, little mouse. It's because you secretly like it. You fucking love how I make you feel. You fucking love that no matter how crazy you get, wielding a fucking knife and trying to stab me, won't scare me away." He leans closer, hovering his lips over mine. "You fucking love how right I make your depravities feel."

A tear I didn't know had formed pops from one eye as I try to swallow the lump in my throat.

"As soon as you start being honest with me, I'll be honest with you and answer your questions." He stands tall and shoves my face away harshly before striding across the room. "Until then, keep pretending you hate me all you like. I'll be back in a few hours to get you for confession."

Swinging the door wide, I leap up about to protest as he steps out into the hall and stares back at me. "I'll have Mabel bring a tray up for dinner."

Frowning at his words, he pulls the door closed, and then I hear it. The snip of the lock as he locks me in.

Vida Loca
Trust

CHAPTER FOURTEEN

Devon

With Jaxcen's phone on my desk, I open it knowing Dom has already disabled the pin code, and I start getting to know my guest better by opening her messages first.

There's one from *Darmal (work)* asking why her fiancé keeps calling their boss, looking for her.

There's another from *Andrea (work- boss)*, asking why she hasn't shown up at work, and then there's a whole bunch more from Eddie.

Thirty three to be exact.

His messages pretty much repeat the same questions.

Where are you?

Why won't you answer my call?

But then there are some that just stick out, making me murderous.

Eddie

I was expecting your call this morning. I don't appreciate being kept waiting.

Eddie

I expect you have a good reason to be ignoring my calls, Jaxcen. Do we need to go over your expected duties as my wife again?

Fucking hell, this arsehole is a piece of work.

Sure, I've been a prick to Jaxcen, but I'm just messing with her to keep her off the scent that I'm actually trying to help. This motherfucker is a legit cockhead.

Opening the call app, I see nineteen missed calls from a few different numbers, and eight voicemails.

Well, now I need to hear this fucker's voice.

Message Received from: Eddie
"Good morning, Jaxcen. I'm a little surprised that I'm having to make this call. It's quite an inconvenience, as I'm sure you already know, so I don't know why you're behaving like this. The rules haven't changed. You call me every morning at nine, yet it's just ticked over to eleven. I'm looking forward to hearing what has you so busy that you can't call your fiancé."

Message Received from: Eddie
"Jaxcen, I'm not sure why you are doing this. Have you been watching those disgusting videos online again? You know how corrupting they are, Jaxcen. I hope you haven't relapsed. I don't think Father Peters will be happy to hear that. In fact, perhaps we should discuss your behaviour with your father. I don't want to resort to that, but I will if you don't call me back soon."

Message Received from: Eddie

"Do you not understand the concept of what soon is Jaxcen? I'm so disgusted with how you are treating me. This isn't the behaviour of a dutiful wife. This is immature childish behaviour that requires strict punishment. I'm coming over."

Message Received from: Eddie

"Stop ignoring me, Jaxcen. I know you can hear the buzzer, and since you aren't at work you must be there. That's it. I'm calling your father."

Message Received from: Dad

"Jaxcen, it's your father. Edward called, and I must say, I am shocked with your behaviour. I raised you to be better than this. If you don't call him or me in the next thirty minutes, I will have to involve Dr Xavier."

Message Received from: Mum

"Jaxcen darling, it's your mother. Your father told me what's happening. Please stop misbehaving. This isn't acceptable. You're about to be married, sweetheart. You can't treat your future husband like this. And those explicit websites... Oh Jaxcen. Why would you look at them? Edward sent your father the links. Why would you watch *such depraved behaviour? Are you taking drugs? That has to be it. Oh dear. We'll have to call Dr Xavier."*

Message Received from: Presley
"Jax, what the fuck? The olds are freaking the fuck out and are on the phone to that psycho doctor they sent you to when you were little. You know I don't care what you do, hell, I fucking love porn, but don't let them get their clutches into you again. I can't bear to see them kill your spark. Not again. Not ever.
"I will try to stall them on my end, but pack a bag and go somewhere. Anywhere they can't find you. Don't use your bank card. If they involve the cops they can track that.
"Shit, Jax. I love you, sis. Please stay safe."

Message Received from: Unknown Number
"Hello, Jaxcen, this is Doctor Alfred Xavier. I treated you at the Holly River Estate when you were younger. Do you remember?
"I was shocked to receive a call from your father. He is extremely distressed. I know I don't have to remind you how hard it will be to return to the facility, especially as an adult. Our adult program is much more intense, but perhaps something you will benefit from. We have merged with a church, and together we do God's work to help our patients. I think this will be of great benefit to you before your wedding. Please call me back. Otherwise, I'll likely show up tomorrow with a community treatment order."

What the actual fuck.

Not only is Eddie a cockhead, but her parents are fucking freaks. They are treating her like a leper. Like she's the one doing something wrong, when her fiancé doesn't even know what's going on.

She's been kidnapped, you fuckhead! Instead of blaming her, you should be looking for her. You should be concerned for her safety, not making it all about you.

What the fuck does he think she's doing? Sitting in her apartment masturbating all day.

Fuck, she probably should if she's going to marry that sap.

I'm fucking furious, not just at what I'm discovering but that Jaxcen actually thinks I'm the type of monster that would force women to marry me and be my sex slaves.

And yeah, I fucking know I haven't given her a better reason to think of me as anything but the monster she's imagining, but fuck, what happened to innocent until proven guilty?

Huh. That thought has me staring at all the voicemails on her phone again.

There's a story here. One that involves Jaxcen and her family not trusting her. Even now, they are judging a situation they don't have any facts on. Jumping to conclusions that she must be misbehaving. Why wouldn't their first thought be for her safety? That perhaps something bad has happened to her?

Now I don't want her to leave here, ever.

"What's the frown for?" Finn asks, stepping into my office and closing the door.

"Where do I start?" I mutter, reclining back in my oversized office chair.

"How about what has you so twisted up about your guest?" Finn smirks, and I shake my head, grinning back because he knows me so fucking well.

"Drink?" I ask, sitting forward and opening the bottom drawer in my desk to bring out my bottle of Glenfiddich Grand whiskey and two glasses.

"Sure." Finn takes a seat in the chair on the other side of my desk, accepting the glass of amber liquid before I pour myself one too. "So, spill, man. What the fuck is going on?"

"It's Christmas. I wanted a treat." I lie and Finn rolls his eyes as he takes a sip.

"Try again. If she was a treat, you would have had her every fucking which way in your city apartment by now, not bailed up here where you actually live. You never bring your fucks here."

Fuck it. I can never lie to my best mate.

"I can't put my finger on it." I admit, feeling more fucking out of sorts than ever before. "I just needed to bring her here and keep her with me. I can't explain it."

"How many times have you fucked her?" Finn asks, and I'd love nothing more than to dodge that question, but he must see my expression because his brows shoot up. "How many times, man?"

"None."

For a moment, I'm not sure he's even breathing. His eyes are open, his gaze on me, but he doesn't blink. Doesn't move.

"Say again." He finally responds.

"Don't make a big deal about it."

"Like fuck." Finn beams, putting his glass down on my desk. "Normally you would have banged a chick at least ten times by now. You mean to tell me you haven't got your dick wet once, and I shouldn't make a big deal about it?"

"That's exactly what I'm saying."

"You fucking like her. Like, really like her. Don't you?"

"That's none of your business!" I snap, and Finn throws his head back laughing.

"So when are you going to tell her?" He grins.

"Tell her what?"

"That you want to keep her." The fucker wags his brows.

"I have bigger fucking issues right now." I grumble into my glass before I take a sip.

"Yeah like the fact she thinks you kidnapped her." Again he chuckles like this is a big fucking joke. And I suppose to him, it is.

Why do best mates enjoy their friends' discomfort so much?

"No, my issues are the fact her fiancé is a controlling narcissist. Hell her parents aren't far off either. Did you read the messages?" I gesture to the phone sitting on my desk, and Finn nods.

"Yep. That prick sounds like he could use a good asswhooping."

"Ain't that the truth," I mutter. "Did you listen to the voicemails, too?"

"Yep."

"What do you think?"

"I think she's safer here with us than her family that's for fucking sure."

"Yeah. I agree. She's so religious but I think it's been forced on her. She has desires her fiancé is making her feel bad for needing. She thinks he's a virgin and she's worried about him finding out she isn't on their wedding night, yet she's so sexually green, I don't know if I believe she isn't a virgin."

Finn frowns at my words. "You think she was assaulted?"

It had crossed my mind, which made me want to kill every fucker in sight just for the hell of it. She was adamant that she's had sex before, yet she was so vague.

"Maybe. She doesn't seem like one to cheat, and she claims to have been with that fucker since they were fourteen, so either she lost her virginity before that, or she did afterwards without him knowing."

"I mean, she's kinda cheating on him now, with you."

I scoff. "Hardly. I'm not giving her much of a choice."

"Given what I heard coming from this office earlier, she didn't sound distressed so I have to assume you are giving her a choice. If she asked you to stop, like if she truly wanted you to, you would. So even though she's probably trying to fight the way she feels, given her outburst with the knife, she still wants you."

"Well, yeah. Her body does. And there's a point of no return that she can't seem to fight."

Finn's lips kick up. "A bit of dubious consent is always fun."

It is, but there's a fucking fine line, and I know it's a fucking blurry one, so I hope I haven't overstepped.

Fuck, have I?

"She'd fit right in here." Finn continues, "It might not be such a bad thing to tell her what's really going on."

"With Mr V or what's going on in this town?" I ask, swirling the amber fluid in my glass before downing the rest.

"Both. All of it. You're holding her here against her will anyway. If you tell her and she still wants to leave, then the only infraction will be forcing her to stay. How she deals with everything else is on her."

"I can't use the threat of killing her then." I point out.

"True, but at least she wouldn't be so terrified of the monster she keeps claiming you to be. It might even give her a chance to get to know you. What would be so wrong with that?"

"Everything."

He throws his head back laughing, his palm slapping against the table. "God fucking forbid you let down that ten foot fucking wall and opened up to a chick for once. How fucking absurd that someone might actually like you."

Fucker.

I hate it when he's right.

"Shut the fuck up. Are Dom and the team ready?"

"Yep. Let's go."

Standing from our chairs, I slip Jaxcen's phone back into the safe, locking it before we leave and head up the path towards the chapel.

I don't know why I haven't knocked it down. For some reason I haven't been able to bring myself to do it. Even now as I unlock it and my men follow me in, I find myself admiring the old structure instead of loathing it.

My gaze shoots straight to the old school confessional at the far end, and not for the first time do I wonder how many secrets have been divulged in its confinements.

It's not like the one built into the wall of St Catherine's in the city. This one resembles more of a change room in a dress shop, with dark velvet maroon drapes covering each entrance, and a thin wall in between.

I guess change rooms don't have a small screen between them to speak through like this does.

My men fill the pews as I stand before them like I'm the fucking preacher, and I suppose in a way I am. I'm the leader in this town, and they look to me for direction. I just preach a little differently than most.

"Okay, as you know, my visit in the city didn't quite go as planned, and some fucker sent unskilled men to kill me." I start, my eyes travelling over my men, all their eyes trained on me. "The man who wants me dead calls himself Mr V, and because I saved Miss Summers, he's decided to make her his new target, since apparently I killed someone dear to him."

Dragging my gaze from my men, I start pacing slowly, my hands behind my back as I frown in thought. "He blackmailed those two men to take me out, using their families' safety to force their hands." I glance back up at my team. "Do we have an update on their families?"

"Yes." Miles clears his throat as he stands warily. "I sent Lenny's team to check on the families."

The way his eyes drop to the floor as he speaks tells me everything I need to know, but we all need to hear the words. We all need the seriousness of this situation to sink in.

"They were all dead. Looks like they had been for a while."

Gritting my teeth, I take a deep inhale to remain fucking calm before I speak. "Then Mr V had no intention of letting my two attackers live anyway."

This knowledge changes everything. It means he's unlikely to negotiate. It means that his threat against Jaxcen is real and if he had found her when he went to her apartment, he would have killed her.

"How many were killed?" I snap, and Miles rushes out.

"Two women and five children in total."

My men shift on the pews as their anger becomes unhidable.

"We need to slaughter this fucker." Finn growls as Miles slumps back down on the pew next to him, and my other men grunt in agreement.

"It's clear the danger to Miss Summers is real. We have her phone and laptop, but since we have no idea who Mr V is, I'm worried he'll dig up information on Jaxcen's family." I pinch the bridge of my nose, knowing I have to tell her. I can't keep it from her anymore.

"Want me to liaise with Riggs? Maybe his team can help get covert protection on her family." Lenny suggests and I nod. "Yeah, do that. I'll deal with my cousins."

They'll want to know everything, and I guess I should stop being a prick and tell them since an attack on me is basically an attack on the whole Marx dynasty.

"Do we have anything on Mr V?" I ask, and Dom stands, nodding.

"The partial number plate is still processing, but we were able to hack into CCTV to retrace the path the Honda took, but we lost it when it travelled west, out of the city."

"Towards Ballarat?" I ask and Dom nods.

"That general direction."

"Could this be Bikie related?" Finn asks, and I frown, considering that.

"Not that I'm aware of, but just in case, reach out to Ringo and see if the Southern Sadists know anything."

Finn nods. "Will do."

"Do we have anything else on this fucker?" I snap, and when no one responds, I dismiss them.

"Let's double perimeter security until this is over." I order and turn my sights to Dom, "You and Finn stay behind and talk to me about Miss Summers."

My men leave, not fucking about as Dom opens up a laptop and passes it to me.

"There's nothing amiss with Miss Summers, other than the way her family and fiancé treat her. This seems to be her personal laptop, so there's no real work on here. I did find some stories she'd written and a few other files saved in a setup folder not normally found in the system folder."

My brows hitch as I look at the screen to understand what Dom is referring to.

"The system folder is generally left alone by users, as it contains all the background files, so by her saving things there, she didn't want them to be found by someone casually looking through her personal files," Dom explains, and I click on the folder to see a few word documents, some PDFs and half a dozen pictures.

Fuck. As each picture transforms into its personalised thumbnail, I can clearly see these pictures are of my little mouse, wearing next to nothing, in provocative positions.

"Did you look at these?" I snap, my glare slamming into Don's wide eyes.

"No, sir. You know I'd never." He shakes his head frantically. "I opened the word docs just to see what they were, and the PDFs too, but I kept my eyes off the pictures when the first thumbnail appeared and I could see they were personal pictures."

"What are the PDFs?" I hiss through clenched teeth, knowing my anger is irrational, yet the idea of his staring at Jaxcen's beautiful naked body without her or my permission has me rather fucking murderous.

"Membership contracts for Cloud 9. Two years worth."

Fuck, she's been going longer than I realised. There's a high fucking chance I've crossed paths with her before. Hell, she's probably watched me fuck.

My lips kick up at the thought, and I will my cock to not inflate any further than it has.

Sporting a semi during a meeting with my men isn't fucking ideal.

"Any idea how we can get her family off her back?" I ask, snapping the laptop shut.

"I mean, you could just tell her what's going on and let her call them. Let her deal with a story to get them to back off." Finn suggests and I narrow my eyes at him.

"She's just as likely to tell them she's been kidnapped and the next fucking thing we know the cops are on our doorstep."

"Would Father Peters help cover for us?" Dom asks, and I look to Finn for his reaction, but as he frowns, I realise that perhaps his little chat with Father Peters didn't go too well.

"I'm gonna say no." Finn shrugs. "He wasn't happy about the threat I made."

Fuck.

It's never good when we have to assert our authority to the ones who have been looking out for us for so long.

"What happened?" I snap.

"He refused to tell us anything about Jaxcen and her fiancé, so I had to insist." Finn shrugs, like it's no big deal, but we all know it is.

Father Peters is one of our biggest allies.

"Please tell me it worked? I don't want to make threats against him for nothing."

"It worked, but he's not happy." Finn shrugs.

"What did he say?" I gesture to the pews and Dom and Finn sit again.

"After quite a bit of insisting, he divulged that Miss Summers and her fiancé aren't original members of St Catherine's. They both came to the city to study and have remained, working full time jobs. Their families are up near the state border, which is where they were both raised. They were members of the local Catholic church until a few years ago, when a new church opened in their area and Eddie's family converted."

My eyes snap to Finn, and his lips thin as he nods knowingly. "Father Peters doesn't know the name of the church since Eddie refused to tell him, simply saying once they are married, Jaxcen will convert to his church and they will move to be closer to their holy community."

"Fuck." I hiss and Finn nods.

"Yeah fuck. You think it's one of those cult churches that keeps popping up?"

"Sounds like it." I grit my teeth, glancing at Dom. "Work with Lenny's connections to get intel on this Eddie fucker. I want to know everything about him. What he eats. Where he eats. Who he fucking shits with if needed. Every fucking thing."

"On it." Dom stands and hurries out, leaving me with my best mate.

"Do me a favour?" I ask, and Finn chuckles.

"Sounds more like an order than a favour."

I roll my eyes, "Fine, it's a fucking order." I pinch the bridge of my nose, willing patience to engulf me. "Go to my suite, collect my guest and bring her here."

"Really? You're gonna fuck her in a church?"

"No, I'm going to issue her penance in church." I smirk.

"So, in other words, you're going to fuck her."

"Just get her and stop pissing me off." I snap, and Finn chuckles as he walks out.

"Like it's hard to piss you off."

I want to tell him the only thing that's hard is my cock, but since it's not hard for him, I keep that to myself and glance over my shoulder at the old confessional.

My little mouse has been a bad girl, and she needs to repent.

Chapter Fifteen

Jaxcen

The rap of knuckles on the door tells me it's not Devon, but it sounds too hard to be Mabel, who was here not too long ago with a tray of food I haven't touched.

I don't bother going to the door. I can't open it. Devon locked me in, and Mabel did the same after delivering me my dinner.

When a key in the lock sounds, I stiffen, sitting up taller on the sofa, trying to ready myself for whatever is about to be thrown at me now, but when the kind eyes of the hulking man, Finn, appear, I relax.

"Expecting someone else?" he smirks.

"Only a monster." I shrug and he chuckles.

"Speaking of, he's requested your presence."

My presence, like he's a damn king and I'm his not so humble servant.

"You can tell his highness, that if he wants to see me, he knows where I am, since he locked me in here."

Finn's smile falls, and a hard expression takes its place.

"I'll rephrase that, since you must have misunderstood." He steps in, his glare hella scary, and for the first time, this man doesn't seem so friendly. "Let's go, Miss Summers."

Huffing, I stand, straightening my dress and feeling somewhat better than I did earlier when Devon made me walk around his town pantiless.

"Where are we going?" I ask, not really expecting a response, but Finn surprises me.

"To church."

My brows shoot up, and I walk faster, because I'm dying to see what the old chapel looks like on the inside.

Finn closes and locks the door behind me, and leads me downstairs and out into the balmy night.

A smile instantly sweeps over my face as the shops come into view, their twinkling Christmas lights starting to engulf the night as the sun sets over Timber Valley.

"Wow, I didn't notice the lights last night," I mutter absentmindedly as we walk up the path.

"All Christmas cheer gets turned off at the stroke of midnight." Finn explains, and I nod, paying him no attention as I glance into the hair salon to see a nativity scene of Mary and Joseph and baby Jesus in the manger.

Huh. I hadn't thought about it until now, but Christmas is a religious celebration. A Christian holiday that gets passed between generations. Easter too. Maybe I should point that out to the monster king, that his town is already practising religion.

A smug smirk tugs at my lips at the thought of knocking him off his high horse.

"He's inside," Finn mutters, dragging me out of my wicked thoughts as he stops at the foot of the path that leads to the chapel doors. "Have a lovely evening, Miss Summers."

With a bow of his head, Finn just stands tall and waits for me to move, so I nod, a little confused about what is happening, and make my way up the path.

Pushing open the door, I glance over my shoulder to find Finn still watching, as if he's making sure I enter and don't try to run.

Where would I run to? Devon always catches me.

Sighing, I turn my back on him and slip inside, noting the row of candles lining each side of the narrow aisle leading all the way up to the confessional where a tall, dark, and unfortunately for my libido, handsome man stands waiting patiently with his hands clasped in front of him.

An eerie chill runs up my spine, like my body instantly recognises the danger I'm in.

That's the devil over there, and he shifts, beckoning me with two fingers.

As if my feet have a mind of their own, I start walking towards him, through the centre of the burning wicks that line my path to hell.

If this is hell, then I'm meant to be here because never have I felt more comfortable in a church than in this moment.

You're sick, Jaxcen. Only God can help you.

My inner voice is yelling at me, but it's nowhere near as loud as the whisper of temptation pulling me closer and closer to the man that has the power to end me with a pull of a trigger.

Devon doesn't speak as I stand before him, but his eyes do. They travel to my lips, before running down the column of my neck and over my clavicle. As if my breasts know, they pebble and I suck in a breath which pushes them towards him.

"Do you know why you're here?"

His voice is so deep and gravelly as he speaks, his eyes trained on the swell of my breasts before finally coming back to lock with mine.

"No," I whisper, too scared to try and speak at my normal volume because then he'll hear it in my tone.

My want.

My need.

My desire.

"The last time you were in a church, you went to confess your sins to God. Tonight, you are in my house. The devil's house. And here, we don't confess our sins." He reaches out, hooking a finger under my jaw and lifting it as he leans in closer. "Here, we celebrate our sins."

My lips part in a silent gasp as he presses his to mine. It's a soft, gentle kiss which is such a contradiction to the monster standing before me, but I don't have time to think too much about it before he's pulling back and gesturing to the confessional behind him.

"Step inside, little mouse, and divulge all of your sins."

My heart flips in my chest, and for a moment, I even think it stops.

What is this?

Am I... excited?

I've never been excited to step inside a confessional before. Only anxious to get it over with, but now, my heart races, and anticipation digs its claws in, urging me forward.

Don't do it, Jaxcen. This is not the path to the Lord's forgiveness.

I still at the whisper inside my head, begging it to be louder than the scream of my temptation to take the plunge and risk it all for the rush of the unknown.

"You can do it, little mouse." His hot breath fans across my cheek as the graze of his finger hooks my hair behind my ear. "Step inside. Divulge your deepest darkest desires and relish in the punishment the devil affords you."

His words, so dark. So sinister, are the final shove I need to slip in past the velvet curtain and drop to my knees on the tuffet as heat flicks over my skin like tiny little sparks.

My chest rises and falls with the race of my heart, my breaths too loud, yet I can't control them. I can't stop them, and they only get more audible when the cover on the screen before me slides open to reveal the shadow of a man sitting on the other side, his crotch level with my eyes, his hands clasped in front, hiding the place I most desire seeing. Touching. Tasting.

A whimper escapes me at the thought, heat pooling between my legs as this utterly sinful situation makes me feel alive.

So alive.

Just like when I'm at Cloud 9.

Just like last night when Devon kissed me.

Or in his bathroom when he touched me until I came apart.

Or today, on his desk, with his head between my legs.

"I'm waiting," he rasps, it's gravel sending a chill down my spine.

"Bless me Father for I have sinned."

"Uh, uh, uh," he tuts. "You are not in the Lord's house now, little mouse, remember? You are in the devil's house. Repeat after me." He shifts, and I watch as those big strong hands unclasp and shift to rest on the tops of his thighs. "My devil."

"My devil," I repeat, my voice husky from my arousal.

"I bestow upon you." He continues, so I repeat.

"I bestow upon you."

"My darkest sins."

I clear my throat. "My darkest sins."

"And ask that you bathe in my debauchery."

I hesitate a moment, knowing how opposite this is from confessing and receiving penance. He wants me to confess and celebrate, and everything I've been taught is rushing at me from all directions, yet my eyes, locked on the way his fingers grip his thighs with impatience, has me opening my mouth, and not only saying the words, but meaning them.

"And ask that you bathe in my debauchery."

"Now say it all together, and I might go easy on you."

A breath escapes me at his words, and I have no idea what he means. Is he going to punish me with pleasure, or with pain?

I should be scared, right?

I'm not.

For some reason, I want to give myself over to him completely, no matter the consequences.

"My devil. I bestow upon you my darkest sins, and ask that you bathe in my debauchery."

"Atta girl," he rasps, and his lips kick up at the corner.

I feel utterly wicked for saying those words. Utterly sinful. They are only words, but they mean so much. So, so much.

"Divulge your sins, Jaxcen. Tell me everything bad you've done."

"I've committed adultery." I rush out.

"And did you like it?" he asks, his palms running up and down his thighs.

"Yes," I admit. "Very much."

"Did it make you feel bad, even while it made you feel good?"

"Yes." I nod. "But..."

"But what, little mouse?"

"But I couldn't stop."

"So you gave in to temptation, and were rewarded with pleasure. If you had stopped, what do you think would have happened?"

I blink at his question, wracking my brain for the answer, but all I can come up with is regret.

"I would have been annoyed, I think. I would have regretted not going through with it, just to see what it would be like."

"But you gave in. You pushed away everything you've been taught, to indulge in sin." This time, I can tell he leans forward by the way his elbows come to rest on top of his knees. "Tell me, Jaxcen. Was it worth it?"

"Yes." The word escapes me before I can stop it, and I can feel the heat in my cheeks flare to life at my admission.

"What do you think your fiancé would say about it?"

"I imagine he wouldn't be pleased," I admit.

"I imagine he wouldn't," Devon agrees, leaning back to clasp his hands in front of his lap again. "Are you going to tell him?"

I frown at that question. I hadn't really considered that, but I probably should.

"Can I ask you a question?" I almost whisper, but he hears and responds.

"Go ahead."

"Do you think he will still want to marry me if I tell him?" I bite my lip, anxiously waiting for his response, but all I get is another question.

"Do you want him to still want to marry you, or are you hoping the answer is no, in the hopes he will break it off with you?"

Dread thumps to the bottom of my gut at his question, and I realise it's because I want him to dump me and leave me alone but there's a big chance he won't.

My lip trembles at the epiphany.

Eddie likes to control me. Not the same way Devon does. I feel like the monster on the other side of the screen challenges me more than anything, where Eddie belittles me to keep me compliant, just so he can save face.

"Jaxcen?" Devon's deep rumble is like a fine red wine. Smooth, filling me with warmth. Comfort. Contentment.

"I don't want to marry him," I admit on a whisper.

"No? What do you want to do then? Go to Cloud 9 and step over the line?"

"Yes…" I shake my head. "Wait, no. I just…"

"You just what?"

My lips seal tight, and my heart aches as everything I want threatens to burst free, yet I know I can't have them. I know my family will never approve.

"Answer me!" he booms, and a squeal flies from my lips as I jump in fright, my knees slipping off the tuffet.

"I just want to do the things I want to do and not be made to feel bad about them," I yell back, my admission exploding from me as more tears burn my eyes, spilling over to my cheeks.

"Then why don't you?" he asks, his hands gripping his thighs again as I reposition myself on the tuffet.

"My family won't approve. They are very religious. I've already brought them so much shame. I can't bear to put them through that again."

"Why are you living your life to please others, little mouse? Why don't you just do as you like and if they don't like it, then they can look away."

"It's not that simple." I sob, slapping at the tears that just keep coming.

"Why not? You only get one life. If you're not getting fulfilment from serving others' expectations, then why not live for your own?"

"Like you? Just shoot anyone who annoys me? Kidnap innocent people for pleasure?"

Lightning fast, Devon disappears from my line of sight before the curtain next to me is pulled back. I gasp, rearing back against the wall as his towering height looms over me.

"You seem to have forgotten that the men I shot were trying to kill us. I haven't heard you thank me for saving your life yet." He steps inside the confessional with me, trapping me against the wall, kneeling before him as I stare up with wide eyes, my cheeks wet with my stupid tears.

"Thank you," I blurt, but he simply chuckles and starts to undo his belt.

"And yes, I kidnapped you, but it's not for the reasons you think, little mouse." He slowly slides his belt off, my gaze dancing between the action and his dark gaze piercing me. "And if you remember correctly, you're the only one that's received pleasure. Not me. But let's change that."

"What?" I'm so confused, yet so transfixed on the way he flicks the button of his jeans open, before slowly easing the zipper of his fly down.

"Just like your Christian God, the devil likes to punish as well, little mouse, just as long as someone is enjoying it."

His tone is utterly wicked, but I no longer stare at his face, my gaze locked onto his hand slipping into his jeans and lifting his stiff dick out, followed by the heavy weight of his balls.

I gasp, unsure if I've seen such a large dick.

Maybe it looks so big because I'm this close to it, yet still, its size isn't scaring me.

No, instead, my mouth fills with saliva and my panties soak through as I realise I want his punishment, in any way he'll give it, whether it hurts me or does the opposite.

What's wrong with me?

"I'm going to punish you now, little mouse. I'm going to make you suck my cock until you start choking and gagging, and I'll only stop when I've come down your throat. Do you understand?"

I nod, my heart flipping in my chest as heat engulfs my entire body.

"Do you know why I'm punishing you?"

I shake my head, risking a glance up at his face to see his hard expression, so fierce. So raw.

"I'm punishing you for not taking what you want out of life. I'm punishing you for letting others dictate how you live. I'm punishing you for denying what you really want for so long." He wraps his hand around his cock which bobs before me, giving it a pump. "And I'm punishing you for eavesdropping on my shower this morning." Releasing his dick, he takes his belt in both hands, quickly wrapping the strap behind my head as he jerks me forward. "Open."

His demand is brutal, yet my lips part, my eyes zeroed in on his hard cock until it surges forward and I can no longer focus on its beauty, but rather feel the silky press of its tip to my lips as it slowly eases in.

"Eyes up," he demands, and I swear my body is his puppet, doing everything he orders like it has no other choice.

And maybe it doesn't, and I'm not even mad about it.

"You've got the most luscious plump lips, Jaxcen. Do you know how many times I've pictured them wrapped around my cock?"

I try to pull away to answer, but he holds the belt tight so I can't retreat. "It was a rhetorical question."

I blink rapidly, as he pushes in further, my tongue brushing over the underside of his dick, as I stretch my mouth to accommodate his girth.

"Are you a gagger, Jaxcen?" he rasps, asking another question I know he doesn't really want the answer to. Besides, he already knows I'm not experienced. This is the first dick I've had in my mouth, so I guess we are about to find out.

As if on cue, I gag, and instead of letting up on the belt holding me in place, he chuckles.

"Breathe through your nose, little mouse. I'm not ready for your dinner to paint my cock just yet."

My eyes widen at that, even as I breathe quickly through my nose, sticking my tongue out as far as it will go in the hopes that it will help.

"You can take a bit more." He pushes in more, and again I gag, this time the action curling my whole body inward which just takes him further, making me gag again.

"Fuuuck, Jax. You should see this," he rasps, and I blink through my tears to focus on his face, loving how he called me Jax and not Jaxcen. "This is the most beautiful sight I've ever fucking seen."

He surges forward even more, and again I gag, his dick hitting the back of my throat, and I breathe quickly, willing myself not to upchuck on his dick.

That would be so embarrassing.

"Okay. It's time," he rasps, and he follows that up by answering the question in my head. "It's time for me to fuck this beautiful mouth."

I kinda thought he was already, but I quickly get what he means when he pulls halfway out, and slips back in quickly.

I gag, the noise loud as he revels in the sound. "Fuck yes, Jax. Let me hear you struggle."

Oh my.... I gag again and again and he starts thrusting in and out of my mouth, my head held in place by the belt, and my hands come to his thighs, ready to push him back because I'm not sure I can do this... but then I see his face.

The way it's contorted. An expression of pleasure and pain mixed together, and it does something to me.

Wetness rushes between my legs, and I give in to his brutal thrusts, my relaxing muscles accommodating him even more, and I only gag on every third or fourth thrust.

"That's it. You're such a good learner, Jaxcen. Such a good filthy Catholic girl." He thrusts faster, and my gag gurgles a little, making me fear I'm about to throw up, but he takes that moment to pull back, popping his dick free as he pants.

"Do you like the way I fuck your mouth, little mouse?"

I nod, gasping for air. "Yes."

His fingers grip my jaw, angling my head so I have to look at him again.

"You're not repulsed?"

I shake my head.

"What about when I make you puke?" He strokes his thumb over the drool on my chin. "Will you be repulsed then?"

I shrug. "I don't know."

A slow sinister smile tugs at his lips. "Shall we find out?"

He doesn't let me answer as he guides my head back to his cock and eases back inside my mouth.

I can't help but love how he watches me. For some reason, his awe makes me feel powerful, even though I'm the one whose mouth is being punished, but I don't hate it. It barely feels like a punishment, and my heart thrashes at the possibilities of what this man could do to me, and how willing I'd be to let him.

With both hands fisting the belt again, he restarts his assault on my throat, and I remain relaxed, my throat welcoming the brutality for the most part.

I watch him watching me as he thrusts, but then he changes tactics, and instead of thrusting, he releases his belt to drape it over my shoulders, and fists both sides of my head before he controls it, forces my head back and forth so quickly that my gag turns into one long retching gag as my body protests the invasion.

Tears stream from my eyes and my nails dig into his thighs as I push at him, and finally he releases me as I gag so hard, I nearly hurl.

"Stop," I pant, gasping for air, and his hand fists into my hair before he tugs my head back to look up at him.

"You gonna lose your dinner?" he asks, still wearing a smirk.

"I didn't eat dinner," I pant, but I can't breathe, "so I'd like not to die."

"Do you want me to stop?" he asks, and for the first time since he started this punishment with me, I see uncertainty in his eyes.

"No." I shake my head. "I want you to cum down my throat."

His eyes darken as a growl rumbles in his chest, and he leans down claiming my lips in a sloppy, drool covered kiss, that doesn't seem to bother him. His tongue dives in, as if he can taste his precum lining my mouth, and hell, the thought causes flutters deep in my core.

Breaking the kiss aggressively, he fists his cock and guides it back to my lips, where I take him in again.

"Why are you so fucking perfect for my cock, little mouse?"

I'm guessing it's another rhetorical question since my mouth is stuffed full of his dick.

"Does it make you wet?" he asks. "Blink once for no and twice for yes."

I blink twice.

Vida Loca
Trust

Chapter Sixteen

Devon

"Fuuuck. Touch yourself while I fuck this pretty mouth."

I've never been this hard in my life. I feel like the skin on my cock is about to split open, and fuck, I don't even care. Not with my little mouse on her knees, letting me fuck those plump lips, her blue eyes bright while tears stream from them.

She's not crying though. No, she's fucking enjoying this, getting off on the way I assault her mouth.

She gags again, the sound gargled, and fuck, I've never had a thing for gagging until now. She's not even trying to push me away as the tip of my cock slides down her throat.

I can see her arm moving, so I lean to the side a little to see those dainty fingers rubbing over her panties so fast, it's like she's mashing the needy bud, desperate for release.

When she moans around my cock, I swear I nearly come from the vibration, so I still, not ready for this to be over yet.

"You like that, Jax?" I rasp before thrusting into her throat again.

Still looking up at me, she blinks twice, and fuck, I love how compliant she is. So willing to let me defile her like this.

"Are you going to come for me?" I ask, even as I feel my balls start to tighten. "Fuck, I'm going to come."

I piston into her then, past the point of no return, chasing my release as pleasure rips through me and I stiffen as my cum shoots down her throat.

She gags again, spluttering this time as some of my cum sprays from her mouth, and fuck, just the sight has more cum bursting from my tip.

Not wanting her to follow through on another gag, I pull out, my gaze tracking the mess I've made as rivers of my cum ooze down her jaw and neck, some dripping between her cleavage.

"That has to be the sexiest sight I've ever seen." I lower myself to my haunches in front of her, my belt forgotten, now laying on the floor behind Jaxcen. "Did you enjoy that, little mouse?"

"Yes," she whispers before her tongue darts out to swipe up a drop of my cum just below her lip.

Fuck.

Where has she been all my fucking life.

"I'm not finished with you yet." I straighten, scooping up my belt and bark. "Stand up."

She takes no care to wipe up the mess I've left on her, instead complying eagerly, like she's excited to see what will happen next.

I should set my phone up and record this. Send it to her fuckhead fiancé and show him how she really likes it.

"Wrists together," I order, and again, she's quick to obey, holding out her wrists to me, her blue gaze intrigued as I loop my belt around them like cuffs, before I reach overhead and pull the strap over the confessional's supporting beam, forcing her arms over her head.

A gasp escapes her, those blue eyes tracking everything I do as I secure her in place and then step back to take in my Christmas treat.

"You know, I'm going to want this every Christmas now that I've had it." I reach out and graze the backs of my fingers down the column of her neck until I get to her dress, eyeing the buttons that run all the way down the front. "Will you come to me every Christmas, Jaxcen? Run off on your husband and let me do whatever I want to you before I send you back to him, stuffed full of my cum?"

Her cheeks flare to life as her plump lips part, her chest rising and falling quickly as my words affect her.

"As long as you kidnap me each year, I won't fight it."

Her response nearly floors me.

Fuck, my dick is rock hard again from that admission alone, and I grin like the cat who got the fucking cream.

"Maybe I'll send you back to him with more than my cum inside you." I grip the front of her dress with both hands and rip it open, the sounds of buttons clattering to the old timber floor louder than I expected as she gasps again, the shock of the action taking her off guard. "Maybe I'll send you back to him carrying my baby."

Her eyes widen and lips part as if to protest, but I silence her words with my lips, claiming a kiss so fucking searing that the temperature feels like it spikes twenty degrees inside the chapel.

As our tongues dance, I taste my cum and I'm not even repulsed by it. Everything this woman does makes me fucking desperate, and I just know there are lines I'll cross for her, that I've never considered crossing before with anyone else.

Reaching between us, I palm her tit, a nice handful, full and plump. My fingers find her nipple, already pebbled and straining as I slide my other hand to the searing skin on her waist, under the dress and around to her back before travelling down to her arse.

She moans into our kiss as I grip her butt, pressing my hips forward to get some friction on my cock, just as she's seeking on her clit.

Breaking our kiss, I nip at her lip hard, and just when I'm about to pull away, her teeth clamp down on my lower lip, not stopping until I can taste the copper of my own blood.

I growl, and she gyrates before sucking my lip into her own, and when she pulls back, her smile is seductive and her tongue darts out to lick the crimson streak of my life source off her own lips.

"Fuck, little mouse. You've turned into a tiger."

She grins, flashing her teeth.

And fuck me sideways, I've never seen anything sexier.

How the fuck does she keep doing that. Blowing my mind with everything she does.

It's like a beast has awoken in her. Like I've stirred the monster and now it wants to play.

And fuck I'm here for it.

Stepping back, I make quick work of tearing her panties at the side seams, ripping them from her body as she gasps in shock, before I dangle them in front of her face.

"Look how drenched they are." I press them to my nose, watching her eyes widen and darken with even more arousal as I inhale her scent. "Fuck, Jax. You smell divine."

Her lips part with a pant, so I gather the wet crotch of her panties in my hand and press them to her lips.

"Open."

She does instantly, letting me stuff her mouth with the wet fabric.

"Suck your juice from them, little mouse. Taste yourself."

She hesitates at first, so I quirk a brow, which is when she finally gives in and the sound of her sucking on the fabric meets my ears.

Fuck yes.

Without a second thought, I fall to my knees, my gaze travelling up her naked flesh, her creamy skin so flawless up to her two plump tits, perky and straining as she watches me from above.

"I'm fucking starving, little mouse."

She whimpers as I lift one of her legs over my shoulder, opening her up to me, and I drag my gaze to her pink flesh, already swollen with desire and glistening with her own arousal.

Like a man starved, I dive in, my lips latching onto her clit and I suck.

She cries out, the sound muffled around the fabric of her panties, and I can already tell it won't take much to make her climax. She's already hovering on the line.

Breaking the suction on her clit, I glide my tongue through her folds, lapping at her juices and the moment she starts gyrating, I fucking let loose on her.

My tongue lashes, my lips suck, all while my fingers travel up to press against the puckered rose of her back passage.

I bet no one has been there either, and just the thought of me introducing her to that level of pleasure has my cock jerking with need.

"Yes," she cries, although muffled around the fabric of her panties, so I press firmer against her back door as I assault her clit with my mouth.

Her climax is explosive, her cries almost screams as she comes apart on my face, her body jerking violently above as she hangs from my belt.

The moment she falls limp, I'm up off the floor, tearing her panties from her lips as I line my cock up, no longer able to hold back, and slam into her.

This has her back arching as she stiffens, her inner walls tight as they squeeze my cock like a vice.

"Fuck, Jax. Tell me you weren't a virgin," I rasp, worried I've just impaled her and brutally torn her hymen.

She said she wasn't, but maybe she was lying. Maybe she really was a fucking virgin and I've just gone and torn into her.

"I w-wasn't," she mutters, as if in pain, but I don't fucking believe her.

Easing back, I assess her face, her blue gaze glistening with unshed tears.

"I don't understand. If you weren't a virgin, then why are you in pain." I go to slip out of her, but she shakes her head frantically, her legs wrapping around me to hold me in place.

"It only happened once with... someone else. I was sixteen. I also tried a vibrator a couple of years ago, but Eddie found it and threw it out, telling me I was beastly and perverted for using it."

"That fucker is going to die," I hiss, and her lips kick up slightly.

"I had the same thought at the time. Well, more or less."

My gaze dances between her eyes for a beat, studying her for a lie or uncertainty, but I don't find it.

"So once, eight years ago, a man had sex with you, and that's it?"

She nods, her cheeks flaring again as her gaze drops in shame.

"Don't do that." I lift her chin with my finger, forcing her eyes back to mine. "Don't be ashamed of your past."

She stares at me for a long moment, a single tear rolling from her eye before she speaks. "If you kidnap me again next Christmas, I might tell you why I'm ashamed of that."

A deep rumble sounds in my chest at the thought of kidnapping her again. Not because I don't like the idea of it, because I fucking do, but because I don't want to give her back to her old life.

"I've changed my mind about that," I tell her, watching her expression fall, but I just smirk, like the prick I am. "I don't think I'll let you go. I might just keep you here as my prisoner, to have as my treat every fucking day."

Her blue eyes brighten, and fuck, I can tell she likes the sound of that.

"Would you let me fuck you like this every day, little mouse?" I ask, slipping my fingers between our bodies to press to her clit.

A moaning gasp escapes her, and she eases her leg lock around me to give me better access as I start circling her needy bud.

"Would you like me to fill you with my cum in every hole?"

"Yes," she admits, so I slowly start moving inside her, feeling her slickness build.

"Would you sit on my face, and smother me, taking everything you need without stopping until I'm drowning in your juice?"

"Oh... Yes." Her lids flutter closed, and I grin.

I bet she's picturing it.

"Fuck, I want that," I admit before latching onto her neck and sucking like a fucking teenager desperate to give my girl a hickey necklace.

And fuck, that's exactly how I feel.

She's my girl, and I'm marking her.

The way her cunt squeezes my cock is unlike anything I've felt. She's hot and wet, and her needy cunt sucks me in like it can't bear to let me retreat.

I palm her arse and give a squeeze as my other hand works on her clit, and just like before, her climax hits hard, so explosive that it clamps down on my cock so tight, milking my own climax without warning.

The roar that leaves me mingles with her screams and jets of cum shoot into her, reminding me that I didn't tarp up, which is something I never forget to do.

I don't know why, but for some reason, the idea of wearing a latex barrier with Jaxcen wasn't going to cut it. My dick and brain had come to the conclusion, and I hadn't questioned it, which makes me wonder. Am I trying to get her pregnant?

I mentioned it to her before.

Why the fuck would I say that?

Even though it's a fucking crazy thought, I find myself not wanting to pull out of her. Not wanting my seed to leak from her and be wasted.

Pressing my forehead to hers, our panting breaths mingle, our gazes locking as we float back down from our highs.

"Are you alright, little mouse?" I ask, my voice husky before she nods.

"That was..." Her voice is raspy too, and I wonder if it's from arousal or the brutal way I fucked her throat before. "That was amazing."

I feel it then, the wetness oozing from her pussy, still wrapped around my cock.

No.

Don't waste it.

Like a fucking psycho, I reach up and unfasten the belt from the support beam to untether Jaxcen from it, and turn with her still wrapped around my cock, taking a few steps out into the chapel where I lower her, laying her on the floor.

Assessing my surroundings, I'm unsure how to make this work, and when my eyes land back on my belt, still wrapped around her wrists, I know what to do.

"Let's get this off your wrists." I reach forward and start pulling on my belt with one hand, while the other holds me up so I can remain impaled inside her.

Jaxcen helps to get her hands free, and I use my teeth to completely unravel the cuffs I made, before glancing behind me.

"Are you... just going to stay in there?" she asks, her voice a little timid now that her arousal has ebbed.

"Yep," I reply simply, shifting our joined bodies back a little until her arse is halfway inside the confessional. "Legs up." I demand, and even though she frowns, she obeys.

I should probably tell her what's running through my head, but then she'll likely run now that the lust haze has faded, so I shift awkwardly, slipping my cock free and watching some of my cum ooze out as well, which only pisses me off more.

"What are you doing now?" she asks as I quickly loop my belt around her ankle.

"Getting you ready for your next position," I admit vaguely, and she half giggles before stopping.

"Wait. You're serious?"

Lifting my brows, I glance at her. "You didn't think your punishment was over already, did you?"

"Well... yeah, I kinda did."

I shake my head, tugging the belt to make sure it won't come off her ankle and then stand, ignoring my jeans as they slip down my thighs while I lift her ankle, forcing her hips up off the floor and secure the other end of the belt to a rail on the inside of the confessional.

"We've only just begun," I admit darkly, making sure the belt is tight enough that she can't get away.

Running my hands down her legs, I dodge her free one kicking out, while the other can't move an inch. My path travels under her thighs and under her raised arse, which I'm sure is an uncomfortable position, but how else am I going to make sure my cum stays inside her?

Gravity can be a bitch, you know.

I'm now sitting so close to her pussy, and the way I have her leg strung up gives me a fantastic bird's eye view of her glistening cunt. With my cum soaked fingers, I circle her clit, watching the way she tries to squirm away, but can't get anywhere on account her leg is tied up.

"Don't you want my cock again, Jax?" I ask, and her eyes flare.

Does she like it when I call her that? Hmmmm... Let's see.

"Answer me, Jax. Do you want me to fill you to the brim with my cum, so much so that when you return to your prudish fiancé that you'll feel my cum trickling down your leg?"

She moans in response, and yeah, it could be from my fingers working on her clit, but I'm pretty fucking sure it's a combination of that, me calling her Jax, and talking filth to her.

I slip a finger into her tight hot heat, feeling my seed inside her as my thumb presses to her clit.

"Do you want to see his face when he realises you've been defiled? That another man's cum runs down your leg?"

"Yes," she pants, gyrating her hips.

"So that's what we are going to do, little mouse. Fill you with so much of my cum that your fiancé will be disgusted. Maybe he'll even call off the wedding." I shoot her a wink.

My cock is ready to go again, and by the flush of her cheeks, and parted lips that release another moan, I can see Jaxcen is just as ready too.

Standing, I quickly remove every inch of clothing on me before returning to settle between her legs. Jaxcen squirms as she watches, and I can tell her brain is telling her to say no, but her cunt is ruling her, given the way her eyes latch onto my cock like she wants to taste it again.

On my knees, I position my tip at her entrance and run it up and down her slit.

"Maybe I'll never give you back to your fiancé," I tell her, pressing my tip to her clit and teasing her, which elicits a moan. "Maybe I'll just keep you like this forever and drown you in pleasure."

As another moan escapes her, I drive my cock so deep into her, that I bottom out and my nuts slap her arse.

The position mustn't be comfortable for her, but I'm fucking laser focused on my goal now, and I'm not stopping for anything. I pound into her hard, the combination of my cum and her arousal making it far easier than the first time, and with each thrust, I watch her tits bounce and her lips part as she moans and pants, her lids falling shut as her arousal claims her once again.

I pound into her over and over, my cock getting wider the longer I go, as I fight to hold on to my release for as long as I can, wanting to make sure it's chock full of my little guys, ready to claim her from inside.

When she palms her tits, her moans filling the room, I press my fingers back to her clit to force her over, and the moment her inner walls squeeze my cock, I explode, filling her once again.

As awkward as the position is that I have her in, I still lean down to kiss her, something I can't seem to get enough of either, and I wonder for a minute if perhaps I've been poisoned or something. This behaviour is so unlike me.

I'm a fuck 'em and kick 'em out kind of guy.

Hell, I usually only coax them with a starter kiss and then they are willing to do whatever I want, and that's it.

Yet here I am, desperate for her lips to be on mine, aching for my cock to recover even though I've only just come, just so I can do it again. And again. And again.

This isn't fucking normal, yet I can't seem to stop.

"That was even better," she pants against my lips. "How does it keep getting better?"

I smirk, feeling like a fucking god, and push back to hover over her.

"Just wait until next time. Give me five minutes." I wink and her eyes widen.

"Again? You want to go again? Aren't you tired?"

I shake my head. "Nope. Besides, making a baby takes time."

She giggles, but it cuts off abruptly as her eyes widen.

"Wait. What!?"

Chapter Seventeen

Jaxcen

He did not just say that! He can't be serious. He was just messing with me before.

"This is a joke right?" I screech, trying to sit up, but with the way my leg is tied to the stupid confessional, I can't get the momentum.

"This is *no* joke, little mouse. I said so before. I told you I might decide to send you back carrying my baby."

Blood rushes past my ears, sounding as loud as thunder.

He's joking. He has to be.

None of this is making sense.

"I thought you were just saying it to…"

I can feel my cheeks betray me the moment I try to say the words.

"To what?" he asks, gliding his fingers through his cum leaking from me, before he starts trying to push it back inside.

"What are you doing? Stop that." I squirm.

"Tell me what you were going to say, little mouse. You thought I was saying it, to what?"

I roll my eyes in frustration, even as he keeps shoving his seed back inside me. "To turn me on."

Chuckling, he shoots me another infuriating wink. "It worked didn't it? You fucking loved it."

Even though I did love it, I'm not going to admit it to this man, who has somehow scrambled my brain into not thinking at all and forgetting that he really has kidnapped me.

"Just imagine your fiancé's face when I send you back not only with my cum running down your thigh, but when you tell him you're pregnant. That the baby you carry was put there by your kidnapper." His smirk is utterly wicked, and damn him, the way he keeps touching me is turning me on again. "Imagine Eddie's face when you tell him your kidnapper made you come so many times that you begged for more."

A whimper escapes me, and he circles my clit, the fire building quickly again.

"Why are you doing this?" I breathe.

"What? This?" He gestures his head to where he's circling my clit again. "Or the part about sending you back carrying my baby?"

"Both," I pant, hating the way he so easily controls my body.

"Well, Jax." He draws out my name, obviously knowing how much I like hearing it roll off his tongue as he plays with my sensitive nub. "I'm doing this because I want to make you come again, so your needy little cunt sucks my swimmers in so deep, they won't ever leak out."

I gasp, even as he sinks two fingers inside me. "And the baby part, besides being a big fuck you to your prude of a fiancé," he curls his fingers inside me, making my back arch and a moan escape my lips as he continues, "I want to know that when you go back to your life, and try to forget about me, you never will, because every time you look at the swell of your stomach, you'll remember how fucking filthy we were together, and how fucking perfect it was."

A strangled moan escapes me as his words do something to me I'm not prepared for, and once again I lose myself in the way this man plays my body like his own personal instrument, sending me over in another crashing orgasm.

"That's it, beautiful. Take my cum deep."

His voice is animalistic, and I've barely caught my breath when he shifts between my legs and eases his dick back in. The full feeling is something I didn't expect to crave so much, but I can't even tell him to stop. There's no way my lips can conjure the word with how good the stretch feels.

Why do I want him so much?

That thought flutters away as he once again consumes me with every thrust, with every dirty word, with every touch of his hands as they roam my body like they own it.

And perhaps they do.

Perhaps I want them to.

The angle Devon is in, pistoning into me with my butt raised off the floor seems to hit differently than before, and another blinding climax rips through me, making me putty in his hands as he once again roars with his own release, throwing his head back.

Even through my daze, I stare at the veins running up his neck and how prominent they are in this moment, like there's electricity running through his body.

Did I do that to him? Is it me, or just sex that makes him this way?

I should be scared, but how can I when those dark eyes meet mine again, devouring me with a look of what I can only attribute to worship.

Worship.

This is a whole different kind of worship than I'm used to, and I don't want it to stop.

Ever.

"Fuck, Jax. Look how full you are," Devon rasps, his eyes going to my exposed flesh. To the place no one has stared at like this before.

It's utterly filthy, yet as he once again keeps forcing this seed back into me when it overflows, all I feel is more aroused.

"Dev," I pant lazily, my lids heavy with exhaustion, yet my libido already ignited and ready to go once again. This can't be normal. "What are you doing to me?"

"I already told you, little mouse. Making sure your body takes all of my cum."

I shake my head, watching him watch me through the fan of my lashes. "No. I don't mean that," I practically whisper, my words slurring a little.

"Then what do you mean?" he asks before gliding his fingers through my utterly soaked folds.

"I mean..." My eyelids flutter closed, as I speak. "What are you doing *to* me?"

I'm not making any sense, but when I feel him move over me and his lips press to my ear, a shiver ripples up my spine as his words register.

"I'm waking you up, little mouse. I'm introducing you to your desires." He nips at my lobe. "I'm showing you it's okay to explore them, and as long as you trust who you're doing them with, nothing bad will happen."

"Do I trust you?" I ask, a little confused as I try to force my lids open, the heat of his breath against my ear has me warming from the inside out, keeping me wanting.

"Not only do you trust me, little mouse, but right now, you trust yourself."

My eyes shoot open at his words, tears pricking them at how hard his words hit, because trusting myself has been hard to come by since I got sent away as a child.

Devon doesn't let me think any more about it though, his lips claiming mine in a kiss that would bring me to my knees if I were standing.

It's slow and sensual. The way his lips nibble and nip, the way his tongue explores every inch of my mouth feels like a claiming, and I never want him to stop.

This time, when he fucks me, it's unhurried, his leisurely pace making it feel like he's savouring each graze of his fingers and each stroke of his dick as he stretches me wide again.

It's sloppy. There's barely any room left for his thick length given how much of his cum fills me, yet he pushes in, going slow, almost too slow, but when I come again, I can feel it build from deep in my core, and when it hits, it's like a never ending tornado of pleasure rippling through every cell in my body.

Despite my awkward position, I'm so spent that I no longer feel it. I no longer feel anything. Even when Devon comes inside me again, all I feel is languid. Lax. Practically numb, and not in a bad way.

Right now, I feel so good. Better than I've ever felt, and I swear there's a smirk on my lips as my eyes close, and the deep gravel of Devon's voice lulls me as everything goes dark, and I succumb to a dreamless sound sleep.

When I wake, I'm wrapped in sheets so soft they feel like a cloud, and a scent so divine I want to bottle it up and keep it for all eternity.

Devon.

I can smell him everywhere around me, yet as I pry my eyes open to find myself back in his suite, in his bed, the man I'm searching for is nowhere in sight.

Slowly, I push myself up, the sheet falling to pool around my hips, revealing my full nakedness. Glancing down at myself, every ache in my body starts making itself known, and images flash through my mind from last night.

The chapel. The confessional. Devon's belt around the back of my head. His dick in my mouth. The feeling like I was going to throw up each time he made me gag, and the way he looked almost drunk, heavy lids, a sexy smirk, so utterly wicked, as I watched him from my knees, knowing I was the one to make him so ravenous.

A lazy smile kicks up my lips, and I rake my hand through my hair, feeling the knotted mess.

I need a shower.

As I shift to slide out of the bed, I find a note sitting on the bedside table and pick it up to read it.

> *When you're feeling human again, you can find me in my office.*
> *x Dev*

My heart flips.

Why does my heart flip?

It's not a love letter, Jaxcen.

But there's an X, and that's a kiss right?

Ugh. Maybe my brain is conjuring up things that aren't even real.

Slipping out of the bed, I dash to the bathroom, quickly showering and spending way too long combing the knots from my hair, before I go to my bag to retrieve a dress.

Today, I choose another button down, wondering if it too will be destroyed by the end of the day, and not even caring if it is. Slipping on some pink lacy panties and a bra to match the dress, I quickly get dressed before sliding on my sandals.

Moving to Devon's full length mirror in the corner of his bedroom, I assess my outfit, but end up staring at my face and neck with wide eyes.

I look a little tired, but there's something about my eyes, their blue hue seeming brighter somehow. My skin looks like it's glowing, my cheeks a little flushed, and my lips, well, they simply look thoroughly kissed.

My neck isn't faring as well, however, with three large marks marring my skin, their deep red and purple tones looking like blood filled bruises.

My lips part as a breath escapes me, and I lean in to get a better look.

Hickeys.

Devon gave me hickeys.

The memory of his lips on my neck comes rushing back, but that's not the only place I remember him sucking.

My eyes widen as I lift my dress to find another mark on my inner thigh, and then another as I peek down the front of my dress into my bra.

He's painted me in hickeys.

I should be mad, right?

I should storm down to his office and slap his face.

Hell, I should suck on his forehead and leave a big purple mark there for the world to see.

I'm not angry though. Strangely, I feel worshipped. I feel owned, and not in a bad way. I feel like he deliberately left his mark on my skin so everyone would know who I belong to.

Even Eddie, when I return to him.

The thought makes me queasy. And so does the thought of returning to my life. Working an office job in a finance firm, entering data like that will ever give me fulfilment.

It hasn't yet. I can't imagine it ever will.

I also can't fathom the idea of returning to that shitty apartment that I keep so simple, just to avoid getting a lecture on greed and how the Lord frowns upon it by my fiancé.

"Well, you know what Eddie, the Lord can suck a big one."

I slap my hand over my mouth, shocked by my own words, but as I slowly release my mouth, I grin at my reflection.

"I fucked another man, Eddie. He made me feel so good. Filled me with so much of his cum that there's no way I'm not carrying his baby right now."

My breathing quickens as I realise how much I mean those words, which is shocking, right?

"He fucked my mouth too, Eddie," I say to my reflection. "Loved it when I gagged around his cock."

My lips thin before I burst out laughing, and holy shit, I think I'm losing my mind.

That thought is sobering.

I know what happens when I lose my mind, and I don't want to ever go through that again.

"I feel trapped," I whisper to myself, tears glazing my eyes. "Why is it so bad to want to feel so good?"

Shaking my head at my patheticness, I blink away my pending tears and straighten up my dress.

My parents and Eddie would frown upon me right now. They would tell me how ashamed they are of my behaviour.

But they aren't here. And until they are, I refuse to let them ruin my fun.

Jutting up my chin, I roll my shoulders back and take in a deep breath before turning on my heel to go in search of my kidnapper.

Just that thought alone has my mood lifting, the thought that I'm favouring my kidnapper instead of being scared of him makes me feel a little unhinged, and right now, I don't care.

When I step into the bar, I'm reminded of my outburst yesterday, when I foolishly went behind the bar and took the knife and threatened to stab people.

Ugh, how embarrassing.

"Good day, Miss Summers." Ronnie, the bartender smiles even though he should probably hate me.

"Uh... hi." I wave awkwardly, noticing the same old guys sitting at the bar, and the same older couple sitting at the end.

Ducking my head, I hurry to Devon's office door to hear a female voice on the other side, arguing with him.

Maybe it's the marks he made on my neck for all to see, or maybe it's the fact I'm thoroughly fucked and feeling a little more daring than usual, but I shove the door open and walk in with all the confidence of a Kardashian, when really I'm nothing but the little mouse Devon calls me.

"But we need a Santa, and everyone loves you so you need to do it." Allegra, the teenage girl from yesterday whines.

"I've told you a thousand fucking times. I'm not putting a fucking Santa suit on."

"Why not?" I ask, butting in before two sets of eyes land on me. "I think you'll look sexy in a Santa suit."

Allegra screws her nose up. "On second thought, maybe you're not the right person for the job."

Devon rolls his eyes at her, a smirk playing at the corners of his mouth.

"Good morning, Miss Summers," Devon rasps, and this time it's Allegra who rolls her eyes.

"I think I'll leave before you make use of the mistletoe." Allegra goes to walk out, but Devon's demanding tone stops her.

"Not so fast, Allegra. You owe Jaxcen an apology."

Sighing with noticeable shoulders slumping, Allegra moves closer to me as she shrugs.

"Sorry for talking smack yesterday. I thought you were one of our new girls and wanted to haze you a bit. It's tradition." She shrugs, but I'm only left with more questions.

"New girls?"

"You know. Devon's rescues." She shrugs like it's no big deal.

"Rescue?" I ask, and Allegra nods.

"You know, like a dog rescue but it's a woman." Again she shrugs like that's no big deal before she walks out, leaving me inside the office with my kidnapper.

My gaze locks onto Devon's, who is lazing back in his big boss chair behind his desk, looking like the king once again.

A playful grin lights his eyes, and they dart up to the ceiling where the mistletoe hangs.

"Where's my kiss, little mouse?" he asks, his dark stare returning to mine. "Come here."

Just like last night, his command has my body obeying, like a puppet made to serve him and only him. He watches me as I move towards him, rounding his desk where he swivels his chair in my direction and reaches out a hand.

Placing mine in his, he tugs me onto his lap, lifting me easily to straddle him, and instantly my body is alight.

"I'm an impatient man, Jaxcen." He reminds me, hinting that he's still waiting for his kiss, so I close the distance, my lids falling closed as I press my lips to his.

A deep growl rumbles from his throat, his hand fisting in my hair as he pulls us together leaving no air between us, and parts my lips with his tongue.

I'd only meant to give him a peck, but his idea of a kiss is slow and searing and all consuming and I find myself once again, putty in his hands.

The kiss is leisurely, and sensual, much like the last time we had sex last night. It's like he's savouring each brush of our lips and each swipe of our tongues, and I swear, I've never experienced anything like it.

Is this normal for him? Is this how he is with all the women he sleeps with?

The thought sends an ache to the centre of my chest, and I pull back, breaking the kiss.

Am I so naive that I've fallen for the first man that shows me how good things can be?

Probably.

Because you're pathetic, Jaxcen.

If Devon knew how into him I am, he'd probably laugh in my face and send me home.

It's so weird. He literally kidnapped me, yet I'm straddling his lap and just last night let him do depraved things to me, even allowing him to ejaculate inside me when I don't even take birth control.

You're going to end up with a disease, you hoe.

Ugh. Shut up, inner voice. I've had just about enough of you.

Eddie says his church doesn't believe in birth control, so I never took it, but now, what if I really am pregnant, and Devon sends me back to deal with the consequences while he moves on to the next woman. Probably the ones here in his town.

"What's going through that head of yours?" he asks, those dark eyes studying my face, and I worry that if he keeps looking, he'll see everything I'm trying to hide.

"Is this what you do with all of them?"

He frowns. "All of who?"

"You know." I shrug, feeling out of sorts talking about this. "All of the women you sleep with. The ones in this town."

That frown deepens and turns into a hard glare.

"You heard what Allegra said right?"

"I heard her say you rescue women." I nod. "But that doesn't mean you don't sleep with them."

"Actually, that's exactly what it means. The women I rescue don't need a man demanding their bodies, Jaxcen. They need a safe haven."

"So you're telling me you don't sleep with the women here? That you're really a good samaritan who is what? Protecting these women?"

"Yes," he barks, clearly annoyed with my questioning. "You're the only woman I've saved that I've shared my bed with."

"What? You call kidnapping, saving?" I scoff and his glare turns pitch black, sending a chill up my spine.

"I made you believe that I kidnapped you to stop you from telling the cops what you saw me do, but really, you're here because the man who sent those men to kill me, must have been watching on the cameras. He saw you there, Jaxcen. He saw how I protected you, and decided instead of coming directly for me, he'd go after you first."

My gaze falls from his, which looks too sincere right now for me to accept what he's saying.

He didn't kidnap me to stop me from talking?

He did it because the man that wants him dead has decided to come after me?

"This makes no sense," I mutter, shaking my head before my eyes lock back onto his.

"If I didn't bring you with me, he would have killed you, little mouse. So I kidnapped you."

"But... You were going to kill me." I point out as heat pricks the back of my eyes. "I was so terrified you were going to take me into the bush and..."

"Yes, I know. Take you to the bush, kill you and bury your body. I remember."

"Why would you let me think that?" I frown, shoving off him and stumbling to my feet. "Why would you deliberately try to scare me like that? It's... mean. So horribly mean!" I cry and he curses, springing from his chair.

"Jaxcen, if I had told you what was happening you still wouldn't have come with me."

I scoff. "Exactly. There's no way in hell I would have gone with a crazy psycho who shoots people point blank in a fucking church!" I scream, and his expression hardens, the monster from the church now in this room with me.

"If you hadn't, you would have been dead by the fucking morning." He sneers, storming towards me so I hurry backwards, nearly tripping over the coffee table. "He went to your apartment, Jaxcen. He went in armed, ready to fucking kill. If I hadn't taken you, then you'd already be dead."

My breath seizes in my lungs at his words, and I find it hard to speak, although I manage it just enough. "How do you know he went to my apartment?"

"When Finn and Miles went to get your things, they planted cameras. It later picked him up, armed and ready to kill before he planted his own cameras."

My mouth drops open as my eyes burn with tears I'm working hard to keep at bay. "That's what you and Finn were talking about yesterday. That was my apartment."

"Yes."

Not only did Devon's men go inside my apartment but they planted cameras, which showed a killer coming for me.

"I have to go," I whisper, tears finally popping free.

"Come on, love. Not this again." Devon sighs, taking another step forward, and I take another step back, my heels hitting the wall behind me.

"No, Devon. Seriously. If you're not going to kill me then I need to go. What if that man goes after my family? After Eddie?"

"Fuck Eddie," Devon sneers looming closer. "I'm happy for him to die."

I don't know why I do it. I don't know what comes over me, but anger like I've never felt engulfs my entire being and I slap Devon's face, hard.

The clap is loud in the office, and his head even whips to the side as I gasp, shocked by what I've done, my palm burning from the contact.

But it's too late. I've gone and done it. I've slapped the monster, and now it's almost as if his presence grows bigger. Wider. Taller. His already dark eyes turning black as his hand whips out to wrap around my throat, slamming me to the wall.

Vida Loca
Trust

Chapter Eighteen

Devon

I want to fuck her until she sees reason. Until she understands that I'm trying to protect her. And if she thinks that fucking slap will deter me, will get me to let her go to fend for herself against a fucking killer, then she's more naive than I thought.

With a growl, I grip the back of her neck, ignoring her whimper and drag her over to my desk, swiping my hand across it to clear the papers off before shoving her face down.

"Stop! What are you doing?" she cries, but there's no way I'm stopping. No way I'm letting her leave my fucking office without knowing how I fucking feel.

Shoving her dress up, I tear the pink lacy panties clean off her in one swift tug, while holding her in place easily with my other hand pressed between her shoulders as she tries to buck me off.

"Devon, stop."

"No. You don't fucking mean that," I snap, sliding my fingers between her legs to find her moist wet cunt already primed for me. "See, little mouse. You want this as much as I do."

"I don't understand why," she whispers, and there's pain in her words which I know stems from the fucked up way she's been raised.

"Let me show you," I rasp, dropping to my knees and spreading her wide.

She whimpers as I position her, exposing her to me, but it's a needy whimper that just makes my cock even harder, aching to bury inside that tight hot cunt.

Surging forward, I press my nose to her bare arse and glide my tongue between her folds, revelling in the way she jolts but pushes back into my face, desperate for what I have to give.

"Mmmm, Jax. You taste so fucking good," I mumble against her cunt, sinking my tongue into her heat as my fingers move to her clit.

"Dev," she pants, and fuck, I like hearing that.

I know she's fucking confused about what's happening here. Hell, so am I, but I'm not letting her slip away. I'm not letting her go until she's sampled everything I can offer her.

And afterwards, I have to hope I can handle her walking away.

I'm not foolish enough to think I can give her a good life.

I live in a gated community that's kept under guard. I take in women. Victims of heinous assaults. I'm a fucking Marx. Danger follows us, and as much as I want to keep my little mouse, I don't want to fence her in. I don't want to put her in danger. I just want her to live.

Like, really live.

And yeah, she might have my kid, and if that happens, I'll make sure they want for nothing, but they'll both be better off living their own life.

Until Christmas.

I meant what I fucking said.

I'll steal her away every fucking Christmas until my dying day, and I'll fucking devour her.

My tongue and fingers continue their assault on her needy cunt, and it's not long before she's crying out, her orgasm ripping through her like a freight train of pleasure.

"Fucking beautiful," I mutter as I stand, quickly freeing my cock and pressing it to her entrance before the last wave of her climax ebbs.

Then I surge in. She cries out again, and I feel it, her walls clenching around my cock, as a second orgasm engulfs her.

I fucking make good use of the way her inner walls clamp around my length, and piston into her quickly, already too close myself to go easy.

"Do you feel that, Jax?" I ask, pounding into her from behind, my gaze zeroing in on her puckered rose, winking at me like a fucking beacon.

"What?" she pants, before I spit on her exposed arse and rub my saliva over her hole. "What are you doing?"

"Do you feel how good we fit together?" I ask, pressing my middle digit into her a little, and she stiffens. "Relax, love. You can take my finger."

"I don't know if I can," she admits, but I chuckle, slowly easing it in a little further as my thrusts slow, my gaze transfixed on the way her flower opens for me.

"Fuck, yes. Open up that filthy hole for me. Let me in."

Another whimper falls past her lips, muffled by the way her face presses into my desk, but she relaxes, and her arse sucks my finger in greedily.

"Atta girl, Jax. You're doing so well," I praise, noting how much more she relaxes when I say that.

Fuuuck. She's desperate for anything I can give her, and fuck, I want to give her everything.

Fucking everything.

I speed up my thrusts again, letting her feel the fullness from both sides. I gather more saliva in my mouth and drop it to her arse, rubbing it in with a second finger, and the moment I slide my index finger inside her arse to join the other, she comes hard.

"Fuck, yes," I moan, feeling my nuts tighten as heat engulfs me, her walls doing what they do so fucking well, milking me, shooting pleasure through my entire body as I fill her with cum.

I still, balls deep inside her, letting each spurt go, hoping it will give me what I want.

And fuck, I have no idea why I want this, to impregnate her, but I fucking do. I've never wanted anything more.

When my hearing returns, the sounds of our panting breaths fill the room, and I collapse over her, peppering the back of her neck with kisses I never give to any other women.

"Why did you do that?" Jaxcen asks, her voice husky, and out of breath.

"Did you not like it, little mouse?" I ask against her ear, just another part of her I can't fucking get enough of, before I push myself up and slip free, rolling her onto her back, still on my desk.

"You know I did," she admits, her big blue gaze coming to mine now that she can see me. "But why did you do that after…"

Her frown is etched with confusion as she trails off, and I'm not sure if it's from whatever is going through her head, or the fact I've just lifted her legs up to rest her knees over my shoulders.

"After what?" I urge, and she blinks a few times, as if coming out of a trance.

"I just slapped you. Told you I want to leave. And in response, you made me come and…"

"And fucked you?"

"Yes," she breathes, her cheeks so red and flushed from the three orgasms I gave her just minutes ago.

"I was just showing you why you should stay." I wag my brows, and she rolls her eyes.

"You only want me to stay so you can fuck me," she quips, and I don't fucking like her tone, or her meaning. Like she's just another fucking notch.

Three days ago, I would never have imagined the last forty-eight hours, but they've happened, and I'm not stupid enough to keep denying how she makes me feel.

Fucking alive.

"No, little mouse. I want you to stay so I can worship you."

My eyes fall to her exposed pussy, my cum glistening on her folds, a few drizzles oozing free.

"Well, that won't do," I mutter, scooping the trails of white jizz up with my fingers, and forcing it back inside her.

"Hey." She tries to squirm away. "What are you doing?"

I lift a brow at her. Did she not hear anything I said last night?

"I'm making sure my cum doesn't leak out." I deadpan and her eyes widen.

"You can't be serious, Devon. You don't want to get me pregnant."

"Why wouldn't I?"

"For one, we don't know each other. We can't have a child together if we don't know one another. Plus, I can't stay. I have to leave."

This time I roll my eyes, my hands running up and down her bare thighs.

"Why, to save Eddie?"

"No," she whispers, her eyes falling from mine with shame. "I'm sorry I slapped you. I don't know why I did that."

I sigh, reaching forward and hooking my finger under her chin, forcing her to look at me again. "You did that because you're feeling trapped."

Her eyes turn glassy.

"Yes," she admits quietly, "but not by you."

My brows hitch as I shoot her a 'really' look, and her face softens.

"Okay, not *only* by you."

I smirk, and a faint one tugs at her lips too.

Sometimes I forget why she's here with me.

She's a decent woman. Kind. Selfless. A little too fucking selfless if you ask me.

She certainly doesn't deserve this shit, or the way I've treated her.

Easing her legs off my shoulders, I lower her feet to my desk and point sternly at her.

"Stay there. Don't move."

She bites her lip, nibbling on the plump flesh, making me want to kiss her and forget about everything, but that will have to wait. I've distracted her with sex far too much. Now's the time for some truths.

Stepping away from her, I move to the Marx family portrait on the wall and swing it open like a door to reveal my safe. Keying in the code, it beeps and unlatches and I reach in to retrieve the black pouch.

"There's something I need you to hear," I say, turning back to her and watching how she tracks my movements, her gaze locked on the pouch in my hand.

Slowly, I pull her phone free, and she goes to grab it, but I shake my head, holding it up high, out of her reach.

"Uh, uh. Not yet, little mouse. Just listen."

Ignoring her confused frown, I open her phone and go to the voice-mails, tapping on the first one to play.

> **Message Received from: Eddie**
> *"Good morning, Jaxcen. I'm a little surprised that I'm having to make this call. It's quite an inconvenience, as I'm sure you already know, so I don't know why you're behaving like this. The rules haven't changed. You call me every morning at nine, yet it's just ticked over to eleven. I'm looking forward to hearing what has you so busy that you can't call your fiancé."*

Red hot heat has engulfed Jaxcen's neck and cheeks, her eyes a little glassy, and it's hard to tell if it's humiliation, or anger.

"So that's Eddie?" I ask, and she gives me a single, angry nod.

Anger is good. Although I'm not sure if she's angry at me or her fiancé.

"He has rules for you?"

Again, she gives me a single nod.

"You call him every morning at nine?"

"Yes," she snaps, her eyes not on me but the phone in my hand.

"Does he always act like a pompous arse?"

She shrugs. "He never used to."

Hmmm. He never used to. Probably before the church, aka a cult, brainwashed him.

I can see she doesn't want to say much, so I play the next voicemail.

Tears well in her eyes and her lower lip wobbles, but her cheeks are still flushed, and I'm pretty sure it's with shame and humiliation.

"So watching porn has corrupted you in the past has it? And now he thinks you've relapsed and gone down the rabbit hole?"

"I guess," she snaps, and I grip her jaw, forcing her to look at me.

"Has he involved your old man in this bullshit before? About you watching porn?"

She tries to sit up and shove me back, but I drop her phone to my desk and pin her wrist to the surface, pressing my nose to hers.

"Are you angry at me, little mouse?"

"Those messages are private. You have no right to listen to them."

"Maybe not. But I needed to know what we were up against with your family. How far they'd go to search for you. And so far, this is what we have. Two voicemails from your fiancé, not even fucking worried about your sudden absence, instead more worried about what depravities you're getting up to."

"It's still not your business," she whispers, tears spilling over.

"Maybe not, but now it is, and for the record, Jaxcen. I'm on your side."

I rear back and hit play on the next voicemail, watching her expression as her fiancé continues to be a dick.

> ***Message Received from: Eddie***
> *"Do you not understand the concept of what soon is Jaxcen? I'm so disgusted with how you are treating me. This isn't the behaviour of a dutiful wife. This is immature childish behaviour that requires strict punishment. I'm coming over."*

"Hmmm. Strict punishment. How does he punish you?" I ask, but she looks away, a sob escaping. "How does he fucking punish you, Jaxcen?!" I yell, and she sneers.

"Not like you... he just... belittles me. Yells at me until I feel like nothing better than a pile of dog shit on the bottom of his shoe."

"He has no right to do that. Don't you get that? No one has the right to make you feel that way."

She shrugs, crossing her arms over her chest while looking anywhere but at me, so I play the next message.

> ***Message Received from: Eddie***
> *"Stop ignoring me, Jaxcen. I know you can hear the buzzer, and since you aren't at work you must be there. That's it. I'm calling your father."*

Her eyes widen at that message, panic contorting her expression. "Oh my God. Did he call my dad?"

"What do you think?" I ask sincerely, and she covers her eyes with her arm. "This can't be happening."

"Unfortunately it is," I say before hitting play on the next message.

She bolts upright, nearly headbutting me, panic gripping her as she
tries to push me away to get free.

"I have to go. Oh my God. I have to go."

"Hold up," I say, gripping her upper arms and holding her in place,
her arse still perched on my desk. "Why does that message make you
want to leave? When you say you have to go, where do you mean?"

"You don't get it. I can't... No. I can't do it." She shakes her head
furiously, the terror in her tone more extreme than when she thought
she was going to die on Tuesday night.

"Can't do what?" I cup her face so she can't look anywhere but at
me, desperately wanting to ease her mind, although I'm not sure what
from exactly.

Is it her fiancé, her dad, or Dr Xavier that has her so panicked?

"I can't do that again. I can't go through that." She tries to shake
her head, but my hands hold her in place. "Oh my god, are there more
messages?"

"Yes," I sigh. "Are you sure you want to listen to them?"

"Yes." She nods. "I need to know what's happening."

Needing a moment, I press my forehead to hers, and the way her lids
flutter closed shows me how much she trusts me. She's not scared of
me. But she is scared of those voicemails.

Sighing, I ease back and release my grip on her face, pressing play on
the next message.

A loud sob escapes her as her mum speaks, and she slaps her hand over her mouth, shaking her head, her eyes pleading with me.

"Please no. No, no no. I can't do it. I can't."

"Hey." I pull her to me, wrapping my arms around her. "Shhhh, love. It'll be alright. I won't let anyone hurt you."

And fuck. The words are the truest thing I've spoken in a long time. I know she has to leave here eventually, but I'll be fucked if I send her back into their lives.

"Why would he do this?" She sobs, and I let her vent, I let her cry, and not once do I break my hold on her. Not once do I let her feel alone.

"Jax," I plead as she falls quiet, easing back to look at her red puffy eyes, and tear stained cheeks. "I promise, I won't let anyone hurt you."

She nods, although I'm not sure if she believes me. Not really.

"I think that's enough," I say, not wanting to put her through any more, but she shakes her head.

"No," she barks, batting at her tears. "How many messages are there?"

"Two more," I admit, and she clears her throat and sits taller, trying to compose herself.

"I want to hear them."

"Maybe later—"

"No. Now!" She glares and I give in, nodding before I press play once again.

> ***Message Received from: Presley***
> *"Jax, what the fuck? The olds are freaking the fuck out and are on the phone to that psycho doctor they sent you to when you were little. You know I don't care what you do, hell, I fucking love porn, but don't let them get their clutches into you again. I can't bear to see them kill your spark. Not again. Not ever.*
> *"I will try to stall them on my end, but pack a bag and go somewhere. Anywhere they can't find you. Don't use your bank card. If they involve the cops they can track that.*
> *"Shit, Jax. I love you sis. Please stay safe."*

This time, her tears are different. Her expression morphs into love and longing.

"Your sister?" I ask, and she nods, smiling at me through her tears.

"Presley. She's my big sister." She shrugs. "You'd probably like her better than me. Most people do."

I frown. "Fuck that," I snap, and her eyes go wide. "She's not you, so no, I won't like her more than you. Fucking ever."

Her brows hitch, and fuck, her expression is filled with a level of innocence I keep forgetting she has.

"I don't get what you see in me," she whispers, and fuck, if that statement isn't heartbreaking.

"I wish you could see yourself through my eyes, little mouse. You'd see a remarkable woman. A woman that makes me want to be a better man."

She giggles. "But we only met a couple of days ago."

"Exactly. How does that even happen?" I graze my thumb over her plump lips. "Imagine how good I'll want to be after a week."

That makes her laugh, and fuck, I love the sound of it. I'd much rather that than these heartbreaking tears.

"I don't know if you should listen to the last message," I admit, and her smile fades.

"Why? Who is it from?"

Maybe I shouldn't tell her, but keeping her in the dark isn't doing her any favours. It might help to keep her here. At least until I can find this Mr V fucker and get rid of him. Then I can deal with her family.

"It's from the doctor."

Panic engulfs her expression, and I realise now, that her real terror is aimed at this man.

I want to know why. I want to know everything, but now isn't the time, and I don't want to force her to divulge that secret. The dirty ones, yes, but the real ones that plague her, that terrify her, no. I want her to reveal those secrets when she's ready.

"Are you sure you want to hear this?" I ask, and she nods, wrapping her arms around herself like she is trying to hide.

I press play anyway.

Message Received from: Unknown Number
"Hello, Jaxcen, this is Doctor Alfred Xavier. I treated you at the Holly River Estate when you were younger. Do you remember?

"I was shocked to receive a call from your father. He is extremely distressed. I know I don't have to remind you how hard it will be to return to the facility, especially as an adult. Our adult program is much more intense, but perhaps something you will benefit from. We have merged with a church, and together we do God's work to help our patients. I think this will be of great benefit to you before your wedding. Please call me back. Otherwise, I'll likely show up tomorrow with a community treatment order."

If I ever had a doubt as to who was the monster in her nightmares, I don't anymore.

She's trembling, rocking back and forth on my desk, her gaze locked on my chest, but her eyes distant.

"Is he the one you really don't want to see, Jax?" I ask, hooking my finger under her chin again to gain her attention, and as her blue gaze meets mine, she nods.

"I can't go back to him. I would rather die." Fury contorts her face. "I swear if you let him come and get me, I'll throw myself off that cliff, Devon. I will. I'll do it. I'm not even kidding."

"Okay." I hold my hands up, needing her to stop speaking that way. "But that fucker will never get in here. He'll never get past my men, and if he even dares to approach our gates, I'll order my men to kill him on the spot."

Even though she's crying, she nods, believing my declaration.

"In fact, if your fuckhead fiancé comes knocking, he'll meet the same fucking fate," I admit, and again she nods, completely content with that.

"Okay."

"Good." I nod. "Okay."

And as if the man himself has heard our conversation, Jaxcen's phone starts ringing, and Eddie's name flashes across the screen.

Chapter Nineteen
Jaxcen

My entire body stiffens at the sight of Eddie's name on my phone screen. He's calling me. This very second, he's calling me, and all I can think is aside from Dr Xavier, Eddie is the last person I want to speak to.

Darting my hand out, I go to hit decline, but Devon's hand wraps around my wrist, stilling it, his eyes hard as he pins me with them, and then he hits accept, and puts it on speaker.

My breath seizes in my lungs.

Why did he do that?

"Jaxcen!" The boom of Eddie's voice isn't concerned in the slightest that I might have been hurt or in danger, and the voice I once adored sounds like that of an enemy.

My shocked gaze darts to Devon, watching as his lips part to speak.

I have no idea what he's going to say to Eddie, but I don't want him to say he's kidnapped me, even though that's exactly what he did.

"What?" I snap before Devon speaks, and his brows shoot up at my voice.

"What? What!" Eddie scoffs. "Where the hell have you been? What's going on?"

Oh, you know, I went to a sex club and then felt guilty about it, so I went to see Father Peters and confessed my sins until some random men started shooting up the church, and this dark knight came out of nowhere, shielded me, kissed me, and then killed the men before kidnapping me and fucking me senseless.

I smirk at myself, knowing I'm not going to say that, but gosh, it would feel good rubbing that in his face.

"I've gone on a little vacation," I say instead, hearing Eddie scoff in shock through the phone, while a slow sinister smirk pulls Devon's lips wide.

I stare at them, remembering how soft they can be, but also how utterly wicked that mouth can be at times. I want to kiss those lips again. And again. And again.

"Vacation? What are you talking about?" Eddie snarls. "You can't just take a holiday at the drop of a hat, ditch out on work without approval and not tell anyone."

"My job doesn't matter." I shrug, even though he can't see me. "I'm going to quit anyway."

"The fuck you are."

"Why not?" I snap, annoyed that he thinks he has the right to tell me what to do. I suppose I've let him do it for so long that is exactly what he thinks. "I'm thinking about getting another job."

"Where." He scoffs. "You have no skills, Jaxcen. You studied Business Administration and haven't even moved out of the mailroom."

Heat flushes my cheeks and I grit my teeth.

"I haven't worked in the mailroom for over a year. And I have plenty of skills," I snap, opening and closing my mouth as I try to think of my skills, but damn him. He's right.

I'm just where he wanted me, telling me just to do a job that won't stress me out so I can focus on my faith and preparation of becoming his wife.

I want to hurl at that thought.

Why am I so easily influenced?

Because you never thought anyone would love you.

"I'm pretty good at blow jobs," I blurt, shocking myself, before I slap my hand over my mouth, my eyes wide in disbelief as Devon smirks and nods, like the cat who got the damn cream.

"What the hell did you say?" Eddie yells, the speaker on my phone crackling.

Oh well. I've gone and done it now. I may as well throw myself right over the edge.

"This one guy really likes making me gag, Eddie. You should see his face when he watches his cock slip past my lips—"

"Shut the fuck up you filthy whore!" Eddie's crazed yell is loud, but not as loud as Devon's.

"You shut the fuck up! You will never speak to Jaxcen like that again! Do you fucking understand?!"

"Oh my god," Eddie gasps. "Are you working in a whorehouse, Jaxcen? Is this one of your clients?"

"No." I beat Devon before he can respond, shooting him a glare, because even though I like him defending me, this is my fight. "He's not my client, but I do serve him. I give him whatever he wants whenever he wants and however he wants it. Even now, his cum is leaking out of me."

The phone goes dead.

My lungs stop working.

The room falls silent.

What have I done?

I stare at my phone, the black screen now all that remains, and my heart sinks.

Eddie will call my dad.

My dad will call Dr Xavier.

And Dr Xavier will take me away and...

"Jax." Devon's large hands envelop each side of my face, lifting my head so I have no choice but to look at him.

"He's going to come here."

"Who is? Eddie?" Devon asks, his deep chocolate eyes staring into mine like he wants to see my soul.

And maybe I want him to see it.

"No. Dr Xavier. He'll come for me now. He'll take me..."

"No, he fucking won't," Devon hisses, pressing his forehead to mine. "I've already told you, if he comes here, he'll get shot. Besides, Eddie doesn't know where you are. Dom already checked your phone for trackers, and you haven't shared your location with anyone, so your fiancé has no idea where to find you."

"Ex fiancé," I whisper, and a smile spreads across Devon's face.

"Well, yeah. I'm pretty sure the wedding is called off now."

I grin too. "What a shame."

Devon isn't usually like this. Soft. Caring.

It's far from the cocky guy that insisted I kiss him before he was about to die, as well as the man that held a gun to his guard's head at the gate after I tried to flirt my way out of this place.

Devon Marx may be a monster, but he's not the same kind of monster that Dr Xavier is.

Feeling more exposed than I did when Devon had me practically naked, my ankle bound to the confessional and his eyes staring at my most intimate place between my legs, uncertainty creeps its way in.

Devon doesn't know exactly what happened in my past, but I'm sure he got a good idea after listening to those voice messages, and after Eddie called.

Will he think of me the same way my parents did when I was a child? Will he decide I'm not worth protecting?

"Where are you going?" Devon's question confuses me, because I'm still perched on his desk, his large hands cupping my face as he stares into my eyes.

"I'm not going anywhere," I point out and he shakes his head a fraction.

"In your head. Where are you going?" His thumb strokes my cheek as his gaze studies me. "I feel like you slipped away there for a moment."

Shit.

I did, didn't I?

"Dr Xavier is a shrink," I admit, but Devon doesn't say anything, continuing to study my eyes like they will reveal everything. "You've already seen how unhinged I can get. Maybe it's best if you dump me on the side of the road somewhere and forget about me."

A savage frown draws in his dark brows, and he flinches back, like I tried to slap him.

"The fuck are you talking about, woman. All I've seen is someone desperate to escape, feeling trapped and in danger. That's not unhinged. That's basic human instinct."

"The knife wasn't normal, Devon," I point out.

"The knife was the most normal thing you've done," he snaps, releasing his hold of my face and stepping back.

I suddenly feel so alone.

Too alone.

"I don't know your story, little mouse, but I can tell you right fucking now, you're not crazy." He points to the wall, but as he speaks, I know he's pointing to a place far from here. "Those fuckers that make you feel bad for having desires are the crazy ones. They've been gaslighting you. Fucking with your head, and because you only want to please them, you believe their fucking lies so easily."

He spins, as if too angry to show me his face before his fist slams into the wall next to the small window.

A squeal of alarm escapes me, and he spins back, showing me that monster I've met a few times now.

"I refuse to let them bring you down any longer, Jaxcen. And I'm fucking sorry for contributing to that. Making you think I was going to kill you. That was fucked, and as fucked up as I am, I'll own that shit."

My lashes flutter with emotions I'm not used to feeling. No one has ever apologised to me before. Not like this.

I'm not used to it and I don't know what to do with it, so I brush it off.

"It's fine. Really. You were—"

"No, it's not fucking fine! Stop letting people get away with it."

He storms back to me.

"Slap me again!" he yells, his deep boom loud, sending a ripple of desire up my spine.

"What?" I mutter, dazed, too transfixed on the hard set of his jaw, and the fury contorting his expression.

What a beautiful monster.

"You heard me! Slap me again! Make me pay for the lie!" His hand whips out to wrap around my throat, much like it did earlier, and I swear heat pools between my legs once again.

There's just something about the way he manhandles me that makes me feel so free, rather than controlled or trapped. Which makes no sense at all, but maybe it's because I like it so much. I want it.

"No!" I curl my lip, pressing my nose to his, my usually quiet voice, loud.

"Yes!" he booms, releasing my neck to slam his hands on the desk either side of my legs.

"No!" I boom back, quickly wrapping my legs around his hips and pinning him between my thighs.

I can feel him. Hard. Long. Ready.

Devon growls, so I growl back, baring my teeth, and feeling every bit the unhinged person I was speaking of only minutes ago.

Hooking his arm behind my back, Devon easily lifts me, forcing me down on his desk as the last of the files and a cup holding pens crashes to the floor.

"Fucking slap me, Jaxcen!"

A bang sounds somewhere behind me, and I realise it's the door flying open before another voice joins our little party.

"What the fuck is going on?"

"Fuck off, Finn," Devon hisses, his eyes staying locked on mine as he hovers over me, the hard length of his cock, although covered by his jeans, pressing deliciously between my legs.

"Nope. Not when you two are gonna trash this whole fucking office," Finn snaps, his voice closer now, and I force my gaze from

Devon's to see him looming on the other side of the desk, glaring at his boss.

"I will smash this whole fucking place up until Jaxcen does as I ask," Devon sneers.

"No." I drag my gaze back to my monster. "Stop it, Devon."

"I'm almost certain I'm gonna regret asking this." Finn's voice is strained, "but what the fuck is it that you're asking her to do?"

Devon growls in that animalistic way he does. "I want her to slap me. Really fucking hard."

I slam my lips together as a moan threatens to expose just how turned on I am right now.

"Dude, why do you want her to slap you?"

"For the lie." Devon snarls, "For making her think she was going to die. Making her think I was taking her because she saw too much."

Finn chuckles. "Fuck man, if you want to be roughed up, I'll do it for you."

"No," Devon barks. "She needs to take back her control."

"Have you ever thought that perhaps I don't want control?"

The words are a shock as I say them, yet I know there's some truth to them.

I'm not sure if it's a result of my past, but it suddenly dawns on me why I was so devoted to Eddie, when I realise now I didn't really love him. Why I never tried to get a better job, instead being content with one with little responsibility. Why I let my parents make all the decisions for me.

I didn't want to control things.

I didn't want to be responsible.

And now, I know why.

Because when I tried to do that, I was made to feel worthless.

Devon's expression is hard, yet confusion plays around the edges of his eyes.

"Is this some sort of fucked up therapy session?" Finn asks, reminding me that we're not alone.

I shake my head. "No. I've been to those before. This isn't the same."

Finn's head comes into view as he leans over to look at me upside down. "Give me the word, Miss Summers, and I'll remove my mate from the room."

Devon doesn't even get pissed about Finn's words, and when I take him in again, I can see he'd let his friend do that.

For me.

Reaching up, I fist Devon's dark hair, my fingers gripping the short strands at the roots, and tug him so we are nose to nose again. "I don't want to slap you, but I do want you to fuck me again, and make me forget everything those people have ever done to me."

Finn curses and Devon growls before his lips slam into mine.

"Wait until I get out of the fucking room!" Finn yells, but Devon is already reaching between us to free his dick, and because I'm still pantiless, he shoves that stiff appendage into me, hard.

I cry out, even as the door closes, and I realise, Finn could have been still standing there watching, and I really wouldn't have cared.

Once again on his desk, Devon makes me forget all my fears.

This time when Devon fucks me, it's not the same as before. Even though he consumed both holes down there before, this time, his entire being consumes me. It wraps around me like a security blanket filled with ecstasy.

Is that even a thing?

It should be.

Because this is something else.

I come twice while Devon pounds into me, giving me everything I asked for and more. His deep voice rasps against my ear, telling me how good my cunt is, and his lips nibble at my neck and ear and lips, like he can't get enough of tasting me.

Afterwards, I'm totally spent. For a moment I fear my limbs have dropped off because I can't feel them, but the moment he scoops me up in his arms, and lays me on the sofa in his office, the feeling returns to my arms and legs.

"You're going to fall asleep on me again, aren't you." He grins, rebuttoning my dress before tending to the mess between my legs, where he shoves his leaking cum back inside like he has so many times.

"We need to talk about your obsession with knocking me up," I mutter lazily, and he chuckles.

"There's nothing to talk about, little mouse."

"If it was a ploy to stop my wedding, then you can stop now," I mutter lazily. "There's not going to be a wedding between me and Eddie." I blink up at him, and he reaches out, stroking some of my hair off my forehead.

"It's not a ploy to sabotage your wedding. I just want to see your round belly and know that you're carrying my kid."

I frown. "You make no sense. We still don't even know each other."

"On the contrary. I think I know you better than anyone else does."

I'd blush if I had the energy, but since all my blood is most likely still near my coochie, there's no rush of heat to my face.

He has a point, though. He does know me better than anyone else.

"Your reasoning has holes in it," I counter and he smirks down at me, those dark eyes appearing more tender than I've ever seen them.

"It's straightforward to me."

I roll my eyes. "I think you're the only one that sees it like that."

Leaning down, he hovers his lips over mine. "My opinion is the only one that matters to you, little mouse." Then he presses his soft lips to mine.

It's another one of his gentle kisses that fills my chest with warmth I've never felt until he slammed into my life.

Is it weird that he makes me feel worshipped from both his gentle kisses, and the devouring ones?

For a little while, we chat about mundane things like TV shows, the best season of the year, and whether or not pineapple should be on pizza.

I'm a pineapple pizza girlie all the way.

At some point, I doze off, and when I wake a little later, I'm alone in his office.

My body aches everywhere, in the best way, and as I sit up, I can't wipe the smile off my face.

This whole scenario is weird, yet I feel so good. I feel like a veil has been lifted and for the first time, I'm truly experiencing who Jaxcen Summers is.

It's a strange thought, given it revolves around sex, but I feel like it's more than that. It's like Devon has given me permission and a safe space to find myself, and I desperately don't want to leave it.

I don't want to go back to the person I was a couple of days ago. She's no longer inside me.

I take a moment searching around Devon's desk and on the floor for my panties and come up empty.

I bet he's pocketed them again.

Cheeky bugger.

Spotting another note in what I'm becoming familiar with as Devon's handwriting, I read it eagerly.

Meeting with my men.
Be back soon.
x Dev

There's that damn kiss again.

My heart flips like I've just received my first love letter. And hell, maybe the one from earlier and this one are the closest I'll ever get.

Eddie sure as shit never gave me one.

Sure he wrote to me when I was in the facility, but they weren't love letters.

He sent me scriptures and things to pray for.

Ugh, why couldn't I see what he was doing?

Just by the note on the desk is my phone, and I glance up at the door, wondering if I take it, will I get into trouble.

Jesus, Jaxcen. Are you going to keep letting people dictate your life, or are you going to own it?

My brows shoot up at my inner thoughts and I grin, deciding that it's my phone, so I'll be the one to be in possession of it.

Going into my contacts, I bring up Presley's number and hit call, anxiously waiting for it to connect, and when it does, my heart does another flip.

"Jax, is that you?"

"Hey, Pres. Sorry about all the fuss. Are you alright?"

"Yeah, I'm fine," she says a little stiffly, and I frown.

Damn, is she angry at me?

"Look, I'm sorry. I'll explain later but I'm okay. Truly," I admit, and she falls quiet for a moment before I hear her wary voice.

"I'm not sure you are." Her tone is hushed. Unsure. So unlike my confident big sister.

"I already told you I am," I mutter, annoyed.

Pres is the only one that has ever fought for me. Not that she had much luck against my parents, but she's always tried and she never judged me. Not ever.

"Where are you Jax? Tell me where you are and I'll come and get you."

I frown. "No, you can't."

"Why?" she asks, her tone sounding way off my normally supportive sister.

Hell, she even left me a message and told me to hide, and what? Now she wants me to come out and potentially get caught.

"I'm doing what you said, Pres. I'm hiding," I explain before a scuffle crackles through the speaker sounding like she dropped it. But then, I hear her yell in the background.

"Don't do what they want, Jax. Stay there!"

What the...

"Jaxcen. This is Dr Xavier. You need to come to me, please."

All the breath whooshes from my lungs at hearing that voice again. His voice.

No.

"You're sick, Jaxcen. You need help. Come to me and I'll help you."

"No," I whisper, feeling like a child again. A teenager with no options.

Dr Xavier sighs. "Jaxcen, I'm not only worried about you, but your sister too. I think Presley could use some treatment too. Don't you think?"

My hand trembles as I squeeze the phone, tears welling in my eyes as panic sets in.

No. No. No.

Not again.

I can't go back.

"Leave her alone," I snap, but he chuckles.

"I'm afraid I can't do that unless you come in. If you want to help your sister then you know what you have to do."

Tears spill over as I shake my head. "Please don't do this. Not now. It's almost Christmas and I want to spend it with my family."

"Christmas is three days away. If you behave and do everything you're supposed to, I might be able to grant you leave on Christmas day."

"Don't do it, Jaxcen!" Presley yells in the background before she cries out like she's in pain.

"Stop! Don't hurt her!" I plead.

"She'll be fine as long as you do the right thing, Jaxcen. Come to your sister's apartment. You have an hour."

"Wait. I can't get there in an hour. I'm too far away."

"You have two hours then, and not a second more." The line goes dead and a sob leaps from my lips.

I have to go. I have to save my sister.

Chapter Twenty

Devon

The minute Dom and Lenny come charging into the meeting room at the back of the Palace, I know they have news. Finn perks up beside me at seeing their stiff postures and serious expressions, his green eyes darting my way.

The fucker is an adrenalin junkie. He loves drama, and loves getting his hands dirty and one thing he hates about Christmas is how the killing business tends to die off for a week or so.

I guess even the scum of the earth celebrate the most ridiculous holy celebration that most people don't even recognise other than gift giving and filling bellies while getting drunk.

The latter is the only perk if you ask me.

"What do you have?" I ask as they sit quickly, and Miles joins us, his hulking frame folding into a seat much too small for him.

"I'm sorry we didn't find the connection until now." Dom starts, our resident hacker looking a little nervous. "We've been so focused on finding Mr V that the pictures you sent from Melissa's phone got pushed to the side."

I frown, about to ask what that has to do with Mr V when Lenny butts in.

"Dom was stressing himself out, so I told him to take a break and work on something else for a bit while I continued searching CCTV footage for the car, and that's when he did a deep dive into the profile you sent him that was from Melissa's phone."

"It's him," Dom continues, tossing some grainy pictures on the table as I stare at the man I killed over a year ago.

"Fit Nick is dead. I fucking killed him myself." I spit and Lenny nods.

"You did, but this fucker..." He jabs his finger onto the grainy picture. "This fucker is Vincent Ballen, Nick's little brother who fucking resembles Nick so much so that he's taken over his social media and kept Nick's profile alive with his own fucking selfies."

Fuck.

"This makes much more sense now," I mutter, and my men nod.

"So Melissa's ex that you killed has a younger brother seeking revenge?" Miles confirms and I nod.

"Looks like it." I turn my gaze to Lenny. "Do we have a location yet?"

"No location yet, but now that we know who it is, we have a better chance at finding him."

"Good. I'd like to get it done before Christmas."

"I thought you didn't like Christmas." Finn smirks and I shoot him a glare.

"I fucking don't."

"Uh-huh. This year's different though, isn't it?" He chuckles and my other men grin. "Wouldn't have anything to do with that feisty blonde you kidnapped?"

I flip him off, and the men erupt in laughter.

I let them off this time. Normally I'd tell them to pull their heads in and focus, but today all I can think about is said blonde asleep in my office, not wearing any panties and dreaming about all the filthy things I've done to her.

Fuck. That thought has my cock waking up.

Down boy.

An alarm tone from not just mine, but all of our phones has me picking the thing up off the table and opening the alert message just as fast as my men.

Their curses fill the room as I read the alert.

Gate Breach - Outbound.

"The fuck!" I yell, standing and charging from the room as I call the front gate. Aaron answers on the first ring. "What's happened?"

"Sir, I'm sorry. She came charging for us in the Corvette, and you said we weren't allowed to shoot her."

"The fuck!" I boom again, "Tell me you didn't just let my guest fucking leave?!"

"She was going to run us down, and she drove that thing right through the gate. They are reinforced to stop that happening from the other side, but not from the inside."

"FUCK!" I roar, slamming my fist into the wall beside me before a hand comes to my shoulder.

"Calm down, man. Try to think clearly," Finn mutters close to my ear, and fuck, he's the only one I wouldn't kill for telling me to fucking calm down.

I end the call to the front gate and bring up my cousin's number before turning to Dom. "Bring up the gate footage in my office now."

He nods and hurries around me, charging down the hall towards my office.

"What are you gonna do?" Finn asks as we follow Dom.

"Well, I gotta tell my cousin his car has just been stolen and hope he doesn't fucking hunt me down and remove my balls from my body."

Finn chuckles, slapping me on the shoulder as I call my cousin.

It rings a couple of times before Conrad answers, sounding a little drunk.

"Sup, cuz? How's my sexy princess?"

Fuck. He calls his car, Princess. This isn't going to end well.

"Hey, yeah, uh... She's currently ripping up the pavement out here in the sticks."

"You don't sound like you're driving right now," Conrad asks, confused, and I grip the back of my neck.

"Yeah, that's because I'm not driving her," I admit, entering my office to see Dom at my computer, his fingers flying over the keyboard as he logs into the video footage from the front gate.

"But you just said…"

"Look, I'll be frank. My guest is driving the Corvette."

"What!" Conrad booms and I pull the phone away from my ear as the speaker crackles. "You're fucking kidding, right?! That's a five hundred thousand dollar car, Dev! Why would you let some chick drive it?"

"I didn't let her exactly."

"Dev." He sneers in warning and I can imagine him gritting his teeth.

Dom waves me over, so I round the desk to look at the screen, watching Aaron and Bruno fly up from their posts, guns in hand as they start yelling before their stance turns panicked. It's then that the Corvette comes onto the screen, so fast I'm a little fucking impressed, right before my men dive out of the way and the Corvette bursts through the gates, speeding off down the road.

"Are you listening to me!" Conrad's voice registers and I realise I must have zoned out as I watched my little mouse make her escape.

Fuck.

I really thought she'd stay.

My eyes fall to my desk where her phone was and the note I left her to see two words written under my message, the handwriting perfectly neat.

I'm sorry.

"Do you have tracking on the car?" I ask my cousin.

"Of course I have tracking on her." He snarls like it's the most ridiculous question ever.

"Good. Track her and tell me where she goes. I'm going to get her." I spit, storming from my office.

"I hope you mean my Princess?"

"No, I fucking mean *my* Princess, and she'd better be prepared for the punishment she'll receive for this."

Chapter Twenty-One

Jaxcen

Not only have I stolen a car, but I've broken so many road laws speeding from Woodall Ridge to get back into the city in time. I can't let them hurt Presley, and I know what's going to happen to me, but I'd rather sacrifice myself than let anyone hurt my sister.

She doesn't know what they'll do to her.

I don't want her to ever know!

My cheeks are still damp with tears, but I stopped crying the moment I reached the inner city, too focused on getting to my sister's apartment without getting noticed by police.

The dent at the front of the Corvette is already getting attention from Melbournians walking on the streets, and I have to hope the car hasn't been listed as stolen just yet.

I just need to get to Presley.

Taking an illegal turn over the tram tracks, I dodge a Range Rover before turning up the wrong way of a quieter one way street, and slam on the brakes, skidding the sleek red car to a stop before throwing the door open, grabbing my phone and leaping out.

My phone rang about five times on my way here. I didn't recognise the number, but I have no doubt it was Devon.

He'll hate me for leaving. He'll think I did it to be stubborn, but I couldn't tell him the real reason why. He would have tried to stop me and then my sister... No. I can't even think about what would happen to her.

Hurrying to the glass doors of the apartment building, I key in the code and the door clicks open. The lift up to the fourteenth floor is too slow. It feels like the longest minute of my life, and when it finally stops and the doors ease open, I slip out and run up the carpeted passage to my sister's apartment.

I have the code for her door too, so I don't bother knocking, keying it in and stepping inside as soon as it opens.

Standing in the entrance of her apartment, I listen for voices but hear nothing, so I click the door closed and slowly walk up the hall that opens to the small kitchen and living room.

"Cutting it close." Eddie sneers from the kitchen counter where he's sitting rigidly on a stool.

I'm not sure why he's here too, but it doesn't surprise me. He's the one that set this in motion, after all.

"Where's Presley?" I ask, my eyes moving through the room to see my father and Dr Xavier.

The sight of the man that haunts my nightmares sends a rush of nausea to my stomach, and I try to force the feeling away by keeping my focus on why I'm here.

Presley.

"Presley went back home with your mother about an hour ago," my dad answers, and I glare at him, my eyes burning as I realise they were never going to take Presley in for treatment.

They knew I'd come to save her.

I've been tricked.

"You don't need me then, do you." I spin on my heel and hurry up the passage, my sight set on the door and just getting beyond it.

"You're not leaving," Eddie sneers from behind me before my hair is yanked back and I cry out, feeling some of my blonde strands rip from the roots, "unless it's with Dr Xavier."

"No!" I scream, hoping to cause enough attention that a neighbour might hear as Eddie overpowers me and drags me back into the living area, where my father and the doctor look bored.

I hate them.

I hate them all!

"You need to go with the doctor, Jaxcen," my father insists, not an ounce of compromise in his tone.

"No. Daddy. I don't need to." I plead as Eddie releases me and I stumble forward, too close to Dr Xavier who I haven't seen in a number of years.

He looks a little older, but I'd never forget those eyes, or that voice.

"Listen to your father, Jaxcen. You know it's for the best," the doctor insists.

"No." I shake my head, wrapping my arms around me as I take a step back, only to bump into Eddie's chest.

"You're not thinking straight," my dad snaps, like this whole thing is an inconvenience. "You've been led astray. Sinned in the worst way, but I forgive you. Eddie forgives you. Just go with Dr Xavier."

"No, Daddy." I sob, my emotions taking over. "You don't know what he does."

"You will go with him now, Jaxcen." My father ignores me, his words clipped.

I'll never be safe around these three men.

Spinning on my heel, I knee Eddie in his junk and take off again towards the entrance, but this time, two men, dressed in some sort of medical uniform, step inside the apartment, their hard eyes trained on me.

No.

I skid to a stop, quickly backing up, realising I'm trapped.

As I step backwards into the living area, ignoring Eddie's groaning, my eyes dart to the glass doors that lead out to a narrow balcony.

My words from earlier flash through my mind. I'd said them to Devon, and I meant them.

There's only one way out.

And it's through those doors.

I charge for them, shoving Eddie to the side and hearing him crash into something, while Dr Xavier's voice yells something I can't make out, not with the way my blood is rushing past my ears.

This is it.

It's time to fly.

Nearly slamming into the door, I fiddle with the latch trying to get it unlocked, and just as I do and pull it open, the sounds of the city rushing in and the light breeze hitting my face, rough hands grab me from behind.

I open my mouth to scream, but the biting sting of a needle pierces my neck and a hand slaps over my mouth dragging me back in before I can jump to my death.

No. No. No.

It might have been death but it would have been freedom to no longer be here and endure this.

I kick out and try to swing my fists, but the two male nurses are beyond strong, and my attempts are futile.

The burn of the sedative runs through my veins quickly, like a rush of heat and relaxation, yet my mind is still panicked. My mind knows what comes next.

"No, Daddy." I slur one last plea to get him to stop this, but he just shakes his head.

"You look like a cheap whore with those marks on your neck," he snarls, and a tear pops free of my eye before everything goes black.

CHAPTER TWENTY-TWO

Devon

"The fuck." Finn mutters as we approach Presley Summers' apartment building in the city, the red Corvette pulled half up on the sidewalk facing the wrong fucking way.

"Why do I get the feeling she was in a fucking hurry?" I snap.

"If she was trying to hide from you, surely she'd hide the car," Finn says what I'm thinking as he eases the car to a stop in front of the Corvette, and I fucking ignore how banged up the front is knowing Conrad is going to lose his shit.

"Call Dom. Get him to check Jaxcen's call records," I snap, opening the door and slipping out. "I have a bad fucking feeling about this."

I thought she'd run because I'd kidnapped her, but now I'm not so sure.

Finn does as I ask, his voice fading as I step up to the driver's side door of the Corvette to find it unlocked. Taking a peek inside, I can see her phone isn't in here, and neither are the keys, so I close the door and glance up at the tall apartment building.

Presley Summers lives on the fourteenth floor. Apartment 1408. Funnily enough, this is a Marx building, although no one would know it. It's owned by a shell corporation which falls under my Uncle Ewan's ownership.

"You know my brother is going to have your nuts for this."

I grin at hearing my cousin, Liam's, voice and turn to see him in a suit, taking a drag of a cigarette with one hand in his pocket.

"He can have them as soon as I find my girl."

Liam's brows hitch. "Your girl? When did that happen?"

I sigh, pinching the bridge of my nose. "I don't fucking know."

"Fuuuck, man. I never thought I'd see the day big bad Devon the devil would be all twisted up over a girl."

"Shut up," I mutter, and Liam laughs. "Why isn't Connie here?"

Dropping his smoke to the path, Liam toes it out and blows the smoke up into the air above his head before responding. "The fucker is too drunk. I promised him I'd handle it."

"I appreciate it." I smirk, knowing Liam is saving my arse.

"You owe me, man." He points at me as Finn approaches.

"Dom said a call was made from Jaxcen's phone to the number registered to Presley Summers. He also said Jaxcen's phone location is here, but Presley's left a while ago and is travelling north towards the border."

"I have a bad fucking feeling," I mutter before turning back to my cousin. "You have the master key?"

"Yep. Got it here." He holds it up and gestures to the front doors of the building. "Let's check things out."

Following my cousin, he opens the doors and takes us up to the fourteenth floor, leading us to the apartment that Jaxcen's phone is located in. When Liam raises his hand to knock, I snatch the key off him and put it in the lock, not wanting to bother with pleasantries.

If Jaxcen is inside then no one is stepping in my way.

I throw the door open, and it bangs against the wall, my eyes darting up the narrow passage that opens into a living area.

"You back so soon, Eddie?" a male voice calls, and my spine fucking stiffens at hearing that fucking name.

Eddie.

It takes me six long strides to get to the mouth of the room, my gaze quickly taking in the space, only to find it occupied by one man.

"Who the hell are you?" he snaps, but I ignore him, pointing to the other passage off the room, and Finn darts past me, gun raised as he heads in that direction to check it out.

On the kitchen counter, is a phone, and I recognise the rose gold trim.

It's Jaxcen's.

And right next to the phone are the keys to the Corvette.

"Keys are on the bench," I mutter over my shoulder, and Liam steps around me to scoop them up.

"What the hell are you doing?" the older man asks, and as I scan the space, I see a few pictures on the walls, one of which has Jaxcen in it, as well as this man.

"Mr Summers, I presume?" I ask, and he frowns.

"Who wants to know?"

"Where's Jaxcen?" I ignore his questions and he frowns.

"How do you know Jaxcen?"

"I'm asking the fucking questions!" I yell, curling my lip and wanting to punch something.

"The fuck you are!" he yells back and I grit my teeth.

"The place is empty." Finn's voice comes from behind me as he approaches.

"Grab her phone from the bench." I gesture my head in that direction, not taking my eyes off the man cornered in the living room.

"Hey! Leave that alone. That doesn't belong to you," Mr Summers snaps, and I smirk, tilting my head to the side to study the slightly overweight man.

"It doesn't belong to you either." I point out. "Where is Jaxcen?"

"Not here." He glares at me, and my lips thin.

"We can do this one of two ways. Either you tell me freely where your daughter is, or I force it out of you." I pace to the glass doors that lead out to a narrow balcony, and notice the smudge of a handprint on the glass.

It could be Presley's. Or it could be Jaxcen's.

I grit my teeth again, turning back to my girl's father.

"You can't just come in here and threaten me."

"Can't I?" I shrug, glancing at my cousin.

"It looks like you already have." He smirks, leaning against the bench, and I nod, dragging my gaze back to Jaxcen's dad.

"Yep. Looks like I have. So what's it going to be? The easy way? Or the hard way?"

"Don't you know who I am?" he yells, but I fucking snap.

"DON'T YOU KNOW WHO I AM?!" I roar, storming forward, my gun raised, and I stalk him as he shuffles backwards until his back hits the far wall. "You'll fucking regret not answering my questions!"

Mr Summers' face turns red in fear as I press the barrel of my gun to his temple, and Liam chuckles behind me.

"Don't you know what happens if you don't cooperate with a Marx?"

"A-a-a M-Marx?"

"Yes." I seethe. "A fucking Marx. Wanna take a stab at which one I am?"

Trembling, Mr Summers shakes his head, but fuck that, I'm gonna introduce myself anyway.

"I'm the fucking devil."

He baulks, the redness washing away from his face as he turns ghost white.

"Looks like he's heard of you." Finn snickers.

"W-why do you want m-my daughter?" Mr Summers stutters again, and I fucking grin.

"Because she gives the best head I've ever fucking had."

Finn curses while Liam laughs and Jaxcen's dad sputters in disbelief.

"Are you gonna make me ask again?"

"You! You're the one who defiled her. You left those marks on her neck."

I nod, fucking proudly, flashing him a cheesy smile. "Wanna know how many times she came around my cock while I sucked on her neck?"

"Stop it." He squeezes his eyes shut like that will stop him from hearing.

"Did she show you the one on her inner thigh, right near her puss—"

A weak punch lands on my jaw, and I fucking roar laughing, before returning the fucking favour.

The crunch of his nose is loud, and blood sprays out, his wailing piercing as he falls to his knees in pain.

"Where the fuck is she?"

Shaking his head in refusal, I realise he's not going to cave easily, so I turn back to Finn and hold out my hand. "My shears."

"Ha-haaa. Now we're talking." Liam celebrates the fact there's about to be a whole lot of blood in the room.

"No. No. Please."

Again I ignore the man, taking the shears from Finn before we approach and Finn wrestles Jaxcen's dad, forcing his hand out to me.

"All you have to do is tell me where Jaxcen is." I remind him, and when he keeps saying no over and over, I pry his pinky from his balled fist and position my shears.

"Here we go." Liam sing-songs behind me before I snap the shears shut, severing the finger as he wails louder.

"Come on, daddy dearest. Tell me where she is." I prompt, but he still mutters no's through his sobbing, so I pry his ring finger from his fist, and repeat the process, severing another finger.

"Where is she?!" I snarl, preparing the middle finger, and when he doesn't answer, that fucking thing goes too.

When I move to his index finger, that's when he caves, his sobs barely comprehensible, so I scoop up his severed fingers and let Finn release him.

"Xavier," he mutters.

"The doctor?" I ask, staring into the terrified and pained eyes of Jaxcen's father.

"Y-yes. He took h-her."

"Why?" I ask, and when he doesn't respond, I move to the kitchen counter and hover my hand over the garbage disposal sink. "You want your fingers back, you'd better fucking answer me."

"S-she's sick. Needs treatment."

I scoff. "She's not fucking sick. You are. That god preaching fiancé of hers is. Not Jaxcen. She's fucking perfect."

"She's behaving like a w-whore."

I grit my teeth, staring at the man that raised Jaxcen and was a part of the damage she carries.

"Well, she's my fucking whore. And I want her back." I snap, letting his fingers drop into the garbage disposal as he cries out, begging for his digits back.

I hit the button, and the loud grinding of his bones fills the room, as the grown man starts sobbing like a fucking baby.

"You don't fuck with the devil," Liam snickers, and I swear, if he had popcorn, he'd be lounging back and eating it as he watches this whole fucking scene.

I take a moment to rinse my hands off as Mr Summers wails about his fucking fingers, and then I glance at my cousin, hoping he's feeling generous.

"I'm gonna need men. More than I have. You think your old man will give me Riggs and his team for a few hours?"

Liam beams, his teeth flashing as he nods. "Riggs always enjoys playing with the devil."

Chapter Twenty-Three

Jaxcen

It's happening again. I can't move. I'm here but I'm not. My body feels heavy yet weightless, and I'm frozen. Trapped inside myself. Inside a dark place that wants to swallow me whole.

Sometimes, bursts of sounds come to me. Voices, male, yet I can't make out what they say. Any time I try to open my eyes, I can't. It's like my lids are sewn shut, but I know they aren't. I've been here before. I know what this is.

It feels like hours that I try to break through the thick haze that keeps me under, and when I finally do, I want to return to the nothingness of the drug induced sleep I've been in. It feels safer there.

I blink rapidly, letting my eyes adjust as I lay still, not wanting to alert anyone that I'm awake. The sterile room surrounding me is white, cold, and barren. My eyes find the window, the familiar sight taking me back to when I was younger.

The grates over the windows allow light to come in, but no way of getting out. I used to spend so much time looking at the framing, analysing how I could find a way to break through.

There's no escaping this place though.

"Good morning." A male nurse enters the room, and I scurry to sit up, making my head spin. "Careful there, Miss Summers. You're still medicated."

I glare at him, I think. It's hard to tell with how numb I feel.

"I need to leave," I slur, hating the way I sound.

"You can leave after your treatment." He smiles, his dark moustache looking like a caterpillar as he approaches me. "Let's go to the bathroom, hey. Time to freshen up a bit."

I shake my head and mutter a no, but he easily takes my arm and leads me off the bed.

"I don't wanna go pee," I slur again and he chuckles.

"Yeah you do. You just can't feel it yet." He eases me across the room and flicks the light on inside the small bathroom, its fluorescent bright, hurting my eyes.

I flinch away, yet he still leads me in, and before I know it, he turns me, lifts my gown and helps me sit back.

"Where are my undies?" I ask, my head feeling heavy as I try to lift it higher to look at the man as he lowers to his haunches.

"You weren't wearing any when you came in." He lifts my gown and peers between my legs. "Besides, you don't need them here. They just get in the way."

I feel it then, the brush of his fingers touching between my legs.

"W-what are you doing?"

I lift my hand to try and push him away, but it's too heavy, and flops back to my side.

"Helping you go to the toilet." He smiles at me, and I think I frown, because I don't know why he'd need to touch me there for me to pee. "Can you feel that?"

I do. I feel it, and it doesn't feel good. I don't want him touching me there, and I know, even with how dazed I feel, that the press of his fingers to my nub is not needed to help me.

"Stop. Please," I slur, and he just smiles up at me. "I will stop once you've gone to the toilet."

The hot ache that engulfs my chest every time I cry seeps past the fog clouding me, but not enough to actually get tears to fall. Yet inside, I want to scream.

Just pee, Jaxcen. Then he'll stop.

Not sure if he meant what he said, I know there's only one way to find out, so I close my eyes, try to ignore how he touches me and focus on emptying my bladder.

It takes a bit, his fingers distracting me more than I'd like, but eventually, the hot stream starts flowing from me, and he stops, smiling at me like I've done a good job.

Mr whoever you are. I would kindly like to take a pen and stab your eye.

When I'm done, I try to clean myself up as best I can, before the perverted nurse helps me up and back out to my room.

My eyes are focused on my bed, so I get a little disoriented when he steers me in a different direction that takes us out of my room and up the passage.

Christmas music. I hear it playing softly through the speakers, but when I glance around, there's not a decoration in sight. All the bedroom doors are open except for one, and when we slowly pass by, I see the lone silhouette of a female sitting over at the window.

"Where is everyone?" I slur again, trying to look up at the man, but that task combined with walking is all too hard, and I drop my head onto his arm as he leads me.

"It's only you and Frankie this time of year. Everyone else has gone home for Christmas."

Frankie? Is that her? The woman sitting in the window that I saw?

I think about asking, but by the time I work the words to my lips, we are walking through another door, and the scent hits me, having more of an effect on me than what I see.

Dr Xavier.

I'll never forget his scent. It reminds me of stepping into a dentist surgery, mixed with something smokey, like cigars.

I try to stop my feet from moving, but the man leading me just tugs a little harder, forcing me inside to sit me down on a seat at the small round dining table.

It reminds me of one I've sat at recently.

Devon's.

Memories come at me then, the dark eyes that terrify most, yet set me on fire. The lips that taste and nibble at me like I'm delectable. Hands that dominate me, yet have the gentlest touch.

I wanna go home.

"There we go, Miss Summers," the male nurse says before leaning over to get in my line of sight. "You have fun with Dr Xavier, and I'll be back to get you later." He bites his lip as two of his fingers press to mine and sink into my mouth. "Hmmm. I have a special treat for you tonight."

"Thank you, Hamish. I'll call for you once we are done."

Dr Xavier's voice saves me from this perverted nurse, but who's going to save me from him?

My lazy gaze moves across the two place settings and the bowl of salad in the middle of the table before Dr Xavier's looming form takes the seat next to mine and I slowly turn my eyes to him.

"You've gone and gotten yourself in a spot of trouble, haven't you, Jaxcen?" he asks, but I don't respond. "And now we have to fix you. Make you compliant again. Make sure you know your place."

I'm glaring. Well, I hope I am. I want to, but I can't feel my face enough to know if it's working.

"You know, Eddie was prepared to take you the way I left you. He's been very aware of the treatment we provide. As is your father. How do you think your mother became so compliant?"

I frown. I think.

Did my mum come here?

"Presley's a different story. She was obedient from the beginning, doing as your parents asked, but you, Jaxcen, have a way of doing the opposite. Look at what happened when you put your nose in where it didn't belong as a child. You were given clear instructions not to speak of what happened in Sunday school, yet that's exactly what you did. And you thought you were helping that girl, didn't you? You thought she wanted it to stop, but she got angry at you, didn't she."

I gulp, remembering something I don't want to.

"And when you took the secrets outside the room, it wasn't only you that was punished, was it."

Tears, I feel them burning the back of my eyes, which must mean the medication is starting to wear off.

Dr Xavier must notice too, because he pushes a glass of juice towards me.

"Drink up, Jaxcen."

My gaze drops to the juice. Orange I think. And everything inside me is screaming not to drink it.

He always asked me to drink the juice at the beginning of our sessions. It took me too long to realise what was happening. I was too young and naive. I thought it was the hypnosis that dragged me into a dark mental cage, trapping me within, but it was the drink. Or at least the drug inside the drink.

I could feel it all. I just couldn't move. Couldn't make a noise.

"Drink the juice," he orders again, but I'm still caught in my memories. Still caught in the nightmare.

It started out simple. Him talking to me softly, making me feel like I was safe, only to stand over me, take his dick out of his pants, and wank it over my head before ejaculating on my face.

After a few sessions of that, the touching began. Over my clothes at first, but then he went under, and I couldn't talk to say no. I couldn't move to push him away. All I could do was experience every second while screaming inside my head and pounding my subconscious to wake up.

I tried so hard to be good so he'd send me home, and eventually he did. I got handed back to my dad and my sessions became monthly outpatient sessions.

I'd go every month and for a while he did nothing. It's like I forgot how much of a monster he was. I figured because I was an outpatient, that sort of treatment was over.

I was wrong.

"Drink it!" he yells this time, becoming impatient, and I manage to shake my head and slur.

"No."

"Jaxcen, Jaxcen, Jaxcen," he sighs. "For this treatment to work, I need you paralysed."

I flinch as he lurches forward, taking the drink and moving to my side.

"You're more experienced now, Jaxcen, so we have to increase the intensity of the treatment. Make sure it sticks this time so you don't step out of line again."

Fisting my hair, he tugs my head back, and a whimper escapes me as his hard hazel eyes bore into mine.

"Open this pretty mouth," he demands, releasing my hair to grip my jaw, the action opening my mouth. "Drink it."

He pours the juice into my mouth, and I start choking, juice flowing over the sides of my mouth and down each side of my neck as he holds my mouth open, and although I fight it, my need to breathe has me gulping down mouthfuls of juice, and I'm almost certain I'm about to drown.

Chapter Twenty-Four

Devon

With guns raised we enter right through the front doors, while some of Riggs' men go through the back. The reception counter is unattended with a sign to press the buzzer for assistance, but we bypass that, Lenny leaping over the counter and breaking through the staff door to release the security doors that let us in.

"We're in," Finn says beside me and we scan the space, the men checking in every room we pass.

"We're in too." Riggs confirms through the small earpiece in my ear, letting us know they have entered the back part of the building.

The facility, Holly River Estate, was mentioned in the voice message left by Dr Xavier, so I knew where to go, since the place borders the Holly River.

The building looks like an aged care facility from the road. The grounds lush. Lots of open air. Manicured gardens. A look of luxury.

Inside is a different fucking matter.

"Hey! What are you d—" the male nurse's voice cuts off a second after I squeeze the trigger, the silencer doing its thing to keep our presence covert.

"One gopher down," I say into my wrist mic, informing Riggs and his men of my kill.

Eyeing the now dead man and the red oozing blood from the bullet hole in his forehead, I pass by an open door and halt.

Unlike the other rooms that have beds with no sheets, this room has a made bed with strewn sheets, but nothing else.

Locking eyes with Finn, I gesture my head into the room, letting him know that I'm taking a look, and enter quickly, checking the bathroom to find it empty.

Approaching the bed, I stare at it and wonder if Jaxcen had been sleeping there. If this is the room they locked her in.

Leaning down, I press my head to the pillow and breathe in the familiar sweet scent of honey and oat milk. It's the shampoo I left for her in my shower.

Fuck. She's been here.

"Anything?" Finn asks quietly from the doorway, and I turn my menacing glare to him.

"She slept here. I can fucking smell her."

"Fuck." Finn steps aside so I can pass.

We now know this is definitely where my girl is, and that knowledge has me moving faster, my urgency to have her back in my arms fucking impalpable.

"We got a lamb." Miles mutters from a door up further, so I hurry forward to the closed door.

There, inside the room, only backlit by the light coming through the grate on the window, is a silhouette of a female, sitting, staring right back at us, which we can only make out because Finn shines his flashlight through the viewing window in the door.

Eyes, dark and sinister stare back, and I have to say, nothing much unsettles me, but this... This woman, or girl or whoever she is, gives me slasher vibes. Or something like that.

"Collateral or rescue?" Miles asks, and I open my mouth to respond, but Finn beats me to it.

"Rescue."

Miles turns to face Finn. "She looks pretty crazy man."

Gritting his teeth, Finn leans in close to Miles, getting in his face. "You'd be crazy too, if you were locked up and endured whatever it is they fucking do here. She's a fucking rescue." He jabs Miles. "Don't fucking question me."

Deciding to leave them to hash that shit out, I keep moving, seeing a sign hanging from the ceiling up ahead, with the name Dr Xavier on it.

Fucking Dr Xavier. I'm gonna gut that fucker.

"What are you doing!" a male voice yells behind us, and the click of a silenced weapon, followed by the thump of a body falling assures me my men have that shit handled.

The moment I reach the door and hear a whimper, I kick the fucking thing open, gun raised as I storm in.

There, across the room is a man, close in age to Jaxcen's dad, practically waterboarding my girl with what looks like orange juice.

"Step away, motherfucker!"

"Who are..." he trails off, his eyes wide as he watches over my shoulder, obviously seeing my men enter behind me.

My gaze darts to Jaxcen, her blonde hair a tangled mess like someone had their hands in it, her already frail body haphazardly covered in a pale blue hospital gown as she sits slumped in a chair at a fucking dining table.

What the fuck is going on here?

"Jaxcen," I call as I approach, but she doesn't answer, too busy gasping for air. "Jaxcen?" I try again, my gaze darting to the doctor as he takes a step away from her.

Rounding the table, my little mouse comes into view, the only colour in her skin is the remnants of juice trailing down her chin and neck, soaking the neckline of her gown.

"Little mouse?" I say, my voice not giving away the fucking panic I'm feeling, and finally, those big blue eyes slowly track to me.

"Dev," she mumbles, her voice slurred.

Fuck.

She's drugged.

I see fucking red and turn my sights on to the man that would dare to harm her.

Two fucking strides is all it takes for me to reach him as he holds his hands out, thinking that will keep me back.

Fucking wrong, arsehole.

Gripping the back of his neck, I lurch him towards the table and slam his face into the surface, hearing his nose crack before he cries out.

"Stop. I was just doing what I've been paid to do."

I force his head up and slam it down again.

My eyes dart to Jaxcen, still slumped in the chair, but her eyes are watching everything that's happening, and fuck if that doesn't make me want to spend hours torturing this fucker.

Dragging him up again, I force him into the chair as Finn approaches with something in his hand.

A pill bottle. Rohypnol. The script made out to Jaxcen Summers. Fuck.

My eyes meet Finn's, and he shoots me a sympathetic look.

"Date rape drug," he whispers, and I nod, already knowing that.

Snatching the pill container off my mate, I turn back to the doctor, who's looking around in every direction, probably trying to figure out a path to his freedom, while I pour a number of the meds into my palm.

"Did I just walk in to find you forcing my girl to drink this juice?" I point to the jug on the table, lift it and start pouring more into the glass he'd used for Jaxcen.

"I...I..."

"The correct answer is yes," I snap, placing the jug of juice back down and lifting the glass. As I round the table again, I nod to Finn, who approaches from the other side, and the doctor starts to panic, his head darting from me to Finn and back.

With rough hands, Finn grips the doctor's face, punching him in the ribs every time he tries to swing a fist at one of us, and the moment the doctor yells, I shove the pills in his mouth and fill it the rest of the way with juice.

"Swallow!" I boom, slapping my hand over his mouth to close it, and he struggles against us, not really enjoying being treated the way he treated my girl.

Too fucking bad, arsehole.

Chapter Twenty-Five

Jaxcen

There's a monster in the room, and it's not Dr Xavier. I'm sad that I'm so hazy. I want to see Devon like this. I want to see him in his devil form, maiming. Destroying. Killing.

Everything feels like it's in slow motion. I know it's not really. It's just the way my brain is processing things with last night's drugs in my system, and I know it won't be long until I'm completely disoriented once the drug laced juice that made it to my stomach kicks in.

I never expected him to come for me. Not here. I know he said he'd protect me, but I betrayed him and stole the Corvette. I left when he asked me not to. He could have left me to my own devices and let me suffer.

Instead, he came for me.

There's a red river of blood pouring from Dr Xavier's nose, and the smell of orange juice is everywhere. Not just on me, but on the doctor too.

When I blink, my lids feel heavier to reopen, and it takes more energy than it should to make them comply.

Don't pass out, Jaxcen.

Don't take your eyes off your monster.

Watch the beast in action.

Watch him make Dr Xavier pay.

There's more yelling, and I focus on the monstrous contortion of Devon's face as he punches the doctor again, smashing his face up with his fist.

He does it over. And over. And over.

I feel a smile. I don't know if my face is actually working, but on the inside, I'm beaming with satisfaction.

In Devon's hand, something glints, and I see it for a brief moment as he lifts it, the sharp edge of a steak knife, coming into view.

Again when he moves, it's in slow motion, but he slams it into the doctor's thigh.

Movement across the other side of the table draws my attention, and I lazily take in the looming man, all dressed in black, his appearance sparking a memory.

Church.

St Catherine's.

He was there the night Devon kidnapped me. He came in afterwards with a group of men in suits, and that really cool woman.

What was his name?

Reed? Rohan? Riggs?

Maybe Riggs.

"Jax." Devon's voice comes from next to me, and I slowly turn my heavy head to find his dark concerned eyes close.

So close.

"Devil," I whisper, trying to grin.

"Little mouse, did he touch you inappropriately?"

I think I frown as I process his words, their meaning taking a little longer than they should to make sense, but when they do, I try to shake my head.

"Not yet," I slur. "Not since last time."

Devon growls.

"The other one did," I slur. "Man. Nurse." I sway on the chair, and Devon's big strong hands grip my arms to keep me in place.

"The male nurse touched you?"

"Said it was to help me peeee." I drag the word out longer than I should. "That's yoursss to touch. Nottt his," I slur, and Devon releases me, lurching up with a roar.

I feel like I'm falling, but another set of strong hands grip me from behind, and I lull my head back to see Finn.

"You're upside downnn again." I think I giggle, I can't be sure.

"I got you." He shoots me a wink, and for some reason it makes me want to cry.

Not that these stupid drugs will let me.

No. They keep me numb. Pliable.

If I could have a big brother, I want it to be Finn.

"Jax." Devon's hands cup my face, redirecting my head back down. "Was this the man that took your virginity?"

"Yesss," I admit, kind of thankful for the drugs numbing my emotions right now since I'm pretty sure there are a number of men behind me, and I would normally be embarrassed to admit that shame.

"Did you consent?" he asks through gritted teeth, and I try to shake my head, but it makes me dizzy.

"Couldn't speak. Couldn't move. Couldn't do anything," I admit.

"He drugged you back then?"

"Yesss."

That's all Devon needs before he stands, turns with his gun raised, and pulls the trigger.

The moment Dr Xavier topples sideways, his stunned expression forever on his face, it's like my body finally relaxes. Finally knows it's no longer in danger, and I start to slide off the chair as everything fades.

The last thing I notice is strong arms scooping me up, and the devil's voice whispering in my ear.

"It's okay, little mouse. I've got you."

Vida Loca
Trust

Wringing my hands together, I can't take my eyes off Jaxcen as she sleeps, completely passed out from whatever drugs that fuckwit forced into her system. Finn and Mabel helped me get her into bed when we arrived back at the Palace, Finn forcing me to shower while he watched over her.

It was the fastest fucking shower I've ever had.

Mabel brought a tray of food, and took my bloodied clothes away, along with the hospital gown that I tore off my little mouse the moment I entered my suite. I'd ordered Mabel to burn it, and I know she will. She's always obedient and never questions me.

"Have you slept yet?" Finn asks, stepping into my suite without knocking. He knows if it's unlocked he can come straight in.

"Not yet," I mutter from the chair I'd pulled up beside my bed so I could watch Jaxcen sleep.

"She's gonna be okay." Finn reassures me, not for the first time since leaving that horrid facility.

I know he's right, but knowing the fucked up things that doctor did to Jaxcen, knowing the things he could have done to her had we not found her... I can't fucking bear it.

"Hey." Finn nudges me with his elbow, so I drag my gaze from my little mouse to my best mate standing beside me. "You okay?"

"Yeah," I lie.

"No, you're fucking not. Talk to me." He turns and sits his arse on the edge of my bed, his concerned gaze locking with mine.

We've been through a lot, Finn and I. Been best mates since we were kids. He knows me better than anyone so I know I can't lie to him. He'll see right through my bullshit.

Sighing, I shake my head, my chest aching in a way I'm not used to.

"I can't keep her," I admit

"Why the fuck not?"

"She deserves better than this life," I practically whisper, my gaze darting to the sleeping beauty in my bed, between my sheets.

"Shouldn't she be the one to decide that?" Finn asks, keeping his voice low, obviously picking up on the fact I don't want Jaxcen to wake and hear this conversation.

"She's too young and inexperienced to know what she wants." My shoulders drop and I pinch the bridge of my nose.

None of this was supposed to happen. I wasn't supposed to find a random woman and bring her to my home. I wasn't supposed to let her see how truly twisted I can be. And I wasn't supposed to want to keep her.

"Fuck," I hiss, shooting wide eyes towards my best mate. "What if I really have gotten her pregnant?"

"What?" Finn's brows shoot high. "You didn't tarp up?"

"Nope." I shake my head remembering how it felt to sink into her bare. To feel the hot silk of her walls gripping my cock.

"She's not on contraception?" Finn asks, glancing over his shoulder at Jaxcen's sleeping form.

"Nope."

"The fuck man?" Finn growls, punching my shoulder. "The fuck were you thinking?"

"You don't wanna know what I was thinking," I growl, rubbing at the place he hit.

"Yeah, I fucking do. Tell me," he snaps and I roll my eyes.

"Fine. But lay off the fucking fists."

"Then stop making stupid fucking decisions," he counters.

"Whatever." I wave him off, trying to figure out how to best explain my thought process from the chapel that first night. "All I can say is I became a little obsessed with the idea of putting my baby in her."

For a long moment, Finn is silent, his eyes wide as he stares at me like I've grown two fucking heads.

"You? Want a kid?"

"I don't know." I shrug, shifting my stare back to Jaxcen. She looks so innocent when she's asleep. More so than normal. "I've never thought much about it. Never thought I'd find someone I can actually tolerate being around for longer than an hour besides you."

"Naw, you wanna have kids with me." Finn mocks and this time I'm the one to throw a punch into his shoulder.

Chuckling, Finn rubs at where my punch landed, before his gaze shifts between me and Jaxcen. "So when you say you became obsessed with the idea of putting a baby inside her, when did that first start?"

"In the chapel," I mutter.

"And that's the first time you fucked her, right?"

I nod, and he grins.

"That's some crazy arse breeding kink."

"What?" I ask, frowning at him.

"Dude, you need to read some of the books the women order in. Breeding kink is a thing. Look." He takes out his phone and I watch his screen upside down, as he searches the internet for breeding kink.

"Here it is." He grins and reads out the meaning. "Breeding kink refers to the intense arousal at the thought of being impregnated or impregnating someone. It means you're literally turned on by the idea of making her pregnant, but it doesn't necessarily mean you want to have a child. Like maybe it's the danger of the possibility that turns you on."

I consider that.

"Nope." I shake my head. "I want my baby to grow inside her and I want him or her to have my eyes and her smile and..." I trail off.

Holy shit, is that really what I want?

"Fuck, man. That's more than a kink. Is it possible you love her?"

"What? No. I've known her for four fucking days," I snap, looking at him like he's grown two heads this time, but he just shrugs.

"Crazier things have happened."

I want to argue that it's beyond crazy that I could love Jaxcen. That love at first sight is a bullshit concept created to sell movies and books, but what else could this be? Just an infatuation?

"You think that could actually be a thing? Maybe I have a brain tumour or something." I frown and Finn chuckles.

"You don't have a fucking brain tumour. But given what you've told me, maybe you should keep her for a bit longer. See where it goes."

"I don't want to take her from one prison and lock her in another." I point out.

"Dude. This place isn't a prison. Hell, she'd probably really like it here if she knows she can come and go as she pleases."

"That's just it. As mine. She can't. She'd need protection everywhere she went."

"So what?" Finn shrugs, standing to clap me on the shoulder, "Griffin made it work with Aggie." He reminds me about my cousin Griffin and the woman he lured into a Christmas game that was borderline stalkerish.

Hell, it worked. They fell in love and got married.

Is that something I can even consider?

Hold up.

Marriage?

What the fuck am I thinking about?

"You wanna leave the town locked down for Chrissy Eve?" Finn asks, bringing me out of my spiralling thoughts.

"No." I shake my head. "We operate as usual, but double the guards. Put them in plain clothes and Santa suits. I want them undercover and on the lookout while we have our gates open to outsiders."

"Got it." He nods, looking at Jaxcen again before shooting me a wink and leaving.

Every Christmas we open the town to the public of Timber Valley. It's only been a tradition for the few years I've been king of this town, but it's become popular, and brings in good money, since we aren't really about tourism and visitors any other day of the year.

People come to see the Christmas lights, and probably to have a stickybeak at the town no one is permitted to enter any other time of the year, and the local women and children love it. They spend months making Christmas themed handcrafts to sell.

It's always a risk though, especially now that Mr V is out for blood, but I'm kind of counting on him visiting since we know what he looks like now. We'll grab him off the street and deal with him swiftly, while the other visitors are none the wiser.

Stirring in my bed, Jaxcen groans, her lids fluttering a little like she's trying to open them. Like she's trying to wake herself up. It doesn't work. The drugs still have their claws in her, and it fucking pisses me off that her father would even consider having her treated that way.

Must be a father thing.

Mine's a prick, too.

I sit and watch her sleep for another hour like a creeper before finally giving in and slipping under the covers with her. Settling on my side, I slide my hand over her stomach and tug her closer, needing to feel her in my arms.

Even in sleep, she knows she's safe, curling towards me, a mutter passing her lips that sounds a helluva lot like, devil.

"Shhh, little mouse. You're safe. I've got you."

They are the same words I breathed in her ear after killing her doctor. Just like then, I don't know if she can hear me or not, but she doesn't pull away, she stays settled against me, her head pressed to my chest under my chin, and I stroke her hair, hoping she feels it. Hoping she knows she's safe.

At some point, I must fall asleep, because when I blink my eyes open again, it's to those big blue eyes staring at me.

I grin, not able to hold back the way the sight of her beautiful ocean eyes finally makes me relax.

"There you are," I rasp, my voice husky from sleep.

"There *you* are," she whispers.

"You're back?" I ask, as if perhaps I'm dreaming and I need the confirmation.

"I'm back."

"Fuck, little mouse," I choke out, dragging my hand from under the sheet to cup her face, pressing my forehead to hers. "Why did you leave?"

"I rang my sister," she whispers before clearing her throat like she's feeling just as choked up as me. "She was acting weird trying to find out where I was but almost like she didn't want to. Then Dr Xavier took the phone. He said he'd take Presley. He was going to do his treatments on her."

Her big blue eyes glass over, and I can tell she's fighting back tears.

I don't want to upset her. I just want to understand.

"So you stole a Corvette and broke out to keep your sister safe?" I ask and she nods, momentarily biting her lip as her gaze dances between mine.

"I'm sorry, Dev. You would have tried to stop me if I told you I needed to leave."

"You're right. I would have," I admit, releasing her face so she can move. "Was your sister there?"

"No. My mum had taken her before I got there. It was only Eddie, Dr Xavier and my dad."

A low growl reverberates in my chest at that whole fucking scenario.

"Eddie wasn't there when I got there," I admit.

"You went there?" she asks surprised, her brows shooting high, just like the tone in her voice.

"Yeah, I did. I wasn't lying when I said you can't run from me, little mouse." I grin and her plump lips kick up. "Serious question... on a scale of one to ten, how much would you hate me if I possibly beat your father up?"

Her brows disappear into her hairline. "Did you?"

"What's your answer first?" I urge, trying not to smirk too much, because the truth may very well upset her.

For a long moment, Jaxcen just stares at me. I can't tell what's running through her head, her expression so neutral that I wonder if she's stopped breathing.

And then she speaks quietly. Almost a whisper.

"I hope you made him cry."

Slowly, my lips spread wider and hers mimic mine.

Fuck, she's beautiful.

"I did," I admit proudly. "He cried when I ground up three of his fingers in the garbage disposal."

A gasp flies from her lips and she presses her hand to her mouth as the dark fan of her lashes flutters.

"You... what?" she asks into her hand, muffling her voice, so I reach out and ease her fingers back, showing me those pretty lips once again.

"Don't worry, his hand wasn't attached to his fingers when I did that. I cut them off first."

"You did not?" she gasps again, but there's a smirk pulling at her lips again.

"I fucking did, little mouse."

"Wow. You really are a monster."

I can't tell if she's unhappy or happy about that. All she can do is blink at me in shock.

Fuck.

"Is that a deal breaker? Me being a monster, I mean."

Slowly, her teeth appear as she smiles, and she shakes her head against the pillow.

"No. I like your monster."

"You do?" I reach forward, having a helluva lot of trouble keeping my hands off her, and I graze my thumb over her bottom lip.

Fuck, they are the most kissable lips I've ever laid eyes on.

"Yes. Your monster calls to mine."

I don't understand her meaning.

Well, I do understand what she's saying, but I don't understand how that refers to her, and not for the first time I have to wonder what happened in her past to have her living the life she's been living.

"Jax... I need to know stuff." I bite my lip, my eyes focused on hers as I ache to taste them again.

"What stuff?"

"I need to know why you started seeing Dr Xavier in the first place?"

I see the moment a wall slams between us, her eyes changing, going distant, and she shuffles back a little.

Fuck.

I don't want to lose her yet.

I'm not ready.

"Jax. What is it about what I just said that is making you want to run?"

"I don't want to run," she snaps, and I sigh.

"You've just looked at the door five times since I asked the question. You want to run. Why? Do I have to take you to the chapel so you can visit the devil?"

That last part manages to put a little warmth back into her gaze, but she shakes her head.

"No. That story doesn't belong in those sessions," she admits, and fuck, I want to kill that fucking doctor all over again.

"Little mouse, I can assure you, nothing you can say will change how much I..."

Fuck... How much I what?

"How much you... love making me gag?"

Her laugh follows her words, and I'm helpless not to join her, because fuck, I wasn't expecting that during this serious conversation.

Instantly, I wrestle her to her back, nipping at her neck as she wraps her legs around my hips, bringing me close to the part I want to drown in.

"I do love making you gag." I grin, leaning down to press my lips to hers, and she nips at them before I deepen the kiss, and for a few minutes, I get lost in her.

I feel like a teenager again, when all that I was interested in was the kiss. When I could kiss a girl for hours and think that was the ultimate.

That was until the sex part took over when I was a little older, but fuck, as much as I love burying my cock deep in Jaxcen, I'd die a happy man if kissing her like this was all there was left.

Slowly, I ease our kiss into nibbles before pulling back to hover over her, looking down at those fucking amazing lips, her flushed cheeks, and those eyes I want to stare in forever.

Fuck.

I can't do that.

"I just want to know you. The bad and the good, little mouse."

Her slight smile falls away, and she remains quiet for so long as I stare down at her that I figure this conversation must be over.

When I go to move off her, she tightens her legs around my hips.

"Don't go. I need you right there when I tell you this."

"Okay." I respond, reaching out to brush her blonde locks behind her ear.

She opens her mouth, and then closes it, her gaze going distant like she is trying to figure out the best way to start. And then, she opens up and starts talking.

"My parents have changed churches so many times over the years. When I was little, we had just moved to a new town and I was at my new Sunday school. They did things differently there." She frowns as she says that, her brows tugging in, making her look so much younger than she is. "Presley had always told me never to let anyone touch my private parts. She said that no one can do that unless I'm sick in that spot and a doctor needs to treat the area."

I stiffen at her words, and her blue gaze rejoins the present, staring into mine, worry flickering through them.

"It's alright, little mouse. Keep going."

She nods, and takes another moment before she continues.

"At the new Sunday school, Brother Eric used to make us all take our pants off. He used to touch everyone like he was a doctor examining. But the girl next to me was different. She was taller and a bit older and she had a few hairs down there." She frowns again, shaking her head. "I didn't know why she had hair there. I was too young to understand anything about puberty. And I didn't understand why he touched her differently..."

She shakes her head, her eyes distant like she's trying to shake off the memory.

"I don't want to go into what he did, but it was wrong and even though it was wrong, I was the one that broke the rule."

"What rule?"

"What happens in Sunday school, stays in Sunday school, I guess." She shrugs, looking annoyed at the idea of it. "I went and told my parents as soon as Sunday school ended, and I did it in front of the other parents. I thought I was doing the right thing by speaking up, but everyone treated me like I was the one that did something wrong."

The fuck!

Now I wish I had killed her old man.

"The real kicker is the girl that he touched called me a sick monster for saying such a thing. She told the grown ups that I was lying. But it was true, and no one believed me." She sighs, chewing on her lip for a moment before continuing. "I started having nightmares about what I'd seen. What I experienced. I kept telling my parents about the dream and about what I saw, begging them to believe me, but they just wouldn't believe anything I had to say after that. They grew more and more concerned and instead of taking me to school one day, they took me to Holly River Estate."

I may not have killed her dad yesterday, but mark my fucking word, he'll be dead by my hand soon.

"What happened there?" I dare ask, and she shrugs, like it's no big deal.

"Exposure."

"Exposure?" I frown, confused.

"I was forced to watch things no ten year old should watch. Things on TV. Magazines were shown to me. And then the real life stuff happened." She sucks in a deep breath, like perhaps she's feeling a little unwell. "Every time they exposed me to something, I would have a session with Dr Xavier the next day, and every time I told him what I saw, I was put in a dark closet for two days in his office."

A deep growl rumbles in my chest, and this time it's Jaxcen who reaches up, her nails dragging through my hair like she is trying to offer me comfort.

Fuck. She's the one that should be offered the comfort.

"Eventually I realised the only way to stay out of the closet was to keep my mouth shut, so I did, and I'd hoped it would get me sent home. Instead the exposure increased from one session to two a day. Then there were the all day and night sessions. I was made to watch. Asked if I wanted to join in." She shakes her head vigorously. "I never did but some of the other girls did."

"Were there boys there?"

"Not patients. All the staff were men. All the patients were girls and women."

Fucking sick fucks.

Now I wish I didn't kill that fucker, and instead brought him back here and tortured him for days, weeks or even years.

"I don't know why, but they eventually started drugging me." She continues. "I didn't notice at first. It was gradual. It was like they were doing it to see if it would coax me into participating in the... sessions."

"And did you ever join in?" I ask, hoping she says no, but knowing it's not her fault if she did. Their manipulation tactics were obviously well versed.

"No, I never joined in, but was always forced to watch, and something about that must have frustrated Dr Xavier because my sessions with him began to change and…" She sucks in another breath, and I can tell this time she's fighting back tears.

"He used the date rape drug on you," I answer for her and she nods quickly.

"I guess that's what it was. I don't want to talk about what he did." She shakes her head again, her emotions taking over. "Please. I don't want to relive that."

"Okay, little mouse. That's enough for today. Or forever if that's what you prefer." I assure her, because fuck, I wish I hadn't insisted she relive that part. "I have one more question though."

She visibly gulps, but nods. "Okay."

"Why do you think you're a monster?"

Chapter Twenty-Seven

Jaxcen

This is it. The moment he learns what sort of person I really am, and he runs away. I mean, I can't actually imagine Devon running away from anything or anyone, but maybe he'll just boot me out on my arse and tell me never to return.

Pressing my hands to his shoulders, I push Devon gently, and he shifts off me, letting me sit up. My head spins as I do, so I close my eyes briefly and let my head get used to my new position.

"Take it slowly. The drugs are probably still in your system," Devon mumbles, sitting up with me and stroking my hair back again.

He likes to do that. And I like when he does that. It makes me feel cherished.

Important.

Seen.

Blinking my eyes open again, the room doesn't spin this time, and I take in the sight of the man studying me with so much concern.

He'll hate me soon.

He'll never look at me like this again.

"I left something out of my story before," I whisper, watching him closely for any reaction.

So far, nothing.

"It was about the reason why I got sent to Dr Xavier."

There's a slight tug of his brows now, but that's it. His dark gaze is still on mine, and he waits quietly for me to continue.

"The nightmares happened. And I kept telling my parents I wasn't lying, but…"

"But?" he asks, his finger hooking under my chin to lift my gaze to his when I try to look at my fidgeting hands in my lap.

"They kept sending me back to Sunday school. And started sending Presley too. She hadn't been before that because she was in the choir, and they rehearsed a lot and received most of her teachings in that group, but for some reason, on this particular day, my parents sent her to Sunday school with me."

Nausea rolls my gut at the memory.

"Presley's innocent eyes, although older than mine, really believed I was lying too, since that's what my parents told her." I remember feeling so alone then. "Brother Eric took a liking to her straight away, and when it came to the *checking of the privates* part of the day, he started with her."

Even though my lower lip is trembling, and I'm not entirely sure I won't puke at any moment, my glare into Devon's eyes is fuelled by the same rage I felt that day.

"He fucking touched her?"

I nod. "I still remember her face when he called her to the centre where he kneeled. She thought she was special. That she was about to receive praise I guess, but the moment he told her to lift her dress," I choke out, a sob lurching from my lips. "I'll never forget the fear in her eyes when she shot me a look."

"Fuck, Jax. You don't have to tell me."

"Yes. I do. You need to know so you can decide if you want me around you or the people in this town."

The frown that creases his forehead is severe, and his tone is harsh.

"There's nothing that will change this." He points aggressively between us. "You need to understand that, love."

Love.

I love it when he calls me that. I love it when he calls me little mouse, that term no longer making me feel meek, but adored. And I love it when he calls me Jax.

"Presley said no," I say, swiping at my tears. "She told him firmly, no you're not allowed to do that. And he ignored her. Simply lifted her dress anyway and laid his perverted hands on her."

My lip curls as rage bubbles inside me, and that familiar unhinged feeling engulfs me.

"The scissors were so close, and before I knew it, they were in my hand, and when I blinked again I was standing over Brother Eric's blood soaked body as he gasped for air." I shake my head, trying to clear the memory, but it's there now. So clear. So engulfing.

"A bloodied bubble kept expanding from his lips. In and out. In and out. I remember feeling happy. I stopped him. He couldn't touch Presley again."

"Come back to me." Devon's deep rasp has me blinking, the sight of Brother Eric's dying body floating away like smoke in the wind, and in its place are those dark smouldering eyes that own my soul with one look.

"I'm back," I whisper, offering him a small smile, even though I don't particularly feel like smiling. "I got sent to Dr Xavier for killing Brother Eric, because of course, a ten year old can't go to prison, and if I could be so violent, I must be crazy, right?"

"Wrong," Devon snaps. "Everything the adults did in your life was wrong."

I shrug. "Even so." I tap the side of my head. "There's a monster in me. There's an unhinged part of me that has the potential to snap."

"It was fucking appropriate given the circumstances, Jax. A monster that comes out to do the right thing, is a monster I want to know."

"You're so weird." I half giggle before my smile falls away altogether.

"Well this weirdo's opinion of you hasn't changed, little mouse. So no more thinking there's something wrong with you."

His warm lips press to my forehead, and I sink into it, letting him hold us there for a long moment before he pulls back to study my face once again.

"I'm sorry I ran off," I whisper, needing him to know that I really am regretful for not trusting him to help me.

"Don't say sorry now." He grins wickedly. "You know where penance happens here."

Heat flushes my cheeks at the reminder, and I grin.

"Is that really a thing?"

"With you and me, yes." He nods, hooking his arm around my back and tugging me onto his lap.

"You like it when I sin." My words are more of a statement than a question, leaving Devon's wicked grin to grow.

"Fuck, yes."

Biting my lip as I grin back, I glide my hands over his shoulders to the back of his neck and admit. "I like sinning for you."

"Good." He nips at my lips. "I expect so many more sins, little mouse. Let's start with some gluttony, hey?"

"Really?" I giggle, as those sinful lips of his trail down my neck.

"Yes, you're too skinny." He pulls back, still smirking and gives my arse a swift slap. "Let's eat."

I nod, feeling my stomach rumble at that suggestion.

"But first, let's shower you," he says right before he lifts me, sliding us out of the bed, and carries me to his bathroom.

He lowers me to the cool tiled floor, and I watch him as he turns the water on in the shower, his hand held out as he tests the temperature.

How did this happen?

Him and me? Me and him?

It's so bizarre to think I only met him a few days ago, yet I feel like I've known him for years.

What a strange thought.

There's still so much I don't know about him, but what I do know is probably the most important thing.

He may be the devil, but he's a good man. To me, anyway. And I guess to the people of this town, if what I'm piecing together is true.

"What are you staring at?" he asks playfully, eyeing me as he holds his hand out for me to go to him.

I don't even hesitate, shooting him a grin as I pull his t-shirt off me.

"Who dressed me?" I ask, having no idea what happened after I blacked out at the facility.

"It was a team effort." He winks, and my brows hitch.

"A team effort? Explain."

"Well..." He tugs me forward, his eyes dropping to my naked chest and the way my nipples are already in tight peaks. "While I stripped that fucking hospital gown off you, Finn got the t-shirt from my drawer, and Mabel peeled back the bed sheets so I could lay you down. Then Finn tossed me the shirt and I slipped it on you while Mabel got a warm washcloth and cleaned up most of the juice clinging to your skin." He grazes his thumb over my cheek, and I can tell he's remembering the sight.

"So, what you're saying is Mabel and Finn saw me naked."

He shrugs. "Finn's my best mate. We share a lot."

My eyes widen. "Um, excuse me? You're not sharing me."

Chuckling, he shakes his head. "Nope. Not like that, but..."

"But?"

"I trust him to take care of you if I can't, little mouse. And I trust his discretion when he helps me with something I consider important. There's no one on this earth more loyal to me than Finn."

Wow. How nice that must be to have that sort of unconditional loyalty. I'm both envious, and happy for him.

"What about your parents? Your mother?"

His eyes darken at my question, and his tone is final.

"We're not speaking about them today."

"Oh... okay." I nod, a little confused as to why it was alright for me to open up and not him.

Not saying another word, Devon strips out of his boxers and leads me into his shower. His rather big shower that has plenty of room for two people. Probably even four.

Tugging me under the water with him, I stay silent, watching his face as he reaches up and runs his hands over my hair, helping the water to soak through, before he does the same to his own.

He's avoiding my eyes. I can tell. His focus remains on pumping out the shampoo and lathering my hair, before spinning me to face the tiled wall where he proceeds to massage my scalp.

A moan escapes me as goosebumps travel over my skin from the way the tips of his fingers dig into my scalp.

"You like that, little mouse?"

"Yes." I breathe, my lids fluttering closed as I give in to yet another way Devon Marx makes me feel good.

"My parents aren't good people," he admits quietly behind me, and my eyes part slightly, as I take in his tone.

I should tell him he doesn't have to divulge this to me, but he continues, and I don't want to be rude and interrupt him.

"I always knew it, even as a young kid. My father disciplined with his fists. My mother disciplined by making sure Dad knew of our transgressions." His fingers leave my scalp, and run through the ends of my hair, slowly stroking, slowly cleaning. "I'm the oldest of five. I have three sisters and a brother. I always made sure I took their punishments. There was no way I was letting my old man lay a hand on my siblings if I could help it."

Not able to bear not seeing his face, I turn to him, taking in his flat expression, and the way he still tries to avoid my eyes.

"You protected your sisters and brother," I point out and he shrugs.

"As much as I could."

"What are their names?" I ask, wanting to know everything about him.

"Lily is the oldest sister, just a couple of years younger than me. I haven't seen her in years. She... moved away."

"Moved away?" I nudge, hoping he'll open up even more.

"Yeah, she lives in the UK. Went on a gap year and ended up getting knocked up by a real douche preppy motherfucker. Our parents being the rays of sunshine they are, demanded she abort the pregnancy, so she never returned. She's been across the other side of the world ever since, raising her twin sons. She thinks Barrett is the only one who knows where she is in England, but I know."

"Who's Barrett? Is he your younger brother?"

"Nah. Barrett is one of my many cousins. He works mostly overseas, brokering deals for the family business. He's been keeping an eye on Lily for me."

"You miss her," I state, pressing my palms to his bare chest, and he nods.

"I imagine she'd be an amazing mum. And I imagine she's happy, no longer part of the Marx empire."

"You sound like you hate it."

He shrugs. "It has its perks and its downfalls, like most things in life."

I nod, fully understanding that now.

"Tell me about your other siblings."

He rolls his eyes. "You really want to know that boring shit?"

"It's not boring to me."

He chuckles, shifting me back under the water and proceeds to rinse out the shampoo.

"Jenaveve and Elise are my other sisters. They live their own lives away from my parents as much as they can. And me too, I guess. I'm not known to be very accommodating."

My brows shoot up. "Aside from your cockiness," I grin, eliciting a smirk from him, "you are very accommodating."

"Depends who you ask, I suppose."

"What about your brother? Is he like you?"

Devon scoffs. "By looks only. Fucker gets into too much trouble. Doesn't have much self control. Life is just one big fucking party to him."

I giggle. "You sound jealous."

"Fuck, maybe I am." He grins, and then his smile falls away.

"I have parents and siblings, but my real family is Finn, and then I guess my men and cousins. They are all that matter."

I nod, standing on my tip toes, and Devon meets me halfway, leaning down to press his lips to mine.

That's all it takes for the heat to spike inside the shower, his arms weaving around me and pulling me flush against his naked front.

This guy here with me now, is so much different to the guy I met at St Catherine's the other night. He's gentle, but rough at the same time. His kiss is claiming, and hell I want him to claim every part of my being. And he's hungry, ravenous as he growls into my mouth, his erection getting harder by the second, pressed to my belly.

"I want you." I breathe into our kiss, and he growls again, lifting me, my legs wrapping around him before I feel the cold tiles at my back.

"I don't want to hurt you," he admits, breaking our kiss to stare into my eyes, his dark gaze melting me like butter.

"You won't." I remind him, "I need this."

The way his lips slam into mine is beyond claiming. They are fevered as they demand mine to comply, and hell, this is exactly what I love about Devon Marx.

He dominates me so thoroughly. It makes me want to give him every last piece of my soul.

"I want to fill you up." He groans, fisting his cock between us and sliding the thick swollen tip at my entrance.

"Yes. Fill me up," I beg, not sure if I just want his dick to fill me, or his cum.

That thought has my pussy aching, desperate to be stretched and dominated. Desperate for him.

I should probably question where my head is at, because his cum could mean a baby, since I've never taken the contraceptive pill, and I know I'm not ready for children, but the risk of it is somehow making this all the more hotter, and I want the filthy version of him that is obsessed with putting his baby inside me.

"I wanna fill you with so much cum that you almost drown in it." He grunts before slamming his dick inside me, and my back arches as I cry out, loving that stretch he gives me with his girth.

"Fuck, Jax. Your cunt is so tight. So fucking hot." He eases out and slams back in. "I don't want this to end."

"Don't stop," I pant, meeting his thrust with my own as he picks up his pace. "Don't ever stop."

A frenzy takes over us, moans, grunts, pants, and wet slaps filling the room as we lose ourselves in each other. His fingers find my nipples, tweaking them as he pounds me into the tiled wall, the press of his pubic bone against my clit sending shockwaves of pleasure through me, hurling me over the edge far too soon.

He doesn't stop though, his dick pistoning into me, his breathing harsh and grunts deep as he claims my insides, and shoots me into a full bodied climax again before he finally groans out his release.

Our panted breathing is loud and echoes in the shower, steam billowing around us as the shower still runs, long forgotten by our frenzy.

"Fuck, sorry, little mouse. That was kind of rushed."

I giggle at his words, pushing at his shoulders so he shifts enough that I can see his face.

"Fast and hard isn't a bad thing." I wink, and his teeth make an appearance as he smiles. Like truly smiles.

Wow.

What a beautiful sight.

"Are you fuckers done yet?" a voice comes from somewhere outside the door, and my mouth drops into an O as Devon grins, and leans to the side to push the shower door open.

"You better not have your dick out." Devon teases as Finn comes into view, and oh my god.

I try to cover myself and realise Devon's body is basically doing that by the way he has me trapped against the wall.

"Nope. Watching you rail your girl isn't my kink, man." Finn smirks, and I bury my face in Devon's neck, mortified.

"So why the fuck are you here eavesdropping?" Devon snaps, almost sounding annoyed at his best mate.

"Play time's over." Finn chuckles. "There are cops at the front gate."

Vida Loca
Trust

Chapter Twenty-Eight
Devon

Leaving Jaxcen to finish up in the shower is a form of fucking torture. I didn't want to leave her wet body, or the opportunity to make sure my cum stays inside her, but when the boys in blue come knocking, it's best not to keep them waiting too long.

"What's up?" Finn asks as we walk silently to the gate.

I glance at him realising I'm lost in my head, thoughts of leaving Jaxcen naked not the only thing plaguing me.

"Why are you so nosey?"

"Because I'm in love with you, why else." He mocks and I roll my eyes.

"Shut up."

He snickers, and I sigh, once again knowing if I don't spill now, he'll just bug me about it later until I do.

"If you must know, I'm feeling..." I trail off. What the fuck is this feeling?

"What? Happy?" Finn teases and I glare at him.

"No. I feel naked."

His brows shoot up, making the scar above his eyebrow crease and sink in, reminding me of the day he fell off the motorbike and needed stitches. Fucker didn't even cry.

"Dude, you have clothes on. You're not naked."

"Not that sort of naked," I mutter, dropping my gaze to the gravel road as we walk.

"Oh you mean the kind of naked when you open up to someone," he says with yet another teasing tone.

"I guess," I admit.

"You told her how much you love me, didn't you?" He laughs, but I don't.

"Well, yeah."

His brows hitch again.

"She needed to know who my family was," I explain and Finn smirks and shoulder bumps me.

"So what's the real reason for your nakedness? Because it's not you admitting to her that you have a man crush on me."

"She asked about my parents."

"And you told her?" Finn asks with a little surprise in his tone.

"Kinda." I shrug. "I gave her the basic run down. She doesn't need to know everything."

"But she knows enough?" Finn asks as he kicks a stone out of his path.

"Yes."

"Huh. You never tell people."

Fucker. Way to call me out.

"I know." I eye him, and his thoughtful expression meets mine.

"Have you decided to keep her?"

Fuck. My heart sinks as I shake my head.

"I can't."

"I think you can. I just think you're scared." Again Finn calls me out.

Why is he my mate again?

"What the fuck am I scared of?" I snap.

"Of letting yourself be happy."

"Fuck off." I shoulder him this time, and he doesn't laugh. He remains serious.

"It's true man."

"I'm happy," I lie and he shoots me a 'really' look, brows high and eyes disbelieving.

"Are you though?"

"Are you?" I snap, wanting the attention off me.

He shrugs. "Maybe I'll find me a Jaxcen of my own."

I scoff. "Not while you have that crazy chick in your house."

He rolls his eyes at me, and as we round the bend in the road, we both eye the town entrance ahead, and the police cruiser sitting on the other side of the closed gates.

"How's that going anyway?" I keep the subject off me, and he happily obliges.

"Well, she's awake. And only tried to kill me twice, so I think that's progress."

Fucking hell. He insisted on taking the crazy chick we rescued from the facility back to his house, determined not to show her the inside of another prison. His words, not mine.

"You're not equipped for the level of care that woman needs, man. Just let me take her to get proper care."

"No," he barks quickly as we descend the hill. "Not yet. Just give me time."

I roll my eyes at my best mate, certain he's already in over his head.

"Fine, but the second you need help, you fucking tell me." I point sternly at him.

"Cross my heart and hope to die." He grins, drawing a cross over his chest with his finger.

Sighing, I turn my sights on the two police officers stepping away from their car to approach the gate.

"Well, let's see who's getting arrested today."

Finn chuckles quietly at my remark, and as we approach my men on this side of the gate, they step aside to allow the officer to see me better.

"Officer Zimora. To what do we owe the pleasure of your company?"

"Sorry for the unannounced visit," Jason Zimora, one of the local cops we have on our payroll peers at me through the gates, "but I've been asked by a Metro department to do a welfare check on a woman. Jaxcen Summers. Her father is claiming that she's been kidnapped."

"Is he? How is Mr Summers?" I smirk, and Jason does too, which his partner, watching on a few metres behind him, can't see.

"It seems he's recovering in hospital. Got his fingers caught in a garbage disposal."

"Is that so?" I ask, feigning surprise.

"Yeah. Know anything about that?" Jason shifts to widen his stance, resting one hand on his belt as he fights a grin.

"What I know is you really shouldn't put your hand in a garbage disposal."

He nods. "No, seems like a bad idea if you want to keep your fingers."

I nod, and lift my brows, waiting for him to get to the point.

"So, can I come in and search for Miss Summers?"

"No need." I take out my phone and call Miles, hearing it ring twice before he answers.

"Boss?"

"Can you please ask Miss Summers to join us at the front gate?"

"Yep. Be down with her soon." Miles grunts and hangs up.

"So she's here?" the second officer asks from behind Jason.

"Yes."

"Of her own volition?" The other officer moves closer and I nod.

"Yes."

"And she'll agree to that freely, will she?"

"Of course." I nod to the other officer before turning my sights to Jason. "You know what I do, Jason. I'm not in the business of forcing women."

"Funny. There's CCTV footage of you chasing her out of St Catherine's Church on Tuesday night." The other officer says smugly, and fuck, I want him to move closer to the gates, so I can reach through and slam his head into the bars. "The part of you throwing her over your shoulder and the way she was punching you didn't appear consensual."

I grit my teeth, slowly taking a calming breath in so I don't lose my shit and kill a cop so close to Christmas.

"You know me, Jas." I smile, directing my response to the copper I know instead of the newbie, obviously not familiar with the way things are done in Timber Valley. "I like it a little rough."

The other officer scoffs, and Jason turns back to him, gesturing for him to join him back over at the cruiser, chatting quietly.

"You confident she won't throw you under the bus?" Finn asks quietly, stepping up to my side and I nod.

"Yep."

"You sure?"

"I said yes, didn't I?" I snap, glaring at my best mate, and he holds his hands up in surrender as the low hum of a golf cart draws our attention.

Turning to look over my shoulder, I watch the cart descend the hill down to the front gate, Miles' hulking form behind the wheel, and Jaxcen's blonde hair blowing from the speed of it as they approach.

"Remain where you are," the other officer orders me, and I see Jason roll his eyes from behind him as they approach the gate again. "Don't say anything to her. Let me do the talking."

This time I roll my eyes and nod, about ready to off this fucker as I turn my back on Jaxcen as she gets out of the cart and moves our way.

"Are you Jaxcen Summers?" the other officer asks, and she nods, coming to stand next to me.

"Yes, I'm Jaxcen."

"Please approach the gate," the officer demands and Jaxcen glances up at me for approval.

Fuck. I like that.

I like that she seeks her approval from me.

Nodding, I watch as she moves closer to the closed gates, glad they are shut so he can't grab her and snatch her away.

"Is there a problem?" she asks, confidence in her tone.

"Please confirm your full name," the officer asks, and I want to punch the fucker for not answering her question.

"Jaxcen Isabelle Summers," she offers.

"The names of your parents and any siblings," he demands, and I ball my fists.

"Remain calm man," Finn mutters quietly next to me.

"My father is John Summers. My mum Isabelle Summers, and I have one sister. Presley Summers," Jaxcen says clearly.

"Are you aware your father is in hospital?" the officer asks, and fuck, I have no idea how she's going to handle this.

Maybe I shouldn't have allowed this questioning, but this guy is new, and it would have ended badly.

For him.

"Yes. I'm aware."

"Do you know why?" the officer asks, and she nods.

"He had an accident."

I bite back my smirk at her vagueness. I'm pretty sure she doesn't know how much she can admit to.

"What sort of accident?" the officer pries for more information.

"With a garbage disposal." She shrugs, like it's no big deal.

"You don't seem concerned." The officer points out and Jaxcen shakes her head.

"Honestly, I'm not. We've had a falling out. If he's going to do something as stupid as put his hands in a garbage disposal, then that's his problem."

Jason smirks behind his officer, who only looks angrier by Jaxcen's response.

"Why are you here?"

"I'm here with my friends for Christmas."

Atta girl.

"And who are you friends?"

"Devon and Finn." She turns and gestures to us, and the officer's eyes darken with anger, clearly not happy that he won't get to arrest anyone today.

As Jaxcen turns back to the officers, I sneak a glance at Finn and he smiles like he's proud she included him on her friends list.

"So you're here of your own free will?" the officer asks and again, Jaxcen nods.

"Yes, I am."

"Can you explain why there is CCTV footage of Mr Marx chasing you out of the St Catherine's Church in the city on Tuesday night?"

Jaxcen's shoulders tense just a fraction. I don't think the officer noticed it, but I did, yet when she speaks, it's with clear confidence, and mockery.

"Well, if you know Devon, you know his cockiness can get a little too much at times." She shrugs like it's no big deal. "So I stormed out, annoyed by his attitude." The little minx dares to grin over her shoulder at me before turning back to the police.

"And he chased me because," she air quotes, "'I'm his.' I swear he's so dramatic."

Little brat. We'll see who the dramatic one is later.

"And how about the part when he threw you over his shoulder and you were punching his back? That didn't look like you were having fun, Miss Summers."

"Oh, that was foreplay." She waves a dismissive hand at him, giggling.

Fuck, my little mouse is a good fucking liar.

"Did he do that to you?" the officer asks, not giving up to try and prove something as he points to her neck.

The fucking hickeys *I* left on her neck.

"Sometimes, he likes to role-play that he's a vampire." She leans closer to the gate, conspiratorially. "It gets him off really fast."

"Okay, that's enough out of you," I growl as my men chuckle and Jason smirks, while the other officer just blinks, dumbfounded.

"Alright, I guess everything seems above board here," the officer says, frowning, his critical gaze scanning over us again.

He spins to walk back towards Jason and the cruiser, but stops quickly, and turns back.

"Oh just one more thing. You wouldn't happen to know anything about the Holly River Estate burning to the ground earlier this morning, would you?"

And that's the moment Jaxcen gives us away, her gasp and wide eyes darting over her shoulder to me, while Jason's partner draws his gun.

Chapter Twenty-Nine

Jaxcen

The sound of gravel scraping from all directions has me moving to the side as guns are drawn, not just from the officer behind the one talking to me, but from Devon and his men.

"Whoa," the officer at the back yells. "Let's all calm down and lower the guns."

"They know something about the facility," the cop that questioned me yells back, his gun raised, shifting its aim between Devon, Finn, Miles and the guards.

"No, they don't. No one said that," the other cop steps closer to his colleague.

"She did," the officer snarls over his shoulder while shifting the aim of his gun again, this time to me. "She reacted."

This isn't good. They are going to shoot each other, and all because I reacted.

"Hey! Don't point a fucking gun at her. She isn't armed!" Devon snarls, and I catch sight of his face, his eyes dark and zeroed in on his target.

The questioning officer.

He does as Devon demands, pointing his gun back at him, and my heart sinks.

No.

Don't point a gun at Dev.

"Make him back off, Jas," Devon stalks forward, his aim never wavering.

"Rick, seriously. Lower your gun." The officer Devon called Jas hisses at his colleague, meanwhile his gaze is on Devon, a message in his eyes like he's trying to convey something without speaking.

"Like fuck," Officer Rick snaps. "They drew on us."

"After you drew on them," Jas points out, trying to calm the situation.

My heart is anything but calm, the organ hammering against my chest as my fear spikes. But it's not fear for myself. It's fear for Devon. Fear for his men.

When did they become important to me too?

What have I done?

"Are we going to have a problem here?" Devon's voice, although calm, is scary as hell, and I can tell his monster is right there, lurking just beneath the surface, ready to come out at any second.

"No, man." Officer Jas or Jason or whatever the hell his name is, shakes his head. "We were just following protocol. Rick is new. He's not up to speed yet."

"Well get him up to fucking speed before someone gets hurt," Devon snarls and Officer Rick snarls back.

"You can't talk to us like that!"

"For fuck's sake," Jas mutters, lowering his gun and approaching his partner to stand between him and us. "Lower your weapon, Rick."

"No," he snaps, and then, to my surprise, Jason's hand shoots out and slams into Rick's face, the crunch of bone loud as Rick wails, his gun falling from his grasp, only for Jason to catch it.

"What the fuck!" Rick screeches, his hands cupped over his nose as blood gushes out, onto his chin and the front of his blue uniform. "Why'd you do that?"

"For not following my order." Jason shoves his shoulders and Rick stumbles back a few steps. "Get in the fucking car."

"I'm gonna report this," Rick cries, but he does as he's told, rushing to the car and slipping inside.

Now I'm really confused.

Why would one officer punch the other?

"Sorry, Dev. You know I had to come and ask." Officer Jason holsters his gun and tucks the other in the back of his pants, and I notice that's when Devon and his men lower theirs.

"I know. Are you sure you can handle him?" Devon asks, his tone less menacing now, like he's talking to an old friend.

"Yeah. I'll take him to visit your cousin before we go back to the station."

"Good idea." Devon smirks wickedly, "Say hi to Griffin for me."

"Will do." Jason smirks back before turning his attention to me, and where I still stand huddled to a tree next to the gates. "Apologies, Miss Summers. Have a lovely Christmas."

"Ah... yeah... you too." I frown, my voice a little shaky.

What the hell just happened?

I watch as the officer gets into his car and starts the engine, starting to drive away.

"You okay, little mouse?"

Glancing in the other direction, I see Devon nearing, his gun gone from his grip as he studies me like I'm a caged animal that might run at any moment.

"I don't understand," I whisper, dumbfounded.

"It's alright, Jax. It's over." He reaches out, snagging my wrist and gently pulling me to him.

"I'm sorry I..."

"It's not your fault." Devon cups my jaw, his dark eyes scanning my face as if he's trying to read my mind. "I'll kick Jason's arse later for coming here and bringing a new recruit."

"But..."

"But what?" He smirks a little, his thumb brushing over my cheek like he can feel its searing heat and he either likes it or is trying to calm it. I can't be sure which, but it's gentle and so opposite of what Devon Marx is.

"But, he's a cop. They are both cops." I point out the obvious and Devon shrugs.

"And?"

"And they are cops," I snap, frustrated as to why he's not taking this more seriously.

"Yes, they are cops, but little mouse, I'm Devon Marx."

His familiar and rather frustrating cocky smirk returns, and I want to slap it off his face for treating this like it's no big deal.

"But..." I try to argue again, and Devon leans close, brushing his lips against mine.

"But nothing." He nibbles on my lips. "I'm a Marx, love. That's all you need to know."

Angling my head, he kisses me hard and deep, his tongue lashing mine like it's trying to remind me who's boss. And I guess it really is him. He's the boss of everyone in this town, and maybe even of the police in the area.

When he pulls back, his dark gaze drops to my lips, and I know he's staring at how swollen they are. He does that to them so easily, and I know he's fascinated by them, more naturally plump than average.

Dazed, I look around as I pull back, needing space to think clearly. His presence consumes me so entirely sometimes, that I forget just how dangerous he is.

I glance over his shoulder at his men. The guards, dressed in a black uniform, armed with guns and knives. Miles, his hulking muscles nearly tearing through the fabric of his t-shirt, his tattoos making him look like an evil villain. And Finn, just as big and built as Devon, his blonde hair doing nothing to make him appear any less scary than the man standing before me.

These men... They are something else.

This isn't just a normal 'rich guy buying off people' type of situation. Not with the danger that oozes from each of their pores.

"Am I..." I glance back at Devon, unsure how or what to ask, or even if I should. "Are you..."

"What?" Devon smirks, like he finds my uncertainty cute.

Ugh. I'll just come right out and ask.

"Is this the mafia?"

I study his face for a reaction, and it's his eyes that respond first, glinting a little as a sinister smirk engulfs his face while he chuckles.

"Probably not the kind of mafia you're used to from Hollywood movies."

"But, it *is* the mafia?" I ask again and he shrugs.

"We don't tend to call it that." He brushes back my hair behind my ear, once again showing me how much he enjoys doing that.

Is he trying to distract me?

"What do you call it? The mob?" I push and he smirks wider.

"No."

"Organised crime?" I continue, hoping I'm not pushing my luck too much.

"I guess you could call us businessmen." He nods.

"Businessmen?" I narrow my eyes and he nods again.

"Yes."

"Businessmen that are in the business of crime?" I try to clarify.

"Exactly." He takes my hand, lifting it to his lips where he presses them to the back, and hot damn, I swoon.

Like, wow. It's such a simple act, but no one has ever kissed the back of my hand before, and there's something about it that sends butterflies straight to my belly, sending ripples of excitement through me.

"Oh...kay" is all I can muster until I remember the church we met in. "Is that why the confessional doors at St Catherine's Church are bulletproof? Does your crime family own it?"

He grins at my question. "We don't own it, but that's where the Marx family worships, and Father Peters is happy for our added security measures as long as we make sizable donations to the charities of his choosing."

My brows shoot up. "Really?"

He nods. "Really." His eyes light up with something that looks a helluva lot like happiness as he tugs on our joined hands and starts walking towards his men.

"Come on, little mouse. Let's feed you."

At the mention of food, my tummy rumbles loudly, and it becomes all I can think about.

He mentioned gluttony earlier, and it's a sin I've found hard to fight often, but knowing that binge eating my favourite chocolates and treats will end up showing on the outside, I tried my best to steer clear of them. Eddie was always the first to see the moment I put a little weight on.

But he's not here and I actually don't care where he is or if he thinks I'm a chubby sinner. I'm hungry, and for once, I have every intention of feasting.

Devon discusses a few more things with his men, that I pay no attention to, and then takes the cute little golf cart, driving us back up the steep hill to the Palace.

When he said he was going to feed me, he didn't lie.

Mabel prepares a feast, and Devon's men join us, sitting at a long table in the back room that looks like it's used for counter meals sometimes.

So we eat. And eat. And eat.

Even though I'm the only female sitting at the table, the men don't look uncomfortable by my presence, their banter and laughter easy to soak in as I watch these men, who seem more like a big family, enjoy a meal and time together.

"Is my little mouse full?" Devon asks, leaning close so only I can hear, and I nod, rubbing my belly.

"I have a food baby."

"A what?" He laughs.

"A food baby." I grin from ear to ear. "Every Christmas, Presley and I would see who could get the biggest food baby belly." I pat my tummy, pushing it out more for effect, and Devon's eyes darken.

"Woman if you keep doing that, I'll throw you on this table and fuck you until I nut inside you ten times just to make sure I see your belly swell like that with my child inside it."

My lips part and eyes widen, his words both formidable and alluring.

"You wouldn't dare," I whisper and Finn leans in on my other side.

"He would."

My brows shoot high and I turn my gaze to Devon's best mate as he chuckles.

"Dev's breeding kink with you seems to surpass the normal realm of playing with the risk." He shrugs, like what he just said is no big deal. "He genuinely wants to knock you up, and he'd have no qualms with fucking you right here in front of everyone while we try to eat."

My mouth forms an O as I shoot my gaze back to Devon, who simply shrugs and shoots me a wink.

I should be appalled right?

I shouldn't want him, someone I barely know, to knock me up. And I absolutely shouldn't get turned on over the idea of Devon taking me on this very table while his men watch.

But I do.

Fuck. I do.

Why do I want that?

Finn chuckles, leaning back in his chair and taking a sip of his drink, while Devon's eyes sear me from the outside in, like he's wielding his dick magic and knows how it's affecting me.

"You want me to fuck you right here, little mouse?"

The table falls quiet at Devon's words, and never in all my life have I felt my cheeks burst with so much heat like they do this very second.

"We could clear away a few plates, make enough room to spread you out so everyone can see." He slides his plate aside, one of his men taking it and passing it up the table, like they'd all be down for this. "I know you like to watch, so you could watch them fist their cocks, getting off on the sight of you shattering around my cock."

I can't breathe. I'm pretty sure my lungs have stopped working, and perhaps even my heart as my gaze roams over each lethal man to see not an ounce of disdain, only lust.

Oh.

My.

God.

Would Devon really do that? Let others see me?

The thought sends a thrill up my spine, and Cloud 9 comes to the forefront of my mind.

How many times have I wanted to step over the line and join in with the action?

How many times have I wished I was the female in the centre getting worshipped by the men, all at once, taking care of her? How many times have I wished it was me everyone was watching and getting off to?

So many times. So, so many times.

But this isn't Cloud 9. This is Woodall Ridge. The gated community run by criminal businessmen.

This is Devon's home.

Clearing my throat, with more than ten sets of eyes on me, I force words past my lips.

"As tempting as that offer is, Mr Marx," I try to keep my tone formal, just like he did when he made the offer, "I dutifully decline."

There are some low chuckles that float around the table, but I keep my eyes trained on Devon, as I stand, pushing my chair back to make my escape before slipping it back into position.

"Where are you going, little mouse?" Devon asks, looking a little disappointed that I didn't take him up on his offer.

"It's Friday afternoon, isn't it?"

He nods, his brow furrowing.

"I believe there are cocktails at Miss Barber's." I spin before he can say anything else, but only get a few steps before his hand engulfs mine and pulls me up short.

"Jax, you shouldn't have cocktails after being drugged yesterday and this morning."

He's right of course. I half expected I'd be passed out for days, but I obviously didn't get as much forced into me as Dr Xavier had hoped.

"I'll have a mocktail." I smile fakely at him, trying to pull my hand free of his but he holds strong.

"I'll walk you there."

Giving in, I let him do that, partially happy that he's with me, and partially certain I need to breathe, which is hard when he's offering me up as a visual feast for his men so he can fill my belly with his child.

We are quiet as we walk through the Palace and out onto the street, the warm December afternoon reminding me how close Christmas is, and how it's unlikely I'll be spending it with my sister.

My sister, who was taken away by my mother so I couldn't see her when I arrived at her apartment.

My sister, who was used as a pawn to try and trick me at first.

She must be so upset.

"I took that too far, didn't I?" Devon's deep rasp gains my attention, and I glance up at him as we stroll up the path, hand in hand like boyfriend and girlfriend. "I'm sorry, little mouse. I shouldn't have done that after what you just went through."

I frown. "I'm not annoyed because of that. I have a feeling anything you do to or with me just helps me forget that nightmare."

My admission has his dark brows quirking up. "Something about what I did has made you quiet."

I mull over what I should say, because I doubt he'll give up unless I tell him something, and he has a damn good bullshit radar, so lying is out of the question.

So I go with a naked truth. "I think I got scared of how much I wanted to take you up on the offer."

Feet halting, Devon spins me to face him. "What scared you about it?"

I scoff and laugh at the same time, the sound more like a snort. "Where do I start?" I shrug. "I shouldn't want people to watch that, Devon. Let alone your men. And there's a part of me that is a little annoyed that you'd want them to see me like that."

He nods, not looking insulted by my admission. "You watch at Cloud 9, but it's natural to want to be the one everyone is watching and getting off on seeing. I imagine you've thought about that when you went to the club."

I nod, not even ashamed to admit that, which is weird in itself. Normally I would be very ashamed.

"And while I am very fucking possessive over you, as long as no one touches you, and you're okay with being watched, I would share that with my men, but it wouldn't be for them, little mouse. It'd be all for you."

His dark eyes roam over my face, locking in on my lips before they travel lower to where his free hand glides down my side and comes to settle on my stomach.

"You have no idea how much I want to fill you with my cum. How much I want this food baby to turn into a real one."

A shiver ripples up my spine, and not one of disgust, but instead excitement.

How does Devon Marx have this control over me?

Reminding me of my food baby, my thoughts shift back to my sister again, and I push any heat I have building in my core aside, for some real talk.

"I'm worried about my sister's safety. My dad might be in hospital, but my mum... well she does everything he asks of her, and I don't trust her with Presley."

"Leave it with me, love. I'll make sure she's kept safe."

I nod, not sure how he'll do that, but certain he's a man of his word.

We walk the rest of the way in silence, but it isn't strained. It's just comfortable. Easy.

Something I'm not used to.

Devon walks me into Miss Barber's backyard, giving the famous Miss Barber strict instructions to only make me mocktails, and the other women engulf me, practically pulling me from Devon's grip to welcome me into their fold.

Devon shoots me a wink, and leaves, and then all eyes are on me.

"Oh my god. He's in love with you." Miss Barber looks nothing like I imagined.

I was sure I was about to meet an older woman with a neat French roll, wearing a suit, but instead I find what I can only describe as a hippy, with dreadlocks.

She's delightful.

Thankfully, with Allegra and Eden here, I'm not the only one drinking non-alcoholic cocktails, and I notice that so too, is Marilda.

Her son is off to the side, playing in a sandpit with a couple of other children, and I wonder if she doesn't like to drink around her son, or if there's another reason... Like maybe she's pregnant. With Devon's child.

Ugh. I don't want to think such a thing and I really have no claim over Devon, but the thought has me jealous as hell, and I hate that Marilda seems so lovely, because I'd love nothing more than to claw her eyes out.

I mean. Not that I know her story, but you can't tell me that her son doesn't resemble Devon.

I wave off Miss Barber's comment about Devon loving me, and instead ask about all of them.

"Tell me how you all came to be a part of this town."

"We all came here for the same reason," a female speaks up, and her familiar smile takes me back to the beer garden at the back of the Palace. I'm sure Devon said her name is Natasha. She played the guitar. "Devon and his men saved us and offered us sanctuary."

I frown. Did I hear that right?

"I can see Natasha has confused you." Miss Barber hands me a mocktail and takes a seat next to me on the wicker bench. "Each of us were in a bad situation. A situation not even the police could save us from. The Marx family were the only ones that could help."

"And Angel Org," the woman that jogged by me yesterday and told me women throw themselves off the cliff adds.

"Angel Org?" I ask.

"Angel Org is run by the Angel sisters. Bec and Amanda Angel. They help women and girls get out of violent situations when the law fails them." Celeste explains. "And they're backed by the Marx family."

"Yeah, Dev and his cousins are the muscle." Allegra wags her brows, and the women snicker. "And then they offered us this place to recoup. Get back on our feet until we're ready to leave and start a life somewhere else."

"Only a couple of women have left." Marilda speaks up for the first time. "Most of us are happy here. It's a simple life. Safe for not just us but our children too."

"Don't you miss your families?" I ask, knowing I would miss Presley.

"We can still see them if and when it's safe," Melissa, the girl who was in Devon's office the first time I went to see him there, adds, offering me a small smile.

"Do they know you're here?"

They all shake their heads.

"No, sweetie. It's safer for them as well as all of us if no one knows our location," Miss Barber says, her smile warm when I glance her way again.

"Don't you get lonely. What about... you know?" I lift my brows looking pointedly at Miss Barber who smirks knowingly.

"Sex? Oh, that's not a problem here, sweetie. Have you seen all the men guarding us?"

All the women giggle and Allegra scoffs. "Speak for yourself. Apparently, I'm too young to be touched. Why can't they save a woman with a teenage son? Ugh." Allegra lulls her head back dramatically, and the women laugh at her. "You can all laugh all you like, but I have needs you know. Just ask my kitty."

"No one here wants to talk to your kitty, Allegra." Celeste cringes.

"I've told you a hundred times, Alle, I'll talk to your kitty." Eden grins, and Allegra waves her off.

"You don't count. We fool around all the time. I want me a dic—"

"That's enough!" Marilda leaps up, glancing at her son before glaring at Allegra. "Mind your language around Damon."

"Fine, whatever." Allegra slumps in her chair and sips on her mocktail

"So what about the women that jump over the cliff? Why did they do that?"

In unison, everyone turns to glare at Celeste.

"What?" She shrugs. "I was just being honest." She doesn't look concerned with their glares and Melissa rolls her eyes.

"Sadie was the only one to do that, Celeste, and she was beyond help. No one could save her from her demons."

They all fall quiet, like they are remembering this Sadie woman who obviously took her own life.

I feel bad for ruining the mood.

"Enough about poor Sadie." Miss Barber waves a dismissive hand. "I'm more interested in you, Jaxcen."

"Oh, uhhh. There's nothing interesting about me."

"Pfft. As if." Allegra waves a hand at me. "Devon brought you here as a guest. A *guest*." She enunciates the word guest like it's important.

"And you stay in his suite." Eden grins from ear to ear, wagging her brows.

"Uhhh. Yes." I'm not entirely sure why this is a big deal, but Celeste, who obviously likes to say whatever comes to mind, fills me in.

"Devon has never brought his fucks back here."

I gape and Marilda snaps, "Language, Celeste. Seriously you women act like we don't go over this every damn week."

"Marilda is right." Miss Barber speaks up as Celeste goes to say something. "We need to remember there are children here."

"I, ah… I'm not his…" I can't string more than two words together, both from the shock of what Celeste said and being called out so plainly.

"Oh we know he's protecting you from someone." Natasha smirks. "I got that out of Bruno the second day you were here."

"Tell them how you got it out of him." Allegra giggles, and Natasha shrugs.

"He can never say no to a blowie."

Marilda glares at Natasha, but Natasha just shrugs. "I could be talking about a blow fly, Ril, calm down. Damon has no idea what we are talking about."

Marilda rolls her eyes, and I remain shocked at this group of women, who aren't at all what I thought they'd be like.

"Devon protects all of us." Miss Barber gains my attention again. "But he's never invited any of us to his suite before." She winks at me, and there's my blush, calling me out like a beacon.

"Have you seen the way he looks at her?" Eden coos. "I want a man to look at me like that one day."

They continue chatting about their experiences encountering Devon and I together like I'm not even here, and my mind feels like it's about to explode from what they told me.

It's hard to believe Devon really hasn't taken any of them to his suite, and it makes me wonder if he's even really a monster at all.

He is though. I know it. I've seen it. I've experienced it. And still, I want him and his monster like I want my next breath.

I spend a few hours with the women, watching them interact, answer questions as vaguely as I can, my eyes always returning to Marilda, and her son Damon.

Is it really just a coincidence that Damon looks so much like Devon?

Were Marilda and him a thing before she came here, and now they are simply co-parents?

I want to ask, but not in front of everyone, so I table those thoughts for another time, which is when my tall, dark and lethal keeper returns to collect me.

Allegra leaps at him and shoves a Santa hat on his head before he chats to the women for a few minutes, and even goes to the children playing, but only picks up one child.

Damon.

They are familiar with each other, Damon kissing Devon's cheek, and when Devon puts Damon down, the little toddler doesn't want him to leave.

Marilda steps in to save Devon, picking up Damon who is crying and reaching for Devon as he approaches me, and my heart sinks.

Even though Marilda doesn't display it, she's affected by Devon coming to me, there's a split second that her eyes meet mine and I'm met with a hint of a glare.

"Ready to go, little mouse?" Devon asks, his hand pressing to the small of my back as he leads me to the gate, and I risk another glance over my shoulder at Marilda, only now her back is to me.

"Where are we going?" I ask, confused by what I just witnessed.

"You've been sinning again, Miss Summers." Devon's deep rasp snaps all of my attention to him, and I glance up to see his dark eyes smouldering with lust. "It's time to confess to the devil."

Vida Loca
Trust

CHAPTER THIRTY

Devon

The candles flicker as I close the chapel door behind us, closing us in, the path lighting the way to the confessional once again. I watch her as she scans the space, her eyes travelling over the candles and the booth, probably remembering what I did to her last time.

She looks a little anxious, and I can't help but think it's because of what that sick fucking doctor had planned for her.

She's been relatively okay, considering, but she can't possibly be, right? Unless those years locked away have desensitised her to the point she doesn't need to deal with the trauma.

Nah. Fuck that. I know she carries those disturbing memories with her, always.

Her big blue eyes dart up to meet mine, and I shoot her another wink, because I don't know what else to fucking do.

This is new.

I'm never at a loss when it comes to matters of sex. But fuck, she's... more than that.

Reaching up to the stupid Santa hat still on my head, I go to tug it off, but her sweet voice stops me.

"Don't." She reaches for my arm, tugging it back down. "Leave it on."

Frowning, I narrow my eyes at her. "I hardly look like the devil with a fucking Santa hat on."

She snickers, facing me fully and her delicate fingers reach up and start unbuttoning my shirt. She doesn't speak, her gaze shifting from the buttons and up to my face as she goes, before pushing the fabric open to reveal my bare chest and abs.

"Now you do."

Fuuuck. Her voice is husky from what I hope is arousal, and her gaze is a little lust drunk as she smirks wickedly, taking a few steps back to gawk at me.

"In the confessional, little mouse."

She hesitates, her smile faltering briefly before she looks over her shoulder at the booth.

She's nervous about going in there.

"It won't be like last time." I assure her, needing her to trust me, and she turns back, frowning.

"Why not?"

"So much has changed, love."

My admission has her frown deepening, and a look of frustration gets shot back at me.

"Nothing has changed," she protests, "I'm not some fragile damsel—"

"I never said you were, little mouse."

"Yet you're treating me differently because of what happened at Holly River."

I stalk towards her, and she steps back matching my strides as we slowly travel up the candle lit path.

"It has nothing to do with Holly River, Jaxcen."

"What does it have to do with then?" she asks, glancing over her shoulder as she hurries backwards, keeping the distance between us.

"It has to do with the fact that things between us have changed."

She stops and frowns. "Have they?"

I nod, closing the gap and cupping her nape. "They have." That's the only answer she's getting from me, so I claim her lips in a kiss that feels like she's the one claiming me, and not the other way around.

A growl rumbles in my chest as I fist her hair, a whimper falling from her mouth into mine as we devour each other, our tongues battling for domination, and fuck, I feel like I'd give it all to her if I were a better man.

But since I'm not, I refuse to let her try and get the upper hand, tugging her hair back and taking control of the kiss.

She's panting by the time I break it, her lips swollen, just the way I fucking love them, her blue gaze even more drunk on the situation as her tits press into my chest, and my cock presses against her pelvis.

"I don't want to confess in there," she whispers, but there's no fear in her words, just fact.

She's strong, but perhaps a confession so soon after being taken to her version of hell isn't such a good idea tonight.

I release her hair. "We can leave."

"No, I don't want to leave. I want to do something... different."

Frowning at her, I watch her eyes, trained on mine as she slowly lowers to her knees before me, and then she lowers her head.

Fuck. Not only is the possessive side of me practically preening at the sight of her in the submissive position, but the fact she still wants to do this fills me with pride.

She understands my brand of crazy.

The fact she wants to do this face to face instead of hiding behind the barrier of discretion and anonymity a confessional provides also does something to me I'm not sure how to explain.

Is it trust?

Does she trust me?

"My devil." Her voice, so soft and innocent, sends my heart racing as she begins. "I bestow upon you my darkest sins, and ask that you bathe in my debauchery."

I growl like the beast I am, my cock joining the party as he too appreciates her words. Her submission.

"Divulge your sins, Jaxcen. Tell me everything bad you've done."

"I've been defiled by the devil multiple times, and I loved it," she admits, her head lifting slowly, her gaze coming up to meet mine as I stand over her, tall and dominating. "There's a possibility I'm already carrying the devil's spawn."

Again I growl, my need to possess her ready to fucking burst.

But I have to wait.

I need patience. I want this to last.

"I stole a car. A slick sexy red Corvette, and I nearly ran over the guards when I escaped. I busted up the front of the Corvette pretty badly."

She licks her lips, her gaze dropping to the hard bulge in my pants, and my cock jerks just knowing she is looking.

"What else?" I rasp, and those big blues lock back onto my eyes.

"I'm pretty sure I broke all the speed limits in the state. I also did an illegal turn and then drove up the wrong side of the street."

I fucking remember the sight of the Corvette half on the path half on the road, its nose pointing in the wrong direction.

"More. Tell me everything," I demand, and her eyes flare.

"I kneed my fiancé in the balls."

My brows shoot up at that, and again I feel pride fill me, glad she stood up to him.

"Actually, he's not my fiancé. He's my ex."

"Atta girl." I reach out and grip her chin, angling her head back more and unzipping my fly, and fuck me, the way she drags her gaze to the sight, the tip of her pink tongue darting out to wet those lips like she's imagining wrapping them around my shaft has precum beading on my tip. "What else?"

"I nearly leaped to my death," she whispers like she's mesmerised by my cock, and it takes me a hot fucking second to realise what she said.

"Hold up. What did you just say?"

The way I squeeze her jaw has her attention returning to my eyes, and she gives me a one shouldered shrug.

"Dr Xavier had two male nurses with him. They came after me, and since they were blocking the entrance, the only other way out was by diving out the doors and over the balcony."

"What!" I snap, ready to fucking murder someone. Anyone, but again, she simply shrugs like it was no big fucking deal.

"I would have rather died than let Dr Xavier take me back to Holly River," she admits easily, but I can't fucking fathom it.

"No," I bark, slapping her hand away when she reaches for my cock. "You need to fight always, little mouse. You hear me?"

I'm met with her glare, as she slaps my hand away this time before wrapping her dainty hand around my shaft. "That *was me* fighting. That was me deciding my fate and not letting them decide it for me. That's my prerogative."

Fuck. I get that. I really fucking get that, but it doesn't make it any easier to accept that if they hadn't stopped her, she'd be dead right now.

My gut sinks at the alternative.

Them stopping her means they caught her and one of them fucking touched her. Touched *my* pussy.

As if she's hoping the magic of her tongue will disorient me enough to drop the subject, Jaxcen's pink tongue darts out as she leans closer and licks up the salty bead on the tip of my cock.

"Fuck, little mouse. You're not playing fair."

She shrugs. "Add that to the list of my sins."

I grin. I fucking grin wide because holy fuck, this woman before me is so different to the one I kidnapped only days ago.

This one is confident. Taking what she wants. And more importantly, fucking fantastic at sinning for me.

"Stop, little mouse," I rasp, fisting her hair to pull her head back right in time to stop her from wrapping those fucking perfect plump lips around me.

As soon as she does that, I know I'm a goner.

"But I wanna suck you," she begs, her voice more whiney, but no less fucking sexy. "I want you to choke me again. Make me gag."

"Fuck, woman. That mouth of yours is dirty tonight."

She shrugs, biting her lower lip as her gaze darts between my cock and my face. "I want to be so dirty with the devil. I want to be filthy."

How the fuck can I deny that?

"Okay, little mouse, but not here. Let's go back to my room so I can spend all night making you regret begging me for that."

CHAPTER THIRTY-ONE

Jaxcen

If I thought Devon was going to let me walk back to his suite on my own, I'm sorely mistaken. How can I be annoyed by the fact that after he tucked his dick away, he lifted me to wrap my legs around his hips, and then slipped two fingers inside me while he walked us back.

The fact that we passed some of his men, and Marilda pushing Damon in the stroller as she headed home from Miss Barber's should mortify me, but it didn't.

I mean, they couldn't see what he was doing, but the sight of my legs around him alone should have sent shame crashing through me.

Finally back in his suite, he slips his fingers free and lowers me to the ground.

"Strip."

I do, without protest, my skin already ablaze and desperate for his touch.

As I peel my clothes off, I watch as he disappears into the bathroom, before returning with an armful of towels.

"What are you doing with those?" I ask, and when his gaze meets mine, I swear it's the most sinful smile I've ever witnessed.

"These are to protect my sheets and carpet a little."

"Oh. Right," I say nodding, but then frown. "Wait. Protect it from what?"

"In case you puke."

Air gets stuck in my throat, and I have to cough to dislodge it, as Devon chuckles, making sure the towels are spread out properly.

His words do two things.

Scare me.

And turn me on.

Which just scares me even more.

I don't want to throw up. There's nothing sexy about that, but something about the possibility of him gagging me so bad that it forces my body to protest, is making my clit throb.

"On the bed, little mouse. On your back, head over the end."

Oh... my...

I've seen this before at Cloud 9. A man watching the shape of his dick as it slides down the woman's throat made easy by her head hanging back off the bed or couch or whatever it is they have her laid out on.

My heart thrashes wildly as I move to the bed, climbing on and getting in position, hanging my head over the end while I look up at him, now upside down.

"If you need me to stop, pinch my leg," he orders, having already removed his shirt and boots, and now working his jeans and boxers down as his eyes travel over my naked flesh. "Understand, little mouse?"

"Yes." I try to nod, but it's hard to do hanging off the end of his bed.

"Remember to try and breathe through your nose. Don't you pass out on me."

"Okay." I watch as he strokes his hard dick, moving closer.

"Open wide, beautiful."

I'm desperate for him, so he doesn't need to ask me twice, my lips parting wide as the tip of his dick slides in. And in. And in.

Damn. I forgot how big he is. How girthy. I have to really stretch my jaw to accommodate him, and in no time, I'm gagging, his size even more overwhelming in this position.

"That's it, little mouse. You can take me."

I gag again, this time the action heaving my stomach, so he eases out, and I take in a deep breath, my eyes watering as I swirl my tongue around his tip.

"You sure you want to do this?" he asks. "I can always pop your anal cherry."

His dark eyes are humorous at my glare, but I reach over my head and grip his hips, drawing him closer again so he sinks deeper as I suck.

"Fuuuck, Jax. Your mouth is heaven." He starts gliding his dick in and out, the sloppy sounds filling the room before he goes deeper and once again, I gag.

"Fuck, I love the way your throat grips my cock when you gag, little mouse."

He pushes in further, and again, I gag and heave, but he doesn't retreat this time.

"Atta girl. I can see my cock in your throat, Jaxcen. It looks as good as it feels."

He thrusts again, and again my body tries to reject it, and I'm a little worried we're about to make use of those towels, but then, he leans over my body, and his lips latch onto my clit, and he sucks.

I moan around his cock and he thrusts in and out in shorter rhythm, and with my mind preoccupied on the heat building between my legs, I hardly notice when I gag again.

"You taste so fucking good," he murmurs against my nub, his tongue swirling over it in small little flicks before he starts sucking again.

This entire thing is so hot. I'm beyond aroused. I feel like I'm entering another sphere and I thrust up against his mouth as he thrusts into my throat, a frenzy taking over both of us.

"Fuck, Jax. You take me so good," he grits out, surging deeper than I thought was possible, my body fighting it even as I chase my own release.

The moment I heave again, he sucks so hard on my clit that I shatter, wave after wave rippling through me, my orgasm so intense and full bodied, that I nearly miss the moment when his seed shoots down my throat, and I fight against my body's reflex to reject it.

Stars start to dance around the edges of my vision as I blink, but I don't tap out. I don't want to make him stop until he's done.

Another climax spears through my clit, making me gasp and suck his seed down, which is the last thing I remember before everything goes black.

Nothingness.

A void.

So light. So free.

Dark.

Nothingness.

A gasp lurches from my lips as freezing cold water engulfs me, and I start hacking up the remnants of cum lodged in my throat.

"Fuck. Jax." Devon pants, not from exhaustion but what sounds very much like fear. "You scared the fuck outta me."

He slumps to the floor with me in his arms, cold water beating down on us from his shower head above, as I spit and cough, gasping for air.

"You were meant to pinch me," he pants again, his arms so tight around me like he's scared to let me go.

"Sorry," I scratch out, my voice husky.

"Please tell me you're alright?" He cups my face, ignoring the cold stream of water, so I nod.

"I'm okay. Promise."

"Fuck." Pressing his forehead to mine, I see it now, so clearly. He really is scared, and not just because I could have died, I suppose, but because he actually cares about me.

"It's a little cold though." I try to giggle, and he hurries to turn on the hot water, and a moment later, steam begins to fill the space as the icy blast turns molten.

"Why did you do that?" he rasps, sounding so far from the monster I know.

"I didn't want to stop you right in the middle of... you know."

His dark eyes roam over my face like he's trying to see if I really am alright.

"Never compromise your safety for a guy to nut, little mouse."

"It wasn't just a guy." I shrug. "It was the devil."

He tries to smirk, but it's weak at best.

"I'm sorry," I whisper, feeling more emotional than I'd like.

His reaction is unexpected, and my need to be closer to him feels like an overwhelming surge of energy I don't know what to do with.

"Fuck me?" I whisper, tears welling in my eyes as shame begins to engulf me.

I took it too far. I realise that now.

"Not tonight, little mouse." He brushes back my wet hair plastered to my face, and even though he looks at me like he'd love nothing more than to have sex with me, he still holds back.

"Why?"

"We should get you to bed. Tomorrow will be a big day." He shifts me off his lap and stands before holding his hand out to me.

"What's tomorrow?"

"Christmas Eve." He tugs me up to stand, gripping both my arms to steady me when I get a little dizzy. "It's my town's busiest day of the year."

"It is?" I ask, curious now, letting him shift me under the hot stream of water as he steps out and starts drying himself.

"Yep. It's the only day we let outsiders in."

"You do?"

He nods, ruffling the water from his dark hair with the towel as he watches me.

"We open the gates on Christmas Eve and people who dare, come and see the lights and enjoy the handcrafts we sell, the music, and food."

Wow. I wasn't expecting that.

"So Mr I Hate Christmas lets other people enjoy it?" I snicker, and he grins and shrugs.

"Keeps them happy I guess."

"You're really just a big softie, aren't you?" I tease, and he glares playfully at me.

"Like fuck." And then he reaches in and flicks the hot water off, laughing at my scream as cold water rushes over me again.

"Arsehole!" I yell, hearing him laugh all the way back into his room.

Quickly flicking the hot water back on, I let it wash over me, feeling the loss of a different kind of warmth Devon brings me so easily.

And no, I'm not talking about the warmth he induces between my legs.

I'm talking about the warmth that fills my chest whenever he's near. The warmth that I can't ever remember feeling until we crossed paths.

It's a warmth I want to hang onto.

I finish up in the shower, hoping that once we are under the covers of his bed, he'll change his mind and want to have sex with me, but when I slip in and he pulls me into his side, I know he meant what he said, and it leaves me feeling perplexed.

Devon Marx doesn't shy away from sex. He'd go all night long if he really wanted to, so, with a heavy heart I realise that perhaps he just really doesn't want to.

Maybe he's nearly done with me warming his sheets.

I may be inexperienced and naive, but I never thought this was more than it is.

He kidnapped me. Lied to me to keep me safe. And has been using my body as his plaything. Nothing more.

His big hands are like magic wands, putting me to sleep by their gentle strokes up and down my back as he holds me close. His touch quickly chases away my worries, and before I know it, sleep is dragging me under to dreams of a tall shadowed man that chases me through the dark, his laugh wicked, but his kiss familiar.

When I finally rouse the next morning, Christmas Eve morning, Devon is nowhere in sight.

Dragging myself out of the comfort of his sheets, I find another handwritten note for me on the bedside table.

Maybe everything is alright. Maybe last night's worries were unfounded, because he wants to unwrap me later.

That has to be a good sign, right?

Not that it matters. I have to go back to my life as soon as he finds the psychopath out to get revenge by killing me. Then it will be back to the daily grind. Working a desk job that brings me no fulfilment.

Eddie wasn't wrong.

I have no skills. Hell, the data entry position is a job share, and when the other lady comes back from maternity leave, I'll be back in the mailroom full time.

God, I want out of that life.

But what can I do? Admin for the rest of my life?

That is my qualification, but I just did that to please Eddie. To please my father.

What would I have done if I wanted to please myself?

I have no idea. I have no interests besides Cloud 9.

Okay, so that isn't true. I love shoes. Like a lot. And fine clothes. Suits that make a woman look powerful, yet exude femininity and tease onlookers, with sexy frills and high split skirts, or a blouse that ties up at the neckline with the satin of a ribbon, but hints to the cleavage underneath through the lace that finishes at the top of the bustline.

Shopping isn't something I can make a living from.

I have no friends. Presley is the closest thing I have to a friend, but I don't get to see her often even though we live in the same city.

Eddie prefers it that way. No friends. No anyone.

People bring their drama, and we don't need it.

That's what Eddie says, but now, I think it's more than that.

I think it's just another way to control me. To keep me naive and dependent on him as my only person.

I miss the boy he was, because the man he is sucks.

Pushing away all thoughts of Eddie and my lack of a life, I decide that for now, I have one, so I quickly shower and dress just as my devil requested, and then I make my way out into the bustling street.

It takes me a minute, but I eventually spot Devon, helping to carry some boxes to the stalls that are being set up along the road.

I grin.

He's wearing the Santa hat again, and he's clearly not happy about it.

Not able to wipe my smile from my face, I walk over to him, and when he looks up, he glares, although it holds no real fire.

"Don't start," he grunts, dusting his hands off before wiping them on his jeans.

"Don't start what? I didn't say anything," I say, innocently batting my lashes.

"You don't have to, it's written all over your face." He lifts an accusing brow and I beam, turning my sights on Allegra who is unpacking homemade Christmas snow globes and placing them on the stall table.

"Hey Allegra." I grin, getting her attention, which is always mischievous. "He looks good in the Santa hat, doesn't he?"

"He does." She nods enthusiastically. "Wait until you see him tonight."

"What's he doing tonight?" Now she really has piqued my interest.

"Tonight is the night all the men in town dress up as Santa, and not the kind with round bellies and wrinkly eyes. These Santas are as sexy as sin."

"What do you know about sexy?" Devon mutters, opening another box for Allegra to start unpacking. "You're twelve."

She gasps, nearly dropping one of the snow globes, but manages to catch it in time and place it safely on the table. "You know damn well I'm sixteen."

He scoffs. "Barely. And sixteen year olds shouldn't be looking at older men and thinking they're sexy."

"Then perhaps you need to hire uglier guards." She sneers, although playfully.

"Perhaps I should just lock you and Eden up for the night to make sure you can't get into any trouble."

Her mouth drops open as she jerks her head back like he just slapped her with an invisible hand. "You wouldn't dare."

"Try me." Devon smirks, leaning in and getting in her face.

"You know I'd escape. I can break into anything. And I can break out of anything as well."

"Should we put your theory to the test?" He quips and Allegra's face turns bright red with anger.

"Ah, Devon. I really need your help with something." I cut in, wanting to save the poor girl from the situation escalating purely due to a battle of wills.

Taking his hand, I tug him away from Allegra, who pokes her tongue out at him before turning her back and focusing on her work.

"Fucking teenagers," Devon mutters, and I grin.

He sounds like a dad or big brother.

I can tell he cares about Allegra, but she's certainly mastered the ability to get under his skin without getting herself killed.

Devon and I spend the day working side by side, helping the town's people set up their stalls and prepare for the night ahead. Devon's eyes travel over me every minute, leaving a searing path that gets harder to ignore each time he does it.

He must like me in red. Or maybe it's because I'm wearing what he ordered.

Yeah, it's probably that.

A few times, we find ourselves under a mistletoe, which I'm pretty sure is care of Allegra. I can hear her giggling each time Devon makes use of the Christmas tradition, taking me off guard and smacking his lips to mine before he whispers something dirty in my ear.

"I want to eat you."

"I can't wait to unwrap you and pash your clit until you soak my face."

Or, my favourite. "I want to rip those panties off and fuck you right here on Main Street."

Very inappropriate given there are minors around, but I'm pretending there are no such things here to witness something that dampens my panties from just the idea of it.

In the late afternoon, Devon and his men disappear to have a meeting, something which I notice they do a lot, so I go up to Devon's suite and find my phone, calling my sister to see if she's alright.

She cries at first, apologising profusely for the role she played in what happened after I got to her apartment, but I assured her I'm alright, and asked how Mum and Dad were.

I didn't really hear what she said, mainly because I don't really care, and eventually, I ended the call, feeling heavy at the fact I won't be spending Christmas with her.

I miss my sister.

Around 6pm, the smell of cooking food draws me back down to the street, where several barbeques are fired up with sizzling meat and vegetables cooking. That's when all the Santas appear.

Cheers ring out from the female community members as the Santas grin, no hat or beard hiding their identity for now.

I have to say, that's one bunch of sexy Santas.

It's weird seeing Devon's men wearing red suits instead of their black clad uniforms. Especially Miles. He's just too big to be a Santa.

"If you keep ogling my men like that, I'm gonna bring out my gun."

Devon's sinister voice rasps against my ear as he pulls me back against him, and a giggle escapes me as we both watch this tight knit community laughing and enjoying each other's company.

"You promise?" I ask, biting my lip to hold back my teasing grin, and Devon spins me in his arms.

"Stop it. You'll get my men killed, and I need them tonight."

"To play Santa?"

"To protect my town."

His words are laced with concern, and I glance over my shoulder again, noticing for the first time that although the men are wearing Santa suits, I can see the outline of some of their weapons underneath.

"Is something going on?" I ask, peering up at him to see his eyes taking in the street.

"It's always a risk opening the gates to the public," he murmurs, as if his attention is caught on something else.

"Are you concerned that the man trying to kill me will come here? Does he know where you live?"

Those deep dark eyes drop to mine now, roaming my face as he speaks quietly. "You're safe here, little mouse."

He tries to assure me with a wicked smile and a wink... So why don't I believe him?

Vida Loca
Trust

Chapter Thirty-Two
Devon

The problem with Jaxcen is she sees more than she should. I don't like lying to her, but from the little I know about her, I know she would try and take matters into her own hands if she knew what could potentially happen tonight.

Or more like, what I'm hoping will happen so I can put a fucking end to this shit.

She'd try and save me, or literally anyone else, but herself.

I employ Marilda to keep Jaxcen occupied after we eat, and by 8pm, Taylor, Alice and Natasha take the small stage at the edge of the street and begin their evening of Christmas carols. A little after, as the sun starts to dip further, we can see the trail of car lights driving up the small mountain, heading our way.

Excitement is in the air, the women practically bursting at the seams to have the town filled with onlookers and those happy to spend their hard earned money on the local handcrafts.

My men are now fully dressed, beards and Santa hats hiding their identity, while some are still dressed in all black, but they are hidden strategically, out of sight where they can watch on, their weapons trained on our visitors, ready for any sign of trouble.

"First cars are approaching the gates now," Finn says, coming to my side. "You sure you want to do this?"

I nod, even though I really do want to pull the pin.

"Open the gates. It ends tonight."

Nodding back, Finn calls the guards at the gates and orders them open.

"Is Dom's team in place?" I ask, knowing they are but needing the reassurance.

"Yep. There are eyes on all cameras. No one will slip away from Main Street without being noticed."

"And Lenny is in the shadows?"

"Roger that. His team is armed and ready." Finn reassures me.

"Okay. Let's keep Melissa safe, yeah?"

"Of course," Finn agrees.

"You got your situation handled?" I turn now to look at my best mate, biting back a smirk he won't be able to see under this itchy as fuck fake white beard.

He has a fucking bite mark on his neck that I spotted earlier today. I want to give him shit for it, but it'll have to wait until I have time to hear the story behind it.

"It's handled for now. I'm still not happy about it."

"You said it yourself. Your visitor was getting too aggressive, and trying to escape. If you didn't drug her food, then we'd have to worry about her causing havoc in the town as well."

Finn nods. "She won't trust me now. I did exactly what I promised her I wouldn't do."

Reaching out, I clap him on the shoulder and his eyes meet mine. "When this is over, you can focus on her. I promise."

I feel like a cunt for demanding he drug his captive. Or visitor. I'm not really sure what to call her since he did save her, but also has her hauled up in his house up on the hill.

Kind of reminds me of the situation with my little mouse. Although, there's zero flirting where Finn is concerned and more trying *not* to get killed by Frankie.

Voices sound in my earpiece, my men at the gates sending updates as cars pull into my town, parking in the front paddocks before they make the hike up the steep hill.

It's not long before my little town is filled with strangers, which puts me on edge more so than any other Christmas Eve.

There's a lot of cheer going on. Children's laughter. Oooh's and ahhh's from women exploring the stalls for last minute gifts, as well as men's laughter while many of them congregate outside the Palace, having a cold beer on me as they chat and watch the live music.

Moving from stall to stall, I help here and there, trying to blend in enough not to be noticed as the king of this town.

Jaxcen easily tells me apart from my other Santas, her eyes catching mine when I assist at Allegra's store and then Marilda's.

I also don't miss the narrowing of eyes Jaxcen sends my way when I talk quietly with Marilda.

It looks like my little mouse gets jealous easily.

Yet another form of sin.

That thought makes me smile.

I think I'm thoroughly corrupting Miss Summers and I'm not even fucking sorry.

"I can't believe we are out of ice again." Ronnie grumbles as he approaches Marilda's stall. "Have you seen Eden? I need her to get some more ice from the cellar."

"She's over there." Jaxcen points across the street, where Eden and Allegra are talking to a group of teenage boys. "I can get the ice for you."

Her offer shouldn't surprise me, but it does.

This isn't her town. In fact, she was brought here against her will, yet she fits in so much like a local after only a few days.

Why do I like that so much?

"Are you sure?" Ronnie asks, even as he holds out the bucket. "I can grab the girls to do it."

"Don't be silly," Jaxcen waves dismissively. "Leave them to their fun. I'll be right back."

Ronnie mutters a thanks and a shrug as Jaxcen bounces on her toes and spins to head into the Palace. "She's a lot nicer when she's not wielding a knife."

Throwing my head back, laughing, Ronnie's grin appears momentarily before he spins and returns to the makeshift street bar.

I assist in yet another sale of Marilda's knitted Christmas jumpers for dogs when Finn hurries to my side and speaks quietly in my ear.

"Melissa is missing."

I jerk back like the fucker slapped me. "What?"

"Dom and his team are reviewing the CCTV, but so far we don't know when or where it happened."

"Lock the place down. No one leaves," I snap, and Finn nods, pulling out his phone.

My gaze darts everywhere, from stall to stall, from group to group, searching for Melissa, our fucking bait.

It was her idea. She volunteered, and I wasn't happy about it, but the idea that we could lure Mr fucking V here, onto our turf would give us the upper hand.

"We're locked down. No one has left since arriving." Finn informs me which means Melissa has to still be here.

"I want a fucking head count!" I snap, and a nearby child's eyes widen at the fact a Santa is swearing.

I'll fucking care about that later.

"On it." Finn moves away, speaking to some of my other men nearby.

My patience waning, I leave Marilda to handle her stall and start looking for Melissa myself. All the town stores are closed and locked, but she could have gone for a walk around the square, or to the cliff, or back to her house.

I don't know why she'd do that though. She knows she's the bait. She was scared shitless even though she insisted on making herself the target.

"Dev," Finn calls, and I spin in time to see him come to my side. "Headcount via CCTV a few minutes ago is short two females, but has an additional Santa."

"The fuck."

"Yeah. The fuck's right. Could Melissa have dressed as a Santa too? Gone and got changed?"

"No," I bark. "Order all Santas to remove their hats and beards and let's see who's left."

Again, Finn nods, talking into his phone, and a moment later, my men start peeling off their red hats and white beards, revealing themselves.

But there's no extra Santa left standing.

"Someone either doesn't know how to count, or something else is going on." I hiss, and my phone rings this time.

"Boss." Dom's voice rushes out. "We've gone back through the video footage. For about an hour there was an extra Santa, we're working through the footage to see when and where he went."

"Make it quick," I snap, ending the call, worried for Melissa's safety. "Hang on a minute." I turn back to Finn, my brows knitting. "You said we were two women short."

"Yeah, Dom's team is working on the two missing now." He points at the camera close by, and I nod, but then my eyes shift to the entrance of the Palace.

Where's Jaxcen? She should have been back with the ice by now.

Storming towards Ronnie's street bar, I scan the area again, looking for my little blonde sinner in her red dress, but come up empty.

"Ronnie, has Jaxcen been back with the ice yet?"

He shakes his head. "Nah. The damn machine's probably bung again. I'll get someone to cover me and go check it out."

"No, I will," I snap, waving Finn over as I walk up the steps of the Palace.

"The second missing female is Jaxcen. She went to get ice. I'll go get her. Be right back." I grumble, and then snap over my shoulder. "I expect an update when I get back."

My best mate nods like an obedient soldier, not thrown off by my snarky attitude.

He gets the seriousness of the situation.

Moving quickly through the bar, I go down the steep staircase into the cellar, and rounding the corner to where the ice machine is, I skid to a stop.

Jaxcen isn't here, but the bucket she carried in is, and it's tipped over on the floor, some of the rapidly melting cubes strewn right across the room like they were kicked.

"Jaxcen?" I call, looking further into the cellar where we keep the wine, and that's when I hear it.

A whimper.

"Jaxcen!" I boom, charging forward past the aisles of shelves to the back of the cellar.

It's dark back here, but not so dark I can't see those big blue eyes, wide with fear, and I'm about to hurry forward when I see it.

She's strapped to a chair. Tape covering her mouth. And attached to her chest is a fucking bomb.

CHAPTER THIRTY-THREE

Jaxcen

Tremors ripple through my body so violently that I fear the bomb will go off on its own. Never in a million years would I have thought I'd wake up from being knocked unconscious to have an explosive attached to me.

"Fuck. Jax."

There's so much pain in Devon's voice as he takes in the situation, his eyes assessing everything as he moves a few steps closer.

"Mmmooo." I cry against the tape covering my lips, and even to my own ears, I can hear that my 'no' came out as a very muffled mo, but Devon understands.

Stepping closer, ignoring my plea, he quickly tears the tape off my lips, and a sob escapes me.

"There was a man. He knew my name." I blubber through my tears. "I thought it must have been the guy that wanted you dead, but he had Melissa down here too. He took her."

"Fuck," he hisses, pulling his phone out, and a few seconds later, he's talking to someone. Finn, maybe. "Jaxcen is in the cellar tied to a fucking chair with a bomb strapped to her. She said a man was here and he took Melissa. Clear the area now. Evacuate the whole fucking town."

Oh my god. This is really happening. I'm going to die. I'm going to be blown up into tiny pieces. There's no way I will survive this.

Hot tears stream down my face as I try to come to terms with my reality.

There's a timer on the front of the bomb. I'm too scared to look at it. I'm too scared to move, let alone see how many minutes or seconds I have left to live.

Holy crap. This is really it.

"Jax. Try to stay calm," Devon says as he rushes back to turn all the lights on before returning to me and lowering to one knee before me, reaching out and cupping one side of my face. "It'll be alright."

"Stop," I sob, "D-don't kneel down. Y-you need to l-leave."

"There's no fucking way I'm leaving you, little mouse." He declares so factually that I fear he's actually lost his mind.

"Y-you can't s-stay. P-please g-go."

"No." He ignores me, releasing my face before taking a closer look at the bomb strapped to me using the flashlight on his phone.

"P-please Dev. It's okay."

His fierce gaze shoots to mine. "It's not fucking okay. Stop asking me to leave you."

"You can't d-die, Devon. This t-town, these p-people need y-you. I'm okay t-to d-die. I know it s-seems weird but in t-the last few days since m-meeting you, I've lived more t-than I ever thought p-possible." My words stutter out around my sobs, and when he goes to speak, I cut him off. "I don't w-want him to hurt M-Melissa. He was s-saying some pretty c-crude things t-to her."

"Don't worry about Melissa. My men are handling that. And I'm here handling this."

Heavy feet coming down the stairs draw our attention to see Finn, his eyes wide as he takes in the scene.

"Fuck."

His words are a whisper, but I hear them.

Yep. I'm fucked. This is it. My last moments are right here right now.

"Call Warrick." Devon barks over his shoulder, and I see Finn's frown as he stares at Devon's back.

"Are you sure?"

"Yes. Get him on the fucking phone!" Devon yells this time and Finn rushes to take out his phone where he calls someone.

"Just keep as still as you can, little mouse. This will all be over soon."

I mean, he's not wrong. It will be. My life will be over.

I'll miss him, which is weird right? We only just met days ago, yet I feel like he knows me better than anyone else.

Finn talks quietly on the phone, before tapping Devon's shoulder with it and passing it to him.

"Warrick," Devon rasps holding the phone out in front of him, having hit speaker.

"You must really want something if you're calling me." The other voice on the phone says with amusement in his tone, but Devon doesn't waste time with pleasantries.

"Tell me how to disable a bomb."

"Daaaamn," Warrick chuckles. "A bomb hey? And why the fuck should I help you?"

Devon's cheeks flare red with anger, but he grits his teeth and responds to who must be his brother. I'm pretty sure he said his brother's name is Warrick.

"You wanna see your kid again right?" Devon snaps and his brother snaps back.

"What do you think!"

"Then fucking help me, damn it. If this thing goes off, it could hurt him, too."

I frown at Devon's words. Warrick has a son, and he's here?

"Come on, man, it's just ticked past three fucking minutes," Devon pleas.

Wait what?

Less than three minutes?

I have less than three minutes to live?

"Oh my god," I whimper and Warrick sighs.

"Fine. Put me on video so I can see what we're working with."

Devon quickly transfers to video call, and a moment later, he holds the phone up in front of the bomb, while his eyes fasten on me.

'It'll be okay,' he mouths, and more tears well in my eyes.

"It's actually not too complicated," Warrick chimes in again, "or, it is complicated but is made to look easy to fool you."

Another sob tries to escape, but I seal my lips shut, not letting this fear control me.

I'm going to die and take Devon and Finn with me. The thought of killing them too is more terrifying to me than my own death.

"Let's pretend it is easy." Devon snarls into the phone, his eyes not wavering from mine.

"Cut the blue wire," Warrick says simply, and Devon's brows shoot up.

"That's it?"

"We'll find out I guess," the voice says through the phone, and Devon looks like he wants to reach into the phone and strangle his brother.

"Take this." He holds up his phone, and Finn steps forward, taking the phone and replacing it with some electrical wire cutters.

"You need to leave," I whisper to Finn, but he shakes his head.

"I'm right where I need to be, Miss Summers."

"Jax," Devon's pained tone draws my attention back to him, and for a moment, he looks lost for words, until he speaks and it's clear he is. "I... You... We..." he shakes his head, momentarily looking at the floor between us.

He's clearly struggling with something, and I'm about to tell him not to worry about anything because I'm pretty damn sure three minutes must be nearly up.

"Fuck, little mouse. What I'm trying to say is... Thank you for waking me up, too."

I frown, confused by his words. By how I woke him up, when he was the one to wake me up. "H-how did I w-wake y-you up?"

"Fuck, baby," he grits out. "You woke me up in every way imaginable."

It's then that he positions the cutters on the blue wire.

"Give us one last kiss then, love." His tone is so cocky, just like that first night at St Catherine's only days ago, and knowing this is my last moment on earth, I do just that, pressing my lips to his in a searing kiss as I wait for our world to explode.

CHAPTER THIRTY-FOUR

Devon

The click of the cutters sounds as loud as a fucking gunshot, and it takes me a moment to realise the bomb didn't explode.

"Shit, that was a gun." Finn snaps from behind me, and a choked sob falls from my little mouse as she realises she's still alive.

Air is trapped in my throat, and I pull back, taking in those blue eyes, still so fucking frightened as I clear my throat, trying to get my fucking lungs to work.

"Here." Finn shoves his phone back at me. "I'll go see what's happening."

I nod and grunt, not daring to drag my gaze from Jaxcen's as another sob lurches from her lips.

Finn's feet pound back up the cellar stairs, leaving us alone, other than the fact my little brother is still on the phone.

Fuck.

I owe him now.

"A-are we really a-alive?" Jaxcen stammers, her cheeks soaked from her never ending tears. "I-is it really o-over?"

Dragging my eyes from hers, I glance down to see the timer on the front of the explosive has stopped, but I can't tell her it's over yet, because it isn't. Not until that thing is off her body and I can be sure it won't explode.

"War," I hiss at my phone screen as I hold it up to see my brother's face. "The timer has stopped, but will it go off when I remove it?"

"There might be a trigger. You'll have to check under it. Slide your fingers between it and the girl. If you feel something shifting in and out then there's a trigger," my little brother, who is an expert with explosives, explains.

My gaze lifts back to Jaxcen, her sobs quieter now, slowly running out of fizz, like a soda that's been left sitting.

"It's nearly over, little mouse. Hold this." I hold out Finn's phone again, and her trembling hand reaches up to take it. "I'm going to feel around the device, okay, beautiful?"

She nods quickly, taking a big gulp like she's trying to dislodge a lump in her throat.

"Say hi to my brother." I gesture my head to the phone, wanting her attention on something else as I do this. It could still go off at any second. I won't be happy until it's off her and a long fucking way from her or anyone else in this town.

Angling the phone her way, I watch as Jaxcen gazes at the screen, blinking and frowning a little before she pulls the screen a little closer.

"Well, hey there, darlin'. I'm Warrick."

I roll my eyes at my brother's cocky tone. He thinks he's so fucking smooth with chicks.

"H-hey." Jaxcen stutters and clears her throat. "Hi. I'm Jaxcen."

"Hey Jaxcen. Are you one of my big brother's rescues?" Warrick asks, and the moment Jaxcen's lips twitch in a smile, I start running my fingers over the device strapped to her, between it and her body.

"No." Jaxcen responds to my brother, but then changes her answer. "Yes. Kinda."

Warrick chuckles. "A bit complicated, is it?"

"Yeah," she responds, lifting the phone higher as I shift closer, wanting to make sure I reach every part of the explosive that's attached to her.

"Tell me, Jaxcen, have you seen my son?"

I stiffen, my eyes darting up to watch her face.

"Your son?" her tone is surprised, and her brows are hitched.

"Damon. He has my hair colour and eyes," Warrick explains, and I want to end the fucking call.

No one is meant to know his son is here. What the fuck is he doing?

"Oh, do you mean the little boy I thought was Devon's?"

I jerk back at her words, her amused gaze darting to mine briefly before she continues talking to my brother.

"He's your son?"

"Yeah. Wait... Why'd you think he was Devon's son?" Warrick asks, and I'm just as fucking curious to find out that answer, so I listen intently and I move my fingers over the top part of the device.

"Well, he looks like Devon, but I guess so do you. You look like a younger version of him."

"But better looking, hey?"

I roll my fucking eyes again as Jaxcen giggles slightly, but then stills, like she's scared her moment of happiness will set off the fucking bomb.

Easing my fingers from around the device, I'm about to take the phone back when Jaxcen speaks again, her tone snappy.

"What did you do to Marilda?" she asks my brother. "Why is she here hiding from you?"

A chuckle rumbles from my chest. "She's got you all figured out brother," I say, but Jaxcen keeps the phone angled her way.

I want to tell them I can't feel a trigger, but there's just something about her conversing with my little brother, and telling him off that has me sitting back on my heels and watching on.

"Look, it's not what I did." Warrick tries to explain, "It's what my wife did."

Jaxcen frowns, her lips parting to speak and then snapping shut before she manages to ask her next question.

"Your wife? As in Marilda?"

It's natural for her to come to that conclusion. Marilda had his son, after all.

"No," Warrick answers quickly, and I'm fucking curious as to why he's giving Jaxcen the time of day to answer. He tends to be cautious around strangers. "Marilda isn't my wife. Amanda is."

I snicker at the confusion sweeping over Jaxcen's face, and decide to put her out of her misery.

"Long story short, Warrick stepped out on his wife, Amanda, with Marilda, who didn't know he was married at the time, since he conveniently left that out," I explain and Jaxcen's shocked blue gaze shifts to me. Fuck, I love her eyes on me. I love her attention. "War got Marilda knocked up, and when she came calling to tell him, she came face to face with his wife."

"Oh," she murmurs and I laugh.

"Yeah, oh."

"Not fucking funny," Warrick snaps, dragging Jaxcen's gaze back to the screen.

"Kinda is," I mutter, standing and moving around the chair Jaxcen is strapped to, checking if there are any more obstacles before I can free my little mouse.

"But why is she here? Who is she in danger from?" Jaxcen asks, and again, most people assume a man is the culprit, but occasionally, the violent one is the female, especially when said female is already naturally violent, and learns that her husband cheated on her and knocked the woman up. The fact Warrick still has his dick is a fucking miracle.

"From Amanda. My wife. She..." Warrick trails off, and now that I'm behind Jaxcen, I can see his face as he looks around, like he is checking to make sure Amanda isn't nearby. "She's very possessive of me."

"Oh." Jaxcen nods, but I cut their conversation off, taking the phone from her grip.

"I can't feel a trigger."

"Cameras have picked him up dragging Melissa around." Finn hurries up the path to us. "Last sighting was of them heading back this way, but we lost them in the woods."

"I heard chatter." I tap on my ear where the earpiece is. "Who was he shooting at?"

"Dunno. Dom seems to think it's a woman. She was chasing them, surprisingly."

Frowning, I glance over his shoulder at the chapel where some of my men are guarding.

"Are the visitors in there?" I gesture my head and he nods.

"And our women and children. All except Melissa and Jaxcen."

"Do you think it's one of the visitors?" I ask and again he shrugs.

Pulling out my phone I call Dom, who answers immediately.

"Boss."

"This other woman. What does she look like?"

"I haven't been able to get a good look. She keeps to the shadows. Her hair is long and dark."

My gaze shoots to Finn, who is frowning now.

"Where was Mr V running from? Do we know where he was before this woman started chasing him?"

"I don't know exactly. Somewhere up near Wattle Way. Near Finn's joint."

Finn's eyes snap to mine, and a slow smirk kicks up my lips.

"Have you checked to see if your guest is still locked up?" I ask Finn, who shakes his head, eyes wide with panic.

"I drugged her though."

"Who's your guest?" Jaxcen butts in, and Finn answers absentmindedly as he looks over his shoulder up the street, as if considering running up the hill to his house.

"Her name is Frankie. We saved her from Holly River Estate before we set fire to it."

Jaxcen starts laughing, like really laughing. The kind of laugh that's full bodied and a little deranged.

"Little mouse?" I ask, and she waves me off, like I'm an idiot before trying to compose herself.

"You drugged her? With what?" she asks Finn, whose brows are pinched.

"The stuff Dr Xavier had for you," he answers.

"And did you use the dose amount on the bottle?" she asks, trying not to laugh again.

"Well, yeah, maybe a little more."

She scoffs, waving her hand. "That woman has been in the facility for years. She would have built a tolerance for the drugs. It would take a lot more to keep her out for an extended period of time."

My brows hitch and Finn looks even more panicked.

"Fuck. She's escaped."

"Escaped yes, but it seems she's hunting Mr V." I shrug, but he still looks panicked.

"What if she... what if she kills both of them?"

He's right of course. We have no real understanding of how unhinged Frankie may be. Hell, there may have been a legitimate reason why she was locked up in that place.

"Dom, did you hear all of that?" I ask, putting the phone back to my ear, having forgotten I was on a call with him.

"Yes, boss."

"Keep eyes on the woods. We need to know the moment they step out. The rest of us are going hunting."

"On it." Dom hangs up, and Finn sucks in a deep breath, accepting his phone back from me, before typing out a message as I turn to Jaxcen.

"Little mouse, I want you in that chapel with the others. Safe and out of the way of harm, okay?"

When she shakes her head and crosses her arms over her chest, my brows hitch.

"Did you just shake your head at me?" I snap and she nods.

"You said under no circumstances am I to leave your side." She lifts a brow like she's winning an argument, but I shake my head.

"You left out the part where I said, unless I tell you to."

Her eyes turn to slits. "You need me there. Frankie will freak out at all the men chasing her. It's been her against abusive men in that facility for god knows how long. She won't trust any of you. But she'll trust me."

"Melissa will be there," I counter, but she scoffs. Fucking scoffs.

"Melissa, if she's not already dead, has no idea how to handle someone who has been locked away like Frankie has. I'm a better bet. Let me come with you. Give me a gun."

I scoff this time. "In no fucking way am I giving you a gun. You might get fucking trigger happy and shoot me."

"Maybe you deserve it."

I square up to her, ready to throw the little minx over my fucking shoulder and give her a good spanking, when a group of my men hurry our way.

"We're ready. Let's go." Miles announces, and I turn to look at Finn, who's smirking my way.

"It's up to you man, but she's right. She might be able to reason with Frankie."

Fuck. He's right. I know he's right but I can't fathom putting Jaxcen in danger like that.

"I'll stay behind you unless I'm needed," she states, her gentle hand coming to rest on my arm.

Gritting my teeth, I glide my tongue over them before pointing sternly at her.

"You'd fucking better do everything I say."

"I will. I promise."

Fuck. I believe her.

"Fine." I turn back to my men. "Let's join the fucking hunt."

Chapter Thirty-Five

Jaxcen

Adrenalin courses through my veins as I hold on to the back of Devon's red Santa pants, trying to match his long strides as we sink into the woods.

I never in a million years would have thought I'd have the guts to do this, and I can only assume it's from the high I'm already on from surviving the whole bomb thing.

That was the scariest thing I've ever had to face.

And now, I'm heading into danger again, my eyes trying to adjust to the dark woods as Devon and his men go hunting for the man that knocked me out and strapped me to a chair with a bomb.

I want to kill him myself.

Snapping twigs are loud as Devon's men creep through the trees, some of them wearing some sort of goggles that remind me of those night vision things I've seen in movies.

Words are whispered and hand signals are used, all of which I don't understand, except for the one where Miles holds his hand up.

That's a clear stop.

Ha! I do know stuff.

Everyone halts immediately, and they are so still and silent, I wonder if they can hear their blood rushing past their ears too.

I'd ask in other circumstances, but this isn't one of them.

I told Devon I'd behave, and since I don't want to cheat death for a second time today, I do exactly what I'm told.

Miles does another hand signal, a swirl and points in one direction and then the other before straight ahead, doing nothing but confusing me, yet the men understand clearly, and start fanning out. Some to the left. Some to the right, while Devon stays with Miles and Finn, and we start moving forward.

We creep further into the woods, the moonlight filtering through the canopy of trees every so often, helping to light the way, and soon, I hear yelling.

A man yelling.

He sounds scared.

Devon chuckles quietly, which makes me smile. I bet he likes the sound of the man he's hunting being scared.

Hell, I do too.

As we draw closer to the yelling, it becomes clearer to hear, and Devon reaches back to where I'm latched onto his pants, giving my wrist a reassuring squeeze.

"Where the fuck are you?!" the male voice yells. "I'm going to kill you!"

Twigs snap up ahead, and that's when my eyes catch on a shadow. A man, alone, spinning back and forth with something in his hand.

"Knife," Miles whispers, and I see Devon nod as we draw closer.

The moment a feminine laugh floats through the air, we all stop in our tracks, and I swear, the sound of it is so sinister that I can't fight the chill that runs up my spine.

Frankie.

Then, as if that wasn't freaky enough, a hauntingly beautiful voice starts to sing.

"Ding dong, I know you can hear me."

"What the fuck," Devon whispers, and another chill ripples up my spine, as the song, so familiar, turns my blood to ice.

"Open up the door. I only want to play a little."

"Is that her?" Miles whispers, turning back to Finn who shrugs as I croak out.

"Yes."

Fuck yes, that's her.

"Ding dong, you can't keep me waiting. It's already too late for you to try and run away."

Another ripple runs through me, yet my feet move, and I step around Devon as my voice joins Frankie's.

"I see you through the window." I step forward again, ignoring Devon as he hisses at me to stop. "Our eyes are locked together."

"Stop, Jaxcen," he snaps again, reaching for me, but I move forward, revelling in the fearful steps of the man up ahead as he spins again at hearing a second voice join in.

My voice.

"I can sense your horror. Though I'd like to see it closer."

"Stop. Baby." Devon wraps his arms around me from behind, his hoarse voice against my ear, and I don't fight him, but I keep singing the song that was played over the loudspeakers every time one of the patients at Holly River tried to hide or escape.

"Ding dong, here I come to find you. Hurry up and run. Let's play a little game and have fun."

"Fuck," Devon whispers again as the man yells at the top of his lungs.

"Stop! You crazy fucking bitches!"

"Ding dong, where is it you've gone to? Do you think you've won? Our game of hide and seek has just begun."

It's then that we see her.

Frankie.

She's across the other side, staring back at us, or perhaps at the terrified man who is now practically surrounded by Devon's men, and two very crazy bitches.

I smirk.

For the first time ever, I embrace my crazy. Embrace the way this world has made me, letting my voice grow louder with Frankie's as we both stare the prey down.

"I hear your footsteps, thumping loudly through the hallways." I take a breath and continue, remembering the terror this song used to bring. "I can hear your sharp breaths. You're not very good at hiding."

"Stop!" he yells, and Frankie steps closer, letting him see her, and giving us a better view of her monster.

My words falter, but her haunting voice continues, her dark hair long, and tangled in waves on each side of her face, falling down past her hips.

"Just wait, you can't hide from me," she sings and I say the two words that were in the background of the song at this point.

"I'm coming."

And she repeats, stepping closer again. "Just wait, you can't hide from me."

"I'm coming," I sing, and the man stiffens, his eyes catching on her.

"Just wait, you can't hide from me." She steps closer and he backs up, closer to us.

"I'm coming." At my words he spins, facing us and starts backing closer to Frankie.

"Just wait, you can't hide from me." Frankie sings and again he spins to face her, waving the knife in his hand.

"Don't come any closer!"

"Knock knock, I'm at your door now." We sing in unison, and he starts spinning back and forth again.

"I am coming in. No need for me to ask permission."

I can see Devon's men drawing closer to the man, none of them concerned with Frankie, who could totally be unhinged enough to attack anyone at this point.

"Knock knock, I'm inside your room now."

"STOP!!" he cries, pressing his hands to his ears as he drops the knife.

Miles lurches forward, as do another two men, taking the man down to the ground, and our singing cuts off.

With my eyes trained on Frankie, I can see disappointment rush over her expression, and I know it's because Devon's men interrupted her.

She was on the hunt.

"Stay down, motherfucker!" one of Devon's men yells, and Frankie's eyes dart from them to the knife laying forgotten on the leafy floor of the woods.

It feels like it happens in slow motion, Frankie leaping from the shadows, her eyes trained on the glint of the blade, the men too preoccupied to notice the threat to their lives is still very real.

"No!" I try to tug away from Devon, whose arms are like talons holding me in place, but at my scream, everyone stills.

"Frankie," Finn hisses, stepping forward and catching her attention.

It's not good attention though. Her eyes are dark. Fierce. Deranged.

"Put it down!" Finn orders, and a slow sinister smirk spreads her lips as her chilling laugh meets our ears again.

"No," she sneers, taking a step closer to Devon's men, who now have the man kneeling.

"Why?" Finn asks. "Do you know this man?"

She slowly shakes her head, flashing her teeth as she sets her sights on the man again.

"Then why do you want to kill him?"

Her head snaps in Finn's direction again, and it looks like she wants to kill him as well, so I'm surprised she answers.

"He was chasing the girl. He hit her. I didn't like it."

I grin.

She's seen it before I bet. Inside that place we both have in common.

I wonder how many times she tried to kill Dr Xavier or his men.

I think I like her.

"Where's Melissa? The other girl?" Finn asks, and a small voice calls to us through the dark woods.

"I'm here!"

Sighs of relief rush through all of the men, and Lenny and another man veer off into the dark in the direction of Melissa's voice.

When Frankie takes another step forward, Miles raises his gun at her, and this time when I pull against Devon's hold, he releases me.

"Wait!" I yell, stepping closer, my eyes darting between Frankie and Miles. "Don't shoot her."

"Jaxcen," Devon sneers, and the twig snapping behind me tells me he's coming closer but I move quickly so Frankie can see my face.

"You want to kill this man?" I ask, and she gives me a single nod.

"What about these other men? Do you want to kill them?"

She tilts her head at me like she's studying me, her gaze running down to my toes and back up again as she nods and points.

All eyes turn to Finn.

"Why do you want to kill him?"

"He lied," she hisses through clenched teeth and a curled lip.

"The drugs?" I put everything I've overheard together from earlier, and her surprised glare shoots back to me.

"He said he wouldn't."

I nod. "I know. He didn't want to. He was ordered to."

"Why?" she snaps.

"Because the king of this town can be a bit of a dick."

Devon curses behind me as his men chuckle, and her eyes find him.

"But, he has people to protect. Women and children. He saves them from bad people and brings them here. His men guard them from men like this." I point to the arsehole that wanted me dead just to hurt Devon. "You're new here, and please excuse me for being blunt, but you're a little cray cray right now. It'll take you a while to adjust to living outside of Holly River Estate, and Finn knows that, but he also has a duty to keep everyone in this town safe."

Her eyes narrow. "I saw you."

I nod. "Yes. I saw you too."

"It wasn't your first time there?" she states more than asks, but I shake my head anyway. "How long ago?"

I know what she's asking.

"Eleven years ago. Then two years of outpatient visits."

She nods. "I need to kill something. Someone."

Glancing back over my shoulder, I take in Devon, and then Finn, who are all watching on quietly, allowing this conversation instead of just killing Frankie and washing their hands of her.

"You can kill him…" I point to the man that strapped a bomb to me, and when he starts to protest, Miles hits him across the back of his head, shutting him up. "If you promise not to kill anyone else here. They only want to help."

Again her eyes narrow at me, before she glances back at Finn.

"Is maiming that one out of the question?" She points to Finn and I glance at him in time to see him baulk.

"Not totally out of the question as long as he doesn't lose any body parts or die. Oh, and leave his pretty face alone."

"Fuck's sake," Finn mutters behind me, even as Frankie nods.

"You got yourself a deal."

"Seriously?" Finn protests, and Devon responds.

"Yes, for now."

"You were the one that fucking ordered me to drug her."

"And every time she hurts you, you can swing your fists at me," Devon declares.

"I'll be bringing more than my fucking fists," Finn sneers, and Frankie smiles.

It's still creepy as hell, but I can tell she's happy with this outcome.

Twigs snapping off to the side draw our attention to Lenny, who's carrying a slightly battered Melissa cradled to his chest.

"You fucking bitch! My brother died because of you!" the man bellows at Melissa, who is sobbing quietly in Lenny's arms.

"Wrong." Devon steps forward, lowering to his haunches so the man can see him better. "Fit Nick got what he deserved, Vincent."

At the use of his name, the man, Vincent, flinches.

"You really think we weren't going to find out who you really were?" Devon chuckles, although there's no humour to it. "Vinny, Vinny, Vinny. Have you forgotten who I am?"

Leaning closer, Devon gets in his face.

"I'm the fucking devil."

Vincent tries to lurch forward, but Devon's men hold him in place before Devon's fist shoots out, punching him in the nose.

"That was for strapping a fucking bomb to my girl!"

For a second I can't breathe.

It could be because he called me his girl.

It could be from the change in his voice, the beast lurking beneath the surface, ready to snap.

Or it could be both.

It doesn't matter, because neither of them scare me.

Nope.

They make me want to run to him.

I don't, of course, staying rooted on the spot as Devon stands and turns to Frankie.

"No one else. Just him. The moment you threaten anyone else here, you'll have a bullet between your eyes. Got it?"

She nods, her eyes flaring with excitement, and Devon turns back to Miles. "Hold him still for her."

"No," Frankie protests. "Let him go. It's better when they run."

I'm not sure why, or what sort of person this makes me, but I'm in awe of Frankie's courage right now.

Yes, I know she's not exactly sane, but there's a power behind her craziness that I know. I've experienced it before when I was ten.

At Sunday school.

When I slaughtered Brother Eric.

Slowly, Devon nods, giving his men the all clear to release Vincent, and the moment they step away, he tries to run.

He makes it three steps before Frankie takes off after him, and only six before her war cry rips through the air as she dives, leaping on his back, the glint of the blade high before she plunges it between his shoulder blades.

He crashes to the ground, and Frankie swings the knife over and over as we watch on, listening to Vincent's pleas for help, before they turn to gurgles.

Devon wraps his arms around me from behind, his deep rasp against my ear as we watch. "You okay with this? You don't have to watch."

I nod, wrapping my arms over his, holding him as he holds me, watching the most brutally monstrous scene unfold before our eyes.

Frankie, in her frenzy, rolls Vincent to his back, forcing him to look in her eyes as his body fights to live.

"Ding dong, looks like I have found you." Frankie sings, finishing the end of the song, "Ding dong, pay the consequence."

She slices the knife slowly across his throat, and it's then that I have to close my eyes, not able to stomach the rest.

I can hear his gurgles, like he is drowning in his own blood, and then when he falls quiet, Frankie's laugh fills the air.

"Fuck," Devon whispers against my ear, and I hear Finn next to me.

"Well, looks like I'm about to find out what maiming feels like."

Frankie's eyes dart over her shoulder, her head shaking as she stands to face us.

My gasp gets lodged in my throat, and Devon must feel me stiffen because he gives me a squeeze.

Frankie is painted in red. Her face. Her hands. Her hair dripping.

"You'll keep," Frankie murmurs to Finn, tossing the knife to the ground before walking past and bumping his shoulder with hers.

"Fuck, man. You wanna stay at mine?" Miles asks, and I can see by Finn's expression that he's considering it, but he shakes his head.

"No. I was the one that wanted to save her. I'll pay the consequences."

Vida Loca
Trust

Chapter Thirty-Six
Devon

Leaving the guards to clean up, I keep my grip firm on Jaxcen's hand as I lead her back to town. My mind is fucking racing. So many different outcomes could have taken place tonight, and in none did we consider a possibility, when we went over our plans meticulously, that Jaxcen would be turned into a human explosive. In none did we consider Mr V would be knowledgeable enough to dress as a Santa, blending in with my fucking men.

The possibility that my little mouse could be dead right now makes me want to fucking hurl.

"Dev?" Jaxcen's sweet voice drags my gaze to hers as we walk up the path of Main Street, twinkling Christmas lights illuminating the way. "What's wrong?"

I take in her big blue eyes, and the concern emanating from them. I take in her cheeks, still flushed on the apples, making her appear even younger and innocent than I know she is. Her skin has a luminescent glow to it, so smooth and creamy, and there's just so much perfection to her that I fear, if I touch her, she'll shatter into a million pieces and I'll never see her again.

I've never thought like this before.

I've never felt like this before.

And fuck, I don't know how or what to do with it.

Because I can't keep her. Look at the danger I've brought into her life since we crossed paths.

No. I can never keep something so precious no matter how much I want it.

"Dev?" she asks again, her brow puckering, and I blink a few times, realising that we've stopped walking, and I'm just staring at her. "Please tell me what's going on inside your head," she whispers.

There's a plea in her tone. It's laced with pain.

How can I tell her what I'm feeling when I simply can't keep her?

I decide to go with the half truth, because I need her to know how important she is.

"He got too close to taking you," I rasp, my voice cracking slightly. And what I don't say is, he got too close from taking you *from me*.

"But he didn't." She reaches up, her dainty hand cupping the side of my face. "I'm still here. You saved me."

"Warrick saved you. Not me," I say bluntly, still annoyed that I had to call my little brother for help. Now I have to deal with that bullshit, which Marilda will likely have my balls for.

Her hand leaves my face to slap my shoulder. "Stop it. You had his help, yes, but it was you who found me. It was you who kept me calm. It was you who knew the right person to call. And it was you that disabled and removed the bomb from me."

"And it was me that put you in that position in the first place," I snap, too fucking pissed at myself as I start walking up the path again, noticing the locals and visitors flowing out from the chapel, now that it's safe.

Fuck. The press will have a field day with this.

"Are you done?" Jaxcen snaps from behind me, and I still at the sass in her tone, slowly turning to face her. "Don't arch your eyebrow at me."

Fuck.

I fight the urge to grin, my gaze raking over the way her arms are crossed over her chest with one hip popped, as she stares at me, deadpanned.

"Am I done with what?" I ask, my voice low and menacing, because whatever is happening here has awakened something inside me, and I get the feeling that was her fucking intention.

"Are you done having a pity party?"

My brows shoot high before they dip, my nostrils flaring at her words.

"The fuck did you just say?"

"You heard me. I'm the one who nearly died, Devon. I should be the one whining about it, but do you see me doing that? No." She twirls her hand in the air between us, gesturing to me. "Yet here you are…"

A low rumble emanates from my chest, which kicks up the corners of her lips in a teasing smirk, like she's fucking happy to be pissing me off right now.

"You might want to check yourself, love," I snap, about ready to wrap my hands around her throat and give it a good fucking squeeze.

"You might want to check *yourself, love*." She repeats my words back to me, her tone almost a mock, but more challenging than anything.

My fucking cock is hard, and given the way her eyes briefly drop to my crotch, she fucking knows it.

Still, she stands before me, no fear, just a challenge written across her expression, waiting to see what I'll do next.

"Maybe I should fuck you right here. In the street. Maybe then you'll fucking remember who you're talking to."

She rolls her eyes. "Maybe you should. And maybe I'll like it. And maybe then, you'll remember that you're the one who brought this version of Jaxcen out in me."

I snicker at that. "It's always been there, Jaxcen. You just needed a nudge."

"Which version do you like better? The demure version of me, still so innocent and inexperienced that you met in the church on a stormy night? Or this one?" She gestures down the length of her torso, my gaze following over the red dress she donned at my request. "Do you like this version of Jaxcen Summers that pushes your buttons? Calls you out on your bullshit? That celebrates her sins to the devil?"

In three strides I'm on her, my hand fists her hair as I force her head back and claim her lips. Her tongue lashes at mine instantly, like she's desperate to taste me, and then she sucks it deep into her mouth like it's my fucking cock as she grinds her mound against my leg.

Fuck, I want her right here, right fucking now.

"Uh, excuse me." A throat clearing behind me makes us both stiffen, and reluctantly, I release Jaxcen's hair and turn to see Ronnie. "The ah... explosive has been removed and is currently being relocated to Timber Valley where Griffin will arrange for its dismantlement."

I nod, knowing these orders would have come from my direct team. Finn, Miles, Dom and Lenny. That's why I have them. They are good at what they do, and at times like this, don't need me to spell everything out to them. They know our top priority is the town's safety, something I've failed at here tonight.

I used my town as bait, knowing the text we sent from Melissa's phone would lure Vincent here.

I used Melissa as bait, something she was happy to do to help get rid of another psychopath. And all because I wanted this over sooner rather than later, because my need to send Jaxcen back to her life is consuming me.

I can't keep her, but the longer she's here, the harder it is for me to accept that.

"Thanks, Ronnie. I'm going to retire to my suite. Call an 8am meeting to debrief and get a media strategy in place."

Ronnie nods. "Will do." He leans to the side to see around me to where Jaxcen is still standing. "Good night, Miss Summers. I'm glad you're safe."

"Thank you, Ronnie," she says sweetly, but there's no shyness in her tone.

Four fucking days she's been here. Four fucking days that feels like four fucking weeks.

She's not only affected me, but she's made an impact in some small way on my men. On the women. On the town.

Slowly, as Ronnie retreats, I turn back to face my sassy little mouse.

"Up to my room. Now," I demand, and fuck, the way her cheeks flare to life has my cock jerking in my fucking pants.

I can tell by the way she bows her head slightly, that this is exactly what she wants. Me, demanding, dominating and confident, and not fucking spiralling out of control.

I will address those feelings tomorrow. Or maybe the fucking day after, but right now, I have better things to do with my night, which involve Jaxcen, naked and screaming.

"Move it," I order, and she does, just like that.

Obedient. Submissive.

My little mouse.

I watch her arse as I follow her up the stairs to my suite. When we reach my door, I lean over her, pressing my hard cock into the valley of her arse as I key in the code, hearing the lock click open a second later.

The moment I push the door open, she hurries inside, through the living space and into my bedroom.

Easing the door shut, I take my time, hearing the rustle of clothing and just knowing she's getting ready for me.

The moment she comes into view as I stalk through the door, I slow my steps, my gaze travelling over her creamy flesh, bare except for the red lacy g-string, and the matching bra with the dusty pink shade of her nipples teasing me through the lace.

"Fuck, little mouse. You look good enough to eat."

She grins as her blue gaze catches mine through the dark fan of her lashes.

She's still keeping her head angled low, showing me that she can be a good girl when she wants to be.

The funny thing is, she's the one with real power here.

In fact, I think it's been that way all of this time.

Look how easily she riled me up. She knew exactly what she was doing.

She wanted this version of me.

She wants the devil.

And fuck, the devil wants her. He wants fucking everything from her.

Stepping up to her as she stands at the foot of my bed, I tug the stupid fucking Santa hat free from where I tucked it in the back of my pants, and when I go to toss it, Jaxcen's dainty hand quickly snatches it off me.

"No."

"What are you doing?" I ask as she reaches up and positions the hat on my head.

"What does it look like?" she asks, a smile teasing her lips.

"It looks like you're putting more clothes on me when you should be taking them off. Don't you want to sin for the devil?"

Leaning back as she lowers her hands from positioning the stupid Santa hat, she admires her dressing skills and shakes her head.

"No, I don't want to sin for the devil tonight." He blue gaze locks with mine then, her pink tongue darting out to wet her lips before she continues. "Tonight, I want to sin for Santa."

I know it shouldn't be, but fuck, the whole sinning for Santa thing sounds fucking hot.

It reminds me of my cousin Griffin, and the borderline stalkerish game he played with Aggie. He called the game, Subbing for Santa, and fuck he made her do some pretty depraved things, but it's the game that sealed their fate. Their happiness.

They haven't been apart since.

I want that.

No. No. No.

I fucking can't have that.

I need to punch myself in my own fucking face and knock some sense into me, yet here I fucking am, leaving on the hat, ready to be her Santa.

"You want to sin for a man in a red suit?" I ask, and she nods.

"Not just any man." She starts undoing the buttons down the front of the red top. "Just you. Naked. Wearing that hat."

Her grin is playful as she parts the red shirt, exposing my chest and abs.

"Does the idea of it make you wet, little mouse?"

"Anything involving you makes me wet," she admits easily, and something about that makes me feel fucking primal.

Like I want to stand out on the balcony and beat my chest for all of the land to hear my claim on this woman.

"Really?" I smirk, before manhandling her to the end of my bed and dropping to my knees. "Let's have a look then."

I grin up at her, those blue eyes wide with surprise, like she is only just catching up with what's happening.

Reaching forward, I press my fingers to the apex between her thighs, the lacy fabric already damp as I glide my digits over her centre.

"You're right. You're already soaked."

She whimpers and nods, her hands bracing the bed behind her as she licks her lips and tugs her bottom lip between her teeth.

"How long have you been like this?"

"There's no end to it when you're around."

"Fuck," I growl, not realising how much I needed her to say that, so I push my head between her legs, gliding my tongue over the damp fabric as she widens her stance.

I tease her with my fingers, pressing into her tight hole, letting the fabric sink in only as far as it will allow, edging her, revelling in her mewling cries as she starts to grind on my face.

Her clit is swollen, easy to find under the fabric, so I tease it too, keeping that barrier there, letting her pleasure build so intensely that it makes her frustrated when she can't take it further.

"Atta girl, Jax," I rasp against her mound. "Fuck my face."

My words send her spiralling, but she still can't get there, something I'm well aware of, and when she least expects it, I quickly tug the fabric aside and latch onto her bare clit.

Her scream is loud as she chases her climax, and the moment I sink three thick fingers inside her, she clamps down around them in an explosion of pulses and spray and cries that I never ever want to forget.

When she slumps back on the bed, I ease my fingers free, standing and pressing them to her lips.

"Open."

She does, her lids darting wide too as she sucks her juice off my digits.

"Look what you did to me, little mouse," I say, watching her gaze shift from mine to my chin and chest as I pop my fingers free of her plump luscious lips.

"Oh... uh... I'll get a towel."

"Nope." I chuckle as she tries to push off the end of my bed, holding her in place. "You'll just have to endure it."

Again, she bites her lip, her eyes locked on my lips before she lurches forward and kisses me.

It's hungry, like she's starved for the taste of herself on me, her tongue not just exploring my mouth, but around it too, sampling her cum.

My hands travel over her near naked flesh, and breaking the kiss, I make quick work of her bra, cupping one tit while sucking the other into the heat of my mouth, feeling her arch back like she wants me to completely devour it. Devour her.

I have her panties off next, my kisses travelling all the way down to her feet before I glance up at her, completely naked and bare to me.

"You're the best present I've ever unwrapped."

Her cheeks flush, just like they do so often, and she tugs me up, spinning us so my back is to the bed, before she shoves me backwards.

"What the...?" I laugh at the sudden role change, only to find her climbing onto my lap, straddling me.

"You're the hottest Santa I've ever sat on." She grins from ear to ear, her words making me chuckle.

"Is that so? Do you normally sit on Santa's lap completely naked?"

She shakes her head, her breath catching as I press my hard shaft against her centre.

"No." She breathes before rolling her hips over my fabric covered cock.

Fuck, I should have ditched the pants, but the way she's starting to ride me has my cock weeping, the friction and sight of her starting to dry hump me a real fucking turn on.

"Do you normally dry hump Santa?"

She shakes her head, rolling her hips again as she watches me from above.

"You're being really bad right now. Sinful. Are you sure you want to be on Santa's naughty list?"

"Yes." She pants, my words spurring her on and she grinds her pussy up and down my shaft.

When her eyes drop to where she's mounted, mine follow to see the outline of my cock under the red fabric, a patch of wetness at the tip from my precum, and a slick trail left behind from her folds as she uses me for her pleasure.

"Fuck, Jax. If you keep doing that, I'm going to cum in my pants," I admit, and her eyes flare like she enjoys the sound of it, so I add. "I'd rather cum inside you."

A whimper escapes her as her hands hurry to my waistband, fumbling with the cord like she'll possibly die if she doesn't free my cock right this second.

I'm right there with her, so I help, and a moment later, my shaft springs free, slapping heavily to my abs.

"I want it," she mutters, almost like she's talking to herself, but I don't stop her as she lifts herself, my cock in her hand, and positions my tip at her entrance.

And then she lowers down, impaling herself.

"Fuuuck." I groan, loving this bit. When I sink in for the first time, feeling the heat envelop me. Feeling her walls squeeze me.

There's nothing fucking like it.

"Dev," she cries. "This... I..."

"Don't try to talk, love. Just fuck me. Take what you need."

Another whimper leaves her plump lips as she rises up and lowers again, teasing us both, over and over before she starts to lose control.

My fingers dig into her hips as she rides me, and I take in the beauty of her in this state.

So free.

So exotic.

Her blonde hair is like a golden halo as she rises and falls, her hands gliding up her body until they find the heavy swell of her tits, cupping them before she pinches her nipples.

A rush of wetness follows, as she does it again, and again, her thrusts coming faster each time.

I'm going to come too fucking soon. I just know it. But I can't. I need this to last.

Fuck! Think of something gross.

I fucking try, but nothing comes to mind, because she's all I can see, feel, hear, smell, taste.

She's fucking everything.

"I'm going to come," I rush out as I feel my nuts tighten, and it spurs her on, one hand moving to her mound, her fingers working over her clit.

I can't... oh fuck, I can't hold it.

A strangled roar bellows from me as my entire body ripples with ecstasy, Jaxcen fucking me with abandon now, her mouth wide, her cries filling the air, her eyes rolling back in her head as she fucks my cock, mashes her clit, and pinches her nipple.

As she climaxes again, her walls pulse around my cock, milking me and extending my orgasm so much so that I don't think it will ever end.

And fuck. I don't want it to.

It does though, basically the moment her climax recedes, her clamping walls ease up, giving my cock a reprieve until we are both a boneless tangled heap on my bed.

Fuck. I want to keep her. I want so much to keep her. To never let her leave this place so I can keep her safe and spend the rest of my days lost in her.

And for a moment, I allow myself to believe that I can do that. For tonight, on Christmas Eve, I'll pretend that she's mine, for now and always.

We remain tangled together for what seems like hours.

My cock shrivels up and goes into hibernation, and even though she's a mess, we're both a mess, we don't move from the sheets.

Does she feel it too?

The end?

I know I shouldn't think like this, yet I can't help but once again hope that my baby is already growing inside her.

I didn't pay all that much attention in sex ed class when I was a horny teenage boy to know exactly how impregnating a female works, other than cock in cunt, but fuck I'd be surprised if she's not carrying a Marx heir.

Fuck. A Marx heir.

Why the fuck do I like the sound of that so much?

"Dev," Jaxcen murmurs, sleeping in my arms.

"Yes, love."

"I don't want to go to sleep," she whispers into my neck.

"Why not?"

"Because I don't want tonight to end."

Her admission makes it feel like a fist is tearing through the wall of my chest and gripping my heart in a fucking vice.

"There's always tomorrow, little mouse," I tell her quietly as she hums in agreement, and the next second, I feel her breathing even out as she gives in to sleep.

I feel like shit.

What I didn't tell her is that tomorrow is all we have. I can't bear to say the words out loud, because then, it would make them true.

Chapter Thirty-Seven

Jaxcen

Wear whatever you like, little mouse.
Today is Christmas.
Find me under the mistletoe.
x D

His note makes me smile, excitement rushing through me and I can't be sure if it's because it's Christmas, or because I get to see him… under the mistletoe.

I shower and dress quickly, my body sore, but the good kind of sore that reminds me of the great sex we had last night.

I'd never felt more sensual. More beautiful than in that moment when he was watching me ride him.

I felt exquisite.

Downstairs in the Palace, people are laughing and rushing around, and through the windows I watch as the women decorate a long table right in the middle of the street getting ready for lunch.

Moving through the bar, and into the open doorway of Devon's office, I see him sitting in his chair, legs up on the desk as he stares at the computer screen in front of him.

A king in his throne.

"Get your sweet arse over here." His deep voice rumbles, even though his eyes haven't moved from the screen.

Grinning, I make my way to him, and the moment I'm next to him, he pulls me down to his lap, a squeal escaping me from the sudden action.

"Merry Christmas, little mouse." He winks at me right before he claims my lips.

I moan into his mouth, linking my wrists behind his neck as I melt into him.

Gosh, I could stay in his lap forever and never need another thing.

"Ah, boss." Ronnie's voice comes from the doorway, and Devon grins against my lips before pulling back to look at him. "Lunch will be ready to serve in thirty minutes, and also, your cousin is just pulling in."

"Thanks, man," Devon says, before planting another kiss on my lips, and then spinning his chair, helping me off him as he stands. "It's time for Christmas."

My heart flutters.

I've never had Christmas somewhere else before, and while I know I'm going to miss Presley desperately, I'm not at all upset that I won't see my parents.

In fact, I think I'll be happy to never see them again.

With my hand in his, Devon leads us out into the street, the warm summer sun already shining high in the sky, and Christmas carols playing in the background from a few speakers scattered around the place.

A black car pulls up towards the end of the table, and a moment later, Liam, Devon's cousin, gets out, his smile wide as he waves over the top of his car at us.

"Hey devil."

I glance up at Devon in time to see him roll his eyes. "Hey, shithead. You pick up the packages?"

"Sure did." He slaps the roof of his car before moving to the front passenger door and opening it.

Rising to my toes, I try to peek in past Liam to see who it is, but can't see anything until a man steps out with a black bag covering his head. The man grumbles something I can't hear, and a moment later, Liam tugs the black bag off his head, revealing dark hair and dark eyes that clearly resemble Devon.

"Was the hood really necessary?" Warrick barks, blinking quickly as his eyes adjust to the bright sun.

"Maybe. Maybe not." Devon deadpans. "Your wife has mad torture skills. I wouldn't put it past her to torture the whereabouts of Marilda and Damon out of you."

"Fuck you. I'd never give them up."

Even though their words to each other are harsh, I can't help but smile, and as soon as Liam closes the car door, I rush forward and throw my arms around Devon's brother.

"Thank you for helping to save my life."

A hesitant awkward pat lands on my back before I pull back to see the eyes so similar to Devon's.

"I guess you're bomb girl?"

I giggle and Devon snarls.

"Do not call her that. Her name is Jaxcen."

Warrick does a bow at me like he's greeting royalty right before he flips his older brother off. "Now where's my fucking kid?"

"He's right here," Marilda's voice startles Warrick, our gazes darting to the path where she stands, her son Damon sitting in the stroller, playing with a toy. "But if you say another foul word in front of our son, Warrick, so help me God, I will remove your tongue from your mouth."

Warrick's eyes soften in an instant, his temperament changing, and the harsh glare he wore moments ago falls away.

He strides towards them, and I think he's about to say hi to his son, but he rounds the stroller, taking Marilda by surprise, lifting her off her feet and smacking his lips to hers.

The stroller, now long forgotten, starts to roll on the path towards the gutter, but Devon hurries forward, saving his nephew as Marilda wraps her legs around Warrick's waist and moans into their kiss.

"Allegra!" Devon calls over his shoulder, and she comes running over from the table where she was pretending to do something, but really she was just gawking at the scene playing out before us.

"Yes?" she asks as she nears.

"Please take Damon for a walk so these two can go *somewhere else*," Devon says pointedly, "to have some privacy."

"Of course." Allegra hurries to take the stroller, pushing it up the street away from the near fornication that's currently unravelling before our eyes.

"Damn. I should have brought popcorn," Liam mutters from beside us, and when I smile up at him, he winks.

I like Liam. He's playful.

"Dev, I could have taken Damon for a walk," I say quietly, and he drags his eyes from his brother to me.

"Nope. I need you here. For your present."

I frown, watching as Devon nods to Liam, who then opens the back car door and helps a woman out.

I know before he even takes the black bag from her head that it's my sister. I'd know her dainty frame anywhere.

She's blinking, trying to adjust to the daylight even as I throw myself at her, wrapping my arms around her neck as I start to sob.

"Hey, sis," Presley says into my hair, weaving her arms around me and running her hands up and down my back soothingly. "Shhh. It's okay. I'm here."

I can hear Devon and Liam chatting quietly somewhere behind me, but I can't let go of my sister. I just can't.

"Hey, Jax. It's alright." She pulls back looking into my eyes, her blue ones matching mine. "I'm so sorry about everything that happened. I didn't want you to hand yourself over to them."

I shake my head, batting at my tears. "There's no way I'd ever let them hurt you, Pres. No way in hell."

"Come on you two. No tears on Christmas Day." Liam grins coming up to stand next to us, and my sister shoots daggers his way.

"No one asked for your advice," she snaps at him, and my brows shoot up.

"Oh come on now. Why are you still so grumpy at me? I told you I would bring you to your sister, and that's exactly what I've done."

She scoffs. "You kidnapped me. That's what you did."

My mouth drops open as Presley pops her hip with her hand on it as she points a Christmas themed talon-like nail in his direction.

"You kidnapped her?" I ask and he shrugs.

"It's a Marx thing."

I roll my eyes as Devon chuckles, but the moment I turn a glare his way, he shuts up.

"She doesn't know Liam, little mouse. She wouldn't go with him, let alone trust him. How else was I meant to give you this gift?"

My shoulders drop as my expression does.

"Literally, so many ways other than kidnapping," I deadpan, and he ignores me.

"Welcome to my town, Presley. I hope you and Jaxcen enjoy spending Christmas with us." Then he takes my hand in his. "Come on, little mouse, let's have lunch."

Presley's brows shoot up, and she mouths 'little mouse' to me before grinning, and I can't help but giggle.

The street fills with the town locals, even the drunks venture from the bar for lunch, as do the Burlingtons, still wearing their typical morbid expressions, but out in the sun like this, they look a fraction less miserable.

Their pain. Their loss. It will never leave them. I can see that, which is really sad.

I haven't asked what happened to them, but I remember their words when I lost my shit and started threatening people with a knife.

They've lost people very dear to them.

Devon ushers me to sit at the end of the table as he takes the head seat, and Presley sits next to me, while Liam sits across from her, shooting her a wink which wins him a glare.

I grin.

If she lightens up, I get the feeling Presley would really get along with Liam. He's playful, something I know my sister is too when she feels safe.

"Wasn't sure if you'd make it," Devon snickers, and I glance up to see Finn pulling out the chair across from me and flopping down in it, wearing a black eye.

"Wasn't sure I'd make it either," he says grimly.

"Is Frankie... okay?" I ask, and he nods.

"She's full of fucking energy today."

"Is she coming for lunch?" I wonder and he shakes his head.

"Nope. Said she doesn't do Christmas or Easter. Only Valentine's Day and Halloween."

I grin. I think Frankie and I could be good friends.

I introduce the people around us to Presley, and the banter around the table is entertaining as we eat, cheers also ringing up an hour later when Marilda and Warrick finally join us.

He scoops up Damon from the stroller and sits him on his lap while he eats, not letting anyone else have him.

It makes me smile.

Obviously their situation isn't the best, and I can imagine there's a lot of anger involved, but it's clear he loves Marilda and Damon. It's sad to think he has to leave them again soon.

After we've eaten way too much, I take Presley for a tour of the town, and we end up sitting on one of the park benches looking out over Timber Valley.

"Have you heard from Eddie since..." I trail off, not wanting to say *since the day Dr Xavier took me*, but Presley shakes her head.

"Please tell me you're not going to marry him."

"Oh, I'm definitely not. My eyes are wide open now."

She nods, angling towards me as she takes me in.

"You seem different. More... real."

My brows shoot up. "As opposed to?"

"Lifeless. A robot. A yes person."

Sighing, I can't even be angry about that truth, no matter how hard it is to hear.

"I lost myself to the treatments... I was still in there," I tap the side of my head, "but scared. Terrified. A little mouse."

"Is that why Devon calls you little mouse?" Presley snaps, looking like she's ready to find him and rip him a new one.

"No. I thought it was because he thought I was weak, but he said he thinks I'm strong."

She frowns. "So, it's like a pet name?"

"I guess." I shrug, still not really knowing the reason behind it myself.

"What's the story with you two?" Presley asks. "He looks at you like he wants to eat you."

I shrug. "That's because he does."

Presley's mouth drops open before she bursts out laughing. "You little hoe." She slaps my shoulder. "I'm so freaking proud of you."

I laugh too, and damn, it feels good. Light. I feel light and... free.

When our laughter dies down, I stare back out at the valley below, wondering how many people in the houses down there are having a good Christmas, and how many are scared, or alone, or on the edge of their own cliff.

"I hate them," I say quietly, before glancing back at my sister. "Mum and Dad. I hate them, Pres. I'll never forgive them for not believing me. I'll never forgive them for putting you into that room with that vile man."

Presley's eyes well with tears. "I know, Jax. I hate them, too. I should have done more back then, and the other day..." She trails off, shaking her head in frustration.

"What could you have done? You would have gotten hurt, either of the times."

"But you sacrificed yourself for me. Twice. I'm the big sister. I should be doing that for you." She sobs, and I throw my arms around her as we embrace.

"Stop beating yourself up for the things our parents have done," I say into her hair. "Now tell me. How pathetic is Dad being about losing his fingers?"

Presley bursts out laughing, leaning back to look at me. "He's so pathetic. It's the best thing that's ever happened."

We both burst into fits of laughter, our giggles floating out over the cliffs of Woodall Ridge, to fall over the town of Fox Pines below.

The day has been wonderful. The best Christmas I ever remember having, and when we rejoin the celebrations on Main Street, Devon is just walking out of the Palace, probably coming from his office or his suite.

We sit and have a few drinks, and finally, Presley stops glaring at Liam and starts laughing with him, and the moment Devon catches my eye, gesturing his head for me to go to him, I stand and leave the celebrations, going for a stroll with the town's king.

We do a walk around the block and I chat away, telling him stories about my Christmases with Presley growing up, and then he leads me through the pub's back entrance, and up the stairs.

I assume he's taking me to his suite, where we will likely disappear for an hour, but then he leads me to the attic door, and up another flight of stairs.

"What are we doing up here?" I ask, remembering the last time we were here.

I'd snuck up here and hidden, watching him freak out down on the street while he and his men searched for me.

That was back when he led me to believe that he was going to kill me. Or at least, could kill me if I didn't behave.

"The view is good from here." He smirks, looking pointedly at me as he stalks towards me while I back up, and grin, making sure he sees me roll my eyes. "Why did you cry that day when I found you praying up here?"

Wow, that day feels so long ago but it was just a few days ago. On Wednesday.

"Remember I told you, the prayer was because the devil was coming for me." I remind him. "I thought you were going to kill me, but then you said you'll always come for me, and I wasn't scared of that. You were the devil and I wasn't scared, but the funny thing is, God, always made me feel scared. Shameful. Not good enough."

Devon nods. "I remember. I also asked you if you really wanted to be saved from me." He shoves me backwards then, onto the box seat much like he did that day. Leaning over me, I'm forced to lay back like last time too. "And then I said, one day soon, I'm gonna fuck you right here in front of this window. I'm gonna let the whole fucking town see how much your cunt craves my cock."

My cheeks flare to life at the reminder of his words, and heat pools between my legs.

"You're not going to do that." I challenge, and he perks a single brow.

"Aren't I?"

There's no need to try and coerce me, I'm right there with him as our lips clash, my hands fisting in his hair and his gripping my arse, squeezing.

In a matter of seconds, he frees me of my panties, flips me on my belly, and hitches up my dress.

"I'm going to punish this pussy, Jaxcen," he rasps, sinking two fingers inside me even as he hoists me up to set me on all fours.

"Yes. Please." I beg like a wanton whore, desperate for him. Desperate for every little thing he wants to do to my body.

I can hear his belt buckle and then his fly as his fingers move inside me, before he removes them and replaces the loss with the thick girth of his cock.

I cry out, my eyes wide as he slams into me, my gaze on the street below, on his men, and the women, and the fact anyone could look up here and see us just adds to the erotic experience.

"Fuck, I love your tight cunt, Jax. It was made for my cock," he grits out, pumping his dick into me as I try to remain upright. "Your arse looks so good. I'd fuck that too if I didn't care about wasting my cum."

"Just do it," I pant, not entirely sure I want that, because I literally have no idea if I can handle it, but my words make him groan, like he's contemplating giving up on the idea of trying to knock me up and fuck my arse, but then his fingers slide around his cock, like he's getting them wet, and then he presses one to my back entrance.

A thrill rushes through me. I really loved it when he did that to me last time. I wasn't sure I could take it, but it was something else entirely, so I can't help but push back against him, taking his finger deep.

"Awww, fuck yesss. I wish you could see how your arse opens up for me. So fucking greedy."

A whimper escapes me as his words work their magic just as much as his dick and fingers do.

"I'm putting another finger in," he says as he presses another digit to my back passage. "Relax for me, beautiful. Let me in."

I moan as I relax, wanting more than his finger there.

I want him to just fill me in every way possible, and I don't even understand that, yet it's a yearning I can't deny.

"Fuck, yes. Open up that filthy hole for me even more."

I fall to my elbows, which seems to help, opening my passage to him, and it's then that I feel him adding a third finger.

"Atta girl, you take me so fucking well."

I moan loudly, feeling my climax rushing at me fast, and Devon must be able to tell, because he starts thrusting faster. His dick. His fingers. Sending me into the stratosphere.

"Fuuuck. I can feel my cock with my fingers," he moans, his voice a higher pitch than I've ever heard it, and so too is his guttural roar as he comes hard.

I've completely forgotten about the fact people could be watching. I don't even care. Let them see. Let everyone see the way Devon loves me.

That thought has my eyes darting open.

Where the hell did that thought come from?

Devon doesn't love me.

I mean, his dick loves me. But he, the ruthless devil. He doesn't love me.

"Fuck, Jax. I'll never get enough of you."

His words are a whisper. Almost like he didn't want me to hear them, and it makes me smile.

Does he feel it too? This thing between us?

Is it more than just sex? Is that even possible after only knowing each other for only a few days?

Lust is a powerful thing. My guess is that it's easy to confuse lust and love when it's as epic as this.

I'm so glad I went into St Catherine's Church on Tuesday night. If I hadn't, I fear I would never have known what it's really like to feel this cherished. To feel this alive.

He's awakened me. Both carnally and spiritually, and I know my life will never be the same.

When he pulls free, he rolls me to my back and repositions me, so my legs are up against the wall.

If anyone looks up, they'll have a weird view of my legs and feet, the thought making me smile.

"Are you really still trying to knock me up?" I ask him, giggling as he nods, not an ounce of shame written across his expression.

"Yes."

"You know, it's probably already happened," I tell him and he shrugs.

"Won't hurt to make sure."

"You're crazy." I giggle, and his dark eyes, lit with humour meet mine.

"Absolutely."

We stay up in the attic for a while longer. Devon lays next to me and puts his legs up on the wall too, mimicking my position as he stares at me.

I feel like he wants to say something, but I don't want to push him. I'm content to be in this moment, feeling the happiest I've ever felt, sharing it with him.

Eventually we clean ourselves up and go back down to the street, where night has begun to fall, the town locals now extremely merry.

I meet my sister out on the street, realising that it's time for her to leave, as Liam leads her to his car.

"Be right back," Devon whispers against my head, before pressing a kiss to it, and Presley grins, wagging her brows.

"Damn, girl. He's smitten."

I beam back, and glance at Liam, who quickly looks away and opens the back passenger door for Presley.

"Time to go."

Presley rolls her eyes at him, and leans in to hug me, but falters, her eyes moving over my shoulder.

Turning to see what caught her eye, I see Devon, coming down the steps of the Palace carrying a suitcase.

My suitcase.

I blink a few times, words not finding their way from my brain to my lips as Devon doesn't make eye contact with me and passes my bag to Liam, who puts it in the trunk of his car.

"Wha—" I glance from Liam to Devon who finally locks eyes with me, and they are full of regret. "What's happening?"

He doesn't say anything for the longest time, but the moment I go to take a step closer to him, he takes a step back and finally speaks.

"It's time for you to go."

Vida Loca
Trust

Chapter Thirty-Eight

Devon

I've never felt like a bigger prick than in this moment. The hurt and betrayal that flashes in Jaxcen's eyes nearly undoes me. Nearly makes me cave. Give in, and ask her to stay.

But that's ridiculous. Five days I have known this woman. Five fucking days isn't enough time for me to be asking her to stay. To ask her not to return to her life and be mine and only mine for what? Forever?

What the actual fuck is wrong with me?

No.

She has to leave.

It's for the best for her and me.

Hell, she has so much life to live now that the blinders have been peeled from her tunnel vision. She's a sexual being and only just awoken. She needs to explore that. She needs to explore everything on her own, out from under the heavy hand of her parents and their twisted religious beliefs.

"Why?" she whispers, tears welling in her beautiful blue eyes as she wrings her hands together, staring at me.

"It's for the best. Mr V is dead, little mouse. You're safe again. You can go back to your life."

"But… I don't want my old life," she protests, taking a step closer, and fuck, like a coward, I take another step back.

I have to. If she gets too close, if she touches me, I'll cave.

"Then change your life." I urge her. "It's yours to control now. Not anyone else's."

Her pained expression morphs to anger and her shoulders roll back as she speaks.

"Fine, then I'm not leaving. That is my decision."

Fuck. She's not going to make this easy.

"Yes, you are, little mouse. Get in the car."

"No, I'm not." She stomps her foot, and fuck if that's not the most adorable thing I've seen her do.

I want to smile, but that will just confuse her into thinking I'll change my mind, so I opt for the truth instead.

"Jaxcen, you're not safe with me."

She frowns, confused, her gaze darting back towards the table where the local woman have congregated. "These women are safe with you."

"That's different. They are residents. They aren't..." I trail off, not sure how to put this, mulling over my words before I speak. "They aren't mine. You saw what happened with Vincent. You were used against me, and if you're mine he won't be the last. I have a lot of enemies, Jax. My family may be powerful, but it comes at a price, and you'll be used as a tool to hit me where it hurts. You can't stay. You have to leave."

"Shouldn't that be my decision? Shouldn't I be the one who decides if that's the life I want to lead?" she snaps, and I shake my head, momentarily looking at Liam for help, but the fucker just looks away.

"It doesn't work like that in my family. There's no point in going around in circles about this, Jaxcen. You have to leave. That's all there is to it."

She stares at me for the longest moment, a fat tear popping from one eye and rolling down her blazing cheek.

"I could be pregnant." She reminds me, and the thought has my heart doing a stupid fucking flip.

"Wait... what?" Presley squeaks from her spot by the car, but we both ignore her, our gazes locked on each other.

"Yes, you could be. I do hope so," I admit and her frown deepens, her anger boiling.

"You make no sense. Why would you want to get me pregnant only to send me away?"

"Because then you'll both be safe."

She scoffs. "You forget, I wasn't safe before you came into my life, Devon. I've never been fucking safe."

Hearing her swear like that is unusual, but warranted. Because she's right. Her life has been nothing but a series of manipulations, distrust, and abuse.

"I can assure you, that from now on, you will be safe, little mouse. Our child will be looked after financially as a Marx heir, although no one but us will know his or her bloodline, and the little tacker will be loved and raised by you. I think you'll be an amazing mother."

Her mouth drops open as more tears spill over, and she bats them away like they are nothing but a nuisance.

"You expect me to be a single mum?"

"Yes," I answer truthfully, and anger flares in her eyes.

"You're insufferable," she snaps and I shrug.

"I know."

"I hate you," she seethes, but I shake my head.

"No, you don't, but maybe you should."

A loud sob escapes her, and then another before she looks to her sister, who shoots her a sympathetic look and holds out her hand for Jaxcen to join her.

Turning back to me, Jaxcen takes another step closer, leaning towards me, and this time I don't move.

"Why would you do this to me? I know it's only been a few days but I really thought... I thought we were happy."

"Jax. You don't need me to be happy. You just need to show the world who you really are and don't for a minute feel ashamed of it."

My words give her no comfort, her glare chilling as more tears spill down her cheeks.

"Get in the car," I order her, my tone unforgiving, but she doesn't move. "Please, Miss Summers. I want you to leave and never come back."

She flinches back like she's been slapped, my cold tone and words so final, that I know she understands this is it.

Slowly, her head lowers, those blue eyes disappear from my sight as her shoulders slump and she turns away. When Liam goes to put a black bag on her head, she slaps his hand away and snarls at him.

"I already know where this place is, fuckwit. And as if I would ever tell anyone about it. I would never jeopardise the safety of the women and children here."

Fuck, the fire in her tone tells me she'll be alright. She'll stand up for herself from now on.

"Alright. Alright." Liam holds his hands up and then looks to Presley. "How about you? You gonna be an issue?" She shakes her head, reaching out to Jaxcen and helping her slip into the back seat, where she joins her.

"Good to see you're still the ice queen." Warrick's fucking irritating voice comes from the side, and by the way he's leaning against the lamp post, I can tell he's been watching this whole thing go down.

"Get in the fucking car, War."

My brother rolls his eyes. "You know, Jen and Elise would love her. Hell, maybe even Lily would come out of hiding to meet this one."

"Fuck off, already," I snap at my brother, annoyed that he'd bring our sisters into this.

Jaxcen has nothing to do with our fucked up family, and I don't like him implying that she'd fit right in.

"Whatever. Until next time, brother." Warrick slaps my shoulder, and nods at Liam as he approaches the car. "I'll need the bag. My wife has torture skills I'm man enough to say I know I'll crack under."

Liam scoffs at Warrick, but bags his head anyway, shoving him in the front seat and closing him in.

"I'm assuming you know what the fuck you're doing?" Liam's brows lift in question, and I scrub my hand through my hair.

"Not at fucking all."

Liam chuckles. "In that case, I'll make sure there's popcorn on the go, since this romantic comedy isn't over yet."

"It's not a fucking romantic comedy," I snap at my cousin who wags his brows.

"Isn't it? Seems pretty funny from where I'm standing."

"Why?" I growl and he shrugs one shoulder.

"Because you think you don't have feelings for her. It's fucking obvious to everyone else but you, and man, I hope you come to your senses before it's too late."

Liam laughs at my hiss, rounding the car and sliding in before starting up the engine.

I feel fucking sick. Like there's an organ dying inside me. I just don't know which one it is, or how to stop it from happening, but I remain rooted on the spot as Liam pulls his car back onto Main Street and drives away with my little mouse inside.

Fuck.

Warrick's wife's torture would be less painful than this.

"You okay, man?" Finn's voice drags my gaze from the fading tail lights as the car disappears around the bend towards the front gates.

"Why does it feel like I'm making a mistake?" I ask quietly, expecting him to say I haven't. Expecting him to reassure me that this is what's best.

"Maybe because you are."

I jerk my glare in his direction, my voice hoarse as I defend my actions.

"She can't be with me. You know that."

"All I hear are excuses. You haven't even tried." Finn lifts a single brow, and I see fucking red.

My fist collides with his face before I even know what's happening, and my best mate stumbles back as shocked gasps float over to us from the table in the middle of the street.

"Nice," Finn snaps, wiping blood from his lip with his finger, before he lunges at me, his fist coming out of nowhere, the smack of his knuckles against my eye socket loud.

"And here I thought when you asked my opinion, you actually wanted the truth. Not for me to appease your precious fucking feelings," Finn snarls right in my face as I square off to him as he does the same back, almost daring me to take another swing at him.

I don't. Instead, I take a step back, my breathing ragged as I fight for control.

"You'll understand if I'm gonna take a few fucking days off," Finn snaps, before spitting a wad of blood to the road by his feet. "You don't pay me enough for this bullshit."

Storming off, Finn leaves me standing there like a fucking fool.

And maybe I am.

Maybe I'm the biggest fucking fool there is.

I'm fucking up everything. I can feel it as much as I know the sun will rise again tomorrow.

But fuck that, and fuck him. I don't need this bullshit in my life. This is why relationships in organised crime don't fucking work. Feelings get involved and people start making mistakes.

With the eyes of many still on me, I turn and head into the Palace, crossing through the bar and into my office where I lock the door and crack open my bottle of whiskey.

It's the only comfort I'll ever get.

Chapter Thirty-Nine
Jaxcen

Even with all the trauma I faced as a child, I don't think I've ever cried this much in my life. I feel pathetic. Out of sorts. I only knew that man for five days. What the hell did I really think was going to happen?

That we were going to stay in that town forever and have sex daily until I had his child, and then do it all over again?

Dammit.

Maybe I did actually think that.

Why am I so naive? So gullible?

It felt so real.

It felt like more than sex.

But what do I have to compare it to?

My relationship with Eddie? The very sexless one where he shamed me for having desires. The one where he dictated my job, where I live, how I live, what I buy and don't buy, what I eat, and where I pray.

My life skills have been stunted. I know that now. But I don't know how I'm meant to live in the real world without those rules. Without those strict guidelines that spell out the difference between right or wrong.

But it's just religion, right? Not the law.

There's no law against gluttony. No law against pride, greed, lust or envy. It's not illegal to gossip, or be lazy, or even commit adultery, and the only time lying is illegal is when it's in the court of law or speaking to the police. Hell, even wrath isn't illegal. I can hate someone, and that's okay, as long as I don't get violent, right?

So really, in religion, or the religion I was raised with, the only sins that should concern me are stealing and murder. Those two are illegal.

So why couldn't I see that before all of this happened? Before the devil kidnapped me and woke me from the spell I'd been under?

I'd been conditioned. Just like at Holly River Estate. Just like with Eddie. I'd been conditioned to conform to behave and believe certain things.

Well, I don't believe in them anymore, but I've never navigated the world with my eyes wide open like this, and I'm scared. So scared.

The drive back to the city was torturous. Liam kept trying to make jokes and lighten the mood, and Warrick, who wore the black bag over his head until we reached the city limits, kept telling stories about the stupid stuff he and Devon got up to when they were little.

It made me realise how little I knew about Devon Marx. I learned more from his brother in the two hour drive than in the five days I spent as his little mouse.

Presley insisted I go back to her place, where I've been staying ever since.

The first three days I didn't get out of bed, but on day four, she dragged my sorry arse out and insisted we go to my place and clean it out.

So that's what we did for two days, relocating my few things and my shoe collection to her apartment.

I found the cameras as we started packing things away. There were two different kinds which I'm guessing one came from Vincent, and the other from Devon's men.

I burned them all.

I also went to the closest pawn shop and hocked my engagement ring. I was expecting the clerk to tell me it wasn't even a real diamond, but it was, and I got six hundred dollars for it, which I used to buy myself some new shoes.

The retail therapy worked for like five minutes.

That little outing made me feel better for a short time, until I had the strange feeling I was being followed, and like a coward, I hurried back to Presley's and locked myself inside for the rest of the day.

Today is New Year's Eve. I've never been to a New Year's Eve party, because Eddie didn't approve, and I'd love to go to one, but when Presley reminds me that she's going to a Marx party that Liam invited us to, I decline.

What if *he's* there? I can't bear to see Devon right now. I just don't think I'd recover from it.

Pres and I venture out into the city for lunch, the air warm, the city bustling with celebrations already starting up.

Melbourne has an amazing fireworks display that happens along the Yarra River each year. I've only ever watched it on TV, but I suppose I might see some of it from Presley's apartment since she's only a block from the river.

"Are you sure you won't come with me tonight? I can ask Liam if Devon will be there. If he's not, you might actually enjoy yourself."

I smile warmly at my sister's third attempt in the last two hours to get me to change my mind, but I shake my head, and take a bite of another fry as a chill runs up my spine.

It's happening again. The feeling of being watched.

I don't know how to explain it. Call it intuition. Or perhaps I'm just crazy. Who knows.

But I can't shake the feeling someone has been following me again. Just like yesterday.

"I'll pass," I say again to my sister, trying to push away my concerns about being stalked. "I want to get my shoes organised."

Presley laughs. "Why didn't I know you had so many shoes? And expensive ones at that?"

I shrug. "Eddie didn't like them." I remind her, then change the tone of my voice, mocking Eddie's voice. *"Shoes like that aren't a necessity, Jaxcen. That is nothing but greed, and greed is a sin. I expect better of you."*

I roll my eyes and Presley giggles. "Your impersonation of him is on point."

I nod. "He did like the sound of his own voice. I heard his lectures many times."

Presley sighs. "I didn't know that, Jax." She reaches across the table and takes my hand. "I'm sorry I didn't know."

"It's not your fault. I thought it was normal." I shrug, and all it does is make Presley stare at me with more concern, and all I feel is pathetic.

"You know, you seem so different now," Pres says, snatching one of the fries off my plate.

"How so?" I ask, glancing around to see if I can spot anyone watching us.

"You just seem so much more... alive."

My gaze darts to hers to see her eating the fry but watching me.

"Alive?" I ask, remembering that's what I felt around Devon.

We'd spoken about this at the cliffs in Woodall Ridge on Christmas Day, and at the time, I did feel alive. Now though, I feel dead inside.

"Yeah. There's this light in your eyes that wasn't there before. It's like you're seeing the world for the first time. Seeing all the possibilities and opportunities at your feet. There's a whole world of wonders for you to explore, and I think you're finally seeing that."

She's right of course. With my eyes wide open, not only do I see what my parents, Dr Xavier, and Eddie did as disgustingly wrong, but I see all the things that are acceptable and right.

Like the woman, two tables over, dressed to impress, her skin glowing with a fresh tan, her nails like claws and her rings sparkling. Her shoes are Jimmy Choo's, and her bag looks like it's Prada. She looks classy. Happy. And even though her style isn't mine, I envy her.

Then there are the two guys in the corner. Happy. Laughing, sharing a plate of food and feeding each other. They don't care about showing their feelings in public. The church frowns upon same sex couples, but it's not illegal, and those two men don't care. They are clearly in love. And scanning the crowd sitting at tables around them shows that they don't care either.

"I see so much now," I mutter quietly, envious of everyone around me. "Why do you think our parents are the way they are?"

Presley's brows shoot up at my question, and she takes a sip of her wine before answering.

"I read Mum's diary last year," she admits, and this time my brows shoot high.

"You did? What did it say?"

"Well, nothing too shocking other than the fact that these BS beliefs they've been raising us with are things she truly believes. And as far as I can tell, it was the way her and Dad were raised too."

I nod, not that shocked. Our parents attended the same church together as kids, so their courtship, as my mother likes to call it, was understandable before they got married.

Were my parents nothing but pawns in their parents' twisted beliefs as well?

Probably.

"There's no changing them now," I admit, wondering how Dad likes living without his fingers.

I wish I had been there when he met the devil.

"Well, we better get going," Presley says, grabbing her bag off the table. "I need to grab a bottle of bubbles on our way back."

I snicker. "I'm pretty sure you don't need to take a bottle of wine to a Marx party. They have plenty of money to supply booze."

"Oh, no. It's not for the party. It's for before the party while I get ready." Presley giggles, and I smile, standing with her as we leave the riverfront cafe.

We chat away as we walk arm in arm the few blocks to Presley's favourite bottle-o, and I stay outside as she goes in, enjoying the sun and the hyped atmosphere of the city today.

In the window of the bottle-o, they have a selection of expensive whiskeys sitting behind the security grates, and my eyes widen at the hefty five thousand dollar price tag.

Gosh. I hope Presley's wine isn't expensive.

As I glance up, a figure across the street catches my eye in the reflection of the window.

Tall. Sandy hair, but wearing a cap.

I stiffen.

Shit.

"I can't believe they've already sold out of my fav," Presley huffs coming to stand next to me, but my eyes remain on the figure over the street. "I should have grabbed it yesterday, but I was worried I'd drink it early and then be without, and now I'm without anyway. This cheap shit will have to do."

"Have a look at this," I say, ignoring the bottle my sister is holding up as I lean closer to the window and point at the whiskey bottles.

"Wait... do you drink whiskey now?" Presley asks in confusion.

"Pres, just keep pretending to look at the whiskey, but instead look at the reflection, and tell me if you can see someone across the street watching us."

A strangled okay falls from her lips, and then I hear her gasp.

"Is that Eddie?"

"Yes. I've had a sixth sense that someone has been following me since yesterday. It's him. We're not safe."

"I got this." Presley straightens from the window and pulls out her phone tapping the screen before placing it to her ear. "Act casual," she tells me, so I stop staring in the window and look at her instead, wondering what she's doing.

"Hi, yes it's me," Presley says into the phone. "You know how you said if we ever felt like we were in danger I could ring. Well, this is me calling."

I can hear a deep voice on the other end of the line, but can't make out who it is.

"Yes, we can start walking that way. See you soon."

Hanging up, she loops her elbow with mine and we start walking back the way we came from only minutes ago.

"Who was that and where are we going?" I ask, and my big sister beams at me.

"That was Liam, and he's just around the corner, so he'll drive us home."

I groan, not wanting anything to do with a Marx man, but I suppose we are safest with them right now, so I let my sister tug me along the street and around the next corner.

We can't look over our shoulder without making it obvious, so we keep our heads forward, and I spot Liam up ahead leaning against his black car.

When he spots us, he smiles, pushing off the car, and I notice his eyes move over our shoulders as we get closer.

"Blondish hair, wearing a cap?" he asks as he closes the distance leaning in to give me a hug, and I nod as he pulls back and then hugs Presley. "Okay, ladies. Your chariot awaits."

I can't help but smile at Liam's typical playfulness, and when I glance at Presley, I can tell she has a thing for him.

Great. The Marx charm is working on her too.

Not that Devon was charming. Not at first anyway, but in the quiet moments, he had a tender side to him that I'll never forget. I'll be dreaming about that side of him forever, I dare say.

My heart hurts thinking about him as I slide into the back seat of Liam's car, and I turn back in time to see Eddie slinking into an alcove.

"I can't believe he's stalking you," Presley says from the front seat as she clips her seatbelt in place.

"I can't either," I mutter, feeling safer now that we are in Liam's car.

"Want me to make him disappear?" Liam asks as he joins us, starting up the car.

Presley giggles at that comment, and I guess she doesn't realise how true his suggestion is. He's a Marx. They could make anyone disappear if they want to. Much like Vincent, although I have no idea what was done with his body. I didn't want to ask.

"No," I sigh. "He'll stop eventually." I hardly believe my words, because quite frankly, him stalking me was never something I considered.

I figured he would wash his hands of me and move on to find some other naive woman.

"Okie dokie," Liam says, pulling the car away from the curb. "You coming to party with us tonight?"

I shake my head when I meet his eyes in the rear view mirror.

"Oh, come on. It'll be fun."

"I've already tried so many times to change her mind," Presley says before the two of them fall into a discussion on their favourite part about New Year's Eve.

I think my favourite part will be that it's the end of a shitty year that I'd like to forget.

After Liam drops us off at Presley's apartment, well, I guess it's mine now too, my sister flits about the place drinking and dancing and getting ready, while I take a soak in the bath and shave my legs, and all my bits.

Presley gets picked up by Liam at six, and I sit on the end of my bed, my hair done, my makeup on, and a mask lying next to me on the bed.

I glance at it, unsure if I should do this. Unsure if going to Cloud 9 is the right thing to do.

I can go there now without shame. I know that. But it's not what's holding me back.

Dev.

Why is he under my skin so much? Why does the thought of watching other people without him there, churn my stomach?

Shit. Maybe I am pregnant.

I should probably test myself, although, I'm gathering it's probably too soon to know. But I guess I'll know soon enough if my monthly doesn't come. Then I'll know if Devon's obsessive attempts to keep his cum inside me have worked.

Standing from the end of my bed, I look at my reflection in the mirror.

Golden blonde hair in long waves. Blue eyes that will only be seen peering through the mask. Red lips that everyone will see, making them look plumper than usual. My neck has fading hickeys, my attempt to cover them with makeup futile, but at least it has taken the harshness away.

My breasts fit perfectly into the c-cup black lacy bra, with a tease of my pink nipple showing through. My stomach is flat, probably a little too flat given my inability to eat much since leaving Woodall Ridge. The black lace panties are a bikini cut in the front and g-string in the back, and my legs are silky smooth, all the way down to the red Louboutin pumps.

I've never worn any other colour than white to Cloud 9. I don't know why.

Was I aiming for innocent?

I don't feel innocent anymore. Not that I dislike that. I rather enjoy the idea that I can be naughty. A little depraved.

I considered wearing red. Men like red which is why I have the red heels on. But my mood is too dark to wear a colour on the rest of me, so I chose black.

Taking the black mask off the bed, I slip it on and examine the full picture.

Is this what I want to do on my first New Year's Eve as a free woman?

I could just stay in and watch the fireworks from the balcony, but the idea of being alone feels almost suffocating.

Perhaps I should have gone with Presley.

"Oh, come on Jaxcen. Make up your damn mind," I snap at myself, and huff, tearing off the mask before moving to my wardrobe.

Fuck it. I can always leave if the Cloud 9 atmosphere doesn't bring me out of my funk.

Throwing on a dress over my lingerie, I order an uber, and with my mask in hand, I leave the apartment.

It's time to see if I'm ready to stop watching from the sidelines and finally join in.

Vida Loca
Trust

CHAPTER FORTY
Devon

Standing, staring at the entrance door of Cloud 9, Jaxcen hovers. She's debating. Wondering if she should go inside. Wondering if it's what she wants.

Just step forward, little mouse. You can do it.

As if she can hear my thoughts, she moves, opening the door and slipping in.

I grin.

Atta girl.

Sighing from the shadows across the street, I watch Eddie, the person I'm actually following, as he hurries to the door. He studies the name and business information printed on the door before he takes his phone out.

I can imagine he's doing a search on Cloud 9, and as he stiffens, I gather he's just realised what sort of establishment it is.

I grin again.

"Go on in, Eddie. I dare you."

Taking the cap off his head, he rakes his fingers through his hair as if to tame it before he shoves the cap in the back pocket of his pants and enters.

I wait about thirty seconds before attempting to cross the busy street, nodding to the far corner where Lenny is standing casually wearing a disguise.

He nods back, and I open the door of the sex club, entering the darkened space.

"Welcome to Cloud 9." A tall blonde woman wearing a gold mesh dress that leaves little to the imagination, smiles at me from behind a counter. "Are you new here or a returning guest?"

"He knows the ropes." The deep voice comes from the side, and I turn to see Marco, club owner and an old friend. "If it isn't the one and only devil."

"Shut up." I snicker as he steps up to me and we bro hug, slapping each other's backs.

"It's been a long time since you've graced us with your presence."

I nod. "That it has. Business still good?"

"Better than ever." He winks. "So are you here for business or pleasure?"

"Unfortunately, business."

"Got anything to do with the blonde that walked in a few minutes ago? She's the one you asked us to notify you about if she came here, right?"

I nod. "Yes her, but it has more to do with the guy that walked in after her."

Marco's dark brows shoot up. "The newbie? Nervous as fuck?"

"Yeah. That's him. What name did he give you?"

Marco smiles at the blonde behind the counter holding his hand out, and she slips the registry book into his hand where he scans it.

"Edward Y." He reads out and I nod.

"That's him. Eddie York. He has a bit of an unhealthy fascination with my girl."

Marco smirks. "Your girl, hey? If she's your girl, then why is she here?"

"I'm a modern man, my friend." I clap him on the shoulder, shooting him a smug grin. "If she wants to explore her sexual appetite, I'm only too happy to sit back and watch."

Marco smirks, but his eyes narrow. "Is shit about to get messy?"

"Only if stalker Eddie touches my girl."

Nodding, Marco turns to the blonde. "Get Melody to put some extra security on the floor with a watch on our newbie."

The blonde nods. "I'll do that now, sir."

"Thank you, Winnie."

Marco's eyes linger a little too long on Winnie's arse as she turns and heads through the door behind the counter, so I give him a nudge with my shoulder.

"You know Melody will be watching you on the cameras right now."

He smirks, glancing back at me. "I know. And how fucking amazing will her angry sex be."

I chuckle. This man speaks my language.

"So was the newbie kitted up? Was he made aware of the rules?" I ask, glancing towards the change rooms which separate us from the main club where all the action happens.

"Yep to both. Had no idea about the mask thing. We even forced him to buy some new boxers, because man, he had granddad jocks on."

I laugh. "He's a religious man."

"Fuck. I was worried about that."

"Got a mask for me then?" I ask, and he grins. "Take whatever you need, and try not to get me shutdown tonight."

I roll my eyes. "Would I do that?"

"Yes," he deadpans, and I laugh all the way into the change rooms, leaving him behind.

Inside, I select a black mask, and slip out of my shirt, leaving my jeans and shoes on, since I have no intentions of getting my cock out tonight, and then I enter the main floor.

The music is loud enough to create a good atmosphere, but not so loud you have to yell to be heard. Part of the ambience is to hear the moans and slapping, after all.

I'm on the top level which opens out to a wrap-around balcony over the main floor below, and I immediately spot Eddie, shifting nervously on his feet as he takes in his surroundings.

What do you think, Eddie boy? Is this a yay or nay for you?

I snicker at my inner thoughts until I see Eddie stiffen, grip the railing and hone in on his prize.

Following his gaze, there, on the level below, I spot my little mouse, standing on the sidelines watching the orgy happening in the middle.

My cock starts to wake up for the first time in days at the sight of her in the black lingerie.

And fuck, her lips are bright red, making them appear more plump than they already are.

Fuck. Maybe I should have sent Finn to do this job.

How the fuck am I going to stay away from her?

I barely take any notice of the foursome in the centre of the room, my focus remaining on Eddie and Jaxcen, making sure I can at least see Eddie at all times.

The three of us remain in our places for quite a while. Me watching Eddie watching Jaxcen. Jaxcen watching the live porn show. Me watching her watch the live porn show.

Fuck. I want to be down there with her. I want to walk up behind her and whisper in her ear.

Just do it, little mouse. Take what you need.

Not that I like the idea of any man touching her, but fuck, I love watching her unravel, and I want her to flourish now that I've helped her unbind those invisible ropes that were holding her captive.

The moment Jaxcen takes a step closer to the action in the centre, the toes of those sexy fucking red heels nearly brushing the line that divides onlookers to those willing to participate, I'm about ready to leap over the railing and stop her.

I don't need to though, because her shoulders slump, and she takes a step back. And then another. And another.

Disappointment courses through me *for her*. She's seeking something and is either too scared to take it, or simply can't reach it, and I hate that for her.

In my distraction, I've lost sight of Eddie, and I stiffen, my gaze darting at every onlooker up on the balcony, trying to spot him.

Shit.

He's not up here.

It's then that I see him, behind Jaxcen, standing in the shadows where I should fucking be.

His gaze is on her, his fists balled, his anger evident, so I start to move.

Hurrying around the balcony towards the stairs, I watch as he approaches her side, and I move faster.

My eyes meet the security detail that is slowly closing in. They can't technically do anything unless something happens, but it's a relief to know Marco's men are on their game, and my little mouse has others looking out for her.

"Let's fuck." I hear Eddie say as I move up behind them, not wanting Jaxcen to see me unless it's absolutely necessary.

"No, thanks," Jaxcen mutters, her voice strange. Flat. Almost defeated.

She doesn't look at Eddie standing next to her. She doesn't even recognise his voice. She just remains standing, staring, at what, I don't know.

Leaning to the side, I see a man's belt draped over the end of the lounge, realising that's what Jaxcen is staring at.

Is she remembering my belt? The one I used on her that night in the chapel. How I hooked it behind her head and controlled her as I fucked her mouth? Is she remembering how I used it as a cuff, to secure her ankle to the confessional so I could keep her hips elevated to ensure my cum would remain inside her?

Fuck. I bet she is remembering that.

How easy it would be for me to take her hand, lead her to the centre and give her what she craves.

"Come on. Let's join in and fuck. That's why you're here, isn't it?"

She shakes her head, still not picking up on his voice as she stares until he speaks again.

"Why not? You're a whore, aren't you?"

My lip curls at his words, and I'm about ready to smash this fucker to the ground when Jaxcen finally snaps out of her trance, jerking her head in his direction.

"Eddie?" There's a tremble to her voice, and she takes a step back, closer to me.

"Isn't this what you've always wanted? To fuck me? Well, here I am, you stupid whore. Let's get this out of your system so we can get married."

She gasps. Taking a step to the side this time, and I see her face better, her blue eyes wide behind the mask.

"Please leave me alone. I am not marrying you."

His lip curls. "Like hell, you're not." He lurches forward, snatching her wrist in his tight grip and starts dragging her over the line into the centre, and just when I'm about to dive on the fucker, and unleash my devil, a strong arm wraps around me from behind.

"Just wait," Marco rasps, and I struggle, hearing Jaxcen cry out as she tries to pull her arm free.

It's then that six security guards are on them, three taking Eddie down, and two quickly escorting Jaxcen away to safety, while one watches on to make sure no one intervenes.

"Fuck." I breathe out, relaxing in Marco's hold to hear him chuckle.

"See. There's no need for bloodshed."

I shove him off me and turn to face the fucker. "I disagree. There should always be bloodshed."

"Fine, just not here."

I roll my eyes at my mate. "Whatever. Make sure she gets home, yeah?"

"You don't even have to ask. Melody will see to that personally."

I nod. "And him? Keep him for a bit, but don't rough him up. Maybe give him a few drinks and send him home in a taxi in an hour."

"Will do." Marco smiles.

I watch as security quickly removes Eddie from the room out a side door, and I turn and leave, ready for the next part of my night.

Taking out my phone, I shoot Theodore Perelli a message, letting him know that I'm on my way, and he responds that he'll see me soon.

In this business, it pays to have friends in low and high places. Just like at Cloud 9, my mate Marco and his wife Melody are the owners of the club, giving me the access I needed to try and protect my little mouse. And now, I meet Theo outside one of the buildings he owns, which just so happens to be directly across the street from Jaxcen's where she now lives with her sister.

It also happens to be the building where Mr Edward York leased an apartment this week, on the fifteenth floor, with a direct view into the Summers sisters' living and bedrooms.

Snide fucker really thinks he can get away with stalking my girl, and then trying to force her into public sex.

What a dick.

Theo meets me in the foyer and hands me an access key to Eddie's apartment.

"You got the payment?" Theo asks, the short man looking expectantly up at me.

"Of course." I hand him the black bag. "Five hundred large. You wanna count it?"

Theo chuckles, accepting the bag. "Nah. I trust you."

"Be prepared for the cops to be here later." I remind him.

"Yeah, I know. All the CCTVs are off in the area, so you're good to go."

We shake hands and I nod, already knowing there's no digital eyes on us right now. I don't trust anyone but Dom to have my back with that.

Taking the lift up, I enter Eddie's apartment cautiously, my hands gloved so no fingerprints are left behind.

Just as expected, the windows and small balcony face Presley's, with a telescope set up in front of the glass sliding door, angled towards her apartment.

I don't touch anything, but a quick glance in the scope shows Jaxcen sitting at the kitchen counter, her fork picking at a salad.

I can see every line on her beautiful face.

She looks sad.

Fuck.

I hate that she's sad.

I want to go to her but I can't. It's too risky, and she deserves better.

My phone vibrates in my pocket, and I pull it out to see a message from Lenny telling me that Eddie's taxi is pulling up outside the apartment building now.

Good.

Time to get this over with.

Stepping forward, I unlatch the lock on the glass sliding door and ease it open as wide as it can go before shifting the telescope onto the dark balcony, and realigning the scope to see inside Presley's apartment again.

When it's in place, I move back inside to the far corner and wait in the dark.

Only a few minutes pass before the apartment door clicks open, and the heavy feet of a man rushes in, muttering under his breath.

His dark silhouette comes into view as he steps into the main living area, his feet halting as the loud city noises float in from the open balcony door.

"What the hell?"

He rushes forward, standing in the open door and scratching his head, before he turns and gazes back inside, his eyes looking directly at me for a brief moment.

He can't see me. I'm shrouded in shadows, and as he turns back and shrugs, I gather the idiot thinks maybe he left his apartment like this. Either that or he doesn't think too much about anything, which is also a possibility.

Turning back to the city beyond his balcony, he steps up to the telescope and glances into the lens.

"You fucking whore. I'll get you. And when I do I'll make you wish you never went to that fucking place."

Red rims my vision as I glare at the back of his head, watching him watch what's mine.

With a level of stealth that can only be learned, I move from the corner towards Eddie, my gun raised and ready in case he turns around.

He doesn't. I move up right behind him and press the barrel of my Glock to the back of his head.

"You like perving on innocent women?" I ask and Eddie stiffens as he registers my words and the gun.

"Wha— Who..."

"Who I am doesn't fucking matter to you," I snarl, keeping my voice deep and quiet. "But, the *what am I doing* is obvious, don't you think?"

"I... Is it money? I don't have much. There's a couple of hundred in my pocket." He starts to sob, and I roll my eyes.

Fucking pussy. Doesn't even have the balls to put up a fight. I shove my barrel hard against his head, and he cries out.

"Please don't kill me."

"Tell me about the woman you are watching through the telescope," I demand.

"H-her name is J-Jaxcen. She's my fiancé."

"Wrong," I hiss, pressing the barrel harder against him, making him whimper. "She's not your fiancé, Eddie. She'll never marry you."

"Oh my god. You're him, aren't you. The man from the phone... with her."

"I am the devil, Eddie. And you are nothing but a waste of oxygen."

"P-Please. I'll leave her alone. I swear."

I chuckle darkly. "No, you won't. But that's okay. You won't be around to harass her anymore."

"But. I..."

"Shut the fuck up!" I snap a little too loud. "Look in the telescope again, Eddie. Have one last look at the woman you'll never get to have."

"N-no, p-please."

"Do it or I'll pull the trigger."

"F-fine." He sobs, leaning closer to the telescope.

I don't bother with the trigger. That will draw too much attention, and quite frankly, I want him even more terrified for the final seconds of his life.

With my gloved hand, I fist the back of his shirt and shove him and the telescope over the balcony railing.

He cries out, screaming all the way down, because he knows there's no coming back from this.

The moment his scream cuts off, I know he's hit pavement, so I slink back inside and leave his apartment, taking the lift back down where I disappear into the night, even as police sirens fill the city streets.

Eddie won't be a problem anymore.

Chapter Forty-One
Jaxcen

Everything feels different. The air. The smells. My appetite. My drive. I feel like a very different person to the naive woman I was back in December. But now I live in a world where there is no more Dr Xavier. No more Holly River Estate or depraved male nurses. And no more Eddie.

I was completely shocked that he'd been spying on me from across the street. The police had photos he'd taken of me, and apparently, when he fell to his death on the last night of the year, he'd been spying on me again through a telescope.

When all the chaos across the street erupted, police and ambulances closing off the road, I'd gone out onto Presley's balcony to try and see what was going on, but with the dark night, and a quickly erected crime scene tent covering the pavement, I couldn't see.

But it turns out it was Eddie. He fell to his death, too busy stalking me through the lens of a telescope.

He'd scared the hell out of me in Cloud 9, but the moment I found out it was him who was dead, all I felt was relief.

He can't hurt me anymore either.

Even though my parents still remain, they haven't spoken to me or Presley since. I'll be happy if I never speak to them again, but I'm not sure how Pres will go. She had a completely different relationship with our parents, so she'll probably cave and visit them eventually.

And that's okay. As long as she is safe.

I spent January trying out different jobs after handing in my resignation at my old one.

I only lasted a day waitressing, and three days in retail. I didn't like the women. They were too catty and sales-target focused and I'm no pushy salesperson.

The bakery down the road is where I've been working ever since. They decided to take a chance on me, even though I didn't have the experience, and now I'm working five days a week, earning just enough money to start saving a deposit to get my own rental again one day soon.

Dianne and Pete are great bosses, and I've made a few friends with the other staff, which is something I've never bothered with before. I've even been asked out on dates by the coffee cart guy, the postie, and a regular customer.

I said no to them all. I'm not sure why. They were all decent looking guys and seemed nice enough, but they just weren't... him.

I've had the urge to return to Cloud 9 more frequently lately, but haven't summoned up the courage yet.

When I last went on New Year's Eve, Eddie had followed me there. He tried to drag me into the centre, but luckily the security guards were on their game, and the ordeal was over quite quickly.

If it wasn't for their good security, I wouldn't be contemplating returning to the club at all.

But I am, even though before Eddie had interrupted me, I had decided to leave. I had no interest in anything there. All I could think about was Devon, and it hurt more than I thought it would.

I haven't seen the devil since he practically banished me from his town. Sometimes I think I can feel his dark eyes on me, but that's nothing more than hope messing with my head.

He said I'd never return to Woodall Ridge, and I'm starting to believe him.

It's now Valentine's day, and Presley has gone out on a date with some new guy she met at a bar last weekend. I kinda thought her and

Liam were starting something up, but she hasn't spoken about him since New Year's Eve, so I guess I was wrong.

I received a special invitation from Cloud 9, inviting me to their Valentine's Evening giving me free entry as an apology for what happened with Eddie in their facility.

It's not necessary to give me free entry, but I've decided to take them up on the offer, and slip into my red lingerie this time.

Feeling bolder.

Feeling a little wicked.

Maybe tonight's the night I'll step over the line.

The club is packed when I arrive, more people in attendance than any other time I've been there. It makes me both anxious and excited. Maybe I can step over the line with someone in the crowd. A gentle caress. A sensual touch. Just... something.

Once my clothes are stored in my locker and my mask is on, I enter the top level, taking my time to watch from the balcony.

There's a couple below. She's spread open for him, while he inserts a vibrator inside her.

When she moans and arches off the chaise, I feel the beginnings of pleasure stir between my legs.

Her hair is blonde, and his hair is dark, and for a moment, I imagine it's me and the devil.

Maybe that's all I have to do. Imagine Devon is the one pleasuring me, instead of some random guy.

With that thought in mind, I move to the lower level, where the crowd is thicker and I see that many couples are going at it in every direction I look.

Oh.

Wow.

Heat courses through my veins and I pretend every man I see is him. I pretend they are the devil.

To say I'm horny is an understatement. Even if I decide not to touch another person here tonight, I'd have no problem touching myself over what I'm seeing.

Absent-mindedly, I cup my breast as I weave through the writhing couples, wanting to get a closer look at the show in the centre where the lights are bright, and you can literally see everything.

I can feel the heat of the bright lights as I approach the line, not getting too close, my eyes watching the couple.

Now the man is lathering his dick with lube while she uses the vibrator on herself, watching him with hungry eyes. They are familiar with each other, and either the wedding bands on their fingers are for each other, or they are married to others who may or may not be watching right now.

Either way, the fact they know each other, and are so turned on pangs at my heart.

I want that.

I had that for a minute there.

And then it was gone.

The tattoos covering the man's back are intricate, and remind me of Devon's, and for a moment I wonder if it's him up there.

But no. Devon's taller. And he has a scar on his left hip, where this man doesn't.

The man presses his dick to the woman's back passage, and she hooks her arms under her knees and lifts them, opening herself up for him more as he eases inside her, even while the vibrator is still inside her pussy.

Ohhhh. She must feel so full.

My lips part as my breathing picks up, heat pooling between my legs at the sight.

I can feel my cheeks heat in one of my stupid blushes that always gives me away, and for a moment I feel like Devon is here watching me, the familiar sensation making me scan the crowd.

I freeze.

My spine stiffening and my lungs completely ceasing as a dark sinister grin catches my eye across the other side of the podium.

No... It can't be.

Surely I'm imagining him again.

Surely he's not really here.

I take a step to the side to see past the couple in the middle, and the bright lights illuminate the man sitting over the other side unmistakably.

It's him.

It's the devil.

Heat rushes through my entire body, and for a moment I want to cry. Tears prick at my eyes, but I force them back. I can't be all pathetic here. This place isn't about feelings. This place is about sex and exploration.

I don't know what to do. Should I stay? Should I go? Should I do nothing?

His eyes are on me though. That much I'm sure about, and then he mouths, 'hello little mouse.'

I spin, giving him my back, ready to walk away but my feet won't move. They won't let me run.

They are traitors, that's what they are!

Glancing back over my shoulder, his eyes are still on me, but a woman is standing in front of him now, partially blocking my view.

I spin back and take another side step, wanting to see what she's doing, when she leans in close and whispers something in his ear, pointing back over her shoulder at the podium.

Wait... Is she inviting him out there?

The moment he nods and grins, I feel a rush of anger burst through me.

Oh hell no.

Vida Loca
Trust

Chapter Forty-Two

Devon

"I'm beginning to think I should have asked for more than five hundred," Quinlan says before she straightens from my ear.

Keeping my grin in place, I glance up at my cousin. "You don't even have to touch me. Just make it appear that you're flirting. That you're into me, and you'll get paid."

She rolls her eyes and leans in close, hovering her lips in front of mine. "Fine. I hope she gets so angry at you that she cuts your dick off and dissolves in it a tub of acid."

"Fuck, cous. You're brutal. You sure know how to seduce a man." I smirk and she straightens again, my eyes darting behind her to find my angry little mouse glaring at us.

"Dude, you're my cousin. My skin is literally crawling right now. Not to mention my brother and his wife are on the podium. I can't unsee that, Devon."

I chuckle at Quinlan's reaction, thankful she at least agreed to help me, since I didn't want any outsiders getting involved.

"It's nearly over," I mutter, my eyes following Jaxcen as she moves through the crowd. "She's already coming this way to fuck you up."

"You are so fucked up," Quinlan snaps, cocking her hip as her hand lands on it.

"I know. That's why I'm your favourite cousin."

"I wouldn't go that far," she scoffs.

"Incoming." I grit between clenched teeth as Jaxcen reaches our side, her glare scorching the side of Quinlan's head.

"Back off brunette barbie."

Quinlan's eyes widen as she turns to look at Jaxcen before shrugging nonchalantly.

"Whatever."

Jaxcen frowns at my cousin as she spins and leaves us, before her hard glare returns to me.

"Why are you here?"

"It's Valentine's Day," I say, like that's an obvious reason.

"You need to leave," she snaps, her dainty hands balled at her sides, and fuck, I'd be happy if she used them on me. A punch. A slap. It's all foreplay when it comes to the two of us.

"Why do I need to leave, little mouse?"

Her nostrils flare, her chest rising and falling in rapid succession as she fights to keep her emotions in check.

Truthfully, I'm feeling out of sorts myself, finally talking to her instead of watching from a distance feels both good, and like I'm crossing a line that I know I drew.

Finn dished me a dose of advice last week, and after a lot of pondering, I decided to take it.

> *"You obviously care about her. Put yourself, her and everyone around us out of our misery and just claim her already. You already have a security detail on her twenty four seven. Just fucking man up."*

Leaning closer, Jaxcen's words are a harsh tone as she speaks truthfully.

"I need you to leave because I don't want to watch you fuck a bunch of other women."

Hmmm. I like this version of her. The woman with fight. The woman who doesn't cower.

"Maybe I'm not here to fuck a bunch of other women. Maybe I'm here to fuck just one."

She glances around, her eyes zeroing in on every other brunette woman nearby as she searches for my cousin, Quinlan.

She won't find her. Quinny is long gone, especially since her brother Griffin is performing anal with his wife Aggie on the podium. I forgot Griffin's wife likes a bit of exhibitionism, and I was momentarily surprised to see them here tonight. I had to get over that really fucking fast when he whipped his cock out.

"Oh right." Jaxcen snarls, "You're just here to fuck bimbo barbie."

"I thought it was brunette barbie?" I counter and she curls her lip.

"Shut up."

My chuckle earns me a glare, and I hold up hands of surrender, hoping she doesn't actually try to kill me before I can win her back.

"Are you planning on watching tonight, little mouse?"

"That's none of your business," she scoffs, crossing her arms over her chest.

"Hmmm," I say thoughtfully, watching how she can't take her eyes off me, their blue searing gaze travelling over my bare chest and down my abs, to my black boxers.

"You know what's better than watching?" I ask, and she narrows her eyes before I stand abruptly, invading her space. "Being the one everyone watches."

As her lips part in shock at my sudden nearness, I grip her throat and press my nose to hers.

"Will you let me touch you right here for everyone to see, Miss Summers?"

Her lips part, but nothing comes out as I start to walk her backwards, towards the centre of the room.

"Will you let me show everyone here how our bodies are made for each other?" I ask, stopping on the bright red line and looking down to the floor at our side.

With my hand on her throat, I guide Jaxcen to do the same, her blue gaze darting to the line that her red heels are now standing on.

"What do you say, little mouse? Do we cross that line?"

A whoosh of air leaves her lips as we both straighten, followed by a whimper, those blue eyes connecting with mine, filled with desperation.

"Answer me, little mouse," I snap, and she tries to nod.

"Yes."

The moment the word passes her lips, I walk her backwards, pushing her over the line and into the spotlight.

Excited murmurs float through the crowd at seeing a second couple join the podium, and I release Jaxcen's neck to lift her legs, wrapping them around me as I take the two steps up onto the cushioned surface.

I claim her lips, no longer able to hold back, showing her with my tongue how much I've fucking missed her.

Something comes over me, and I kind of wish we were alone, because there's so much I need to say, but I chose this scenario, because I knew she wouldn't run from this.

She's wanted to do this for so long, but she didn't realise she couldn't do it because something was missing.

Me.

I lower her to the surface and press my body into hers, letting her feel my weight as I start grinding between her legs.

My cock is stiffer than it's ever been, hard as stone, aching to find its heaven inside her, but for now, my focus is on her. I want to make her feel treasured. I want to remind her how explosive we can be together, because after this, I'll never send her away again.

I break our kiss to move to her ear, my voice deep as I rasp, "I'm going to strip you little mouse, for everyone to see, but only I can touch you. You're safe with me."

She nods against my lips, so I pepper kisses down her neck, my hands peeling the lace straps of her bra down her arms, bringing the cups with it to expose her perky tits.

Her nipples are peaked hard, and I mouth them, sucking each one in between my lips before trailing lower and making quick work of her panties.

I watch those stormy blue eyes behind the mask, how they shift from me to the people watching. There's no fear in them, only excitement, and when I spread her legs wide, knowing many have a good view of my girl's flushed pink pussy, I glide two fingers through her folds to find her soaking wet.

"Fuck, little mouse. You're drenched."

The moment I ease my two digits inside her, those blue eyes roll back and she arches off the podium, palming her tits.

More excitement travels through the crowd. Moans. Chatter. Fucking. It all adds to the atmosphere and what's happening to Jaxcen's body. How ready she is to take everything I want to give her.

Starved for her taste, I dive down, latching onto her clit and sucking, flicking my tongue and revelling in how swollen the little bud is for me.

How swollen it is for *this*.

Curling my fingers inside her, I lave at her clit, my eyes locked on her face, her parted plump lips as she pants, her gaze, so bright around her nearly blown irises.

She could be watching the crowd to see how they are reacting to her, but she can't take her eyes off me. Off what I'm doing to her, until the pleasure builds so much that her eyes roll backwards before they close, and she lets herself go.

The moment her hands fist in my hair and she starts grinding on my face, I nearly come, but by some miracle I'm able to hold it back, knowing the only place I want my cum is deep inside her.

The moment I add a third finger into her heat, she skyrockets, her pleasured screams egging the entire room on, and I swear most of the people climax themselves, given the wave of moans and cries that sweep across the space.

I don't stop my assault on her until she starts trying to slap me away, and then I grin up at her, my lips and stubble lining my chin damp with her juices.

"Atta girl," I tell her, and I just know, if I were to tug off her mask, I'd see those pretty apples of her cheeks turning red.

Kissing my way back up her body, I come to hover over her lips, our eyes locking once again as she continues to take in large lungfuls of air, trying to catch her breath.

"You still with me, Jax?" I ask, needing the reassurance. "Are you ready for my cock now?"

Biting her lip, she nods, keeping her voice to herself.

I wonder why.

Perhaps she's scared her voice will say the opposite of her nod.

That thought just makes me even more determined to remind her what happens when we come together.

Easing back off her, I help her stand, noticing how shaky her legs are.

Seeing that Griffin is using one of the harnesses hanging from above, I decide that's a brilliant fucking idea, and reach up to the one hanging over Jaxcen's head.

"Are we doing syncronised fucking?" Griffin chuckles from a few metres away where he is helping Aggie into the straps.

I shrug and grin at my cousin, "Apparently."

"Who's that?" Jaxcen whispers, glancing over her shoulder at the couple she's never met before.

"That's Griff. My cousin."

Her lips part in shock as I start securing the harness on her, and I can't help but notice she's really paying no attention to what I'm doing to her.

"Another cousin? How many do you have?" Even as she asks this, she wraps her arms over her chest like it's alright for strangers to see her tits but not my cousin.

"In that family, there's eighteen. Well, nineteen if you include the girl they adopted."

"What?" she squeaks, glancing back at Griff as he hoists Aggie up, her naked flesh spread open and exposed for everyone to see.

"Griff is one of Liam's many brothers. But don't worry, they have three different mums. My uncle didn't make one woman suffer through all of that."

She gapes at me as I finish securing the straps, and squeaks in surprise when I start hoisting her up and her feet leave the ground.

"Wait... what's happening?"

"Do you trust me, little mouse?" I ask, as I lock the harness in place on the beam off to the side, and even though she nods, I can see her looking down at herself and how exposed she is.

Me... well I just stand there and admire her for a moment.

She's fucking stunning all strung up for me to devour.

I'd like it a helluva lot better if I could actually see all of her face, but since we are here, I'm happy people can't see that. Only I know what she looks like underneath her mask.

The way the harness is rigged up, her back is supported, her arms are free, but her legs are bent with feet drawn close to her bare arse, and her knees are wide open, giving me all the access I need.

Glancing over to the side of the room, I make eye contact with Marco, giving him a nod before he moves our way and holds out the gift I have for my little mouse.

"Thanks man," I say as I take the box and he grins.

"I should be thanking you. This is the best show we've had in a long time."

I chuckle, moving back to Jaxcen and holding up the box.

"What's that?" she asks quietly, her body slowly turning one way and then the other as she hangs like a planter swaying in the wind.

"A gift for my Valentine." I grin, lifting the lid on the box to reveal the shiny object.

Her lips part, her head leaning closer to get a better look, before those blue eyes dart to mine.

"Is that... A plug?" she whispers the last part and I beam.

"Yes. You're going to wear it while I fuck you. You'll feel nice and full."

"Oh." Her lips part and her breathing quickens, so I decide not to drag this out.

She wants it. She wants me. Right now, anyway, so there's no point in holding back anymore.

Pulling the butt plug out of the box, I use the antibacterial wipes to make sure it's clean, even though it's new, and then douse it in lube, watching my little mouse the whole time as she watches everything I do, hanging there ready for me.

With a good dose of lube on my fingers as well, I approach my prize and spin her so her back is to me as I press my lips to her ear.

"Look at them, Jax. They're fucking salivating over you. Look at the men, jerking their cocks, fucking someone else but watching you. Even the women want a piece of you. They want to taste your sweet nectar." I press my fingers to her back passage and nip at her ear as I slip two inside. "They want to devour you."

She moans, and I'm surprised how relaxed her puckered little hole is given this new experience of being watched. But maybe that's helping. Maybe all the eyes on her have her trapped in an intoxicating lust haze.

Fuck, I hope so.

Lowering to my haunches, I slip my fingers from her arse and press the plug to it, watching her take it in greedily, her moan loud.

Once it's inside, I stand and give her arse a slap before spinning her to face me and letting her watch me free my cock as I tug off my boxers and kick them aside.

"You want this, little mouse?" I ask her, fisting my cock and pumping it, watching her greedy little eyes soak it all in.

"Yes." She nods quickly. "Please."

Ahhh, I do love it when she begs.

Stepping between her widely parted legs, I watch her as she watches my cock pressing to her entrance, and I leave it there. Waiting. Hesitating for no other reason but to draw out her hunger.

"Please. Put it in." She cries and fuck, I can't deny either of us any longer.

I drive hard inside her tight hot cunt, her cry loud as she throws her head back, and I grip her legs, letting the harness do all the work and I push and pull her back and forth onto my hard cock.

"Fuuuck, Jax. Your pussy takes me so well," I rasp as she nods quickly in agreement. "I've fucking missed it," I admit, feeling way more fucking emotional than I thought I would.

She nods again, her eyes coming to mine, a glassy sheen over them as I fuck her fiercely.

My hand runs up her front, coming to rest at her neck as I draw her closer so she hears my next words without mistake.

"I've fucking missed you."

A whimper passes her lips, and those blue eyes start to water, so I claim her lips, needing to remind her again, that when the two of us come together like this, nothing else matters.

My hands move to her arse as I break the kiss, my hips thrusting as I pound into her, the plug in her back passage working well to fill her and add pressure to all her sensitive places.

"You're mine." I grit out as I start to lose control. "You are all fucking mine."

She whimpers, and I feel her tightening around my cock as she tumbles over the edge again, another orgasm ripping through her as I piston so fast that I nearly see fucking stars.

I explode inside her, my cock jerking hard over and over as I fill her pussy with my seed, reminding me how much I've missed this. Missed her.

When the ripples of pleasure subside, I find my arms wrapped around her, my head tucked into her neck, and my cock semi-hard, but nowhere ready to retreat just yet.

I feel it before I hear it. Her body shuddering. A sob passing her lips into the crook of my neck.

Easing back enough to cup her face, I stare into those blue tear-filled eyes and the sight fucking hurts.

I hate to see her tears. Her pain. I want to take it all away so she feels nothing but warmth, love, and happiness.

"Jax?"

"Please get me down."

"But—"

"Please, Devon. Just get me down from here."

Fuck.

I nod, moving quickly to remove the plug, tossing it in the box, before lowering her down and letting the harness unravel until her feet touch the floor. The moment she can stand, she helps me get the rest of the harness off, before she quickly picks up her bra and panties, clutching them to her chest.

"Hey." I grab her arm when she turns away from me, and those blue pained eyes glance up to lock with mine.

"Leave me alone, Devon." She snarls with so much pain lacing her tone before she wrenches her arm free, and runs off through the crowd.

CHAPTER FORTY-THREE

Jaxcen

Completely shaken by what just happened at Cloud 9, I dress and flee by foot, running the five city blocks back to Presley's apartment. I've been holding my tears at bay as much as I can. Some escape every now and then, but I wrangle them under control, completely confused over seeing Devon again.

Why did he go there?

Why did he do that?

I'd been doing so well, or so I thought, but I was fooling myself. Big time.

I'm not okay, and I haven't been ever since Devon booted me out of his town.

The moment I close myself inside the apartment, I want to break, but I keep it all in, needing to shower. I need to get his scent off my skin before I completely lose the little control I have.

"I've decided Christmas isn't enough."

The deep voice startles me, and I scream, whirling around to see Devon sitting on the lounge suite dressed in black pants and a black shirt, looking devastatingly handsome. He's leaning forward, legs wide the way men sit, his elbows resting on top of his knees.

"What are you doing here?" I squeak. "How did you get in?"

"Since this building is owned by the Marx family, and I'm a Marx, getting in isn't that hard." He stands, his height and frame making Presley's apartment feel small. Too small as he stalks closer. "And I'm here for you."

"I... I don't understand. What do you mean Christmas isn't enough?" I whisper loudly, taking a step back.

He smirks that wicked way only Devon Marx can. "Have you forgotten how I said I'd come for you every Christmas? That I'd kidnap you every year?"

I frown. What the hell is he talking about?

"I remember you rambling about that at one point, but then you forced me to leave, Devon. I figured playtime was over."

His eyes darken at my words, and he steps closer, making my retreat end against the wall by the hallway that leads to the bedrooms.

"Rambling?" He smirks, arching a dark brow. "You call my promises rambling?"

"There's a lot of things I could call them, Devon, but never once did I consider them a promise."

Sucking in a sharp breath, he cages me in, a hand on either side of my head as he leans in.

"I've decided to keep you."

My brows shoot high before I scowl at him.

"I'm not a possession."

"Aren't you?" He tilts his head to the side, his gaze dropping to my cleavage.

"I don't want to be your sex slave, Devon."

Those dark eyes dart back to mine. "Don't you? Why not? You enjoy it so much."

My nostrils flare at his insinuation, even though he's not wrong, which just pisses me off even more.

"I need more." I dare to admit the truth, and he shifts to lean on one elbow, as his other hand reaches out, his fingers brushing my flaming hot cheek.

"Like what, little mouse?"

"Dates. Dinners. Couples things," I admit, knowing Devon Marx isn't that kind of man. "I may crave the kind of sex you can give me, but I also crave a companion. Someone who sees me for me."

He jerks back like I just slapped him, his hand falling away, and god damnit, I miss it.

Shit.

"You don't think I see you?" he asks, sounding a little hurt. "Has nothing during our confessions shown you that?"

"That was role play," I scoff, pressing my hands to his chest to shove him back, but he doesn't budge.

Instead he peels my hands from his chest and holds them there, his big palms engulfing mine.

"Sure, the submission part was role play, but the confessions themselves, my interest in them was real. If that part was simply role play, then the confessions would have been made up for the sake of the scene we were playing. Not real truths, little mouse." He presses his lips to the back of my hands, first one, and then the other, he kisses them. "It was more than kink for me."

His admission is real. I can hear it in his tone. See it in his eyes. Feel it in his searing touch as he holds my hands like he's worried they'll disappear.

Crap. He's right. Those confessions with him were the realest thing I've ever experienced.

I've been exposed and vulnerable before. Made to feel so alone that nothing I cared about mattered.

But Devon, those moments we shared were brutally honest, and he wanted my truth, not to use against me, but because I needed someone to hear me. Just once.

Tears well in my eyes as I let myself remember how he made me feel. How safe I felt even when he was pushing me to step over the scary line.

But that's not enough. Sure he's missed having sex with me and the way I push his buttons. I can tell he likes that about me. But I need so much more than confessions of sins, and sex so intense that I allow myself to pass out.

"It's not enough," I whisper, my lip trembling as I fight not to shatter in his presence.

"What more do you need?" he asks, releasing my hands and cupping each side of my face, tilting my head back so there's nowhere else to look but at him.

"Love," I admit, and he frowns.

"You don't think I love you?" he grumbles, and I try to shake my head, but his grip is firm, and I can't move it an inch.

"No. I think you want to possess me. Control me. Own me," I admit, seeing his frown deepen with each word I speak. "You obviously can't handle the idea of me going to Cloud 9 or you wouldn't have gone there tonight. You wouldn't be doing this. That's not love."

"I disagree," he growls, pressing his forehead to mine. "I think possessing you is the realest love there is. I don't deny how I feel about you. I may be a bad man, but fuck woman, you make me want to be good."

He kisses me then, his lips hot and soft and intoxicating. I'm powerless to deny him so I part my lips willingly, our tongues clashing in a kiss that feels like he's trying to claim me.

Then he pulls back, his gaze on my lips momentarily before locking with mine. "And as for Cloud 9, I went there *for* you, so you could finally step over that line. So you could feel what it was like to have everyone worship you with their heated eyes and their writhing loins. The reason you've never been able to do it is because you didn't have me."

I want to scoff, but a lump the size of a cricket ball is lodged in my throat, because I think he's actually right. I've been to Cloud 9 so many times, and I couldn't make myself step over the line.

I used to think it was because of Eddie and those twisted beliefs we had, but now, although that did play a role in it, I really think I just didn't trust anyone enough to touch me. To make sure I enjoyed it. To make sure I was safe.

Fat tears spill over, and I finally work the lump down enough so I can speak.

"You sent me away."

"Yes." He swipes at my tears with his thumbs.

"And now you want me back?"

"Yes," he admits easily, staring into my eyes, his lips so close to mine that we are sharing the same air.

"Why? I thought you said it was too dangerous," I whisper.

"I made a mistake. I can keep you safer if you're with me."

My brows shoot up. "Devon Marx, the devil. Made a mistake?"

"Yes." He gives a single nod, ignoring my mocking tone.

Why is he doing this now?

I don't know what to do.

I don't know what's right or wrong.

I can't think straight when he's so close.

Relaxing my knees, I drop down out of his hold, escaping him, and I don't miss the surprise on his face.

He thought I was about to cave.

It hurts to think about. I hate that I fell so hard for a man I hardly know. I hate that it was so easy for him to get under my skin. And I hate that all I want to do is run back into his arms and forget the loneliness I've felt every minute of every day since he sent me away.

But I can't.

There's more than my heart at stake.

"Please leave. I need... time."

He scowls, but doesn't follow me as I retreat backwards, stepping into the hallway that leads to my bedroom.

"Jax," he rasps, but I shake my head.

"Please make sure the door is locked on your way out." And with that, I turn and hurry into my bedroom, closing myself in.

I stand with my back to the door, holding my breath, trying to keep my tears at bay until I hear him leave.

I wait. And wait. And wait.

Finally, the sound of my apartment door opening and closing floats down the hallway, and my shoulders sag as the first sob escapes me.

I take the five steps to my bed and fall face first, holding my breath as the pain feels like it's going to shatter my heart on my next breath as I start to cry.

The sound of my bedroom door opening has me stilling, before I roll around to see Devon storming in.

"I'm not taking no for an answer," he snaps, his eyes locking onto mine as I gasp. "You can have all the time you need in my fucking bed, in my fucking town, where you belong." He rakes his hand through his hair before continuing, his eyes giving my bedroom a quick scan.

Oh no.

"You can... can..." He frowns, his eyes leaving me to the far bedside table, and I know exactly what he's looking at. "Is that..." His gaze darts back to me as he points. "Is that what I think it is?"

I shake my head, my eyes wide, tears still searing my cheeks and I reel with panic at how to explain this.

Or better yet, get him out so I don't have to.

"It fucking is," he yells as he starts to round my bed, and I scramble to roll over and crawl across my mattress to reach the bedside table before he does.

My hand grips it, and I'm about to snatch it away, but Devon latches on, his strength far outmatching mine, and he tugs it from my hold.

"Devon!" I yell, pushing up to my knees on the mattress as I try again to snatch it back, but he steps backwards, the frame gripped in both of his hands as his eyes study the picture.

Shit.

SHIT.

"Devon," I cry, and finally his gaze lifts from the framed picture to look at me.

"Are you... Is there..." His wide eyes drop to my stomach, and my heart melts like butter on hot toast.

He looks so adorable right now. Those big eyes, normally so harsh, are wide and round, making him look younger. Making him look so hopeful.

Wait.

No.

Stop.

Don't think that way about Devon.

I can't let myself care.

But then, his lips spread wide, his teeth flash as he beams, a smile so big I've never seen him wear it, and oh lord, it's something else. Something miraculous.

Something I want to see again. And again. And again.

"I did it," he whispers, still grinning from ear to ear, his gaze darting back to the picture in his hand. "You're having my baby."

Dammit. This isn't how it was meant to go. He was meant to leave me alone. I'd only just started to accept that. I'd only just embraced the idea of being a single mum, and now he comes in and does this.

I'm so confused and annoyed and I just... I just need him to leave.

"No, Devon. I'm having *my* baby."

He doesn't hear me though, or if he does, he doesn't acknowledge it, moving to my closet and opening the door.

"We need to pack your things."

"What? No!"

"Yes," he snarls over his shoulder, so I scramble off my bed and try to stop him as he starts taking my clothes off the hangers.

"No, Devon. Stop. Put them back."

"Oh, wow. For a moment there I thought you'd totally lost it and were talking to yourself."

Presley's voice makes us both freeze and look over our shoulders to see her grinning from the doorway.

"Hey, Presley," Devon says, and I frown, turning back to him and slapping his arm.

"Don't speak to my sister."

He frowns at where I slapped him, but then completely forgets about it as his mind goes back to the baby.

"Find a bag, Jaxcen. Stop wasting time."

"I said no!" I stomp my foot and ball my fists while Presley giggles from the doorway.

"I guess he knows about Apricot, then?" she asks, and I send her a *'you're not being helpful glare'* as Devon stills, glancing back at my sister.

"Apricot?"

"Yeah. That's this week's name since Jax is ten weeks pregnant. The baby is the size of an apricot," Presley explains, sitting on my bed with a big goofy smile.

"Really?" Devon asks, clearly surprised. "The size of an apricot?"

"Yep." Presley nods, popping the P before Devon drops to his knees before me, his large hands engulfing my hips as he stares at my tummy.

"Hey there, Apricot."

Oh fuck.

If I weren't already pregnant, I would have just conceived right in this moment.

Why is his fascination so adorable?

I glance back at Presley to see her beaming, looking so damn happy.

Why is she looking so damn happy? She knows this can't happen.

"Stop." I try to take a step back, but Devon holds me in place.

"When's the baby due?" he asks, his dark gaze darting up to mine, and hell, I've never seen so much hope in his stare before.

"None of your business," I say quietly as Presley speaks over me. "September."

"September." Devon smiles at me before looking back at my stomach, even though all he can see is my green dress. "A spring baby. Fucking perfect." He nods before leaning forward and pressing his lips to my fabric covered stomach.

I hear Presley sigh from where she's sitting on my bed, and I shoot her a glare, but she's too busy looking dreamily at me and Devon.

Great. Now she's lost her mind too.

"Pack your bag," Devon says for the hundredth time, standing up and turning back to move to my closet, digging more clothes out.

"No," I sigh, my shoulders dropping.

This argument is exhausting.

"Fine." He nods, more to himself than anything, his eyes coming to mine. "I'll send my men for your belongings."

I'm about to argue with him once again when he starts stalking towards me and I try to skitter away.

"Stop, Devon. I'm not going with you." I hold my hands out, my heels colliding with my bed as I fall back, but Devon stops his chase, sighing and shrugging.

"Fine. I'll just stay here. I'll get Finn to bring my clothes."

"What!" Presley finally speaks up, her voice pitched high as she launches herself off the bed. "Uh-uh. Jax, you need to go with him."

"What! Whose side are you on?" I protest, bolting up from the bed to stare at my sister.

"I'm on *my* side. Firstly, I don't want a man in my apartment. Men are pigs." She glares at me. "Secondly, you've been pining over him ever since you left. Stop being stubborn and just decide to be happy."

"You've been pining over me?" Devon asks and I snap.

"No!"

"Yeah, you have." He brings out his shit-eating grin which makes me want to be irrationally violent.

"Get out!" I point to the door but he shakes his head, stepping up to me and taking my hand in his.

"Come on, love. Decide to be happy with me."

"Stop," I whisper, and he shakes his head again.

"No, I'll never stop fighting for you."

"Oh my god!" Presley's voice draws our attention to see her gesturing to us. "Do you have a brother like you? I'm single and ready for all that."

"Presley!" I squeak, and she shrugs.

"What? At least I'm being honest, which is more than you're being right now."

She has a point, but even so, why isn't she on my side right now?

"Come on, little mouse. Come with me. Let me remind you of how much my town adores you."

"But... You broke my heart," I whisper, and for the first time I see the regret wash over his expression as he reaches out and cups my cheek.

"If it's any consolation, I broke my own heart too."

It's hard to believe a man like him could ever be brokenhearted, what with him being so tough and all, but I can see it. The truth is in his eyes. The pain he's been suffering.

"Did you cry?" I ask, needing the truth.

"Nearly," he admits, and shit, I hate the thought of him being so sad that he nearly cries.

I know that pain all too well.

"Did you day drink and get wasted?" I ask, and he nods quickly.

"Many times, little mouse. Many, many times."

"Did you think about calling me?"

He gives me a sad smile then. One that doesn't reach his eyes as he responds. "I've stared at your number every fucking day since I sent you way. Hell, I even got rid of your piece of shit ex fiancé for you."

My mouth drops open as I gasp, while Presley giggles.

"You owe me fifty bucks, sis. I told you it was no accident."

"Are you serious?" I whisper, and again Devon nods, doing that thing again where he presses his forehead to mine.

"Yes. He'd been following you. Stalking you. Spying on you from across the street. He even grabbed you at Cloud 9. He had to go. I needed to do that so you could be safe."

Holy. Fucking. Shit.

He actually murdered my ex fiancé.

And why aren't I mad about that? What is wrong with me?

You're a scandalous sinner, Jaxcen. Stop fighting it.

"You know about Eddie coming to Cloud 9?" I ask, and he nods.

"Come back home with me." He cups the other side of my face. "Let me make my shitty decision up to you. I promise you won't regret it."

Should I really forgive him?

I want to, but is it the right thing to do?

What if it's not?

But, what if it is?

What if going with Devon, giving him this chance, is my happily ever after?

What if it turns out better than I ever thought I deserved?

What if he's the best dad, loving and protecting, giving our child a life without any of the horrors I've endured?

I stare into his deep dark eyes for a long time as he waits patiently for me to respond.

A warm calm rushes through me from head to toe and I know... I already know what I have to do. What I want to do.

I lick my lips and suck in a deep breath as I take a step backwards, putting some distance between us.

"If you want me to come with you. You'll have to make me."

That absolutely wicked grin only Devon Marx can pull off, kicks up his lips, and he starts to slowly roll up his shirt sleeves.

Damn, why is that so hot?

"I'll do it, little mouse. I'll kidnap you over and over until you come to terms with the fact that you belong with me. In my bed. By my side."

I give a non caring single shrug of my shoulder as I continue walking backwards getting closer to my bedroom door, ignoring Presley's excited giggles and claps.

"If you can catch me, you can keep me."

My words elicit an animalistic growl, and I spin with a squeal, running out of my room and down the hall towards the front door.

I can hear his wicked laugh before those heavy feet and long strides start chasing me, and my heart almost leaps out my throat as I grip the handle of the apartment door and throw it open, bolting out into the passage.

As I dash past the lifts, I press the button but keep running, knowing it won't get here in time.

With my eyes trained on the exit sign, I hurry forward, hearing his heavy feet closing in as I shove the stairwell door open, ready to bolt down the flights of stairs.

Devon's strong arm latches around my waist, his hand slapping over my mouth as I scream, my heart thrashing wildly like it's ready to gallop off without me, and leave the shell of my body behind.

"You're mine now, little mouse." Devon growls against my ear, dropping me to my feet and spinning me before hoisting me up so my legs wrap around him.

"Why do you call me little mouse?" I ask, hoping he'll finally tell me, and he smirks, his dark eyes piercing as he cups my cheek.

"Because I am the predator, and you are my prey. I'm the big scary cat, and you're the sweet little mouse."

I barely have a second to react before his lips are on mine, his weight pressing me into the cool concrete wall of the fire escape as he fumbles with his pants.

I moan, grind on any friction I can get as he frees himself, and then, with skilled fingers, he slips my panties aside and drives into me hard.

We both cry out, our moans echoing all the way up to the twenty sixth floor, and all the way back down to the bottom as he pounds into me, and all I can do is hold on, lose myself in his lips and tongue and the sparks of electricity that dance from his skin to mine.

There's no extra stimulation needed. This right here is fuelled by more than lust. By more than sexual desire.

We fit. It makes no sense to me, but at the same time it makes all the sense in the world, and as he sends me to new heights, breaking our kiss, he draws back, pinning me to the wall with his hand around my throat to claim me completely. Mind. Body. And soul.

"You're mine now, little mouse. I'm never letting you go."

CHAPTER FORTY-FOUR

Epilogue 1 – 6 Months Later

Devon – Part 1

She's radiant. Glowing. Her hair is thicker and shinier. The swell of her breasts has grown considerably. And her belly is round and ripe with my child inside. She's never looked more stunning.

"You look like a creeper," Finn mutters from beside me as I watch Jaxcen out in the street being showered with gifts by the people in my town that have now become her friends. Her family.

"I don't care. I'll never get enough of her."

"Yeah, I've picked up on that." Finn chuckles. "You look exhausted though."

This time I drag my gaze away from the baby shower celebrations and face my best mate.

"She's so horny all the fucking time. We have sleep sex, like a lot."

Finn's brows shoot up. "What the fuck is sleep sex?"

I shrug. "I dunno. It's just what I'm calling it. One minute we are both asleep. The next minute our bodies have gravitated together and we both wake aroused as fuck already groping each other."

"Fuck. Really?" Finn asks. "That kinda sounds... hot."

I nod. "It fucking is. Especially with how far gone she is when we finally wake. She's like, possessed or something. All I have to do is let it happen."

"Shit. Pregnancy hormones?" Finn asks and I shrug.

"Maybe. I hope it's not just that though. I wanna keep waking up like that."

We both chuckle before I turn my sights back out onto the street, watching Jaxcen's sister, Presley dote over her.

"Last night, she was already well awake when she woke me. My cock in her hand, stroking me as her lips closed around my tip." Fuck, my cock twitches at the memory. "She told me to go back to sleep, that she'll be done soon, and then she rose over me and sat on my cock."

"Fuck. You gotta stop telling me this. I'm getting hard which is not something I want to be doing from words that fall from your fucking lips."

I laugh at Finn as he shifts uncomfortably and continue anyway.

"Dude she was making me hard so she could ride my cock and she thought I'd just fall back to sleep. As fucking if. Then we were at it for three fucking hours."

Finn laughs. "Is that why you look so tired lately? You too old to keep up with your young baby mumma?"

"Nah, I'll never be too old for her. She keeps me young."

And it's the truth. For now anyway. I may be in my early forties and Jaxcen in her mid-twenties, but there's something about our union that makes me feel more alive than I've ever felt.

"How are you still standing, man?" Finn asks curiously, and I shrug.

"Why do you think I lock myself in my office every morning when she goes into the bakery to work? I'm catching up on sleep on that shitty old couch."

Throwing his head back, Finn laughs before clapping me on the back.

"I was gonna ask why you don't just go up to bed in your suite, but my guess is you don't want to risk her catching you having an old man nap just to keep up with her."

"Shut up," I grumble, even as my lips kick up. "So, is it ready?"

"Yep, here are the keys." Finn dangles the keys between us and I accept them, slipping them in my pocket before I turn and walk out of the Palace.

"Let's do this."

Jaxcen - Part 2

My cheeks hurt from smiling so much, but I can't help it. I feel so full with life, love, and happiness. Marilda and my sister Presley conspired and planned the most wonderful baby shower and gender reveal I could ever hope for, and I've been made to feel so much more special than I ever imagined.

It's been a beautiful day, Main Street closed off as they do so often for town celebrations, decorated in all things baby.

There are so many gifts. Clothes, blankets, cute teddies, all for this bump that keeps kicking me from the inside. I have no idea how we will fit all the gifts up in Devon's suite.

Today is an unusually sunny August day, hinting at spring, ready to kick winter to the curb. Spring is the season my baby is due to be born.

In less than a month.

I'm more than ready to meet the little future soccer player or karate expert given how well he or she kicks. Every time I sit to relax, the little devil starts using me as a boxing bag.

"Are you ready?" Marilda asks, smiling at me as she rests her son Damon on her hip. "The next part of today's events are happening at the cliff."

I beam at Marilda as Presley insists to everyone else to go ahead, and excited anticipation rushes through me.

The reveal.

We are going to do the reveal soon, and I'll finally know if this baby is a boy or a girl.

"Where's Devon?" I ask, glancing over my shoulder to look for him, but can't see him anywhere.

"I think he's already there." Presley beams, offering me her arm where I hoist myself up off the chair, my free hand rubbing over the eight month swell of my belly.

"Well, let's go and find out who this is in here."

Presley and Marilda beam, walking with me slowly towards the grassy town square that leads to the cliffs.

We chat as we walk, talking about all the gifts I've been showered with today, and it takes me a moment to notice that the lush green grass under foot starts to become covered with rose petals.

Frowning, I glance up to see that we are at the foot of a rose petal path, lined with our friends from the town gathered along each side, and up ahead, standing all the way over by the cliff's edge on his own, is Devon.

"Why does this gender reveal feel like I'm about to walk down the aisle?" I whisper to my sister and friend, who both giggle, but don't answer me other than Presley saying, "Go to your man."

Feeling rather exposed with all eyes on me, I start walking over the rose petals and quickly forget about everyone, because up ahead is Devon, and the closer I get, the more I can see his eyes locked onto me, onto every step I take, and I'm drawn to him like a magnet.

Behind him there's some sort of box I noticed Marilda and Finn setting up this morning for the gender reveal, but my attention goes right back to the way Devon is looking at me, making me feel this is something more.

"What's going on?" I whisper as I near him, and Devon takes my hand, tugging me closer before he lowers to one knee.

Devon - Part 3

I'm so fucking nervous. I don't know why, but fuck, I want to get this right.

She looks stunning walking towards me, her stomach swollen, her skin glowing.

She's like the sun.

Warm. Bright. And burning for me.

"What's going on?" she whispers as she nears.

I simply smile, reach my hand out to her and tug her closer, impatient to close the distance.

Then, I lower to one knee.

A gasp escapes her, her trembling free hand coming to her chest as her eyes turn glassy.

"Dev?"

"You know I love you, little mouse. You know there's been no other to steal my soul like you have. You know I'd burn this entire world to the ground to protect you and keep you safe and in my arms, always. And you know that I'm a powerful man, yet there's no other that walks this earth that can bring me to my knees, other than you."

Reaching into my shirt pocket, my fingers clasp the ring and I pull it out as I take in her wide blue gaze, glassing over with unshed tears.

There's no box, just the twelve carat pink oval cut diamond sitting atop of a thin rose gold diamond encrusted band, and those big blue eyes widen even more as she takes it in.

"In less than a month, our little family will begin." I continue, drawing her gaze from the rock I'm holding, back to my eyes. "You've made me happier than I ever thought possible, giving me an entirely new purpose that I can't wait to share with you until we are old and grey with grandkids and great grandkids."

I don't say that perhaps I'll be gone before I can see great grandkids given my age, because that shit doesn't belong in this conversation.

Tears finally pool over and stream down Jaxcen's cheeks, yet her smile is wide as she stares down at me, taking in my words.

"And now I ask you for one more thing, my sweet Jaxcen."

Returning my gaze back to her slender fingers, I position the ring at the tip of her nail before peering back up into her ocean blues.

I have to clear my fucking throat. There's a lump lodged there, sticky and persistent as my own emotions run rampant inside my chest.

And then, I say the words that have been on the tip of my tongue for months.

"Marry me."

Jaxcen - Part 4

It's not really a question, but it doesn't need to be. I'm already nodding, a string of yes's flying from my lips as he slips the ring onto my finger.

It fits perfectly, and I don't even care to look at the rock. It could be a scrap of old metal for all I care, because nothing else matters but this man right here and the moment we are sharing right now, in our own little bubble even though the entire town is watching on.

His dark eyes flick up from my finger to my face, and I leap at him, my belly getting in the way as I try to reach him for a kiss.

Chuckling, Devon repositions me onto his raised knee and claims my lips thoroughly as we kiss, our tongues dancing with hunger and excitement.

Cheers ring up all the way over where the town watches on, and as we kiss, a countdown starts up, chanted by everyone watching.

"Five, four, three, two..."

Devon and I pull apart on "one" to hear a loud pop and then a huge arch of hot pink dust shoots up into the air, blocking out the view of Timber Valley, while an embarrassing sob leaps from my lips.

"Fuck, love. It's a girl." Devon's voice has taken on a higher pitch, and I nod, blubbering, trying to speak but unable to as he holds me to him, our eyes trained on the vaporising pink dust.

There's so much cheering, and it's getting closer, and I know our little bubble is about to be invaded, but I don't care, because every one of these people mean something to me. Even the town's folk have become close friends in the months since Devon 'kidnapped' me again and brought me back into his fold.

Drawing my gaze away from the open air that is now revealing Timber Valley again, Devon and I stare at each other, and I cup his face, pressing our foreheads together just like he loves to do so often.

"I can't wait to grow old and grey with you."

Even at this close proximity, I can see the huge smile that lights his whole face.

"I fucking love you, Jax."

"I love you too, Dev."

Devon - Part 5

After helping Jaxcen up off my knee, we both accept congratulations from everyone, on our engagement and the news that our little bundle growing inside Jaxcen is a girl.

When the celebration dies down and the sun starts to set, bringing with it a cool breeze that reminds us that winter is still here, I take my fiancé's hand and lead her away, towards the chapel.

"Are we really doing confession tonight?" Jaxcen giggles, and I shoot her a smirk.

"Not tonight. I have a different gift for the mother of my child."

For the last six months, my men have been building a house next to the chapel. It's a four bedroom double story home, and all of this time, Jaxcen has thought it is to house newcomers since the town's houses are basically full up.

While that's true, and my men have started on some smaller cottages further up the mountain, this one is our new home. Fit for a family of five or more if needed. I'm not sure I'll ever tire of putting a baby in her belly, so we may need to extend it one day.

Confused, Jaxcen frowns, which deepens as I lead her to the path of the new house.

When she turns her confused gaze to me, I dangle the keys between us.

"Our new home, little mouse."

"What? But I thought..."

Fuck, she's adorable. Her puckered brows. Those plump lips as she nibbles on them, trying to put two and two together.

"You thought this was for new rescues, yes I know." I grin. "I lied."

She gapes at me and then slaps my shoulder.

"No more lies, or I'll... I'll..."

"You'll what?" I smirk.

"I'll have surgery to get my pussy sealed shut so you can't knock me up again."

Fuck. She plays a hard fucking game because now I'm the one gaping.

"You wouldn't dare."

"Wouldn't I?" she challenges, and fuck, that's not a challenge I'm willing to accept.

Her smirk is utterly evil, having learned from the master, after all.

"Fine. No more lies. Now get your sexy arse inside our new home. I want to christen every fucking room tonight."

Even as she smiles she bites her lips, those hormones working in my favour as she snatches the keys off me and hurries up the path to unlock the front door.

My cock is already hard as I follow behind, my pregophilia kicking in once again.

I never realised I had so many fucking fetishes, but the thing is, they start and end with Jaxcen. *She* is my fetish. My addiction. My reason to fucking breathe.

But fuck, can you blame me?

She was put on this earth just for me, that I'm sure of. And now, with her body changing, even though she feels like an oversized hippopotamus—her words, not mine—I do everything I can to make her feel as sexy as she looks to me.

The moment I close the front door, she pounces on me, but I manage to steer her to the stairs, up them and coax her into our bedroom because I know the bed is the safest place for an eight month pregnant woman to be railed.

I have her naked within seconds as she wrestles to get me bare, and when I have her positioned on the end of the bed, her legs over my shoulders and my cock disappearing inside her, I see the glint of her engagement ring as she tweaks her own nipples, and I want to pound my chest like a fucking caveman, declaring his ownership over a woman for all the land to see.

She is mine, in every fucking way, and I'll never tire of possessing her.

CHAPTER FORTY-FIVE

Epilogue 2 - Four Years Later

Jaxcen - Part 1

With my hand over my heart, I study the security monitor watching Devon as he stands looking dapper in his light grey suit on the balcony just off our living area.

He's waiting, and my heart flutters with excitement as I hear the cutest little voices flow through on the speaker.

"Come on, Harry. Daddy's waiting to see us."

Izzy's sweet voice elicits adored sighs from my bridesmaids Presley, Marilda, and Allegra, as they watch beside me.

"In you go." I hear Devon's sister Jen urge off screen, before the two little heads of my children appear, Izzy's hair in a long cascade of dark curls, while Harry's shorter blonde curls are a little more tamed today thanks to Devon's sisters working their magic with product and telling Harry it was magic lotion to help him grow so he can be just like his daddy.

"Daddy!" Harry calls as he sees Devon standing by the railing, and as Devon turns for his first look at his two children ready for our wedding, I see him stagger back a little, and I know he feels it too.

Floored.

This life. These kids. How lucky are we?

So damn lucky.

All we need is each other. Nothing else matters.

"Buddy, look at you." Devon coos, dropping to one knee as Harry's little three year-old legs move quickly before he leaps into his daddy's arms and Devon stands holding his son.

"Oh lord. I think I just got pregnant," Presley says, and Marilda and Allegra giggle.

"Don't you look smart in your suit?" Devon remarks and Harry nods.

"Just like you, Daddy."

Devon beams. "Little man, you look better than me."

Proud of that fact, Harry wriggles to get down, and the moment his feet hit the deck, he does the most ridiculous dance that brings out a deep rumble of laughter from Devon.

"Girl, you're totally getting knocked up tonight." Allegra giggles, and I glance at her quickly to see her brows wagging. "The way you are eye fucking your husband-to-be right now should be illegal."

I giggle back, not even bothering to deny that Devon and I will likely not come up for air after today until he's satisfied that I'm bearing his third child.

He's wanted another for a while, but I begged him to hold off so we could enjoy Isabelle and Harry for a bit, and so I could get into shape to fit into my dream wedding dress, of course.

Devon agreed, but I know as soon as we hit the sheets tonight, all bets are off. I'll be his cumdumpster once again, and I'm not even a little mad about it.

"Daddy, do you like my dress?" Izzy's voice draws my eyes back to the screen to see her walking towards him, her pale pink dress like a little Cinderella gown, just the way she wanted.

She stops and does a twirl in the centre of the balcony as Devon falls quiet.

He nods quickly, before spinning to face away from our four year old daughter, and I can see the side of his face, and the way he brushes away a tear.

"Oh my god, that's it. I'm now pregnant with twins." Presley groans and we all laugh.

Turning back to face his daughter, Devon holds his hand out to her as Harry continues to dance off to the side in his own little world.

Rushing forward, Izzy takes his hand, smiling up at him as he lowers to one knee again.

"My beautiful Isabelle. You look like the most beautiful princess of all the lands."

She beams.

"Thank you, Daddy, but you are wrong."

"Oh?" Devon asks while she nods.

"Mummy is the most beautiful princess of all the lands."

"Nawwww," my bridesmaids coo as my eyes turn glassy.

Don't cry. Don't ruin your makeup before you've even walked down the aisle, Jaxcen.

"Oh I bet she is," Devon agrees. "But Mummy is about to become the queen, which means you are the princess of all princesses."

Izzy nods, like she's accepting that responsibility with pride. "Until I have a little sister, and then we will share being the most beautiful princesses of the land."

Devon cups her little cheek. "You have your mother's heart. So big. So sweet."

"Are you going to cry, Daddy?" she asks, and damn it, there goes a tear from my eye.

I hear sniffing next to me, and Marilda swipes at her eyes. "Crap."

I smile and wrap her in a hug as we continue watching the screen.

"Today, I just might, princess." Devon admits, not too masculine to show his feelings.

"That's okay, Daddy. I have tissues. My dress has pockets."

Laughing, he pulls her in for a hug, and she squeezes her little arms around his neck the way she does to me when she thinks I need an Izzy hug.

Devon's sister Jen comes onto the screen then, ushering my children out and ordering Devon to get his arse to the altar, so I drag my gaze from the screen to face my sister.

"Have I ruined my makeup?"

"No. It's still perfect." She smiles.

My attempt to catch the tears must have worked.

"Are you sure you're okay about our parents not being here?" Presley asks, her eyes kind as she stares at me.

I nod. "They aren't my parents, Pres. You know this. Nothing about the way they raised us was parental as far as I'm concerned. All I need is you."

The words are bitter on my tongue, because even though part of me means them, there's still a part of me that wishes things were different. That wishes they were here today to celebrate with us. To accept the life I've chosen and simply be proud.

But they are who they are, and there's nothing I can do to change them.

Presley smiles, believing my lie, and we hug as Allegra fusses with my train, before Marilda claps her hands to gain our attention.

"Places ladies. Let's get you married, Jax."

My heart flutters and it's almost too overwhelming to feel this much love and happiness after the childhood I experienced. Sometimes I find myself waiting for the other shoe to drop. Like I'll wake up one day and find everything that made me happy gone. Like it was all just a dream.

But that day hasn't come yet, so I will keep embracing each and every second I get with my family, and hopefully one day, I'll find myself wondering when the last time was that I wondered when it would all vanish.

Walking from my house, we make our way to the town square, and the cliff front that I got engaged at over four years ago, our presence hidden by tall partitions on the grass, lined with white sheer fabric and twinkling lights, so the guests can't see us yet.

"Everyone is seated and ready." Allegra beams after peaking around the partition. "Are you ready?"

Am I?

Yes. I nod easily, smiling at the three women I chose as my bridesmaids, and Jenaveve, Devon's sister as she approaches us with my two beautiful children.

"I have two very eager children here ready to walk their mummy down the aisle."

Two big smiles beam up at me from my children's faces and I hold my hands out.

"Let's get married then." I giggle as Izzy jumps in excitement and Harry hurries to my side taking my hand.

I decided to forgo holding a bouquet of flowers. They just seem unimportant compared to the need to hold my two children's little hands in mine as they walk me down the aisle to their daddy.

A piano starts playing, the tune Devon chose for me to walk down the aisle to. I wasn't sure what it would be. He wanted to keep it a surprise, but as the tune hits my ears, I become aware of what it is.

One by one, my bridesmaids start their walk down the red carpet laid out for the event.

Allegra goes first, and then Marilda, while Presley stands waiting for her turn, her eyes already tearing up as she takes one last glance at me.

"Love you, sis," she whispers, and I kiss the air before she starts walking.

Taking some long deep breaths in, I try to keep my tears at bay. I don't want to be a sobbing mess as I walk to Devon. I want to see everything. Everyone.

I especially want to see my soon to be husband's face as I approach, and I want to lock that memory away to cherish over all of my days.

The moment Taylor and Alice begin humming, I know it's time, and I move onto the red carpet, looking down towards Devon whose back is to me.

"Every time our eyes meet," Taylor starts singing the opening line to Amazed, and I start walking as Devon turns.

He is a hard man. A scary man. A devil many fear. Yet right now, the moment his eyes land on me, walking towards him with his children, his strong facade breaks.

He looks up at the sky briefly, Finn offering him comfort with a hand on his back as he blows out a breath, his dark gaze returning to us as we walk closer.

I need my own moment, looking away from him and glancing down at our beautiful children, my eyes meeting Harry's mischievous smirks, much like his father's, before moving to Izzy's, her eyes warm and she gives my hand a little squeeze like she is silently telling me she's here for me.

Gosh, how can a four year old be my little rock?

Now a few metres from Dev, I return my eyes to his, to find his smile wide and his gaze glassy, pride written all over his expression.

I know how he feels. This life we have built together is everything.

That's the moment Harry breaks away from me, closing the distance to run to his daddy, who picks him up immediately, pressing a kiss to his cheek as they both watch me and Izzy as we reach them.

"Hey, beautiful," Devon says softly as I stand before him, my smile wide as I respond.

"Hey."

Devon - Part 2

The music fades out, and another rush of excitement bursts through me as Izzy takes my hand and places it in Jaxcen's.

How can a four year old be so in tune with what's happening?

That kid is smarter than I thought possible. She never misses a beat, and today is no exception.

"Here Mummy and Daddy. It's time for you to get married."

Jaxcen's smile is warm as she leans over and places a kiss on Izzy's cheek, who beams and reaches out for Harry's hand and I lower him to the ground.

Jen and Elise are nearby, holding their hands out for their niece and nephew who happily go to them, finally allowing me and Jax to face each other and drink each other in fully.

I thought seeing my children all dressed up would be my weak moment, but nothing prepared me for seeing my wife-to-be, wearing an intricately beaded ivory gown with the sun shining overhead, lighting up the gold in her hair as she walked down the aisle, accompanied by our children.

"You're the most beautiful sight I've ever seen," I say, not caring who can hear.

Leaning forward, her hand presses to my chest as she stands on tip toes to reach my ear.

"The devil has never looked more handsome."

I chuckle quietly as she shifts back into place, and the celebrant begins the service.

I'll be honest. I don't listen to most of it. I'm too taken by the sight in front of me. By the woman that came into my life on a stormy December night in a church nearly five years ago, and even though I stole her from her life, she's the one that stole me. Stole my heart.

We say our vows, having chosen more traditional ones, not really thinking our guests would appreciate the ones we'll likely share during our confession rituals we still do to this very day.

We say our 'I do's' and then I finally get to kiss her, before completing the formality of signing the forms and what not.

The service turns into a party not long after, something my little town does so well, and given we have a large number of extra visitors, mainly Marx family members, the partying goes well into the next morning.

I, however, leave my family and friends to it, leading Jaxcen away to the Palace, passing the suite we used to share before Izzy came into the world.

We usually keep it for guests these days, but since we need a night off from the kids, thanks to Jen and Elise staying in our house, I'm about to give Jaxcen her wedding gift while we can be alone to enjoy it.

"I thought we were going to the suite." Jaxcen giggles as I usher her up the steep stairs into the attic.

"We'll go there later. First, I have a surprise for you."

She grins wickedly over her shoulder at me before we reach the top, and her eyes widen at the transformed attic space.

"Is this what I think it is?"

When those blue excited eyes dart to me, I nod.

"It is, little mouse."

"You turned the attic into a sex dungeon?"

"Not a sex dungeon," I chuckle. "A sex attic."

"Same thing." She counters, although she is smiling, her eyes wide with fascination.

"Using the chapel was getting a little…" I trail off, remembering how Izzy had come looking for us when she had a bad dream last month. It was one in the morning. We hadn't expected her to wake up, and she knows we spend time in the chapel, although thankfully, she's never asked us what we do in there. We were lucky the doors were locked.

"The chapel is dangerous," Jaxcen agrees. "So regular babysitters then?" she asks, smirking over her shoulder at me as she runs a finger over the St Andrew's Cross in the centre of the room.

"Absolutely," I agree, and she spins to face me.

"So Mr Marx. You kidnap me, possess me, turn me into your sex slave, knock me up, twice, marry me, and now lure me into your sex attic. What are you going to do with me now?"

Slowly undoing my shirt, I move to the wall of tools and instruments, and study the array of floggers, whips, cuffs, ropes and various other tools I can use on my little mouse.

Shucking off my shirt, I select a braided leather whip and turn back to face Jaxcen as I slap it against my palm.

"I think we'll start with making that fine arse of yours nice and red."

She nods, a very willing participant these days, our kink games having evolved quite a lot since the first night I made her confess to me on her knees. We have upped the intensity of our sessions together over the years, so she's not at all shocked by what she sees.

Making quick work of her wedding dress, she drapes it over a chair and stands before me completely naked, not bothering with any fabric barriers, and that's how I know she's already primed for me.

"Give me a level?" I ask, and her cheeks heat as she considers it.

She's normally faster at choosing what sort of session we will have. I leave it up to her to decide how severe she wants it. When she's pregnant, I refuse to do anything but mild BDSM, but outside of that she mostly chooses moderate, only selecting severe a couple of times when she was struggling with those demons that sometimes creep in, making her feel guilt and shame.

"Jax?" I urge, and the moment her gaze drops to the floor, I already know what she's going to say.

"Severe."

I've never questioned her need for me to actually deliver her real punishments before, but right now, I'm confused as fuck, because today is our wedding day. She should be happy. Celebrating. Not wracked with shame.

"But—"

Her eyes, brewing with a storm I'm not privy to, glare at me. "Severe." She repeats and all I can do is stare at her for a moment.

"Please," she asks quietly, and even though I'm confused, I know I'll find out through this session what's plaguing her so much that she wants to be punished on her wedding night.

"Bend over the bench." I point to the padded bench that has links for restraints on it. I won't use that now, but I can't fucking wait to give everything in here a thorough test run eventually.

Doing as I ask, Jaxcen goes to the bench, bending over its A-frame so her arse is up in the air, and I move up behind her and tap my feet to the insides of her ankles.

"Wider."

She shifts her stance wider, holding on to a bar near her hair as it dangles down, and I take the nearby lube and gloss up her arsehole, before hunting down a nice big plug, and lathering it up too.

When I part her cheeks and press it to her puckered rose, she relaxes, opening her tight hole to me, and I slip the plug inside.

"Oh," she moans and I chuckle.

"Yeah, you know what's coming, don't you?"

She wriggles a little over the bench, like the idea of me fucking her arse is turning her on.

She's become accustomed to my cock in that part of her, especially during the time of the month she could be ovulating over the past few years since she wanted to hold off on having more children until after we were married, and since I need to fuck her daily, during those days, her puckered rose is all mine.

"I do know what's coming," she admits. "But I thought you'd want to save all your cum for... well, you know."

I chuckle. I do know.

"I never said I was going to cum in your arse, little mouse. Just fuck it."

My words make her squirm, and she gets impatient.

"Oh, come on. Just looking at you all day has been edging me," she moans, so I give her what she wants, and strike the whip.

"Are you begging already?" I snap, and she squeaks, and wriggles her arse some more.

"Yes, I am. I'm aching for you."

Slap.

Another squeak.

"Begin," I demand, and she does.

"My devil. I bestow upon you my darkest sins, and ask that you bathe in my debauchery."

Her words are rushed, her desperation already present, but tonight, I won't let her rush this. She'll get her pleasure soon enough, just as long as I find out why she wants this punishment to be severe.

"Divulge your sins, little mouse. Tell me everything bad you've done."

I repeat the words I have so many times since that night in the chapel, our little ritual already making my cock hard.

"Lust," she begins, using the seven deadly sins as she does every time now, like she revels in disobeying those religious rules that were drummed into her head. "I've had excessive sexual thoughts today. I'm so horny for the devil. I ache for him to fill me with his cum. I want every last drop he can give me, in every hole, a thousand times over. I want to drown in his seed."

"Fuck," I snap, whipping her bare arse again and this time she moans.

Since I'm going easy on her for now, she's using her words to tease me, using my obsession with giving her my cum to get me riled up to fuck her.

"Gluttony," she pants. "I went back for thirds at today's wedding dinner. I took an extra bread roll," she breathes, stopping for a moment before she tries to push me again. "And I considered slipping the chocolate covered strawberries inside me so you could eat them out of me tonight."

Slap.

Another moan.

"Continue." I bark, my cock as solid as stone now.

"Greed," she moans, already squirming for more. "Last night, I ordered the Double Dipper I showed you online even though you told me I don't need it. Because even though I don't need it, I want to feel it inside me."

SLAP!

A scream.

My cock weeps, and I know that lashing gave her the bite of pain she's clearly trying to get me to give her by admitting to buying the sex toy I told her not to get.

"You'd better tell me when it arrives," I hiss, recalling the two pronged device she wanted to try out after I mentioned I'd considered buying it to edge her. Now, she's going to fucking regret going against me and buying it anyway.

"Yes, devil. I'll tell you as soon as it arrives," she pants, arching her arse up higher like she's hungry for some friction.

"Continue." I remind her, and she does.

"Sloth," she whispers, and I can tell she's fighting how aroused she is right now, because there's something she wants to get off her chest, but clearly couldn't do it outside of this session. "I pretended I was asleep this morning so you had to get up to do the kids' breakfast so I didn't have to, and when you were busy, I threw my birth control out."

I growl, whipping her harder than I'd like to as she nearly makes me snap, knowing too well my desire to fill her with more babies has been a constant for the last eighteen months.

Fuck. She's desperate for the pain.

Her scream is loud and long, and I rub my hand over the red raised skin on her arse as I force her legs wider with my feet.

She's panting, and probably wondering if she should use the safe word, because I've never whipped her that hard before, which naturally makes me feel like shit, even though it's what she asked for.

"Wrath!" she yells, sounding really pissed now, and I undo my pants and slip out of them as I wait for her to speak.

I want to be ready for her, because it's only going to get worse for her before it gets better, and she knows it.

"I want to take that whip and slap your face with it," she snaps, and I smirk, aiming for her other arse cheek this time as I whip her hard.

"Ouch, fuck me, Devon. One day you're gonna wake up tied to something and I'm gonna see how much you like it."

Frowning, I move to the other side of the bench and lower to my haunches, brushing back her hair to see her teary eyes.

"Little mouse, say the word."

"No."

"Why?"

"I don't want this to stop."

I frown at her admission.

"This here or the whole thing? Because you know we can take a break and move on to something else."

"I want to finish my confession," she whispers.

"I'll put the whip away. I can use something else."

"No," she grabs my wrist as I go to stand, keeping me in place on my haunches. "I can take it. I need it. Please."

I stare at her in disbelief. I know she can take it, but what I don't understand is why she wants to.

"What's going on?"

"Nothing. Please finish. I need to finish."

"Fuck," I hiss, fisting my hand into her hair and angling her head to me even though she's still in an awkward upside down position. "I fucking love you, Jax."

"I love you too, Dev." She smiles at me. "Please let's finish this and then, I want all of your cum. I want you to make me forget my name."

Sighing, I nod, and reluctantly stand.

There's a reason she wants me to finish this, and since I know her so fucking well, I know I'll find out what it is in her last confession, so I can't end it prematurely.

Jaxcen - Part 3

The whip comes down hard on my arse again, and hot tears fill my eyes as I get punished for my envy. I cry out, letting myself feel the pain, because I need it.

We used to celebrate the sins differently in the beginning, but after some time of settling into life here, I still had so many unresolved issues relating to my upbringing, that I asked Devon to punish me for my sins instead on occasion, and we came up with a level system.

At first, he was against it, but I told him how much I needed to feel that pain, that it was a way for me to release it. Not to mention, Devon likes to punish, so in my eyes it was a win win.

But today, our wedding day, although so beautiful and wonderful getting to share it with our son and daughter, something was missing, and I just admitted to Devon that I was envious of him, because he had more than one family member sitting on his side of the aisle.

"Jaxcen," he barks, clearly angry, and I know he's trying to reel it in since we make a point not to bring our disagreements into this part of our life. "They may not have your blood, but my family is your family. You know that."

"Yes, devil," I whimper, trying to remind him we are in a scene.

Emotions are high right now for both of us, but instead of letting him say anything more about it, I continue.

"Pride."

My voice is loud, not a yell but close to it, so I can finally admit what has bothered me so much about today.

"You asked me this morning, last night, last week, and last month, and my sister even asked me before the wedding today, if I was really alright with my parents not being here."

Devon rubs his palm over my arse, right where I know he will hit, probably harder than before, but I need it. I just really need it.

"I said I was okay. I said they weren't parents to me. I pretended that they didn't matter, because my pride wouldn't let me admit that I really just wanted them here, and I still want their acceptance, even after everything they have done to me."

I brace myself, already crying, waiting, waiting, waiting.

"Do it!" I scream, and the whip scorches my arse as it slices over my flesh, a piercing scream ripping from me.

Before the sound has even finished leaving my lips, Devon has me up off the bench and curled into his chest as he sits with me on the lounge near the window.

"Fuck, Jax," he whispers into my hair, peppering kisses to it as I cry. I hate that I brought that in here. My parents don't belong in this room, but the moment after we were married and we turned to face everyone, I realised I wanted to see their faces. I wanted to see their pride and acceptance, but the truth is, it would never have happened. They haven't spoken to me since the day Dr Xavier took me from Presley's apartment. They only speak to Presley if she calls them, and I feel like that's my fault.

I've already come to terms that I'll always deal with their ghosts. I'd been doing fine too, but getting married brought up memories of little girl Jaxcen, before everything went wrong, who used to play dress up and dream about her wedding day when her parents would look lovingly at her.

At some point today, that little girl turned up in my subconscious and wouldn't go away.

Until now.

"I'm sorry," I breathe into Devon's neck. "Can we redo this? I feel like I've fucked it all up."

I hate that I let that part of me get in the way of our happy day. Devon's parents weren't here either, but you don't see him punishing himself over it.

We both have fucked up parents. The difference between them was that Devon's used their fists to punish, while mine used other people to deliver my punishments so they wouldn't have to.

Forcing my head back with a gentle fist in my hair, Devon stares into my eyes.

"Nope. There's no redo's, and we do that because you need it, and obviously today was hard. I'm sorry I didn't notice."

I shake my head. "Dev. I didn't let anyone see until now."

"I've always got your back, little mouse."

"I know. That's why I can do this now with you. Only with you."

"I hate that you want to be punished like that." He admits. "I'm sorry for hurting you."

Shifting in his lap, I straddle him, running my fingers through his hair.

"You didn't hurt me, Dev. You helped me. I feel free of that burden now."

He studies me for a moment and then nods.

"Get on the Cross. I've got so much cum for you, I'm about to burst."

I smile at him, knowing he's probably not joking, so I do as my husband says.

CHAPTER FORTY-SIX
Epilogue 3 - Christmas (a few weeks later)

Devon - Part 1

It's clear to me that my little mouse has a Santa fetish. Every fucking Christmas Eve since the first one, she insists I wear the fucking Santa hat when we fuck, and now, she's brought the whole fucking Santa suit to our sex attic.

"Yes," she cries as I pound into her where she's restrained to the St Andrew's Cross.

It's top of the range, the lower part of the cross adjustable to get the ultimate spreadage, and right now, I have Jaxcen's legs wide, unable to move from where they are locked in place, completely at my mercy.

Her arse is full, a dildo protruding from it, giving a cramped feeling as my cock surges in and out.

"You gonna come, little mouse?" I rasp, my fingers digging into her hips, and she nods, her plump lips parted as she pants.

The moment I press down on her lower abdomen, while tilting the Cross further back, she explodes around my cock.

I piston inside her, chasing my own release and a moment later, ropes of cum are shooting inside her as a wave of ecstasy ripples through me.

Thanks to a little blue pill I took earlier, I know my cock won't go down anytime soon, something I decided is important until I know she has my baby growing inside her again.

I need to be able to fuck as many times as possible during our sessions, since we have to arrange sitters just to get this uninterrupted time together, so I fucking make the most of it, and I won't stop fucking her until the blue pill stops working.

Pulling free, I tilt the Cross upside down on a forty-five degree angle, making sure my cum can't leak out, and then I press the button to lift the Cross higher until my little sex slave is at just the right height to suck my cock.

"How are you doing?" I ask, since the only noise that's come from her are her cries and pants.

"Is that all you've got, Santa?" She smirks, fucking egging me on, from upside down.

"Open those pretty lips," I demand, and she does, giving my cock entry to her hot little mouth.

"Oh fuck, that feels good," I tell her, pushing deep until she gags. "Can you taste yourself, little mouse?"

She mumbles a yes around my cock, and fuck, this blue pill has me as horny as she gets when she's pregnant.

"Pinch my leg if you can't breathe, okay? No fucking passing out on me."

She tries to nod around my cock as I release one of her wrists, even though there's a fifty fifty chance she'll disobey me.

She does that sometimes, letting herself nearly suffocate. It happens at least once a year, and since the last time was only a couple of months ago, I'm fairly confident she won't disobey me tonight.

When I feel her hand on my leg, I brace the timber of the Cross behind her hips and lean closer, latching onto her clit.

And then, I give true meaning to fucking her mouth.

It's savagely brutal, and she pinches me at least three times needing air, but fuck, she's learnt how to take it so well over the years, her gag reflex getting more and more desensitised, although, when she's pregnant, it has the opposite effect.

We learned that through her first pregnancy, and her fear of throwing up became a reality, so I don't go to this extreme when she's knocked up.

Thankfully, since she's not yet with child, I'm able to push her limits while sucking her clit hard.

She comes twice, her own kinks helping to get her over the line since she gets a huge lady boner when I fuck her mouth like this, while I return the oral, sixty-niner style, making her detonate, on repeat.

When I feel my nuts descending, I pull free, and quickly turn her the right way up, slamming into her awaiting cunt, her legs still spread apart on the Cross where I fill her with more cum.

If she's not yet pregnant, then she will be after tonight.

Jaxcen - Part 2

This Cross has to be my favourite thing ever. Not only does it adjust for Devon to spread my legs to the angle he wants, but the leg extensions also tilt up and back into different angles, so now, my legs are spread and up, exposing my arse to give him good access as he eases his huge cock inside.

"Fuuuck, little mouse. Has this hole gotten tighter?"

"You have a Girthmonster dildo in my pussy." I remind him through pants. "That probably has a lot to do with it."

Far out. The dildo is like a fist, something I never considered I'd want to do, but when he showed me that thing, and lathered it with lube, I was desperate for it.

He chose this dildo because he was adamant that it would still keep his cum inside, and I think he was right.

It's not a long dildo, like some. Its purpose is for the stretch, to feel full, and hell I feel so full right now.

"You're such a filthy little mouse," he rasps, knowing what his dirty words do to me.

"Yes." I agree, because in this moment, I want to be the filthiest I've ever been.

The things this man does to me is utterly addictive.

I'm hooked.

"Oh fuck, Jax. Smile up into the camera baby."

My eyes find the camera over head, an addition he installed two nights ago, making our own little movie that we used as a visual when we fucked each other while we watched it later.

"Who's watching?" he asks, pumping a steady rhythm into my arse, and I grin, knowing what he's asking.

"Your men," I say, even though they aren't. Just pretending that someone is watching us gets me off.

We haven't been back to Cloud 9. I realised I didn't need that place, only Devon, but he likes to whisper things in my ear about his men watching us all the time, and although I'm fairly certain I'll never take him up on that, there's always the possibility, and that's enough to send me into a frenzy.

"They all have their cocks in their hands for you," he rasps, moving faster, his fingers pressing to my clit and circling. "They want to cum all over your naked body." He uses his free hand to push the dildo a little deeper while rubbing more friction against my clit.

"Yes. I'm nearly..." I hold my breath, squeezing my eyes tight as I chase my orgasm.

"Fuck yes, that's it," he pants, easing out before sliding the other dildo from earlier back into my arse. They both have gentle vibrating capabilities, and this time Devon uses it, keeping me on edge.

My lids fly open, two dildos protruding from me as Devon shifts to my side, returning his fingers to my clit.

"Look into the camera, Jaxcen. Watch the men watching you."

My eyes shift to the lens, and I imagine them. They are all faceless men, it's only their dicks in their hands that I picture surrounding me.

"Open your mouth, baby. Get ready for them to cum on you."

I open my mouth, my climax speeding at me quickly and I hear Devon grunt before the first jet of hot cum hits me, and I detonate.

"Fuuuck, Jax. They're cumming into your mouth."

His words are strangled and they send me into a double orgasm, another slamming into me before the first one has stopped.

It feels like the ripples rush through me forever, and when I finally open my eyes, it's to see the Santa devil standing over me, dick in hand as he squeezes every last drop of his cum from his hard length into my mouth.

"Swallow," he demands, and I do, desperate to please him.

"Dev," I pant, as he smiles down at me. "You... you came in my mouth."

He nods. "That I did, little mouse."

"But, I thought..." I have to catch my breath before finishing. "I thought you were saving it all for..." I point to my pussy which is still stuffed full, and he shrugs.

"This scene was too good to interrupt for me to get you pregnant. Besides, I like trying to get you pregnant. I'm in no hurry." He winks, before moving between my legs. "Relax for me."

I do as he says, and he eases the dildo from my arse, his eyes wide with excitement as he stares hungrily at my open passage.

"You want me to get this on camera so you can see how fucking hot this is?"

I nod, knowing how utterly fascinated he is with my arse, so naturally I'm curious.

"You're wicked." I grin.

"And you're filthy." He beams with pride as he moves the Cross back further so my open arse is in clear view of the overhead camera. "Fuck, baby. Filthy as sin."

When he's satisfied that the camera has recorded the way he's opened me up, he tilts me and the Cross horizontally.

"I'll always be filthy for you, Devon and your inner devil." I smile, and he leans over me, still restrained to the St Andrew's Cross, at his mercy.

"Will you always sin for me, little mouse?" he asks, hovering over my lips.

"I'll always sin for my Santa." I smile, and then we kiss, our lips claiming each other all over again.

The End

Do you want more naughty dark Christmas filth?
Check out SUBBING FOR SANTA.
This is story about Devon's cousin, Griffin Marx, and the naughty Christmas game he played!
It's a dark mafia Christmas romance with stalker vibes and serious kinks!
https://geni.us/subbingforsanta

ALREADY READ SUBBING FOR SANTA?
Continue reading to check out Sarah JD's other dark stories.

Sarah JDs Books

READING ORDER

NOVELLA

SINFUL DESIRES

-FOX PINES SAGA PREQUEL-
A SPICY HIDDEN IDENTITY WORKPLACE ROMANCE
NOVELLA

TROPES: MF – Friends to Lovers – Workplace romance – Religious Trauma – Hidden Identity – Femme Dom – Kinks – Explicit - CONTENT WARNING!

SINFUL DESIRES:
https://geni.us/sinfuldesires

THE HEAVY HEARTS SERIES

A DARK NEW ADULT ROMANCE

TROPES: MF – Tortured Souls – Kidnapping – Trauma – Violence & Bullying (not between FMC & MMC) – Blackmail – Found Family – SERIOUS CONTENT WARNING!

HEAVY (Book 1):
https://geni.us/heavyhearts1
DEEP (Book 2):
https://geni.us/heavyhearts2
BURIED (Book 3):
https://geni.us/heavyhearts3

BREAKING THE SILENCE

A DARK NEW ADULT ROMANCE

TROPES: MF – Tortured Souls – Secret Identity – Organised Crime – Assassin – Kidnapping – Violence & Gore (not between FMC & MMC) – Blackmail & Coercion – Non-con – Found Family – SERIOUS CONTENT WARNING!

SILENT HUSH (Book 1):
https://geni.us/silenthush1
SAVAGE SCREAM (Book 2):
https://geni.us/savagescream2

SUBBING FOR SANTA

A DARK CHRISTMAS ROMANCE WITH STALKER VIBES

TROPES: MF – Stalker – Secret Identity – Mafia/Organised Crime – Violence (not between FMC & MMC) – Found Family – SERIOUS CONTENT WARNING!

SUBBING FOR SANTA:
https://geni.us/subbingforsanta

SINNING FOR SANTA

A SPICY DARK MAFIA CHRISTMAS ROMANCE
SINNING FOR SANTA:
https://geni.us/sinningforsanta

THE CRUZ KINGS MC SERIES

A DARK ENEMIES-TO-LOVERS MC RO-MANCE
by B. Lybaek & Sarah JD

TROPES: MF – Motorcycle Club – Tortured Souls – Organised Crime – Kidnapping – Violence – Blackmail & Coercion – Dub-con – Non-con – SOMNOPHILIA – Found Family – Bets – SERIOUS CONTENT WARNING!

MAKING THE KING
https://books2read.com/MTK1
TEMPTED BY A KING (Book 1):
https://geni.us/cruzkings1
WANTED BY A KING (Book 2):
https://geni.us/cruzkings2
CLAIMED BY A KING (Book 3):
https://geni.us/cruzkings3

CHECK OUT ALL OF SARAH JD'S BOOKS HERE:

https://sarahjdauthor.com/books

Sarah JD's Books

Stay Connected

Want to find out all the Tea before everyone else?
Join my VIP readers list to hear more about Sarah's books, characters,
and special announcements.

SIGN UP HERE
https://dashboard.mailer-
lite.com/forms/602430/100269803983341506/share

Want to join the conversation about your fav characters?
Join my Facebook Readers Group
SARAH'S VICIOUS KITTENS

JOIN HERE!
https://www.facebook.com/groups/
sarahjaneduncanreadersgroup

For more information on books & book signing events please visit:
https://sarahjdauthor.com

SCAN
ME
STALK ME

Sarah JD

Sarah JD, also known as Sarah Jane Duncan, is a dark romance author living in Australia with Mr Duncan who stole her off the market back in high school.

Sarah can be found in her writing room plotting out her next smut filled romance filled with angst, violence, and themes so dark you should probably question why you love it so much.

Sarah writes about strong females who have to fight against the odds to find their power, their voice, and their truth. Her heroines possess the strength that only comes from being a survivor, and through their trauma, battles and struggles, they learn to trust again, and find love.

There's nothing easy about their stories. They are hard, gritty, and painfully heartbreaking at times. But what doesn't kill us makes us stronger, right? And when you throw in a swoon worthy guy, or an alphahole that you just want to slap, but also fall to your knees and obey, it's the recipe for a rollercoaster ride.

So buckle up. Read the warnings. And let yourself get lost in the dark stories Sarah creates.